BILLY CHILDISH was born in 1959 in Chatham, Kent, and left school at sixteen. After working in Chatham Naval Dockyard as an apprentice stonemason, he went on to study painting, which proved to be unsatisfactory.

Billy Childish was diagnosed dyslexic at the age of 28. Despite this, he has published more than thirty poetry collections and three novels. He has recorded over one hundred albums on a variety of independent record labels and exhibited paintings all over the world.

D1440062

Billy's Website: *www.billychildish.com*

MY FAULT

Billy Childish

This edition published in 2005 by
Virgin Books Ltd
Thames Wharf Studios
Rainville Road
London
W6 9HA

First published in 1996 by Codex Books

ISBN 0 7535 1061 8

Typeset by TW Typesetting, Plymouth, Devon
Printed and bound in Great Britain by
Mackays of Chatham plc, Chatham Kent

CONTENTS

The greatest defeat in anything, is to forget, and above all to forget what it is that has smashed you, and let yourself be smashed without realising how thoroughly devilish man can be. When our time is up, we people mustn't bear malice, but neither must we forget: we must tell the whole thing, without altering one single word – everything that we have seen of man's viciousness; and then it will be over and time to go. That is enough of a job for a whole lifetime.

L. F. Céline

For the whores and thieves everywhere.

INTRODUCTION

*M*y *Fault* was started in 1982, just after I was expelled from the painting department of St Martins School of Art for self-publishing a poetry booklet that was described as 'the worst type of toilet wall humour!' I signed back on the dole and carried on painting in my home town of Chatham.

Later that summer I met Tracey Emin, who was studying fashion at the local art college, and our ensuing love affair became the first parts of *My Fault*. Filling notebooks in longhand, the first draft (working title, 'King of the Cunts') was completed in 1984. The first part of the book, covering my early childhood and teenage years, was the last part to be written.

In 1986, I revised the longhand manuscript, laboriously typing out the novel one fingerdly in my backyard over the summer. For the later drafts, my then girlfriend Kyra, learned to type and it was her work that transformed my badly typed, scrawled pages into readable copy.

At the time, I certainly viewed *My Fault* as my life's work. After a childhood of abuse at the hands of family and teachers, I couldn't be 'shut up' any more and had to tell my own story in my own way. My anger was such that if *My Fault* hadn't been written then, quite seriously, I would have killed.

My Fault is a creative confession, an 'I' novel, based in my experience. As my self-published poetry had been received with open hostility (I was expelled from art school, banned from readings) I was quite sure that no one would touch *My Fault*, so

I didn't even bother sending the manuscript to publishers. Then, in 1995 a chance conversation led to Codex Books approaching me and asking to publish it.

A first edition of two thousand copies was hastily printed and appeared in some book shops in 1996. These quickly sold out through word of mouth.

Now, they're warming up the fires and want to do it again. For this second edition I've fixed printing errors and restored some missing fragments from the archive that the manuscript was drawn from.

Is *My Fault* autobiography or fiction? All our most dearly held truths are fiction and our fiction tells us everything there is to know about ourselves.

PROLOGUE

I 've been raving again, prattling on like an idiot. It's always been
my problem – I'm a loudmouth. I can't remember places, dates
or people, but still I keep harping on about my crummy past,
trying to prove that I existed, that all this really did happen. It's
a mish mash, anarchy and confusion from cover to cover. I should
know, a vile hicking monster, I even bore my friends with it. The
truth? Oh, I doubt it, but I try ... I rack my brains, rewriting,
rethinking, and now here I am with thirteen, fourteen drafts, is it?
And not even a sniff of a publisher. Oh no, I don't delude myself
on that score; if this manuscript should ever see the light of day,
it will be through yours truly digging into his own pockets. I've
done it before, on several occasions ... Publishers only ever
publish what flatters them, and do you have to be polite? Awfully!
My betters have been drumming that one into my bonce for years,
for decades, but it still leaves me cold.

'If you're hankering after success – success, accolade or even
just a humble crust, then at least be polite! You'd better wise up
kid, we've got whore-houses stacked to the rafters with clodhoppers like you, shelves full of the bastards! And not the obnoxious
upstart types either, oh no, these boys are shiny, clever and
sophisticated. Greater understanding, deeper compassion, fine-
tuned. Syntax! Novellas! Encyclopedias! And their wives and kids
too, gushing wells of miracle children, high-powered women that
can do almost everything a man can do, only better. Teeny-
boppers with their fingers jammed right up the pulse ... Shelf

3

after shelf of the bastards, shit carts full to the brim, overflowing with bestsellers, the coffee tables of the world buckling!'

Hey just look at my heading there, standing up for itself, as proud as can be: 'Prologue'. Not bad! It has to be read that way, you see my great fear is that you'll think me conceited, but I'm trying, that's all, in my own fashion to say something close to my heart.

'Lies, bullshit and claptrap! And it's supposed to be English as well, humph! He's pissing on the lavatory seat and shitting on the floor! Where's our great literary traditions? Our Heritage? No description, no punctuation? Why, the stinking upstart can't even spell! Go on, piss off creep, you're polluting our market, no one's interested in your perverted little day-dreams, your toilet wall humour!'

There, is that crazy enough for you? 'Toilet wall humour', that's an actual quote; yes, I've been maligned from the cradle to the dockyard . . . Please control the frustrations that I'm about to put upon you. All I ask, dear benefactor, is that you read me with thought. The first word is fact: 'desperation'. You know, to have to yield to such a word today, to get through . . . The meaning of my work is bad, I know, but please if you can forgive me my cheek . . . I say that with head bowed. Just let me get down one tenth of the facts and that will be enough; that will be my proof, my evidence so to speak. I know the true essence of this testament is to communicate an emotion, human and universal . . . That sounds pretty grand, doesn't it? But that doesn't necessarily make it pretentious . . . To relate to this matter, I have to rely on my own profound thoughts and discoveries.

Evidence! That's my little preoccupation: the history of a nobody . . . I keep notes, I make lists. Remember, a fact is a fact, no matter how hard the liars amongst you might try hushing it up. You've got to gather your evidence, and be methodical about it. Trust your own memory (I'm an elephant on that score) and try not to be duped again . . .

So here I am, ready to die for my beliefs as it were: yes, useless in effect, but I carry on . . . There it is in a nutshell. Please, please, no tears! A joker? Perhaps, we'll get to know each other later . . . But above all, one must stay away from boycotts . . . Yes, I'm blacked, but tell me, do you have my guts?

I'm quite serious in this endeavour, even if I do smirk whilst saying it, and I'm also aware of the risk I'm taking in exposing the lie of my family. You see, by compromising my loved ones (those people as lost and quivering as myself) I'm committing the ultimate sin, because I refuse to carry any further the lie that we were ever loved or wanted.

So the little darlings will get upset? If they get upset, they get upset. Facts give them one royal pain in the arse! All they want to hear are reassurances, beautiful lies, baby food . . . After all, a lie, when told beautifully, will always outshine a mere truth; and now that all the million and one distractions of the head and heart have been set into place, they don't give a tinkers cuss! We've created a world full of sophisticated know-alls, a day-glo world, homogenised and double-sterilised. A spineless cocktail that slips down your throat and out into the pan without a hiccup!

Have you heard of me yet, trying to establish my views on our future? Oh, so I'm alienating my poor readers? Believe me, sorrow breaks through from my saddened heart. (Wipes eyes, coughs slightly.) OK, let's just say that some of these people might be living and some of them might be dead, whatever, they have moved on, they are no longer attached, the thread has been broken . . . What more can I say? After all, I am only a man, yes alone, and what possible harm can one man do in a world filled with experts?

1. THE THREE PENNIES

People are always out to lose themselves: in books, in drink, in sex and clothes, in crowds and in each other. So much for their precious personal identity. For such vain self-serving bastards, people are pretty sick of themselves. We set out into this world full of bluster and fine ideals, but slowly, bit by bit, that most delicate heart is eaten away. We stagger on, we buy and we sell, we grow ever more extravagant, desperate to lose ourselves, to try and forget what we once were, to dull ourselves to what we've become ... And then the night, pacing the boards alone, full of remembrances, sick to the core, sick of our own chatter, of our own mirthless mugs.

I'm sorry, it's the drink: I blow hot and cold, I laugh as if to cry, I grow melancholic. One minute I'm reeling and fighting mad, the next I come over all friendly again, I go all lovey-dovey and the sun wears a smile on its lips. I won't quit talking, I repeat myself, I fall to the ground, I taste the little pieces of grit. I walk with one foot dredging the gutter. I hop all the way down to the end of the alley, away from the high street, out from under these sickly street lamps, hideous hues of orange, dazzling ... To crawl in here and lay my beer sodden head on the pavement, a balm ... This is better, back there I thought I was a goner, but in here it's nice and cosy. I drop my lashes and the world swims ... I have to sit up or I'll puke.

You see I can't bear being in the house – a young writer has a million sites to see, but he can't face the page. The evening comes and the pubs open, I sup on my soup and play with my coins, I jangle them in my pocket, I weigh them, I let them slip between my fingers. I'll write another day, on a perfect sunny day in the invisible future, the right typer, the right girl, the right paper. I'll kick the booze and the ciggies and write immortal lines, poetry carved in marble. They'll be great days, glorious days . . .

I go to the bar and order Scotch – a young writer doesn't drink to his future on any old blend. A malt, golden. I knock it back, straight and no water. That's the type of man you're dealing with! Here's to you Hemingway, you ineffectual skunk! And to you Sartre, you groundling! Poems to break the hearts of impossible princesses. Boy, those wankers better watch out for me!

I count my change, my little stack; I feel the faces with my fingers, then place them on the bar, my three pennies. 'Warm beer and wet change, the definition of a London pub in the blitz.' That was one of my mother's many pronouncements. But this is whisky, mother dear, and it's burning a hole right through Johnny's sorry guts. A little poison to warm him through this sour night – no money, no friends, in autumn time, that melancholic time of year.

It's cold on a street like that, cold and lonely for a young writer who's down on his luck, to be heading home at half eleven without a friend in the world, not even an innocent bottle, and only three pennies to jangle in his pocket. Such injustices shouldn't be allowed, and then to taunt someone with it, to make fun, a mockery.

I eye the bottles, sitting behind the plate window . . . Row upon row of them, draped with fairy lights, jewel-like. A million glitterings. A thousand different hues, delicate shades, just beyond my reach. To do such a thing to an honest fellow, a young writer. I shake my head in disgust, shivering. When I think of myself like this, my heart fills with such pity that I want to walk straight up to myself, thrust thirty pounds into my disbelieving hands, kiss both cheeks and wish me all the luck in the world. Then to just turn and walk away, to melt back into the crowds, the shadows, back-handing a small tear.

I stare down at my three pennies and back into that window. My heart thumps under my jacket and all of a sudden I know exactly what I'm going to do. I pull my collar up round my ears, check up and down the street and march straight in there. I hit the door and make for the bottles. There's only these two night-owls sat here filling their pouches, conversing, downing their gut-rot. If you don't calculate your risks in this world, you're finished. I see these two bozos slumped at the bar and I know they won't lift a finger. I'll be walking back out into the cold night clasping my nightcap before those greybeards even bat an eyelid. I ponder the situation, I weigh the ifs and buts, then I'm doing it, I'm walking in through the doorway.

I bite my lip, duck my head and slip in there. Even before I get to the bar those bastards have rattled me. I see them jump to attention as soon as I cross the doormat. I ignore them and head straight for the bottles. I lift one, cold, heavy, golden . . . I tuck that baby under my arm and turn to leave. I've got what I came for – now adios amigos, time to depart, to say our fond farewells.

Those fish jumped so quick I scarcely saw them move. I lift the bottle and before I can even read the vintage I feel his damp little mitt curling round my throat. He pulls and turns me, that skinny one, and pushes his face right into mine. Not a kind face, not the face of a man who understands the rotten luck of a young writer. An altogether unappealing face, small and bitter, built round his nose. I look into it. I see it looking back at me.

'What do you think you're up to, you little shit! Right, I've got him Bob, you call the police!'

I hold up my bottle, I show him my prize.

'I only want a drink.'

I hear the latch go. Beaky's mate throws the bolt, now they've got me. I miscalculated. I should've listened to my heart instead of my head. It's too late to start reminiscing now; you dip your hand in then have to accept the prize. That's the way it is in this world, especially if you're just some arse on the dole, heading home on a cold night without a bottle, and three miserly pennies rattling in your rotten pocket. He comes for me, shoving me this way and that. I let him play Mister Big. He grabs my throat and bangs me up against the bar. His crony throws the bolt and my goose is cooked. I think of decking him with the bottle: I take aim, I weigh it, but the moment passes.

'Look all I want is a drink, OK?'

I reason with him, I explain the situation, but there's no use talking with a cut-throat like that, a boss-man, a taxpayer, with all the booze in the world, well fed and fleshy, with a gut full of fine brandy. He barges straight into me, just for the fun of it. He juts his chin. He shouldn't have done, not to the likes of me, not to a young writer on the dole. I measure up that hooter of his, if I had half a mind I'd sit this coot on his tail!

'Where's your money you little shit! Come on! Empty your pockets! I said empty 'em!'

'I only want a drink.'

I try and placate him but he wants to dance – he keeps lifting his knee, I parry, but he's insistent, he jiggles up and down, a fox-trot . . .

'All I want is a drink, you sell drink don't you?'

It doesn't wash, he's out for revenge, he's determined to show me what for! He puts his hand inside my jacket, feeling my wallet, totally unabashed. He goes through all my linings, he checks it right down near the bottom, in all the corners. He's getting my goat, this fellow with his rummagings and his liberties. He extracts them, one by one. He counts them out onto the bar in front of him, my smiling faces, profiles, three coppers, worthless . . . I'm sick of his waltzing and give him the brush-off, a gentle shove, just to make a point, to show him that I've got heart, too. I watch the bar shudder, it sways, tips and spills itself onto the boards. He knocks against it, spins across the room, pirouettes and knocks it for six. The till goes through the window and hits the tarmac. A tinkling of glass, a special music. I saw it bounce. All three of us take a look; we peer through the busted pane. He rubs his chin, screws up his face and waves it under my nose, like a dirty rag. Things are going from bad to worse. He wants damages, he demands compensation. Justice must be seen to be done! He re-empties my pockets there and then, he rakes around in the linings, he isn't at all discreet. He wants money, hard cash!

'Sit down and put your hands on your head!' He points to the corner.

I saunter over and find my armchair.

'This is going to cost you! This is going to cost you dear!'

He takes them under the light, brandishing my threepence, holds them up to the lamp, revolving each coin individually between thumb and forefinger. He stops grinning, and lets them clatter to the floor.

'Oh dear, this isn't going to buy you out, is it? Not by a long chalk it isn't! Deary me no!' He shouts at me, he talks with his eyebrows.

I need a drink – that jig has left me gasping.

'How about a little glass of Scotch?' I ask politely; I reinforce it with a smile. He strokes his hooter, and eyes me from behind his smashed barricade. But no answer . . . He's taken an instant dislike to me.

'You're in deep trouble, deep trouble . . .' He repeats it purely for the effect, to hear himself in charge.

The meat wagon rolls up, my friends rush to the window, the pretty flashing blue lights, a million segments, a cobweb of busted glass just for me . . .

'He's in here, officer!'

A face shows behind the broken pane, moustachioed, helmeted. Another joins it – two of them, their badges shining like beer cans.

'You alright in there, sir?'

'Yes officer, we've apprehended the villain!'

They start right aways dismantling the fortress; they rattle the portcullis, they nod, they discuss, then they get to it. They spit on their palms and start pulling at the top layer; I keep in my seat and watch the wall coming down. They lift the till, it takes two of them to do that, staggering under its weight. They totter, crab-like, towards the table, then place it down gentle as a baby – they mind their fingers, then get the door. They re-find it, throw the bolt and let the cavalry in. The one with the tash surveys the bomb-site, he wags his helmet and lets out a low whistle. He cocks his head at me.

'Is this the fellow-me-lad?'

He asks it but he already knows it. He ambles over through the matchwood.

'And what have we been up to then, Sonny Jim?'

I twist my neck and take a look at my interrogator: three stripes and a moustache, more like a beard. His whole head jammed into his helmet, shiny blue. I lean in under its peak – I know a sympathetic voice when I hear one, and this cop is a good cop, the type of cop who'll give a young writer a break. I smile to let him know that I'm not drunk. I breathe my brew all over him, I try to suck it back in but it's too late, I'm reeking of it.

'You see officer, sergeant, sir . . .' I concentrate on what I'm about to say, I don't want to go rushing into this and mess up my lines. I look into his little grey eyes – he blinks to reassure me. I put my tongue in the right place and start all over again. I explain my predicament, the whole misunderstanding, the attack, the mugging, the stealing of my thrupence.

'I called in at this night spot, this brothel, for a little night cap, officer. The barman was indisposed, so I poured myself a wee dram and placed my money on the bar.'

I worked out my whole monologue in my head as I went along, and no slurring. I got my big fat stupid tongue out of my cheek and blabbed the whole story. I got it off pat.

'A terrible misunderstanding officer. This pair here, the gentleman with the big nose, and his friend who stands here now, laughing at me . . . Well, quite frankly, they attacked me . . . They jumped in arse first, your lordship, and stole all of my money! so to speak . . . as is plainly evident.'

A little piece of spittle flies from my lips. We watch it revolve between us, it catches the light, then dances onto the end of his nose . . . His knuckles whiten on his truncheon.

I back down, I can see that I've made a misjudgment. I knew from the outset that he was going to be a tough nut to crack. There's no sympathy in this one, he's cold, a hard-nose with no understanding of a young writer who's down on his luck. In fact I'd go as far as to say that this simpleton has never read a book in his life. He doesn't know his Baudelaire from his Bukowski. His eyes glaze over with disgust, a hideous battleship grey. I brush at his stripes, three of them, intricately embroidered, silver thread, a delicate weave . . . It's plain that I'm cutting no ice – this cop is a stony one. I may as well go sing it to the birds, 'cos no matter how I plead, I'm never going to get a fair trial out of this hangman.

'Yes, officer, clean through the window, my till and a full bottle . . .'

He emphasises, draws pictures through the night air, he gilds the lily. My mouth drops, I can't believe my ears. Shit! I may as well wave goodbye. A young writer versus the righteousness of the bourgeoisie? My word against his? A shop owner and a magistrate to boot? I hold my palms to the sky, I've been set up good and proper this time; old double bracket here has framed me and there's bugger all an innocent man can do about it . . . Just some kid wending his way home, alone, on a cold and bitter night. No silver hip flask for company, no floozy on my arm or fat wallet, just the three mugs of Elizabeth wearing a hole in my pocket.

They slip the cuffs on me and lead me out to the meat wagon. The doors go, they clang them behind me and hit the siren.

It's the drink that did it, definitely the drink; it destroyed my family, it runs through us like a great river. A curse, a whole lake of sadness. Bottle after bottle of the stuff, revolving, spinning . . .

row upon row of the little bastards! Halves, quarts, flagons, barrels, all the brands. I tell stories, I explain, I elaborate, I get carried away – my whisky philosophy. But I have my vocation . . . They shouldn't be allowed to do that, to tempt a humble writer, cold, homeward bound, with not so much as a tipple to see him to bed. Just three miserly coins rattling around in the depths of his pockets.

We pull in round the back of the nick, we swerve all the bends, he jams his foot down. We play cops and robbers, we get there in the end, through the night, the tradesmen's entrance . . . He slams on the anchors, I've no arms to catch myself; they've cuffed me up behind my back. I can hardly feel my fingers, don't these bozos know about gangrene?

I blink, I stumble – two of the cops keep me between them, they manhandle me into the cell-block, they go to great pains to make my life uncomfortable, the cuffs pinching, my fingers numb . . . I try to explain to them, my fingers, that I'm a writer, an artist, but I can see from their expressions that they're deaf. They jostle and shove me, they make me trip, they swear at me for that.

This must be the charge room. I get pushed from behind, that's what makes me trip. I apologise, I fall into the light, I focus through the neon. Three or four of them, in uniform – they steer me to the desk, I stagger, I regain my balance.

'Another cunt for the gallows, sarge!'

I heard that, I get the message. And the one behind the desk, stooped at the shoulder, the braid glistens, he adjusts his little peak and announces himself. I recognise him right away. I have to screw up my eyes and squint . . . I'd know that mug anywhere: swallow cheeked; the oily little tash, moth eaten . . . He bristles with pleasure, licks at his pencil, and smoothes out the charge sheet. He's never been so pleased to see anyone in his life. He rubs his mitts together with glee – clouds of scurf rise up, little flakes, a snow storm in miniature. He dusts the flakes from his lap, stands and peers at me as if he's never seen me before in his life. He walks round back, tugs at the bracelets, then nods for them to be taken off . . .

'You said he was a cunt, Jeff, and that's what we've got, a right cunt! Who's been a naughty boy then?'

I can't bring my hands back round front, they have to be lifted. I nurse them, massaging my wrists. I flex and unflex them; slowly they come back to life, all ten, hot and burning, a dull ache.

'Empty your pockets! On the table!' The air blossoms out of his mouth. I fumble with my hanky . . . I try to please him . . . but it's cold in that dump. You'd think those bozos would run a couple of heaters on a cold winter's night? I stick my hand back in my pocket; I clasp at things but can't feel a thing. I fish out a key and let it tinkle onto the desk, then some fluff . . . a comb . . . my notebook . . . His eyes light up and he snatches it up. I feel that I have to speak up, to make my point.

'Excuse me . . . that's my notebook . . . a diary. I'm a young writer. It's personal.'

He licks his fingers and flicks the pages. I watch them turn, I open my mouth and go to speak but it's pointless. He narrows his eyes, screws up his mug and digests.

'Did you write this drivel?'

'It's mine, it's personal . . . a diary . . . I'd rather you didn't read it, actually.'

'You'd rather I didn't read it? Oh, pardon me! Did you hear that boys? Sir would rather I didn't read it!'

That raises a laugh, a couple of sniggers – actually, it makes me blush . . .

'Is this supposed to be English? 'Cos if it is, you can't fucking well spell, my son!'

I keep my chin on my chest.

'Speak up, let's hear you! Cat got your tongue?'

I clear my throat, I say it out loud: 'It's a poem.'

That cracks his face into a fearsome grimace, he stares into it, he scratches his bonce, he mouths my lines and he jams his mug so close to mine that we're almost rubbing noses.

'You call this a poem?'

His skin shimmies under the surface. He licks his lips, little pools of spit in the corners, white scum, his moustache twitching in and out of the foam.

'I'll tell you what this is sonny! It ain't nice, that's what it is! And it don't rhyme . . . Are you a subversive? 'Cos you stinks like one to me . . . Your clothes stinks, your ideas stink, your poems stink, and you stink! You've been smoking pot? Hashish? Ganja? Have you been at the wacky-baccy, boy?'

I shouldn't have answered back, not like that; you can't go back-chatting gentlemen of the constabulary, not if it's an easy ride you're after.

'Scrumpy and kebab, officer.'

I can hear his teeth cracking under the weight of his grimace.

'Get your arse out of them clothes! Empty your pockets! Keep your hands on your head! You need to learn some respect boy! Some respect!'

I fumble with my belt.

'So you likes anarchy, do you? You enjoy riots and public disorder? You'd like to stab a bobby, wouldn't you? Come on then, I'm waiting! Give him your knife Jeff, let him have a go . . . Come on! Come on, or are you too fucking yellow?'

I step out of my trousers, pull off my pants and socks and stare down at my nakedness. He doesn't even help me with my jacket, my knees knocking with the cold. He smiles, but not with his eyes, just the corners of his mouth, then he picks up my comb from the little pile of my personal effects . . . He picks at it gingerly, wrinkles his nose . . . He holds it up to the light, then lets it go from between thumb and forefinger. We all watch it rattle down onto the concrete. He cuts his smirk dead.

'Pick that up!'

Those other bastards all moo at each other, they're absolutely delighted; big louts, dressed in blue, except for their bovver boots, black, shiny. They egg each other on and play with their truncheons . . . They catch me pogging them and stare me down . . . I have to lower my eyes, my hands in front, covering myself . . . The cold concrete floor, shifting my weight from foot to foot. I study it, trowel marks, and my little toe, reddened, a corn . . .

'You heard the sergeant, now pick it up!' A little chorus, two baritone and one bass.

I look at the comb and back up at those mouths working away in all the flesh.

'On your knees!'

I go down, I crouch naked, I lower my body, the smell of boot polish comes up to me, the smell of their maleness.

'Down!'

They twitch their toecaps, steel, next to my nose . . . I see my reflection, I swallow . . .

'Pick it up!'

I feel for it, my fingers in the dust, I close them around it.

'What's that tattoo on your arse say, boy?'

He delights himself and turns to the others. I tremble on my knees . . .

'I don't know, I've never seen it before, officer.'

I felt myself going to say it, and then out it comes of its own accord. He grabs me by the neck, digs his fingers in, and pushes me down, forcing my face into the concrete. I feel his boot, the toecap, he sticks it into my kidneys.

'What's that? Answering back! I can see that we're going to have to teach you some manners! Aren't we! A little boot massage! Come on, say it again, come on! Speak up so's we can hear you!'

'I think I have the right to remain silent.'

'Oh, oh, it thinks does it? Hark at that lads. It thinks! Well, you think an awful lot don't you boy, but you don't know much do you? In fact you know fuck all! The only rights you've got are the ones I say you've got, and that's none! Got it? You ain't allowed to shit unless I says so, got it?!'

He extracts his toecap; I scramble to my feet, shaking. To be honest I felt pretty vulnerable stood there starkers between those bruisers, dark blue, grinning, tapping their boots. I keep my eyes averted, I have to. You see I've got this look, the jaw line, the arrogance that I can't hide. He stares me out then turns his face in disgust.

'OK, book the cunt!' They write my name in the charge book then rough-handle me through to the lock-up. The jailer wags his keys like a bunch of bananas.

'Is there a toilet? please? I need to go to the toilet.'

That's exactly how I talk – straight, clear, precise, without a hint of sarcasm.

'Pardon?'

'Is there a toilet, please?'

'Oh yes, we've got a toilet for you your lordship, a very special toilet, just you follow me, right this way, sir. A real nice shit hole, deep and dark, so's you can get right down in the pan and curl up at the bottom, 'cos that's where you belong, isn't it? In the shit!'

He shoves me through the doorway. Hey, that's no way to go speaking to a young writer! He throws the bolt, double locks it, the keys rattling. Growing quieter ... walking up the gangway, another door, another lock, receding ...

I take a piss in the bucket, read the wall, and shake off the little droplets. Not so many luxuries in this hotel, and that bastard hasn't even killed the light. Not even a blanket, no mattress, just a couple of slats, hard, stone-like. And the wind comes at you. How's a fellow meant to get his head down? I pace the concrete floor, naked, and prance like a flamingo. I swap feet, I have to keep moving. And no bed, not even a blanket . . .

OK, so I slipped up: can't a fellow make an honest mistake? I only wanted a wee dram, for Christ's sake, a humble little nip . . . And let's face it, that fat cat had plenty to spare . . . Bottles of the stuff . . . whisky galore! row upon row . . . Why should he have everything in the drinks department – a cosy fire, a full brandy bowl in one hand, and a fancy cigar in the other – whilst all I've got is three worthless pennies to rub together?

I got to know that floor pretty well during the course of my visit. Concrete, grey, with a piss trough running to the little drain in the middle. I counted all the ridges, different undulations. Then I have to crawl onto the bench. I collapse, I lay on my front and tuck my legs up under my body, I stick my arms between my legs. A hundred contortions to hold in the heat, to not die from the cold, to last the night . . . I trembled so hard that I almost jumped off the bench.

'Oi, you! Wake up!'

I look up and there's a pair of mirthless eyes grinning at me through the grill.

'Are you playing with yourself?' I keep schtum. 'Oi, I'm talking to you, you little pervert! Are you wanking in there? Are you wanking in your pit? Do you want me to come in there and give you a good kicking?'

I say nothing. I've learned humility. Anyway they're below me. For my friends and loved ones I will suffer and endure 'til the bitter end . . . A young writer . . .

I see his mug at the peep hole, I will memorise it for posterity. I mumble, I go to speak, I have to ask it, I'm delirious with the cold.

'Can I have a blanket, please?'

'Can you have a what?'

'A blanket . . . please . . . I need a blanket.'

'Did you hear that, Jeff? Did you hear something squeak? I think we've got mice in here.'

'I need a blanket, I'm cold.'

'Say "please".'

'Please.'

'No!'

He's delighted himself. He dances down the corridor, I hear his forced laughter, it echoes . . . He rattles my cage. I count time by his visits ... every half hour ... just to make sure that I'm not getting comfortable, that a fellow doesn't get his head down ... He carries on right to the end of the night, hoping for the excuse to give me a good kicking. Right up until it starts turning grey outside ...

2. THE MAN WITH WHISKERS

H e wasn't happy; he felt cheated and he deserved better: my father. Christ he deserved better alright, better than all of us!

They lock me in the bedroom so I scream. I scream and scream until my mother comes in.

'For crying out loud shut up! Just bloody shut up!'

She lifts me from the cot and carries me downstairs. I watch the walls . . . They come up to you then they shrink away . . . Railings, banisters, a special effect: on off, on off . . . I'm watching the stairs, we go down and they go up . . . You see I'm being carried that way, and that's the effect.

She sits me on her lap and I nuzzle her breast.

'For God's sake, he should be eating solids! Think of yourself, Juny!'

The man with whiskers shakes his napkin at me. I'm lifted, dumped in the high chair and handed a crust: I suck on it. The man with the whiskers tells me not to play with my food, but to eat it. I look at that crust, I take a special interest in it: three or four different colours, some black bits, and these holes, hundreds of them, some kind of intricate garden.

'He's got to learn to eat solids, how are we meant to lead a normal life if you insist on breast-feeding him?'

I play with the Weetabix . . . I dribble it back out . . .

'Eat your food, Steven, don't play with it!'

I look from my mother to the man with whiskers – he must be talking to me. He repeats it, mouthing his words.

'Eat up your porridge, come along, Nichollas, you too!'

'He's had enough, haven't you darling?'

'He asked for it so he can finish it.'

'But it's cold, he doesn't like it when it's cold, do you, Nichollas?' She fusses and she smoothes his hair.

The man with the whiskers stands and flings down his napkin. He walks out then turns and storms back in again, he makes a grab at the porridge bowl.

'You're spoiling the children, woman!'

A blaze of whiskers, old yellow beard, plucking invisible fruits from the skies, arching his eyebrows until they look like viaducts.

'Look at your dress woman, you're pissing milk! I will not have you breast-feeding that infant in public! As for you, eat your bloody porridge when mummy makes it or I'll force it down your bloody throat! Give me the bowl, come along now! You asked for it, now you can eat it. Eat it!'

He picks up the spoon and waves it under his nose like a tomahawk, leaping up and down in front of us, doing a little jig, hanging his arms for effect. Ape-like, chimpanzee-ish . . . Nichollas starts to blubber, he stands and wets himself. He grabs at the table cloth and goes down. The table subsides under the avalanche. He crawls through the porridge; the old man splutters, falls to his knees and rolls in it.

'Shit and damnation! A sea of porridge, that's what I'm swimming in! A sea of piss and porridge! You've turned my very children against me! Well, I'm carrying you monkeys no further!'

He grinds his teeth so hard that he spits powder. A filling falls to my feet and rattles across the linoleum; silver, black, heavy, irregular . . . I crawl over to it, just a kid, on my hands and knees, no kidding . . . He holds out his hand to me.

'Give it here! Give it me!' He slips in the milk and crashes into the sideboard, his head bouncing between the shelves. He pulls himself out and smashes his head into the chimney stack, breaking the house down into matchwood. He swivels and bites at his back, then snatches up my stool. The cute little stool I sit on whilst my mother makes pastry in the afternoons. He raises it high above his head and crashes it down onto the cooker. A million particles . . . hundreds and thousands . . . spinning, little orbits . . . Down onto the mat . . . busted . . .

We blink through the sawdust, his peroxide hair shimmering above his head, a halo of gold: old snow ball . . . And his delicate

kisser, mincing between his whiskers . . . My breath is locked in
my heart, shamed to silence. This is his tantrum and, by God, no
one better try stealing his wind, or else! He shakes his fingers at us;
they rattle in their joints like teeth. I crawl under the table cloth,
following my brother. He sticks his boot in my face, he pretends
it's an accident but it's on purpose. We crouch beneath the drapes,
watching their feet. His shoes shine like gravy, and her in flipflops.

'Christ, Juny, you must hate me! Do you, is that it? Come on
answer me!'

He slaps her.

'Stop looking at me, and you!'

He pulls at the table cloth, 'til it billows above his head, like a
spinnaker.

'Mind the porridge!'

We hear her shout, but it's too late, it somersaults through the
air, it sticks to the ceiling, droplets, clots . . . It falls like rain. The
old man kicks at the bowl.

'Shit the porridge! Shit it, I shit it, me, the great provider!'

He scoops up a handful of the stuff, and slaps it into his hair.
We don't know if we're meant to laugh.

'Yes me, the great provider! My great sin? To provide and to
cherish, that's all! And who's to say I don't? Answer me that?' He
defies us with his nose. 'Come on, speak up! Don't be shy! We can
talk it over like adults. Do I or don't I?'

My mother let out a little sob.

'Oh, I see, I get the picture, of course, I get it now, that's it, I've
been blind . . . I haven't provided enough, that's it, isn't it? You
want more, don't you? You want blood! Well, step right up and
open a vein, come on be my guest, why don't you? That's it, is it?
Oh yes, lovely . . . I must have been blind. You want blood, that's
it, my fucking guts! Fuck and damnation! I apologise, unreserved-
ly . . . on my humble knees! And I thought that I'd done enough,
that I'd been pulling my weight, working my fingers to the bloody
bone!'

He rattles them at us again. It's absolutely true, nothing, no skin
on them whatsoever, just clean white bones . . .

'My giddy aunt, Juny, you bastards stick worse than dog shit!'
He mimes it, he scrapes his shoe across the mat, he comes barking
in under the table cloth on all fours . . .

'And as for him, yes you, you little shitter! I caught you
bouncing on my sofa again, didn't I? Yes daddy! Yes daddy! You

must think I was born yesterday! Well, I want to hear it from your own lips, an admittal, an apology, and don't bother lying to me ... I saw you, I caught you red-handed! So come on now, own up! Do you know how much that sofa cost? And it hasn't even been paid for yet, not a bit of it! Well, come on speak up! Juny, come here, Juny! I want you to hear this. Look, this smelly child of yours was caught bouncing on the sofa! On my sofa! Weren't you, Smell? Look at it woman, look at it, brand new, wrecked! Scarcely a month old! Thread-bare, your children!'

He kicks at it.

'A write-off, a total write-off! With his shoes on mind, do you understand me? Bouncing with his shoes!'

He calls her to witness, he grabs at the offending foot.

'What size are they? Where did he get such feet? And look at them, they're scuffed! Scuffed, I tell you! He's been playing in his best shoes again! Haven't you? Look at them, ruined, ruined! You see this pair of mine, look at them, feast your eyes! Bought last week? A month ago? No, ten years old! That's right, ten years old, going on fifteen!'

He bounds over the sofa and smashes his head into the lampshade, he lets off words like fire-crackers. He starts in again, arse first.

'Who's to stop me?'

He bounces up and down.

'Who the hell's to fucking well stop me?'

Higher and higher he goes, somersaulting like an acrobat ...

'Aren't – I – the – one – who – pays – for – every – thing! – And – not – just – the – hard – boiled – eggs – and – nuts! – Every – thing! – House! – Clothes! – Furni – ture! – My – facili – ties! – My – sofa! – Every – thing! – All – of – it!'

He catapults off sideways, a little trampolining, then he flies through the air and crashes down on top of my mother. They bounce and land in a heap – arms, legs, pieces of his beard are on the carpet. He scratches at the tufts, a rash, we see red ... He drags my mother to her feet.

'All of it! All of it! My facilities!'

She lets out a little cry and he releases her. She drops to her knees and sobs, she gags ... Blub, blub, blub ... blub, blub, blub ... She pleads, but not loudly, inwardly, and she wrung her hands with weep ...

This is the first scene of violence that I can remember. And I remember realising that my father wasn't happy, and my mother looked tragic. She made a profession of it over the years. In the end no one could beat her at it; no matter how hard we tried she could always go one better. She prided herself on it . . . It was a whole new era for her.

'Brup, brup, brup . . . brup, brup, brup . . .'

When it comes to tragedy, no one can outdo a woman; they are the eternal sufferers. Periods, childbirth, hysterectomy and decay, and they always coming up smiling, but sadly, at the edges . . . She cried silent tears, my mother did, great torrents of them. They're the real tears, none of your yelling and boo-hooing. I had to sit and watch her, my heart frozen. I didn't want her to die. I tried to hold her hand. She drooled like a sick calf. Real misery is silent, I should know, I've seen it from an early age.

3. THE SMELL

The old man pissed off, but never formally left . . . He still used to show up now and again, but begrudgingly, just to check up. Just to make sure that we weren't having a good time, that us kids hadn't been dropping little bits of litter . . .

'For crying out loud, shut your bickering or I'll bang your bloody heads together!'

Slam! Nichollas was four years older than me and twice my size – he used to launch himself as our heads came together. I used to see real sparks, stars and comets, a whole light show! And his head wasn't just bigger than mine, it was as heavy as a rock. It crippled my mother when she had him, twenty-two internal stitches and then some more . . .

'No wonder he split you like a fig, Juny, look at the size of the head on young Nichollas!'

He stands back admiring it like a new piece of furniture . . . And then Slam! straight into mine. And it wasn't just bone, oh no, it was crammed full of brains, as they were always at great pains to point out.

'There's brains for you, Juny, such an intelligent head.'

Then Slam! That's the sound of our heads coming together . . . Slam! My little head up against that great slab of bone? Not much of a competition. Crack! That's justice for you . . . My little head, fine featured, blond hair, not much chance of fair play. And him supposedly the intelligent one, the one with all the brains. 'Big Brother' and Crunch! That's what I learned, and the way Nick used to launch himself, gleefully, at my expense. It was as if they were already in cahoots and no matter what, I'd come off the worse . . .

And now he's surprised that I don't forget. Bang! That kind of memory, it stays with you. My big brother was petty and vicious alright, already stomping round like the pompous little prick he's grown up to be.

Once you get used to being on the receiving end like that, it doesn't take too long before you start learning to inflict some misery of your own. Because whatever else you might say about us humans, even the most stupid of us have some kind of imagination when it comes down to spite. In the realms of laying on pain and suffering, we're unsurpassable, we truly are world beaters . . . How to dole out acres of misery and suffering? If we learn nothing else in this world, we learn that much.

'Do you want the police to come and arrest you, Steven? Do you want me to have to call the police?'

I drew on my plimsoll with a bit of chalk.

'Would you like a little sister to play with?'

Then the snow came and I went up the stairs to their room and there was a cat sitting with her in bed. I wasn't allowed in their bed, but the cat was. It was a girl cat but it had a boy's name, it was called George. Then it got cat flu and we had to walk quiet and the snow got deeper and deeper until the river froze over and our tortoises died in the shed.

Then the cat came back to life; my mother nursed it under the kitchen stove . . . She made it a little lead and let it sleep in her bed again. Then I accidentally stood on it. I held onto the banister and put my foot on its back, I lowered my weight and it squawked . . . I felt the old man's hands on me. He saw the whole thing. He throws his hat down and jumps the stairs four at a time. He shakes me 'til I see stars. I can't feel the ground. He gave me 'what for' – I was just one big mistake, I was a scab and should have died at birth! I wouldn't stop crying and I wouldn't stop sucking my mother's tits.

'This child will amount to nothing, Juny, nothing!'

Once they did manage to get me weaned, I'd only eat chocolate and chips. I had attacks of boils, and bruised like an apple . . . I couldn't move. My mother had to hold me down whilst my father burst the pus out of me. They didn't want to be seen with me in public – I was a disgrace, I had a shitty arse and my teeth were totally rotted. My family called me: 'The Smell'. I was dragged into the bedroom and thrashed.

4. TINKER-BUD

It's no picnic being a kid, and it's even tougher being the younger brother: you learn to yelp before the punch, and then everybody gets the same idea and decides to join in.

I really was a nice polite kid at heart, there was still some joy left in me in those days, but then experience wipes all that out . . .

The trouble was that by the time I got to being born, my brother and the old man already had it all sewn up, they saw me as an outsider trying to muscle in on their scene. I was viewed with suspicion bordering on outright contempt. Just the look of me gave them the willies, they made loud remarks and insinuations: apparently my pallor left a lot to be desired, my particular smell.

'It's the biscuits he eats.'

My mother defended me, but that only stocked up their loathing still further.

'The biscuits!' My father scoffs, pulling out his handkerchief, he flourishes it, he shakes it to the four corners then blows, he takes his hooter in both hands and trumpets it. Honk! Honk! Honk! Reverberating, his morning reveille . . . Honk! Honk! Honk! He used to deliver some vicious blasts on that neb of his. That's the way he used to blow that thing, that's what all the noise is about, you understand me, now? Honk! Honk! That's him sounding his fog horn. He looks down at me, past both barrels, he gives it a last tweak, it wobbles, he flares his nostrils . . .

'Would you like to go away, Steven? A boarding school or borstal, which would you prefer?'

I stare into the carpet, I look for my marble, the golden cat's eye, the best one of the lot, lost for good more than likely . . . He consoles me, he pats my head, he lifts his hand, he sniffs at it.

'My God, Juny, this child stinks!'

'It's the biscuits,' she stutters it out. 'Bourbon, his favourites . . .'

He can't believe his ears, he smacks the side of his head with his fist.

'The biscuits! The biscuits! Juny, the little tyke stinks, so don't try and tell me any different! Don't give me biscuits, he doesn't wipe himself properly! Don't try and break my heart with your biscuits! He's making a mockery, a fool of us both . . . Boarding school, that's the only answer, they'll install some discipline! Steven . . . Steven! Look at me when I'm talking to you! Do you want to go to prison? Do you want me to have to call the police? Is that what you want? Do we have to lock you away?'

Children belong to their parents, that's a fact. You don't need a licence, just a cock and a pair of balls . . . In our world my father was omnipresent, he exercised his will from afar. He came and he went. He stayed away. He turns up and bosses us like dirt.

'Look at him, Juny, he's crawling in boils, there's so much pus in him that it can't get out quick enough!'

It was true, I couldn't move. I was swathed in bandages and calamine from head to foot. 'Hop-a-long Cassidy', Nana Lewis calls me – that hands everybody a laugh. 'Hop-a-long Cassidy' . . . I hobble about . . .

She used to bring us fruit, Nana Lewis, fruit on Wednesdays . . . And once a little tortoise called Charlie, she found him in the vegetable patch, a cute little fellow. I sat naked in the sun and his neck was cold and he had a mouth and eyes and everything, and his tongue was pink and came out when he ate and he lived in his own shell. And we saw big Caroline next door in the paddling pool and she had no clothes on and she didn't have a willy.

I put Charlie down on the grass, squat down and look between my legs, I put my head to my knees in shame. And then the snow came and we put Charlie in a cardboard box in the shed, but when we took him out in the spring, he was dead.

'The frost must have gotten to him.' Caroline pushes me on the swing. 'You see everything dies . . .'

I lift my feet up off the ground and swing, I study my ankles, fawn socks, black slip-on plimsolls. I lean back and Caroline smiles down at me.

'No one lives forever, everyone has to die . . . Then the soul goes up to heaven.'

'Where's heaven?'

'In the clouds with God.'

Now that I've got to see, to see a dead man floating up into the sky on his back, like a plank.

'The body dies and the soul floats up to heaven.'

And I got the devil in me and my legs came out in boils, they spread up from my knees and out across my back. My mother holds me down whilst the old man squeezes them out, yellow worms, vicious attacks, not very lovely, unasked for. I was humbled but still rancid, a little retarded maybe? Possibly, possibly . . .

'He won't speak properly! He won't close his mouth when he eats! He can't piss straight! He can't wipe his own arse! Look woman, look! He pisses directly up the wall, and not a drop of it in the basin mind! Why do you always have to urinate on the floor, Steven? And don't tell me it's the biscuits he eats!'

'He tries, but it's difficult to aim when he's standing up.'

'How in hell would you know woman! Christ, if he isn't pissing the bed, he's shitting his pants, and now this! The floor's thick with it. He's rotting the linoleum, look at it, clear up the wall!'

He points at the stains, the discolorations . . .

'In the toilet basin, Steven! Urinate in the toilet basin! Not up the wall, for crying out loud! And wash behind your foreskin! What did I tell you to do? When you go to the toilet, pull your foreskin back, do you understand?'

He yanks my shorts down. He orders me. I have to show him, to pull it back. I try to aim but it goes both right and left, two separate streams, a snake's tongue . . . golden droplets. It hits the old man square in the eye, a terrible jet. He jumps back.

'Jesus Christ Almighty!' He dabs at his eye. 'You little pig!'

I shake it off and go to pull the foreskin back, but it won't budge, it's jammed . . . I give it another tug, but it's honest to God stuck. The old man folds away his hanky and has a go himself, at first gingerly, then with both hands. He gets stuck in, but no movement, not a sausage. He looks kind of quizzical. He pours himself a triple Scotch and passes out on the sofa.

Next morning I go to piss but nothing will come out. I try to pull back my foreskin but the nob's as swollen as a plum. So we have to go and see the quack, Baldielocks and his Three Hairs, he licks them flat . . .

'The trouble,' as he points out, 'is that the end's swollen, a kind of balloon effect.'

I stand there with my trousers round my ankles whilst he walks around playing with his face, moulding the flesh, great caskets of it, hanging down below his ears . . . He re-approaches the problem, he daubs at it with cotton wool, he applies some soapy water and gives it an experimental tug. There's a little ripping sound, that brings me up on my toes.

'Shush, Steven!' The old man's like a sergeant. 'Shush!'

A spot of blood, but otherwise no change.

'For Christ's sake, stand still, Steven!'

I try to tell him that it hurts.

'Shush!'

His answer to everything: 'shush!'

Our doctor puckers his lips, kissed with a quizzical smile.

'We'll have to keep the little chap in overnight for observation, to see if there's any further developments. I think it's for the best.'

He agrees with himself, walks behind his desk and lights one up, he puffs on it . . . Pretending to know what he's talking about . . . He studies his cuticles . . .

'He'll be on the Children's Ward, he'll need pyjamas, dressing gown and his slippers. He motions to me with his great white dome . . . discussing my future. That's nice, pleasant, educated – me just a piece of furniture . . .

I run as fast as my little dick will let me, I have to gyrate my hips like a spider to stop the cloth chafing. I kind of fart all the way up the road and in through the main doors. Then I have to hang around for ages, waiting for those two loafers to catch up, the pair of them still chewing at each other's throats. I can hear the old man barking a whole block away. It's obvious that if I don't get him out of the quack's face there's going to be some blood spilt. It seems that the only chance I've got, is to usher him in off the street before he gets his head bent. I was left holding that door 'til doomsday.

There aren't many places that smell worse than hospitals. I hold my breath, and try not to breathe: bleach battling with piss and decay. It hits you as soon as you walk in there. I count to thirty then I get shoved. This nurse leads me to my bed, iron, chipped, forty of them in two rows. The faces of the unknown, pale-faced kids and a roaring noise, like a swimming pool.

I have to undress, change into my pyjamas and get into bed, even though it's the middle of the afternoon.

The kid in the next bed's got appendicitis, so I get to eat his cold sausages; I help myself to his grapes as well. His mother reckons I'll get appendicitis because I swallow the pips. She walks in and she's got one leg shorter than the other. She asks me my name and tells me that Simon isn't allowed tomatoes at home, because the skins don't agree with him . . .

'I don't eat tomatoes,' I tell her, and she raises her eyes to the ceiling.

'I see you're a spoilt little boy,' she says, which means that I am bad.

I just have time to tell her that my father's going to buy me a squirrel for my birthday, when a load of white coats come marching up the ward. A crashing of heels . . . They make straight for my bed, pull the screens round and crowd in on the inside. They loom through the darkness. All their faces, ghastly, jammed into mine, hot mouths, discussing . . .

'You've eaten, you shouldn't have been allowed to eat.'

They pull the bedclothes back and tug at my foreskin, they fight over the stethoscope and bicker like kids. They prod and swap notes. Young men mostly, red-faced and pimply, shavers, and one greybeard. He takes his thumbs from his waistcoat, an elaborate silk. First he powders his hands, then he blows into the gloves, he huffs through the talcum powder, stretching the fingers like elastic bands then lets them go Thwack! One at a time, five on each hand, ten in all, then nursy helps him into them. He flexes his fingers, he strains them, he pulls at each little pinkie individually, he makes like a pianist, he orchestrates – suspenseful, we're caught watching.

It seems that the time for deliberating has passed, no more dilly-dallying or chewing it over in Latin. He takes my knob between thumb and forefinger, he twists it to the left and to the right – it's positively blossoming with blood – he polishes it up purple as a toga . . . He nods his head and nursy passes him the syringe . . .

'Now this won't hurt, just a little prick!' He looks round, he milks his audience, they blush into their waistcoats, cheap woollen affairs. 'And that's all you'll feel. You're a big boy now, aren't you ...' He reads my name tag, '... Steven? You have to be brave now.'

He checks the syringe, he goes cross-eyed, a little jet of clear fluid caught in the strip lights, a delicate arc ... A mole on his cheek, a clot of blood and two grey hairs. He eases it in, and I scream. It jumps out of me, long, drawn out, wrenched from the pit of my stomach ... I writhe, my toes curl and I grip the sheets.

'Tut-tut, you're not a little girl, are you?'

The tears sting my eyes ... That's rich, him and his 'tut-tut', then Slam! with his hot stiletto, right into the helmet, right where it was most swollen, the most sensitive. I bite the pillow and whinny like a horse.

'Tut-tut.'

He hands nursy the empty syringe and holds up his hands to be de-gloved ...

'There might be some slight bruising, just keep it clean and dry ... You can go home in the morning.'

His lackeys pull the screens back and they all head off down the pub. And him calling me a little girl, him with his six inch syringe! They depart and I'm left holding myself. Then I remember Tinker-bud and I hold onto him as well, a little koala bear, a glove puppet, kids stuff. We play peek-a-boo under the covers, we survey the damage, gingerly, my burst balloon. We sneak a look when the other kids aren't looking, I don't want to let on ... My shame ...

The bruise spread right down to my balls, and lasted for a month. My mother was dead proud of it, she wanted everybody to know. I even had to show it to Bert, who ran the general store at the end the road. He wouldn't sell me fireworks ...

'You're under-age,' he said.

And I ran home crying, that was regular.

He winces at my bruises ...

'Nasty,' he tells my mother. 'Very nasty.'

They closed him down that summer ... He asked a little girl from the council estate to come behind the counter and take off her knickers.

'Nasty,' he said.

Me with my shorts round my knees.

'Very nasty.'

That cheered my mother up no end.

5. OVER THE BACK

If I tell you exactly how it was, then nobody will be able to accuse me of lying. That's my hollow dream, that's how I kid myself. I'll stay terrifyingly honest, helping myself to understand, to come to terms . . .

'Young gentlemen' that's how our father used to address us, us sat scrubbed and helpless in the back seat of his car. And somehow the old fool really seemed to believe it: 'young gentlemen'.

We lived under the constant threat of his impending visits, and the silent misery of my mother. Once the old girl tidied up we aren't allowed to romp around or move so much as a hair. No more fun and games for us kids, no sir! Double scrubbed and no messing.

And every night our mother sat at her place by the window, waiting for the car headlamps to show, sniffling to herself . . . Then the sobs . . . Then it got totally dark and she chucked the grub away. It was the same pattern night after night, week in week out, until the old buzzard finally rolls up.

'Was that his lights? Did you hear a car door?'

Me and me brother look at each other: now she's seeing things. And then the crying, swallowed down, hollow sounding, unwinding, then winding up again. The same old tune, wheezing in the dark, at the far end . . . near the Venetian blinds. Each night, hoping, expectant, then resigned . . . Each night she makes believe as if he's gonna show up, and we have to go through the whole charade again. She tidies up, combs her hair and paints a smile on her face ... Then the clock watching, 'til finally she chucks the grub away and opens a bottle of Guinness. Then the phone goes ... She chucks the moggy off her lap and leaps to it ... He's pissed ... He'll be on the next train ... The pips go ... then nothing ... We sit and wait ... Neither hide nor hair, and us double scrubbed and no playing in the garden ... And off to bed early.

'Your father's at the station, he'll be here in fifteen minutes.'

She fiddles with her throat and stares earnestly into the garden ...

'Is that some rubbish up by the fir tree? You didn't drop any sweet wrappers did you, Steven? You know what your father's like!'

We sit around twiddling our thumbs, and not getting dirty. We play in the back room – we're not allowed in the front room on account that I kind of fucked up the sofa by bouncing on it, so we're not allowed in there. I paint a bird in purple and a picture of war, then my brother punches me and knocks the paint water over. I writhe on the floor screaming 'til the old girl comes in and does her nut.

'Soddin' bloody kids! Look at it! And for Christ's sake stop whining! My God, that voice! It's high time you learned a few facts of life!' She looks at me meaningfully.

Then we hear the car door go and a blond shadow at the window, ghost-like ... We have to look twice, to be sure ... We have to see him coming, first his titfer, then his beard. Then he comes into full view, throwing his brolly about, stabbing at toffee papers. He stops, about turns and stoops, he takes a closer look, making sure ... He picks something up between thumb and forefinger, holds it up to the light, sniffs at it, then carries it off with him at arm's length and presents it to my mother awaiting him on the door step. We watch out of the window. He floats up the garden, picks up the toffee wrapper and walks straight up to her. He goes out of sight, then comes back into view; he kind of looks at me, and I do the same ...

'Hello Nichollas, Steven.'

He nods and walks past, his head thrown back, eyes averted. He goes into the front room, and the door closes.

'Hello father,' I say.

The old girl runs to the kitchen full tilt and ditches the toffee wrapper, Plop! into the waste bin, it rattles around down there, amongst the potato peelings and tea leaves – she chucks it in there, the offending wrapper. Then shuffles about in the kitchen fiddling with the skin round her throat . . . He comes back out the front room practising his scowl.

'What are you fussing about with now, Juny?'

'Would you like something to eat, darling?'

He stops and stares at her, he looks her up and down from head to foot.

'Yes, Juny, roast beef and Yorkshire pudding, please!' She puts the lid on the bread bin. 'Roast beef please, Juny!' . . . That's how he answers her.

We haven't got any roast beef, so we have to go out to dinner and that means we have to be double scrubbed.

'I could do you some cheese on toast . . . I didn't know that you'd be coming . . . Or I could do some egg and chips.'

He shakes his head in disbelief. No playing over the back woods, double scrubbed and no dilly-dallying. My mother chucks the cheese on toast in the bin . . . And then she has to go and get tarted up. I see her naked in the bathroom, then she gets out the talcum powder . . . The stench of lipstick and finally her mother's old fur coat . . . It was always a signal when she put that rag on, that meant we were going out.

'Can't I go over the back instead . . . I ain't hungry . . . I won't stay out late . . .?'

'Absolutely not, Steven, it's a family meal!'

That's tough. My brother backs the old man up. 'No way kid!' That's how everybody speaks to me. I look resigned, I kick at stones.

'What's the matter with that child of yours, Juny? He's totally unappreciative.'

I toe the ground and I look at him, then I don't, that's the way it's always been. Bored, moseying around, waiting for that old git to show up, then the phone goes . . .

'Oh shit bugger arseholes! Oh, for heaven's sakes stop it the pair of you, I'm trying to listen! Shut up or I'll bang your soddin' heads together! Oh, hello darling . . . yes . . . yes . . . the 8.15 . . . yes . . .'

And then the tidying up . . . Getting our knees clean for a start, and not going over the back . . . Then that bozo would show, clasping a toffee wrapper. His nose in the air, he walks in, and deposits it in the bin . . . Bravo!

'Come along, Juny, chop chop! I haven't eaten since luncheon. Nichollas! Steven! Look at your knees! For Christ's sake, chop-chop! Really, Juny, there's no food in the house, and now you want to keep me hanging around all evening. I expressly rang you in advance, why can't you be ready? Come along you boys, get in the car now! And for God's sake mind the upholstery! Christ, Juny, you're prepared to use my facilities but do I get any respect!'

Me and my brother traipse out, and head for the car, it's still warm and stinking of leather . . .

My father starts it up and then we have to sit there in silence for fifteen minutes whilst my mother runs back indoors. She checks that the cooker's turned off, that the cat has been put out, makes sure that she's left a light on and checks that she locked the back door. We watch her coming and going in slow motion. She slams the front door and pulls it violently, almost wrenching her arm from its socket, just to be sure. To be certain. Is it locked? My father drums on the steering wheel with his root-like fingers.

'Good God, woman, for Christ sake's get in the bloody car! I hope that child is not going to puke in the car again! You're not going to do a Technicolor yawn, are you, Steven?'

'Wot?'

'Not "wot", "pardon"!'

It's my opinion that he swerved all those corners on purpose. He chucked the engine into fourth and never bothered to come back down again, his hands flailing at the wheel like a juggler. I feel my collar and suck at the inside of my mouth. It's the special combination of the leather and the old girl's lipstick, the car reeks of it, and her swathed in that stinking fur coat of her mothers. She turns in her seat and smoothes my hair back, a cat lick, and then the smell hits me, it clings to the roof of my mouth, I gag. She feels my forehead, and rattles her cheap jewellery at me. The gold of her ring, it glitters in my eye socket. I gag, I vomit and re-swallow, I grit my teeth . . . I need air, I want the woods, I want to be a Tyrannosaurus Rex or a squirrel. The old man hits the brakes and swerves the roundabout at full throttle. My stomach heaves, it trickles through my nose, sour, some bean sauce – I have to let it go. I open up and let it pour, in hot jets, six different types of tomatoes.

'My God, Juny, stop him! I don't believe it! He's done it again! The little stinker!' My father grapples with the wheel, yelling over his shoulder. 'Why didn't you tell us! You did that on purpose, didn't you? Well, he can clear it up! He's your child, Juny! Shit and damnation! You stinking little bastard!'

He slams on the anchors and I smack my nose on the handle on the back of his seat, a little dinner tray. I swallow another mouthful . . .

'It's the way you drive, he can't help it . . . can you, Steven?'

My mother dabs at my nose with a handkerchief, starched at the edges. I fumble with the door-catch, fall to my knees and crawl onto the verge. My father's hands grip the steering wheel. He stares out through the windscreen in disgust . . . I breathe the grass, the hedge. I feel the dirt and dig in my fingernails. I don't want to go out to dinner. I don't want to eat, I don't like eating, it's a trap, just another torture set up to destroy me . . . I gurgle in the dust. Please let me stay here, please leave me to die, I can't face the leather. My mother, a giant lipstick . . . I let go, bitter, two or three mouthfuls, sweet and clinging . . .

'Dad, Steven's being sick again.' My brother sings it out triumphantly.

I lick at my snot, eyes stinging. My legs are thin and white, I don't know what I am doing here or why I came, but these people have control of my life. I am their property to do with as they wish, I am under their spell, the spell of the tongue and fist . . . I crawl onto the back seat . . . The trouble is that I got some dirt on the upholstery.

We drive on through the silence and the smell. A topic for conversation, but for later, and my bad teeth, my boils. We drive on in silence, waiting . . .

'Young gentlemen . . .' That's how my father spoke to us after his brandy, his face glistening.

I breathe through my mouth, avoiding the stench, I stick my mug up against the glass.

'Can you hear anything?' He turns to face us over the back of his seat. 'You can't? Well, that's it! That's what you pay for! Listen, Prrrrrr . . . That's all . . .' He minces his moustaches together and purrs like a cat. 'Prrrrrrr, that's what you pay for, engineering! Mister Rolls and Mister Royce, the finest engine in the world! Is the engine turned off? No! I assure you, the engine is running, listen!' He puckers his lips. 'Prrrrrrr . . . There you have it, the Rolls Royce engine! Quality my young gentlemen! That's right, gentlemen, young . . . You're both fine young gentlemen!'

We sit there in the car park, the car cranking away beneath our feet.

'You're both fine young gentlemen ... and when you grow up, you're both going to be good-looking chaps!'

My brother's face swells like a football, scowling with pride.

'Fine, handsome young gentlemen!'

I sit there, my teeth sticking out in eight different directions, still chewing on bits of carrot.

'Fine handsome young men, aren't they Juny?'

My brother gives me a horse bite on the leg and I have to squeal.

'Now shush the pair of you before I bang your bloody heads together! If you can't behave like adults, you won't be treated like adults!'

My brother smirks down at me. I use my hand to cover my teeth, fucked up ... I wanted to believe, but I can't. I honestly can't ...

6. A CAT'S ARSE IN HIS HEAD

Me and Jeffrey caught bumblebees in our bare hands, and I fell and grazed my knees every day that summer. Then the girls in the white house left and went to live in Australia and I fell off the bed and cracked my head open and my mother told me to shut up blubbering or she'd call an ambulance. 'Did I want to get taken away?' And the sun came in hot through the front window and the green out front of the council estate looked sad and yellow and she just kept on ironing.

She didn't want to carry me, so at the shopping arcade I get lost on purpose. I talk to myself, I play with a lolly stick, she tells me to drop it, it's dirty . . . Then she just walks off, she lets go of my reins and I stand by this oak tree . . . Then she storms back, snatches hold of my hand and drags me along behind her.

'Do you want me to have to pull your trousers down and smack your bare bottom in public?'

I walk on, quite fragile really, crying.

It seemed that they'd been mapping out my future in private and my feelings don't even enter into the calculations . . . I watch their mouths . . . My father walks around naked with his big willy out . . . Nobody else in the world has bum cracks but my family; everybody else's are filled in . . .

My father takes me down town and they make me sit on a plank and have my head shaved. My mother buys me new socks, shoes and a tie, my little bow on an elastic has to go . . . Actually, my brother flicks it into the fireplace and I have to watch it burn. Apparently, I cry too much.

I try to follow the whispered conversations, but everyone quits gassing as soon as I cock an ear.

Next morning my mother comes in, clicks the light on, pulls the covers off me, and forces me into the new clothing . . . I rub my eyes, I whimper . . . That stuff's harsh, freshly starched . . . It's still dark outside, I start to blubber.

'Don't be a baby, Steven! You're not a baby are you? You're a big boy now, you're going to school.'

'I don't want to go to school . . .'

'Of course you do, you'll meet lots of new friends.'

'Is Jeffrey going?'

'No, you'll make new friends.'

'I want to stay here with you . . .'

'You can't, you have to go, it's the law, you don't want mummy to be arrested, do you?'

'My stomach hurts . . .'

She yanks my shorts up and buttons them, stern faced, a regular Judas, nothing but a turn-coat. I'm dressed, my face wiped, a cat-lick, then I'm taken outside. I fight all the way, tooth and nail, right up to the front steps of the school. I kick at her and shriek like a whistle . . . The bush, I want the bush! She unclasps my fingers one by one, knuckles whitening and I sob from the bottom of my heart. I'm losing my life, I have to wave goodbye; she pulls me by my arm up those steps . . . I stagger and trip, I plead . . .

'For God's sake stop dragging your feet, Steven! Now stop your crying or I'll give you something to cry about!'

That's tough, I trusted her and she dealt me a dud. I suck my snot, I try and let her know my feelings, deep down, heart-felt . . .

'You have to go to school, you've got to learn to read and write!'

I bite at my tears, stinging, blinding . . . 'I don't want to read and write.'

'If you don't go to school, you'll be taken into care and I'll be arrested!'

'I don't want to go.'

'It's the law!'

'Why?

'For Christ's sake shut up!'

And so I let them destroy my specialness.

She left me in that place, echoing corridors, banging doors. Everything in hideous miniature and a smell that goes straight to your bowels, the smell of beatings and betrayals. There's scarcely any love in those classrooms, just hapless kids: row upon row of us, gummy and diseased, just waiting to be lied to. And the teachers banging it out day in, day out, year after year: '2 + 2 = 4', 'animals don't really talk' and 'gentle Jesus' ... All those sad stumbling lies that have as little to do with the spirit of man and the love of God as can be humanely imaginable.

My hatred of school was absolute, a rare and beautiful hatred, almost perfect. They murdered us behind closed doors, sat at evil little desks: kid-sized.

At eleven o'clock they hand round the little milk bottles and one drinking straw each, all apart from the kiddie at the end, the one with the busted specs held together with dirty pink sticky plaster. Old four-eyes got no drinking straw; he got a kick and a pinch if he was lucky! Then he gets dragged out front and has his legs slapped for losing his drinking straw. Good! We're all in agreement, us, the teacher and the world, we nod, we understand the mentality of the class-room. We finish our milk, we suck it right down to the bottom, then follow it round with our straws, we blow bubbles to see who can make the loudest racket, then we get told to shut it.

Mrs Lamb claps her hands, and orders us up off our seats. We go single file up to the front and drop our bottles into the crate, we clank them, we throw them in there 'til they bust. Then we go sit down again and play with the toys 'til dinner time. You go to the shelf and choose for yourself, little plastic soldiers, some metal fish in a cardboard tank with little fishing rods with magnets on the end ... Some busted jigsaws in numbered boxes ... I get the lid, with a number that doesn't exist. I have to stare at it, to try and find its friend ... Fifteen minutes go past, an hour ... An upside-down five, a two that isn't a two or a three. There is no such number ... The window, a dirty patch of tarmac, a few trees in the distance battling in the mud.

Then the dinner bell, Mrs Lamb waves it above her head. That means that we have to go out and stand about out there in the fresh air. We get up and file out like little soldiers, then we run, we scream 'til it hurts, competing with the birds. I walk up the little path to the toilets, past the school gate ... I stare out into that other world, a police car goes past and a man with a tree under his arm. I find the toilets and there's this kid in there with one of his ears missing, just a rim of gristle and a hole like a cat's arse in his head. I sneek looks at it whilst I pee . . . Some of it goes on my sandals.

In class we do God, make dinosaurs and sing baa-baa black sheep. Then it's home time and my mother meets me at the gate, and the peanut man's there on his bike, and she buys me a toffee apple. And I begged her not to make me go back to that place, I dropped my toffee apple and I cried.

It seems that it was imperative that I learned to read and write, that I forget my life up until that moment. I stared into the books, but I couldn't make head nor tail of it: their letters and numbers were meaningless to me. I was singled out and shamed for my ignorance and general stupidity . . . I just couldn't understand why I should change, why I had to learn this foreign language.

My mother sat with me going through the lists.

'Cat! Sat! Mat! Your brother could read and write at your age. Just look at it, at its shape . . . C-A-T, CAT!'

We sit cross-legged in a neat little semi-circle and Mrs Lamb plays the piano. 'Nick-knack-paddy-whack, give the dog a bone, this old man came rolling home.' And we sing along, we have to, we're orchestrated. We have no choice in the matter, everything's been decided in our absence, no democracy, just liberal hell. In the end, it seems that you have to do everything that you don't want to do in this world, and then you have to pretend that you actually enjoy doing it, that you've at last grown up, that it's exactly what you've always wanted all along. That's the type of people we are.

7. THE LANGUAGE OF ALL THE ARSEHOLES OF THE WORLD

'Juny! Honk, honk! Juny!' His morning reveille, a double blast, both nostrils ... 'Have you starched my handkerchiefs?' He walks downstairs.

'. . . Garage,' he says to me. 'Garage!'

I look up at him.

'Garage, repeat it after me, garage! Are you listening, Steven? Not 'garige'. Garage! Garage, garage! For heaven's sake if you've got something to say, then say it correctly: garage! Bought, not 'brawt'!' He pulls at his whiskers and coughs slightly. 'Have you been playing with those council estate hooligans again? Has he, Juny? I thought I said that he wasn't allowed over there! That's where you get this filthy talk from, isn't it? Well, you might think it sounds clever, but it doesn't, it's vulgar! Now look at me.' He puckers his lips and crosses his eyes. 'Garage! Bought! Ga-rah-je ... Ga-rah-je! Got it? Really, Juny, what's the point? Can he spell yet? Not really? A little? Now and then? Well, say it then damn you! Re-mem-ber, not 'renember', remember! Remember, remember, remember! Garage, garage, garage! Bought, bought, bought! Jesus Christ! What are they teaching this child? It's that school, I warned you! Nothing but riff-raff! They can't even teach him to speak properly! Remember! Not 'renember'! Not 'brawt'! Not 'garige'! Garage, ga-rah-je! 'Garige'? Oh, you don't mean the ga-rah-je, per chance do you? You 'brawt' it, what's 'brawt' mean? You couldn't possibly mean that you bought it? Bought, bought, bought! Got it? Bought, bought, bought! Satisfied?

'Renember', do you? 'Re-nem-ber'? Remember, remember, re-member! Steven, are you listening to me? Come along, say it after me, ga-rah-je! What's wrong with this child of yours, Juny? He looks unhappy.'

I'll tell you something for free, you needn't bother trying to talk with anybody in this world, especially when you're just a little kid. You're still shitting your pants, and nobody's the least bit interested. All this talk about communication and understanding? It's all hokum. Your opinions are not required, the only thing grown-ups are enchanted by is the sound of their own voices, they go gooey-eyed, they've got three fingers jammed up their own arses.

You want to talk to my father? Have you got your cheque book? You'll need it! You wish to have a voice in this land, to keep on the right side of law and order? Well, cough up kid! If it's preferential treatment you require then put your money where your mouth is cock-sucker! On your knees! Bow down to the democratic voice of money! Cheque books at the ready, credit cards cocked! The only real language? Money! – The language of all the arseholes of the world! And forget your loose change, tosser, spondulicks, and nothing less!

You write and paint and you can't hold down a real job? It doesn't look too rosy down at the local nick. Your credit rating? Your National Identity Card? The murdering computer, that's where we'll all wind up! Dialled and filed, down on their super-tech memory bank. The rich, the poor, the damned and the dead, nothing but ciphers. Did I say the rich? Pardon me! Of course the pompous and the opinionated will never die, they fuck around as if they'll live forever, immortality guaranteed, and never a moment's doubt!

I really did try talking to him, my father, but when it came down to it, he had a very limited style, Edwardian and bombastic. He had a way of looking in the mirror, re-fixing his whiskers, checking his time piece and trying another flounce in his bow-tie. The whole lot of righteousness was so thick and clinging that you couldn't knock it from between his ears with a hammer and chisel (that's a joke). It would take his own death to pull him up and start him reasoning ... People can become pretty lucid when they're staring over the edge of eternity, it knocks the bullshit right out of them double quick! All of a sudden they start making pretty good sense. Then they quit blubbering and they're dead.

8. CRABS AND BUTTERFLIES

'You've got it coming to you!' That was levelled at me pretty regularly, that and, 'You'll be for the high jump!'

They point at the blackboard, they reiterate, us sat yawning. That chalk made a special sound when it screeched those letters, and a choking dust . . . But no matter what I just couldn't get myself interested in their fancy calligraphy. The difference between a 'p' and a 'q'? Don't even ask . . .

If they'd have just let me spend a little more time mixing with the crabs and the butterflies, I'd have been a sight happier. Have you ever seen a crab walk? Now that's something to see, they walk sideways. They lift themselves up and head off in that direction, like that! They pick up their skirts, shake their heels and they're off! Style, finesse and individuality: crabs. That's what I'm talking about, the little fellows you got on Seasalter beach before the big freeze of 1963.

And the big girls from the caravan site used to come and take me by the hand and lead me out across those mud flats. I knew all the best places to look – the mussel bank, out around the reef. You have to approach them from behind, that's the only way to avoid their pinchers, and then you pick them up, like that! The same goes for butterflies, you've got to have finesse. You can't just go busting up their wings like Kevin Harding did: gently does it and don't throw a shadow! You try explaining that to the ignorant and they won't listen. They know it all, they just barge in there and smash everything up. It's all the same to them; poetry is meaningless! There's nothing I didn't know about butterflies in those days. The only person who knew more than me was Caroline and she was five years older than me and went to the big school.

'You have to be very still and quiet, and don't go between the butterfly and the sun.'

Big Caroline had a picture book, Butterflies of the Chalk Downs, page after page in full colour, from caterpillars to chrysalis, from chrysalis to butterfly. Intricate hues, and not all of them common, the chalk blue for example, you don't see that little fellow any more.

All that went out the window, twenty-odd years back, when big Caroline moved, my father walked out and my brother stepped into his shoes. The woods came down and the estates went up, people with no understanding of natural habitats, kids who'd sooner crush a thing of beauty than take a second look at it, kids with chips on their shoulders this big! Butterflies? Forget it! Smack!

'You can't even read 'n' write?'

My brother drops a brick onto my head ... He tumbles them off the big stack in Nigel Forman's front yard. Smash! There goes my head again.

The world was becoming mighty serious for me, my brother made sure of that.

And to think that when I was a kid I knew that animals could talk to each other, I absolutely knew it, and now I know next to nothing, zilch! Just a handful of crummy memories, the destroying blackboard, the world that knows best! I lie awake at night and think of those woods, I see how far I can go into them. I search them in memory, the big beech tree, a certain hollow stump, I keep them all alive, I have to, now that I'm a fossil.

9. THE SILENCE OF WORDS

'That's a fine arse you've got on you, Juny!'
My father walks over and slaps it and I go out into the garden. My brother won't let me in his tent so I sit on the grass and make a daisy chain. I put it over my head and watch a flying saucer come up over the trees . . . It revolves lazily in the clear blue.

'Look Nick, a flying saucer!'

He undoes the ties and comes out on his hands and knees, and shades his eyes.

'No it ain't, it's a jet.'

'But it's spinning.'

'I tell you it's a jet, alright!'

He kicks my knee and I fall . . . I start crying.

'Arse!' I say.

'What?'

'ARSE!'

I hear him running . . . The old man comes across the lawn at me, I squeal as he pulls me to my feet and starts slapping my legs . . .

My brother stands by the little green tent and folds his arms. The old man dragging me back towards the house.

'What did I hear you say! I'll teach you to speak such filth! You can go to your room until you're fit to mix with other human beings! Do I make myself clear? Now get moving!'

He twists my arm, my face filled with snot . . . And I saw a flying saucer as true as I write this . . .

* * *

If my father had just truly upped and left us, we'd all of been a sight happier. But as it was, we couldn't relax, he kept hanging on, on account that we were occupying his collateral. That's what it amounted to. 'You're using my facilities!' That was his catch phrase ... One thing you could be sure of with the old man was that he would never tire of roasting the same old chestnuts.

'You use my facilities, but you're not prepared to contribute a thing! You could mow the lawn, paint the shed, but no! You use my facilities but contribute positively nothing, nil!'

He's letting us know his feelings, putting us in the picture. That's him alright, I'd recognise that dandy anywhere, the one in the whiskers, the blond bombshell! Side-buckle shoes, and the big opinions, stable, never changing. Three years go by, he shows up, another six months and there he is, in all his finery, resplendent, clasping his brolly.

'There's no food in the house! We'll have to go out to dinner. Wah!'

I step on his corns, I'm at that age ... I bang into things, uncoordinated, gawky ... I had them all out in one go you see, twelve of them, and now I've got new tusks, they stick out over my lips. I have to use my hand to grin and I breathe kind of heavy, I can't breathe and eat at the same time.

'For goodness sake close your mouth and breathe through your nose when you eat, Steven!'

They kept telling me, but I couldn't, it was blocked or something, I honestly tried but I made a snorting noise.

'Take him to the doctor if he can't breathe! He isn't a pig, is he? Breathe through your nose, Steven!'

'I can't,' I said.

'Well, try!'

My brother punctuates it with a kick in the ankle, to be sure I've heard, that I am paying attention to our father. Boot! And the anger in his eyes, directed at me personally, you understand. Then he looks up to his father, an apologetic smile, one of love and confusion, desperate to be liked, to be appreciated.

I tried breathing through my nose, I concentrated on it, I snorted and slapped my chops. That's what they went to great lengths to point out: apparently, I wasn't that lovely, and then there was the smell.

'Can you smell something?' My father beams.

'It's stinky Steven,' chants my brother. 'He stinks awfully father, Steven smells!'

'No,' my father corrects him, 'not Steven, you mean The Smell, Nichollas, The Smell!'

He smiles at his joke and pats his kisser with his handkerchief. It was the old girl who lit his fuse asking him what he'd like for dinner.

'I don't want to eat, Juny, I don't care if I never eat again! There's never any damned food in this house anyway!' He marches out, then turns and sticks his head back round the door. 'Roast beef and Yorkshire pudding! You haven't got it? You haven't got it!

'Roast beef, Yorkshire pudding', that's how he always answered, and he knew damn well that we didn't have three pennies to keep each other company, let alone forking out on luxuries. 'Roast beef and Yorkshire pudding, please, Juny.' And us living on a few mouldering potatoes, and the occasional sausage. We haven't got 'roast beef', so we have to go out for dinner.

He rings up in advance, just to keep her on tenter hooks. She's got no time for us kids, we have to tidy our lives away. Then his mistress rings up, dishing the dirt – it became a regular occurrence. Every evening, six o'clock, the phone goes and the old girl sits there chewing the fat. I play on the rug driving my toy Batmobile, but she won't talk to me, just, 'Shush! In a minute! For crying out loud!' Finally she serves up the egg and chips, and she's crying into the yolk . . . Then she sags at the knees and drops the plate, a big string of snot . . .

'I'm going to have a nervous breakdown,' she tells me, and I know that she means she is going to die and leave me.

Every time I come in from school I look to see if she's been strangled, lying naked on her bed, face down with her crotchless knickers stuffed in her mouth. That's what they were. I found them at the back of the drawer.

'Come along, Juny, we're going out for dinner. I haven't eaten since luncheon. Are those children ready? Come along, chop-chop!'

The trouble is, I've got these teeth, I have to use my hand to grin on account of the monstrous effect, and I breathe kind of heavy, I can't eat and breathe at the same time. And then there's my teeth, it all gets mixed up, it antagonises people.

'For God's sake, breathe through your nose and close your mouth when you eat, Steven! If only you could see yourself!'

'It's his voice, I just can't stand his voice,' my mother chips in. 'It's that whining. You don't have to listen to it. My God, his voice!'

They repeat themselves, they're waiting for it to sink in, to penetrate my thick skull. Eating silently, that was a tough one, and speaking the Queen's English ... I had to hear about it regularly, in detail, the list of my inadequacies ...

'The thing about steak,' as my father explains, 'is you mustn't be able to see any blood, none of it must come out when you cut it ... It must be well done, not even a whisper of pink.'

No juice, that was his point, he didn't like the juice, the fact that is was an animal, he picked at it and sniffed ...

'Steak, please, very well done ... And Smell, what would you like, egg and chips?' He raises his voice, he looks to the other tables and waves his wallet around.

'Anything on the menu ... Have anything you wish.'

Then he turns back to us. He whispers at us with venom, but silently, without words. I stare into my plate. This is his great moment of grandness: the family meal ... misery located on a table top. He swigs at the claret and explains all about the butter, the specific type of flock wallpaper, sharks.

'They couldn't take the man's wet-suit off because it was the only thing holding him together. Then there was the blood!'

He peers at his meal, hideously charred ... His crisp little steak, he picks at it and blows kisses ... Phut! Phut! He thinks it over, nibbling at his fingertips, then he sniffs and pops his eyes, he's found something ...

'This isn't well done! Look, Juny, it's perfectly raw!' It's true. In the depths of the brittle piece of meat is a thread-like vein of pink. 'You heard me make my order, didn't you? I specifically asked you for well done! I can't eat that! What do you think? The chips?' He loosens his collar and coughs, his studs ping off like shrapnel ... 'It's raw! Look at it! Waiter! Waiter!'

I eat the skin of the chip first, then blow on the white stuff inside ... The waitress shows up, clutching her breasts.

'Look at this, and I ordered well done.' He speaks evenly and succulently, a gentle, authoritarian whisper, charm itself ... 'I don't like to complain my dear, but I did specifically ask for very well done, didn't I, darling?'

My mother nods into her fish and chips, she's caught with a mouthful of hake. 'Oh yes he did, he specifically asked for very well done . . .'

My father looks at her with great distaste and waves his napkin in her face . . .

'Please, Juny, let me handle this.'

'I'll take it away and change it for you immediately, sir . . .'

'No! No! It's too late now, I've lost my appetite, anyway. No, don't worry yourself. I didn't want it anyway, I just thought I'd point it out to you, that's all.'

He tugs at the plate, his thumb skids in the gravy . . . He relinquishes his hold. He lets her win: the tug of war of the plate . . . She adjusts her headgear and retreats, plate in hand. The little burnt steak, it goes back to the kitchen.

'Stupid girl, I didn't want it changed. You saw it, Juny, blood red! I don't know what all the fuss is about.'

He consoles himself with a roll, playing with the butter, still griping, justifying himself to the grave. He rolls the dough round in his gob, his tongue following just behind, then takes another gargle on the red stuff and swills the whole thing between his teeth. He questions the rest of us with his eyebrows, little blond crescents. He swallows and gags, then another slurp.

'It was raw! Perfectly raw!'

10. PLASTIC ELEPHANT

All my troubles date from my first life. I ate nothing but chocolate bars up until I was eighteen. It contributed to my overall smell, black teeth, green teeth. Holes so deep I could feel right the way through to the centre, using my tongue, rough edges, busted, then hard shiny gum. A little platform, right in the middle, a kind of courtyard inside the crumbling tooth . . .

The dentist was a half hour bus ride up to Gillingham. They gave you cocaine in those days, and my mother bought me a plastic elephant with removable tusks and ears, just to cheer me up, to stop me being quite such a pain in the arse. Anything to do with wild animals is alright by me. We bought it from the shop next door, the one that used to have the money flying across the ceiling on wires. You don't see that sort of thing these days, Zing! It went right over your head, Zing! That's the cash box, magical. Wee-zing! Right over your head, real money, on strings.

11. THE SMELL OF DOG

We only occupied the smallest room in that mansion of ours, on account of the cold. Between his visits the old man was starving us out ... We lived under the constant threat of repossession ...

'We're on an economy drive!' That's what the old girl kept repeating, that and, 'I'm going to have a nervous breakdown!'

I lived my whole life on one of her economy drives.

I draw a picture of her crying, with the cat on her lap.

We sit huddled round that antique oil stove smouldering away in the corner. An acrid stench, glowing through the gloom, a glimmer of warmth, defused, candle-like. Apparently it 'conserved energy', besides we aren't allowed to so much as set foot in the front room on account of my bouncing. The sofa was a wreck, I was banned, it was unanimous; on that one count everyone was in full agreement.

'He's been bouncing on the sofa again, Juny! I don't want him in there! Do you understand me? Use the front room? Waste coal on an open fire? Have we got money to burn? And think of the furniture! It's already thread-bare without your kids clambering about all over it!'

I push my Dinky car about on the floor, I examine the tyres – one of them keeps coming off.

'Can you put my tyre back on for me?'

He rolls his eye into the back of his skull.

'Shhh, your father's busy!'

He massages his sockets . . . I pick at it, the little tyre, rubbery, a loop.

'If I find out you've been bouncing!' He bites down.

Yes sir! The smallest room for us, and no wasting precious gas or electricity! We sat holed up in that cave for the whole winter, bleak, enduring, twiddling our thumbs, the oil stove creaking out noxious gases, thick and oily. My skin turned waxy to the touch, a ghostly grey, a little green round the gills, but otherwise yellow. Not too much chance of getting any fresh air, not in amongst that soot, great plumes of the stuff. And me with my boils, sort of illuminations, glistening through the smog . . . Me, me mum and me brother, huddled over the wick . . . Paraffin I think it burned on, just one miserable dribble left in the whole can, to last 'til the end of January.

What gave the old man his blacklist moods, was the stench, it permeated everything, it was absorbed into the furniture and fittings.

He rolls up out of the night, his feet sounding on the gravel, a visitation . . . white, bearded, a face at the window. My mother hits the panic button and we drop everything . . .

'Oh my goodness! Put the stove out! Nichollas open the window! He'll smell it!'

She flaps her arms about in the murk, trying to dispel the fumes. She ushers the smoke out of the window. The room turns to ice . . . That was his ultimate trick, turning up on the doorstep, completely unannounced, stamping his feet through the frost, teeth gritted, his nose in the air.

'Have you been burning that stove again? My God the place stinks of it! Come along woman, admit it! You don't need to, I can smell it. My whole fucking wardrobe reeks of the stuff!'

It was the idea that we'd actually been keeping warm that antagonised him, that me and Nick had been roasting a few harmless chestnuts in the dying coals, windfalls, gatherings in the leaves. The shells are pretty messy, it seems we fucked up the carpet. It was obvious that he'd have to put his foot down.

'You've been burning that stove again, haven't you, Juny? Christ, I can smell it from down the end of the street! As soon as my back is turned! I've told you a thousand times, leave it in the shed woman! You've got coal, you've got electricity! I provide for everything, don't I?'

It's cold, damp, real fog, winter-time, gusts of ice and snow, regular drifts, and us huddled over that burner, a little blue flame, blushing, eerie-looking. We keep our heads down, we daren't answer back. No back-chat! Not in the slightest, it ain't worth the aggravation. And smiles are out of the question, too, or any kind of talking . . . That would just crank him up into new crescendos . . .

'Have you been peeling chestnuts on the carpet? 'Ain't'! 'ain't'! What sort of language is that?'

We hear him barking down the phone, making all kinds of threats, promises about his imminent return. He hasn't shown his face in the last two months, but still he yells his tirades. We hear him woofing in the distance, little sparks of electricity. He hasn't paid the bills – the constant fear that we'll be disconnected.

'Don't I give you house-keeping, Juny? What the hell are you spending it on down there? Because I warn you, there isn't another brass farthing coming from me, my good woman! You've already bled me dry! The lot of you! Shit and damnation! I've been in a terrible accident, the car's a write-off! A man was killed! I'll be ba . . .' Prrrrrrrr . . . The pips go . . . he loses his tuppence . . . We're left dangling on a string, under the constant threat of his appearance . . . or possible eviction.

'You'd better not be burning that infernal oil stove, Juny! Because don't say I haven't warned you! I can smell it from here!'

He bites at the mouthpiece and shakes it between his teeth like a bone.

'I'm coming straight down there and putting the whole lot of you out on the street! Do you hear me? That's my fucking oil you're burning down there, Juny! My fucking oil!'

He bounces the receiver in its cradle, he pulls the whole thing out by the wire and dangles it from the wall. He imposes his rule from afar: geography holds no boundaries. He exercises his will for the sheer hell of watching us jump!

We sit blowing on our hands. I take one of the chestnuts; my brother clobbers me.

'Fuck off, that's mine!'

He undoes my fingers one by one, then gives me a chinese burn. I let out a cry, a little whimper.

'For God's sake stop your whining!'

That's my mother speaking. She sips at her Guinness and quakes gently in the gloom . . . Then the door goes and the old man marches in. That's our signal, we drop everything and jump to attention. We hear footsteps echoing down the driveway, a car door slams. He announces himself, brisk, stinking of the bottle. He wrinkles his nose . . .

'Can I smell dog, Juny? Juny, I smell dog!'

That's when everything turned sour: the smell of that oil stove was one thing, but me bringing home a harmless little stray was another . . . The old girl did her nut, she made me promise to take it over the back and lose it in the woods, somewhere desolate, the back of beyond . . .

'Your father won't hear of it! And besides, the cat . . . the cat won't like it!'

12. HEARBOY

I dressed hearboy up in my anorak and hid him in the garage. I patted him. I threw him a stick, my new-found friend, black and white, a stray from the council estate, and not at all snobbish. He looks at me in that special kind of way, his tongue hanging. He wants to play, to make friends, with these funny eyes, blue, mottled, but not blind. And he knew how to beg all by himself, he didn't take any kind of training. He just mucked right in with us kids, as if to say, 'we all want to have some fun, so let's go to it!' We all run hell for leather over the back woods and have a good romp.

That's when the old man shows up: he makes his threats over the phone, he promises repercussions. He tells the old girl that he's just leaving, he's on his way at this very moment, his arrival is imminent. We've heard it all before, it's for the birds, ramblings of a wino, then, lo and behold, the old coot really does show up. We clamp our jaws and hold onto our hats. It's bound to bring out the worst in him, the stench of that stove and me with my new mutt.

Right away he orders the dog out. He banishes him from the house for forever and a day. And the stove, we have to shut that down for a start, on account of the fumes, great plumes of burning oil . . .

Then he has to go picking on Hearboy. Not only a dog, but a stray! That was pushing things too far! No breeding! Neither fish nor fowl! He waves his hands about like a bush. 'Out! Out! Out!' He barks like a mongrel, he sends out signals, he bosses the dog, and the dog does just like he tells him. The old man turns and marches away, then he stops and scratches his bean, he sits on it like an egg. Then slowly he turns around and calls the dog back over. Hearboy wags his tail, runs right up, sits and licks at the old man's mitt. The old man lifts his hand to his face, he studies his palm and dips his fingers in it, puzzled, then he regains his composure. He reaches down and pats Hearboy's head gingerly, just a stroke at first, then more playfully, he tussles his ears. Hearboy smiles back up at him. They cock their heads at each other. The dog's ears go like that!

'Woof,' he says. 'Woof woof!'

'Sit!'

'Woof woof!'

'Roll over!'

'Woof!'

'Beg!'

'Woof woof woof!'

'Stay!'

'Woof!'

'Lie boy, lie!'

The old man's pleased as punch, he looks around grinning, trying to find an audience . . .

'Did you see that, Juny? Look, watch . . .'

He directs it, a whole new toy, he's warming to the mutt.

'Hearboy!'

And over he comes, running at full tilt, funny coloured eyes, a pink tongue hanging out. That knocks the wind out of him, the old fake. He troops off to the other side of the garden, he finds a toffee wrapper, he stoops, he pockets it, and not even a reprimand! Then – 'Hearboy! Hearboy!'

And Hearboy does it again, the dog I mean, he bombs over, tongue lolling, little trails of drool, good as gold. The old man's mask pinches at the side, it almost cracks his mug.

'Hearboy!' That was the command. 'Hearboy!' That's what we got to call him, my stray. 'Hearboy!' And here he comes. Style! The style of the dog. 'Hearboy!' No bashfulness, no snobbery, just friendly and true. Enthusiastic, out for some fun, whipped.

'Collect his lead, Steven, we're going over the woods to test Hearboy's obedience in the open country!'

He talks to me! He's talking about Hearboy, my mutt, my little stray. I stare up at him open mouthed.

'Come along, chop chop!'

I jump to it, I have to be quick before he changes his mind. I call the mutt over, I get Hearboy's lead on . . . I take off my belt and loop it through his collar. That sends him wacky – you have to yank on it and holler blue murder.

'Can I show you the big beech tree, dad? Can I show you how to climb it, the big beech tree?'

He pulls at his whiskers, stares thoughtfully at the dog and says nothing. First of all he has to climb into his wellingtons, and then wax his Rolls Royce. It's half six before we actually set off. I even offer to show the old man the big beech tree, to show him how to climb it. He sort of saunters along, recalcitrant. When we get past the old scout hut, I figure it'll be alright to let Hearboy off his lead. I unloop his lead and buckle it back round my shorts. He goes super-wacky again; he yelps and butts me, puppyish . . . He gets his lipstick out, cocks his leg then darts off double quick, on all fours, sideways, crab-like, looking for rabbits. He sniffs and takes another piss, he looks back over his shoulder, wonky eyes, he wants encouragement.

'Go on boy, go on!' I shout it, I grin and stamp my foot at him. Then he makes a dash and disappears into a bush, he runs back out at ten different angles, he circles us. The joy on his doggy face, his tongue flying like a banner, pinkish, dripping . . .

The old man bites his lip and takes command . . .

'Hearboy! Hearboy, heel!'

The old man barks it out. He slaps his thighs. He fills his voice with hate. He booms it out. He opens his lungs and yells. But Hearboy's lost to the world, everything's a game to him. The old man's opinions? Bollocks!

I pick a blackberry, sneek up behind my father and slap it on the back of his neck. I pick two or three, I eat one, then I toy with the other. I run and jump and get him right in the back of the neck, just above the collar. Then I run on and turn, but he doesn't chase after me. He just stands there rigid, then lifts his hand, wipes the back of his neck and stares at the pulp. He peers into the little seeds, in amongst the juice, then lowers his jowls, a countenance of doom. I just wanted him to join in that's all, to feel part of the fun . . .

I run up behind him and Slap! with a ripe blackberry. He wipes it off, looks at it, then turns on his heels and marches off back towards the house. I trail along behind him, following in his wellingtons, trying to tell him, trying to get him to speak to me. You see, it was only a prank, some harmless fun. Me and the mutt scamper along between his strides, his face turns black. I start to blubber but he keeps marching, mask set, face to the front. I was only going to show him the big beech tree, that's all. How to climb it, the way there, the special way, a short-cut, a secret short-cut. I drag at his shirt tails, I beg him to stop, to come back, to see the big beech tree with me and Hearboy. But I may as well cut my throat.

'I promise that I'm sorry, truly, truly sorry, cross my heart and hope to die!'

But he won't even look at me, not a second glance, not even for Hearboy. Me and the mutt slow down, he's got us beat. We watch him 'til his tail disappears, the blackberry stain on his collar, red, kind of blue-ish, purpley, running down the back of his neck . . . He disappears out of sight, crosses the little clearing, then he's gone . . . past the old scout hut at full gallop . . . disused wells . . . the brambles . . . heading towards the driveway. Golden locks flouncing in the breeze, and his neck, blue-black, erect, dignified, unforgiving: my father.

13. THE FACTS OF LIFE

E aster time we went down to the old shack on the beach. A-roads, the trees ringed with white, instead of street lamps. They had to pull over five or six times to let me out so's that I could puke. And I remember the sky was always blue and there was this church with a little field and a donkey; my mother would ask the old man to pull over, so's I could stroke it. And the donkey would walk painfully over to us, his back like an old carpet and his ears twitching. And there was a big dark tree, a blue sky, and his sad eyes blinking away the flies. I stroked his velvety ears and fed him a handful of dandelions, and the old man revving the motor, telling us it was time to go.

That was some place, a little line of shingle marking the end of the estuary ... A road, a general store, two dikes and no main drainage, and there was always the wind. We used to sit 'n' watch the old girl empty the septic tank into the sea every morning.

Walking across those pebbles made you wince – my brother forced me to put my whole weight on those razor shells ...

And the old bat with curlers who owned that shack, shrills out across those hot stones, 'My God, isn't he horrific!'

And my brother pipes back, 'Oh yes, rather!'

It seems I've got a lot of evening-up to do, a lot of scores to settle. I stick my tongue in my jaw. The beach stank, the sun stung, and I sweltered under the weight of my betters, my elders, my superiors.

Ah, just to speak with my pen and breathe, to lay this ghost to rest. I shan't bathe my brow until all the humiliations I've suffered have been spoken in full.

The old man blew us out; he packed us off down to Seasalter, then absconded. We couldn't afford the rent on a shack by ourselves so we chipped in with a friend of the family, Norman, and his daughter Sue. Nick kipped on the couch, Sue slept with my mum, and I have to sleep in the big bed with Norman.

And that's when he got it out. All night he keeps asking if I can keep a secret, he rubs my tummy and repeats it.

'Fred, can you keep a secret?'

Of course I can keep secrets. I tell him loads of times. Then he groans and gets his willy out, he slaps it in my palm, like a sausage, brown and hot, and all these crinkly grey hairs. That's odd, all those hairs, I haven't got any of those. Then he tugs my knickers down and plays with my little pecker. He sucks on it 'til it goes hard, then he starts grunting and kneels over me and wags his thick one in my face. I can feel the heat coming off it – he slaps my arse with it, hot, denuded, growing . . .

It went up and out like a stick. I look at it; that makes me go cross-eyed, he plunks it into my hand and I remember something my brother told me about, 'wanking' . . . about rubbing your willy until this stuff comes out of it. So I do it. I kind of move it a bit and he starts dribbling. This must be what they call 'wanking'. This must be 'the facts of life' that my mother keeps going on about . . . 'It's about time you learned some facts of life!' Must be that my father can't tell me the facts of life because he's too busy at the office. My mother must have asked Norman to tell me. I wondered if that's what it was, if me mum hadn't asked old Norm to show me 'the facts of life'.

He slaps it into my palm, then starts having some kind of fit; he jiggles about all over the shop, his eyes popping. That's something I couldn't get used to, his eyes without his specks on, like some kind of hideous dwarf, snorting through his nose. I had to look away out of pity for him. And that thing sticking out of all those grey hairs, that sausage between his legs, hot and steaming. I let it go, I drop it double quick, just as soon as he starts moaning and dribbling. I thought that I'd hurt him. That maybe I'd done the 'wanking' wrong – it seemed that way. He was a school teacher – you go messing with them and they're just as likely to put you on a detention, or hit you or something. And that's when he does it, he flips me over onto my belly and puts his thing between my legs, he noses it in there, he sweats on me, he gurgles, he trembles at the knees. And the sound of the shingle, that's the waves . . .

I used to have to go to the bedroom in the afternoons, I didn't breathe a word to no one, I was guilty as sin, I kept schtum . . . I was implicated just by virtue of being born. That's sad.

So now I talk, I dare him to come back, old Norman, I dare him to come back here and try to shut me up! I'll give him juice! We can talk about his dick and the crummier aspects of his intricate personality. I know his address, I have contacts. And his daughter, sweet Sue, in the nut-house by all accounts. Well, I remember and I won't forget. The sun slanting in through the drawn curtains, pale blue sea horses and cockle shells. Afternoons, you could hear the kids playing outside, the beach, the seagulls . . .

14. DIDICOIS AND GYPSIES

Norman gives me this little crucifix, he hands it me through his car window. I see the crinkly hairs on the back of his hand, then he winks at me and calls me Fred.

'I'll be round to see you, Fred!' Then the wink through his specs.

I admit that I was oversensitive as a child, that I pissed the bed and that I cried 'til I was sick, but I had certain jolts. I had to have the light on, I couldn't sleep without the light on. I had to stare into it, to concentrate on it, holding my crucifix ... trying to breathe through the covers, hiding my neck.

The ant's making clicking noises with his antennae, right alongside my bed, horse-sized, signalling to his brother ants on the other side. That's what the throbbing noise must be, the bass notes, they agitate the air, shaking it up, up into a billion dots, dragonflies with four foot wing-spans and teeth. I suck at the roof of my mouth, dry, itching ...

I can hear breathing, more like retching ... a man leaning over my bed wearing a gas mask. His nose goes on for ever and ever, it goes out through the window and into the garden. I want to get up, to tell my mother, to stop the night. I crawl onto the floor, pull on my plimsolls and follow his nose, out into the garden, right round the house, three times. I count the laps. Moonlit, I run naked and trembling, with a little hard-on; I slip in a cat's shit. Then somebody sees me from the road, a man and a woman, arms linked, staring right through me. I freeze, stock-still, statue-like.

They walk on and I slip back indoors ... I make a breathing tunnel, my head way down beneath the covers, sweating in fear. I have to keep the air hole as small as possible to stop the spiders crawling down it and laying eggs in my mouth.

I ask my brother to hold my hand. I whisper hard ... He pretends to be asleep, then he grabs my hand and rubs it around the hairs on his dick ...

Next day, I nick a tube of glue from the garage, shave off my eyebrow, and paste the hairs round my little dick. I too will be a man.

I try to be true to my little heart. I try, but everything comes out back to front, I stammer and piss the bed ... I read everything backwards: no matter how hard I flex my eyes I can't distinguish my 'p's from my 'q's. It ties my mind into knots ... My mother tried with me, she really did, she read me bedtime stories right up until my teens, even when it hurt her throat to carry on. I wet the bed to repay her.

I tried to conceal it, I tried pissing down the side of the mattress where no one would notice. I started walking backwards, heaping more and more shame upon myself.

When my father came to hear of this new development he threw an epileptic fit – he was absolutely one hundred per cent up in arms.

'So now he's a bed wetter! Urinating all over the floor wasn't enough! Now at last you see what this toad is made of! It's your own fault, Juny. Don't tell me that I didn't warn you! You spoil him! It's the company he keeps! Christ he should never have been allowed to set a single foot on that council estate! My words or somebody else's? They're all didicois and gypsies, Juny, every goddamned one of those Irishmen is on social security!'

As far as my father saw it, I was crawling around in a cesspool of my own making, raking through the shit with the lowest of the low. Every last one of his fears and predictions had been fulfilled, four times over!

'So that's how you repay your mother is it? In piss! The little pig pisses his bed does he? Exactly how old are you, Steven? One? Two? Three and a half, maybe? A baby, and I thought you were a young man! Look at him, Juny, he's swimming in it, it must be those biscuits he eats! Well, how many buckets of urine do you want exactly? Full to the brim! Ten! Fifteen or twenty maybe? When we're swimming in piss, then will you be satisfied?'

It was agreed that I was pasty, had legs like matchsticks with the wood scraped off, and that I smelled. I probably had a criminal nature and was heading for a good pasting. It was unanimous. And my father left. And no matter how hard I laugh, it is only to shed this wounded self, and how bitter it tastes.

My mother, my brother, and my nan too; none of them asked about my life nor thought to protect me. And I cried and I told them I wished I was dead . . . And no matter how hard I sobbed, they laughed at me. And I ran to the toilet and smashed my head against the wall, cracking the tiles . . . 'til I fell sobbing to my knees, the door locked.

15. JAM-RAG

T he big fear of my childhood was that I'd find my mother murdered, strangled in her bedroom. Whenever she was out, I immediately assumed that she was dead. I shout for her from downstairs, I walk through the kitchen, the hall, the back room, then started climbing the stairs. Talking loudly to her, as if she was there all along, trying to sound jovial, my mouth turned to dust. I approached her bedroom, convinced that she was lying in there, naked and dead, strangled by the hands of my father, her knickers stuffed in her mouth.

I stare at the back of the door and shout, 'Hello mum, are you in there?'

I bang on it extra loud, grab the brass handle and barge straight in. I force myself to look at the bed, then I check the other side of it and underneath, then the airing cupboard and the wardrobe. No sign of her anywhere, nothing. She must have been run over by a lorry on the way back from the shops.

'Nick! Nick! I think it's mum! She must have cut herself, it's blood!' I hold one up, I present it to him; he looks at me, he does a double take and jumps up.

'Get out my fucking room!'

'But look, I think she's hurt.' I hold out the blood heavy towel, stinking. 'I found it in the bathroom.'

'Get the fuck out!' He kicks at me. 'And take that fucking jam-rag with you! Go on, piss off! Put it fucking well back!'

He knees me – my leg goes numb, I hobble. He shoves me and bangs the door behind me, it rebounds twice. I whimper to myself,

I sit on the bathroom stool ... Then I find some blood on the toilet seat, and a packet of her sanitary towels in a box. I put one up my jumper, go to my mother's room, and undress in front of her mirror. You hook the ends onto this little belt, and it goes between your legs. I try my dick in four different positions. I admire myself. I pull at it, it goes hard, but the poor little fellow's bald. I hobble about, trying on her suspenders ... a bra ... panties ... stockings ... I put on lipstick and one of her dresses and tie my hair in a silk scarf. Last of all I paint my nails and venture outside ...

I put the Hearboy on his lead and take him for walkies, clacking in my high heels. A bus passes, I hike up my skirts and expose myself, daring people to recognise me, to spot that I am not a lady but a boy, that I've got a dick between my legs under the jam-rag.

I take the mutt up under the fir tree, get my dick out, take a piss, and let Hearboy lick at it. Shit, that stings! I suck my breath in hard, then a little bit of juice comes. The dirty mutt loves it, he laps at it – it must be the salt. Then he starts jerking himself off and I have to kick him in the ribs, three or four times. Actually, I have to strangle him a bit until he looks sad that he's going to die. Really, I would much rather have been touching little Elizabeth from over the council estate: tasting her and licking her sticky-out bottom. I yank Hearboy on his chain; I pull him along, his claws scouring the pavement.

Now that I come to think of it, my mother was the only one who showed any care for that dog. 'Hearboy!' we named him, some kind of half-breed Collie with these manked-up eyes. Friendly, loyal, everything that a human being isn't. Puppyish as well. And a flincher. 'Hearboy!' My mother was the only one who looked after him – I lost all interest. He got old and dotty, he pissed himself and walked round in little circles. In the end she took him away and had him gassed. 'Hearboy!', the little stray dog, out of pity. She didn't bring the corpse back, they did something with it, they must have burned it.

'I should of brought him back and buried him here.' She tells me about it. 'He was wetting himself all the time, I didn't have any choice, I had to have him put down.'

I nod, I have no argument.

'But I wish I'd kept his body, I wish I had him buried here.'

He disappeared out of our lives. We were friends once, but sex made me want to kick him. I hated that dog through guilt. That's about all you're left with in the end. The love flitters away, but guilt? It's weighty, it's resilient.

I pretended to strangle him, I wait 'til he starts choking, then I let him go – and his sad eyes, he must of trusted me . . . Goodbye doggy, nice to have met you, but now it's time to shift your gears, friend of my childhood.

And me dressed up in drag, dick inside my Y-fronts, brought up on my father's pornography, filched from his briefcase. I didn't know who I was or what I was turning into: my delicate self had been ruined and there was an uproar of bad blood. The confusion, that one so young – me it seems, because I remember – should be so damaged, that no one looked out for me or cared. And even now, I grin and mock myself out of fear. But I hold the truth aloft, a golden torch, sacred, because no one else dares to.

By this time it was obvious that with a mug like mine, and my low-life nature, that I was a dog molester of the lowest instincts. My brother looks me up and down, whistles through his teeth and shakes his mangy head.

'You're just the sort that gets acne!' he pronounces.

He stings me in front of his friends, his entourage of admirers, in front of his cuties in fact. I check my mug in the mirror, you see, I've got this jutting jawline and hollow cheeks. I examine them with my fingers; how I craved for some cream puffs like my brother's. I hated my face, I cut into it with razors. No woman could ever love such an ugly customer.

I lie in bed and kiss the pillow. I kiss it, cotton and feathers; it sucks the spit right out of your mouth. I put a toilet roll in there; I cram it full of Vaseline, stick my little dick in and really start to run. I get a regular gallop on, chasing little Elizabeth's arse. I guess I made quite a racket, shaking up the whole house, careering round the room, skidding on the carpet. I was banging my head into the wall: that's what all the noise was about. You see, I have to put an extra spurt on – her delicate little arse, that special type of shape, it protruded, throbbing. I just had my nose in there, and that's when I look up, to see my mother standing in the doorway, with a cup of tea in her hand . . .

'You're going to have to learn some facts of life, young man!'

That knocks the steam out of my little engine. I slam it into reverse, I shield my loins. Her with her, 'you're going to have to learn some facts of life' routine. That's what she said. I've heard it a thousand times over; she repeats it in every situation, totally out of context. That and her, 'it's a question of survival!' She's kept that one going. It's still doing the rounds, 'sure as eggs are eggs', an evergreen, she'll take that one with her to the grave. That and her, 'when you're older, then you'll see!' 'Bloody soddin' kids!' And, 'the way you cried, my God, your voice. You were clingy and you wouldn't eat anything!' There you have it, the wisdoms of a lifetime.

But me lying there, with my dick in that toilet roll – I have to admit that I blushed.

16. THE GREEN BOOK

I 'll come clean with you, I've had it in for religion from an early age: for schools, religion and anybody else's half-arsed dogma. I've no nose for that type of bullshit.

Lordswood Primary School: the vicar's son sat right opposite me. I eyed him timidly. A fringe, eight little freckles and a perfect little nose. He stutters, he can't get his tongue round his 't's. He purples up, sucks his cheeks in then spits it out. We sit round holding our breath, waiting for the show to begin, for the big announcement. No one dares pre-empt him, or put words in his mouth. He sits there laying an egg, he waves his hands about like a diver. The truth of the matter is he bullied me. No kidding, even this bible-basher got one over on me: God's kid! He wore Chelsea boots and a black rollneck sweater, he reeked of style, Johnty, the vicar's son.

And they sat us down at the same desk, the 'them', the teachers. Mister Jones, six foot two or three. I remember his mug, Welsh with a shaving rash, bad breath and sincere.

'Good morning, class.'

'Good morning, Mister Jones.'

'Now come along, you can do better than that. Good morning class!'

'Good morning, Mister Jones.'

He drags it out of us, we shuffle to our feet, scraping our chairs: nine o'clock and knackered already ... 'Good morning, Mister Jones.' We sing it out and drop back to our seats.

'Now then, that's much better!'

He studies his wrist watch, looks up at us meaningfully, rummages around in his eye socket, then places his brief case on the desk top.

'I wonder if any of you can tell me what this is.' He put in his hand and extracts a flat square packet. He holds it up for all to see.

'It's an LP!' he announces to himself. 'Now can anybody tell me what LP stands for?'

He nurses the record from its dust jacket and holds it up between his thumb and forefinger, 'hahs' on it and gives it a quick scuff with his cufflink. He peers into all those little black grooves. He reads them like they were a book, mouthing all the notes, then slings it onto the turntable, crunches the arm across and forces the needle down in the plastic. As ham-fisted as a Dutchman. He's certainly got all the gear up there, all the gadgets, a little turntable, a speaker, and two or three knobs to play with.

'We killed these people!' he announces. 'These people were red skinned people. Can anybody tell me where the red-skins come from? America!' he answers himself. 'Long before Christopher Columbus even dreamed of the New World! Take that out of your mouth, boy! Come along, spit it into the bin! The white people annihilated the red people!' He stands there flexing his feet, size twelves; he lets us know his opinions.

He gives us a moment to let it all sink in . . . We sit behind our little desks . . . His face, a blank of flesh, millions of intricate little specks, and the rash, the whole thing mushed in together.

'The white man killed the red man; we systematically eradicated his culture!'

There he goes, sounding off again. Well, I knew I hadn't killed no Indians. If anyone had done any killing it was more likely to be the likes of him with the big feet and the rash – old know-all, stuffed behind his desk. He clicks off his rotten music and hands round the pencils.

'Alright class, pass them round!' He pulls out his little white baton and conducts us like a chorus, 'That's right boys and girls, all the way to the back. Has everybody got one? Good, now what book are we on?'

The hands shoot up, eager beavers, they clamour for attention. Old Johnty can't get his foot out his mouth . . . I slouch below my desk, long haired, reticent, not understanding the words, the numbers.

'The Green Book, sir! The Green Book, we're on the Green Book, sir!'

That's the way they sing it, a chorus, keen, blonde, glittering eyes, Johnty too. 'The Green Book, sir, we're reading the Green Book!'

I listen in, I sit up, say, me too, the Green Book? Yeah, me too. They hand them round, a big stack of green: I take one and pass the rest on. I look it over, this Green Book of theirs. Green, definitely green, but a bit thick, a little on the robust side. And that's strange, all that weird calligraphy on the spine, that got me thinking. Hey, wait a minute! What's going on? My colour rises, I go to speak, but my tongue goes thick, I can't swallow. I go to replace my book, to tell sir, to let them know, but the moment passes. I wave my hands about but no one's in the least little bit interested. They're all engrossed, the whole lot of them, heads down, mowing, nothing but a bunch of sheep. I try and attract their attention, my class mates, heads bowed ... I make little movements, I pout and wrinkle my forehead, but it's no good, no one could give a fig. And our Welshman, our Mister Jones? Picking through his scabs with one hand and scratching his balls with the other, totally engrossed.

I look to the pages, that book was some size alright, like some kind of hideous bible, totally unfathomable and hardly a picture in sight. Gross, indecent, never-ending. And every page crammed full of them, they marched on like an army of little insects. Hey, what are those things? Spiderish, intricate, detailed, repetitive ... letters? Letters, shit! I finger my collar and swallow my puke, sour, bitter-sweet. This ain't the Green Book, this is a green book, volume eight or nine I shouldn't wonder. Green yes, but after that the similarities are pretty thin on the ground – a green book but not my faithful little volume one, the Green Book, the one with the cute little black and white mices on the front cover. No! These bastards have stitched me up, the whole stinking lot of 'em are in cahoots. Who the hell are they trying to kid? I want a recount, them with their 'Green Book!' Green Book my arse! Green Book bloody volume three hundred and twenty-one more like!

I had to go into that classroom, nine o'clock sharp every morning and sit behind that desk 'til half-three in the afternoon, and all the time making out to be reading those hieroglyphs, for two whole stinking weeks. I moved my lips, and stared sweating into that mess of spiders legs, sweating, trying to come to terms with the hatefulness of life, the seconds clocking. Sometimes moving a page, folding it back and peeping over into the beyond.

There was more of it, exactly the same, page after page of the stuff, disappearing into eternity. I turned back double quick, it said something, something, something, then there was a number: a number 'one' I think it was, like a line, a stake! Tree-ish, but without the branches. I stared at that stroke, that line, I studied it and held onto it. I knew what that line meant, that line was a number. I took furtive glances at the other kids, my pals, the prodigies of the word, just their fringes and a bit of their noses showing. And that Johnty kid, the vicar's son, sat opposite me. All I could hear all day long was the sound of his pages folding back, it seemed like every three minutes he finished one of those pages and started on another. That made me stare at him, his freckles and his superior little kisser mouthing the words, running sentences. I'd fill that for him! I'd teach him some fucking words!

The point is, you see, is that I didn't want to let on – I was ashamed, me being thick and all that. You see, I was told it every day, my brother liked to remind me, he used to rub it in.

'You're thick, you are. You can't read and write and you wet the bed!'

It was true ... I stared down, kicked the dirt 'n' played with my buttons ...

'Mother, Steven can't read or write yet! I could read and write when I was five! He's thick! Aren't you, thicko!'

You see, I didn't want to let on about the Green Book, the one with the mices on, 'cos that was an infant's book, a beginners book, for stupid kids, for retards.

Mister Jones made us take turns to read out loud in class, and slowly his little white baton worked round the room until finally it's pointing straight at me. I sit dumb and stupid, choking back a tear. I wanted to speak, to come out with a wonderful story, a story to break the hearts of impossible princesses, for the veil to suddenly lift and for me to magically understand their game. I cleared my throat, as if to begin.

'Number one,' I said, quiet, low down, into my jumper.

'Could that boy speak up? Come along ... what did you say?'

'He said nur-nur-nur-number one, sir!'

'Yes, number one ... and?'

I peered under my desk at my feet.

'Come along, boy ... What's your name?'

'He-he-his-na-na-name-is-Ham-Ham-Hamperson, sir.'

'Is that your name? Come out to the front, Hamperson ... Would that be a Christmas Hamperson or a picnic Hamperson?'

He smirks to the ceiling, he grins round the room so's that the class know that they can laugh. I push my arse off that seat, kick my sandals onto the deck and approach his desk. Oaken, grainy, I stare into its molecules, and that fat-faced Jonesy boy sat stuffed behind it: sir.

'There seems to be a problem, Christmas, can't you read this book?'

He shows the class the cover. I open and shut my mouth and stare into the scuff marks on my sandals. I try to say it, to broach the subject, 'the Green Book', to tell him about the white mice, to open my dumb stupid mouth.

'Are you on Green Book five, then?'

I shake my head, a tear hits the dust.

'Green Book three? Come along speak up! We haven't got all day! Green Book two, or three, which is it to be?'

I find something under my nail, like dirt, but sort of white coloured, sort of clean dirt.

'Look at me when I'm talking to you, Hamperson! I said what book are you on, two or three?'

'The one with the mices, sir,' I whisper it.

'Pardon!'

'The one with the mices.'

'The one with the mices?'

The classroom grows hushed ...

'It's a-a-a-an infant's book, sir!'

'The one with the mices?' Jonesy's incredulous. 'The one with the mices?'

He 'tut-tutts' me and bends his baton almost double ...

'The one with the mices! Dear, oh dear ... My youngest daughter has already read book six, and she is still in kindergarten! I'll have to bring her in to give you reading lessons, won't I? That will be a turn-up for the books, an infant teaching a junior!'

He turns to the class and milks them again and again. He shames me with his English rose, the stuck up little bitch.

From then on I have to go to the retard classes in the afternoons, the dump for the no-hopers, backward kids, clodhoppers ... That made me start pulling some faces, sat in that room full of thickos, and me the best drawer in the whole school. They told me to cut out the doodling and start drawing the alphabet. Single letters, one at a time, row upon row of the little bastards. You had to sing them out, to repeat them parrot-style.

'Small, smell, smile ... Small, smell, smile ... Small, smell, smile ...'

I draw a mousy-mousy, a couple of the little fellows, jolly, full of fun, noses, little whiskers, tails. And then the bell goes and we have to go and hang around the school gate waiting for Johnty's old man to pick us up.

'My fa-fa-fa-fa ...'

His face purples up, his eyes hideous. Come on, spit it out! His fa-fa what? He hangs his tongue out and bugs his eyes.

'Ma-ma-ma, fa-fa ... my father's a vicar, wh-wh-wh-what's yours do?'

'He does drawing'

'Wh-what's he draw?'

'Cats 'n' stuff?'

'Where's he w-work'

'I dunno ... I don't renember ...'

'Y-y-you-you mean "remember".'

'What?'

'You said "renember"! You-you-you sh-sh-sh-should say "re-member".'

'Renember.' I try to say it, but it comes out wrong.

That makes his day, he holds onto himself. I look at the bushes, at the passing cars. I kick at a slug, black, creeping, a trail of slime. I split its guts, yellow, I toe it; then his old man shows up.

'Hello fa-fa-father, th-this is Ste-Ste-Steven ... He-he-he ca-ca-can't say remember ...'

'Yes, I can! I just forgot, that's all.'

'Forgot? Can't you "renember"?'

Old God Squad smirks down at me. Oh, so the vic's got a sense of humour! Johnty's positively beaming.

The wrong book for two whole weeks, and me just a kid, still in shorts, too shit-scared to tell Mister Jones, or to let on to the other brats, my superior classmates. I stared that Johnty kid down, despite his old man being there.

'You shut it, Johnty!'

'Johnty? What's this "Johnty"?' Jonathan! That's his name! Jonathan! I suppose you can say that alright? Jonathan! He wasn't christened Johnty! Jonathan is his name, so use it!'

I looked to Johnty and back to that prick in the dog's collar.

'Johnafun,' I say.

17. 5 PARK DRIVE

I showed him my crucifix, I took it into school with me, and showed it to God's kid. Wooden with a brass inlay, dangling on a bit of old rope. I dig it out my pocket and show him it after assembly.

'It's real wood, with gold! This man made it for me, his name's Norman, he's a woodwork teacher in the big school. He knows my mum. It's for scaring off vampires, smart in't it? He didn't buy it or nothing, he made it by hand, all by himself! It keeps off vampires – here, take it, go on. You can spit on it if you like. Go on, spit on it!'

That makes him look at me, his delicate little gob doesn't look quite so superior anymore, he puckers up his lips like a cat's arse
. . .

'Go on, spit on it!'

'I-I-I-I ca-ca-ca-nn't, my fa-fa-fa-father's a vicar!'

'So what, don't mean you can't spit on it, does it? You don't believe in God, do you?'

'I ha-ha-have to, my father's a vicar.'

'Don't mean you have to, just because your dad does, does it? Go on, spit on it! I spit on it, I spat on it this morning. I keep it under my pillow, it keeps off vampires. Give us it here.'

I snort one up, I suck my cheeks in and gob. I hold it under his nose for inspection.

'Come on, don't be a wanker!'

'Wha-wha-wha-what's a wa-wa-wanker?'

I look at him sideways. What's he trying to pull? Him with his 'what's a wa-wa-wanker?'

'You don't know what wanking means? Really?'

'N-n-n-n-no . . .'

'Well, it's . . . it's wanking, isn't it? You do it to women 'n' things. You see, you have stuff, spunk . . . After the wanking . . .'

'Wh-wh-what?'

'It's like, you know, weeing . . . Only you do it up 'em.'

He gives me a blank one.

'The women, you do it up the women and that gives them a baby . . . You put it up their cunt for a white one and up their arse for a black one.'

That took him aback, his stupid little kisser mincing about, chewing on it. I knew I had something over on him. I lean in, and say it right in his ear.

'How long's your winkle on the donk? You have to rub it; look I'll show you . . .'

I looked about, checked the coast was clear and unbuttoned it.

We got good at that game – we used to lock ourselves in the toilets and get a stiffy by looking through my old man's porno mags. Once we got a donk-on, we measured them up and played sword fights, and put them against each others arses. The idea was to check each week to see if they'd grown. But that God's kid used to have a half hard-on, and then swear blind that it was still on the soft. You have to watch those religious types, any chance they get they'll cheat. They think they've got the whole universe sewn up: they've seen it and they've fucked it, they know the whole show!

There was no doubts that he fancied himself, what with his freckles, rose-bud lips and his literary genius. Him with his Green Book volume eighteen. And what with his 'remember' not 'renember', he got to thinking that maybe he could 'boss' me! I had to drag him down through the shit, to out-dirt him on every count.

'You can come round my house after school if you want, we've got these woods 'n' fields over the back, 'n' these ants nests. You get a spade 'n' bucket 'n' dig up a red ants nest, then you chuck it on top of a black ants nest 'n' watch 'em fight . . . The red ants always win, they're smaller 'n' slower, but when they get hold of one of them black ants, they rip its fuckin' head off! It's smart! You gonna come? Go on, say you'll come, 'n' I'll show you me wasp collection! They're still alive, I feed 'em on flies! They sting 'em 'n' carry 'em around, hanging underneath whilst they're flying ... We can go and see Terry, he's gonna be a Hell's Angel!'

'A Hell's Angel?'

'They ride motorbikes 'n' piss on their jeans, 'n' they don't wash 'em, 'n' you mustn't let your mum wash 'em either. They piss on 'em 'n' rub oil 'n' stuff into 'em, my brother knows all about it, he's got the book. And Terry, the man over the road, when he gets his licence he's gonna be one, 'n' he says I can have a go on the back of his Triumph, when he gets it. You see, they have smaller people on the back, 'cos then it makes the one on the front look bigger. But you have to piss on your jeans, it's good, 'n' you rub oil 'n' stuff in 'em. There's some in my dad's garidge ...'

That took some convincing, getting God's kid to piss on himself. I have to build him up to it, that and the gobbing on the crucifix. The fucking king of the Green Book!

After school I take him down Smelly Al's, and both of us chuck in for a pack of 5 Park Drive. I show him how you're supposed to smoke. You hook your thumb in your belt loop and suck it all down 'til it hurts. We light up inside my old man's garage. Johnty couldn't do it as good as me, so I had to finish his for him. Then we got our dicks out and measure them up with a steel ruler. Johnty reckons his has grown half an inch since last week, which is bullshit.

We go into the garage, piss on each other's jeans, then head over the back into the woods. We go the short way round to the big beech tree and set up the crucifix and the melted action men. You burn off the arms and legs and stick the knitting needles through their heads. Then you pour in the red paint, like real bullet holes. I arrange one either side of Jesus, then get the big jar of jaspers out. I shake them up to make them dizzy.

'Look at these bastards! You see that one? That's the queen!'

Big, holding in mid-air, revolving her antennae, spinning like radars, a special glow, orange-yellow.

'I caught her by the dustbins with a cigarette case. You snap it shut 'n' catch 'em mid-air! That's a special one, that one, probably a hornet or something.'

I take a lug on my ciggie and blow the smoke in on top of them, just to be on the safe side.

'If that bastard gets out she'll sting you to death, she's specially trained!'

I empty them out onto the deck, black and yellow, creepy-crawling, little circles, testing their wings.

'Quick, put the hornet back, we'll save her 'til last.'

I get out my jack-knife and hold it under her legs, 'til she clings on, heavy, bloated. She sticks her sting into the blade, she unsheathes it and flexes her abdomen . . . I flick her back into the jar.

'Give us the matches before they fly off!'

I squidged a bit of Evostick onto the heads of the matches, glue them onto the jaspers' backs, then stake them out in a nice little row. Six in all, feet kicking.

'You yellow faced Jap bastards, we got you now!'

I squint right into their faces, their little hands wiping their jaws, outraged, cursing, showing their teeth.

'Look, they're trying to kill 'emselves, but they can't reach! Don't worry little jaspers, you'll know death soon enough! But first you can watch your comrades die!'

I snatch up the little plastic bomber, camouflaged with black crosses, chuck it on the ground and squirt it with lighter fuel.

'Right, burn the wasps. Now! Come on, quick, like this!'

I strike a match and let it burn up the stake. The wasp kicks, his wings singed, jaws going, his body doubles back trying to sting himself, the little spike throbbing in and out, then the match explodes.

'Did you see it? Did you see it? See, come on, it's your turn now . . .'

I chuck the match on the Heinkel and squirt more lighter fuel, the plastic curls, giving off black smoke.

'Look, the fuckin' Nazis, they're burning!'

I speak to the action men. 'Come on Frank, Joey, do the rest of 'em, torch 'em! 'I can't Frank, I'm dying, it's my arm, arrghh!' 'Joey, Joey speak to me!' OK men, the flame thrower, torch 'em!'

We fumble with the matches, then one by one the jaspers flare up, legs blackening, their antennae droop, they gnash their jaws, their abdomens Crack! and Pop! Six in all, maybe seven of them, burned alive at the stake. Captured and shamed, my power supreme! I pick up the action men, make them salute, and knight them with my jack-knife.

'Well done men, it's been a great day for peace and freedom! You Frank, and you Joey, you're heroes, an inspiration to your country. You have served bravely and wisely, with God on your side. So now, let us pray for the glorious dead!'

I kneel them down in the dirt and put their stumps together.

'God in heaven, gentle Jesus 'n' all the other ghosts, we thank you for this victory . . . Remember the glorious dead . . . Never let them stray from the path of righteousness, Amen!'

We unbuttoned our hoses and let go a stream of hot piss, it hisses and steams, frothing up the black dirt. It's a race against time to see who can piss out the most wasps. Life and death, little channels, pools of piss. We roll in it and kick those mean little bastards back into the black earth! We stamp them back into the sod, teaching those jaspers a lesson, letting them know who's boss! The Judgement of the Christ, that's what, that's who, and that's what! The game of the little yellow and black ones.

We lie back, covered in shit, breathing in fits and starts. 'Those bastards won't come back in a hurry!' I light a ciggie, draw the smoke in deep and cough, my eyes watering. I lean forward and spit on the cross, yellow juice.

'Go on, spit on it!'

Johnty looks up startled.

'Come on, God's kid, fuckin' spit on it, you fuckin' Christ lover!'

I jump up and shout it in his face. I swing his action man round by its dislocated ankle. I wag it right under his nose blood-red, stumps for arms, neck broken, a quarter inch shell hole right through his bonce.

'Jesus ain't gonna save you now, so spit on it! Spit on it, you wanker!'

I watched his mug crumble, the lips twitching, the freckles, the delicate eyelashes. He chews his lips and blubbers, a tear rolling down his smoke-blackened mug. He doesn't talk about his 'Green Book' now, nor his 'renember'. No, he isn't such a big kid now. He's implicated – he pissed on the dead – he's measured, and he's burnt, and his poxy god has deserted him! He sucks on his spit and twiddles with his tongue.

'M . . . m-m-m-m . . . fa-fa-fa . . . m-m-m-fa-fa-father says I'm not to p-play with you no more!'

He goes to get to his feet. I shove him hard in the chest.

'Yeah, 'n' your old man stinks, just like his fucking church!'

He swings round and slips in the piss, he picks himself up, he looks at me, then his face explodes and he runs howling through the woods . . . I watch him go . . .

'Johnty! Johnty!'

I call after him, but nothing . . . just his banshee, decreasing . . . a few blackbirds, nothing . . . I chuck his action man onto the heap . . .

'OK, Joey? Joey! Joey!'

'I don't want to die, Franky, I don't want to die!'

'It's got to come off, Joey, it's gangrenous.'

'Arrghh!'

'Here, bite on this . . . I've got to do it Joey, I've got to cut it out!'

I kneel in the leaves, black dirt, a few twigs, crap . . . I open my jack-knife, cross myself, kiss the blade and swish the queen's head clean off . . .

18. NANA LEWIS

I f it hadn't been for Nana Lewis keeping us going on handouts, we'd of all starved to death on the spot, years back even. That was my mother's opinion, and she never tired of repeating it, quietly, to herself. That's the way she talked, in whispers, repetitively, trailing off. She never ever finished a sentence in twenty-five years of marriage.

'The thing is . . .'

I sit waiting, I look at her face, ageing, then stare out of the window. The silence grows, there's a thousand different types of silence in this world, but hers was total, apart from a few twitterings in the branches, in the distance, on the edge of hearing. I'm still waiting, suspenseful, the penny that never dropped. It was sure to wind the old man up, her pronouncements. He staggers in drunk, half two in the morning, pulling at his shirt studs, hopping round the bedroom on one leg. He walks into the wall and pisses in the wardrobe. What really gets his goat is that it's all perfectly true.

'Love-a-duck, Juny, you can't live off fresh air alone you know! My poor little angels! Here take this, Juny, no I insist, spend it on the kids!'

She forces a bluey into the old girl's mitt.

Nana Lewis had imagination alright. She not only kept me and my brother in pocket money, but she paid off half the household bills to boot. She forced half crowns into our hands; she knew us kids needed a little treat once in a while.

'Rationing isn't the norm these days, you know Juny, there isn't a war on anymore, you know!'

The old man got tired of hearing it; he bit his lip and stared up at the ceiling. He finds a boil in his beard, he scratches at it, raking his fingernails through the bristles, he lances it, walks to the cabinet and pours himself a stiff one. He downs it in one and scowls round the room.

'That mother of yours! I'm a stranger in my own house! Why don't you all piss off and live with her?'

Once he caught wind that Nana Lewis was bringing in fruits and supplies, he almost choked. He popped his eyes at us and flung his hands around like bundles of sticks, he refused point blank to sink another brass farthing into the upkeep.

'OK, that's it, Juny! Do you hear me? Out! You, your kids, the oil heater, the mutt, the whole stinking lot of you! Out, out, out!'

He shakes it at us, dripping paraffin, he storms in and out the hallway, he marches round the garden with it . . . He flings it left, right and centre, he interrogates it.

'You're thick, the lot of you, thick and bone idle! Money doesn't grow on trees, you know! You imbeciles! You'll end up blowing yourselves sky-high!' He rattles its cage. 'Well, I tell you this much for free, I'm not slogging my guts out, dragging my arse up to London every day, just so's you lot can lie in the lap of luxury, abusing my facilities! Who's going to pay the telephone bill? The electricity? Well, no longer am I going to bear the brunt of your ridiculous extravagances! Come along woman, all of you, out! Chop-chop! You don't like my hospitality? Fine! Clear out and take those snivelling brats with you! It's time to call a halt, for you to learn to shoulder your own responsibilities! Enough is enough, as they say! I'm afraid you've bled me dry, now go see how your mother likes having a bunch of bone idle loafers cluttering up her doorstep! I wash my hands of you, here and now!'

He dips his hands in the wick and he crosses himself with the oil, he absolves himself, walks to the garage and climbs into his bus. We stand agape, staring after him. A winter fly wakes up and bangs into the lampshade, Hearboy comes out from under the table and bites at it. We look at each other, I go to breathe, I forgot. Just as we think the hurricane has blown itself out, we hear another crash and he emerges from out of his little house.

'How low do you want to crawl, exactly? What sort of ground teat do you want to suck on? Come on woman, answer me!

Because I'll tell you this much, a sow's is too high, that's plain as day!'

We make him sick alright, we don't budge an inch, we know our rights. We sit tight on our wicket, electricity or no electricity, we refuse to be intimidated.

So it gets pretty cold in England round about Christmas time. Nothing too extreme, but you get to notice it. The damp, the fog, the pea-soupers, every type of downpour, and then there's the frosts . . . The oil stove is banished, we get the message: 'it stinks!'

'It's as senseless as burning money, you may as well walk to the gutter and chuck it down the drain!'

That's his opinion. We've heard them all in duplicate – he's delivered his tirade, he's made his point. He winds down, takes a swig at his bottle, he chucks it back in great golden glugs, then spits it back out again. He slams the door, we can hear him crashing about in the garage. He takes the oil-stove with him, he's axing it once and for all, he rips into it, he lets it know who's boss, he gains control.

'How do you like that? You bastard!'

My mother tugs at the skin on her throat. We haven't seen the old coot for two months, and then here he is, laying down the law. He turns up completely out of the blue, as righteous as a priest. He quits dismantling the flue and we hear him in his jalopy, gunning the motor; he reverses in and out of the garage, grinding the gears. He accelerates, then slams on all four brakes. He isn't going anywhere, it's all for effect – he's got a two year ban, a drink driving rap. He's just winding her up, trying to get the old girl's goat. He jumps out his seat, slams and re-slams the door – it rebounds so hard that it hits him in the shins. He turns jet-white, grinds his maulers into dust and spits out the fillings. He implodes, he gets out the car and rips the door off, he bites at the wing mirrors.

'Eighteen thousand tons of stinking shit! Fuck and damnation!'

He hurls himself onto the bonnet, pummelling it with his fists. He whimpers and farts with the exertion, hugging the silver lady, shimmering, acres of gossamer . . . He kisses her and licks at her wings, her drapery, silver, dignified, always serene, glimmering in the moonlight. He goes all romantic on her, sucking at her toes, her little feet. He whispers sweet nothings, blows kisses, baby talk.

Suddenly he sits bolt upright and stares back at the darkened house. His eyes travelling from window to window, 'til finally

they come to rest on my room, my little night light flickering . . .
I stand back behind the curtain. I see him climb down off the
bonnet, he adjusts his bow-tie, and reins in his temper. He tunes
it like a motor, finely, with care. He rewinds it, he stamps and
curses, he wipes the drool onto his cuff – that makes him wince.
That's funny, his cufflink must have scratched his nose. He checks
for blood, pawing at his face in the wing mirror, bent, drunk,
skyward . . . He has to stand funny to do that, at a jaunty angle,
to check his nose. He scratched it on either his signet ring or his
cufflink, one of the two. He gives his hair a cat-lick, re-straightens
the wing mirror, then studies himself in the glass. Buttons his
waistcoat, pulls out his onion and has a time check.

I see him from the top window, my little bedside lamp burning.
I have to have the light on, a reassurance, otherwise I see things
– there are vampires, real. No kidding, I need the light, something
to keep my spirits up.

Just as we think he's passed his vortex he starts drumming
again, hammering the doors, he huffs and puffs. He blusters round
the garden, does a couple of little circuits then comes in through
the back way.

'Juny! Darling! I'm home! I had to work late! The office! Is
there any food in the house? Are the children in bed? Steven?
Nichollas? Children! Juny, was that a light I saw burning? Answer
me, woman!'

He grabs at her, he pulls at her arms and drags her out into the
night, her in her night dress.

'Look at it woman, look at what you've done to me! Feast your
eyes on that and don't forget a single scratch!'

His Roller lies wrecked before them. The panels hopelessly bent.

'Now are you satisfied? Something to cheer you up. My
complete and utter downfall! Something for you to smile about!
Look at it, it's a wreck woman! A man was killed! It's a write-off!
A complete fucking write-off!'

He spits it out through his beard, brandy flavoured.

He wrote off four cars in three years, ripping down miles of
crash barrier, re-moulding them into weird and wonderful art
forms . . . He had the intellectuals guessing. 'Could it really be art?
And if so expressionist or romantic?' 'Anarchic Realism', was one
school of thought, 'Auto Dadaism', pronounced a second.

Drunk and disorderly he would emerge from amongst the
wreckage, a slight scratch on his left wrist and two bruised knees.

He dusts himself off and replaces his titfer . . . He has to go back in to fetch his brolly from the parcel shelf, he opens it up and checks the ribbing, there seems to be a slight nick out of the handle . . . Then the old bill roll up and he gives them the special handshake. They help him to sit on the curb, he's hurt his shin but otherwise he's completely unscathed.

The old girl lets out a scream and runs howling into the drive, her arms flailing, the old man socks her one right in the eye, and drags her back into the house . . . He jams his mitt into the fuse box.

'My fucking electricity!'

The house goes black, there's a frothing noise, then everything goes black. He's illuminated in the sparks, his teeth glint, all his pearls, every last one a cap. Then darkness, it rushes in and surrounds me! My little light goes off, that's how I know he's home. He must have ripped out the fuse box, that was the noise I heard, and the bang. It goes black! I call out for my mother, the old man screaming down the driveway. We can just make out his peroxide hair floating in the moonlight, and his bloodshot eyes.

'You're abusing my facilities! Squandering my fucking electricity!'

He dances, elfin-like under the boughs of the trees, moonlit, a cloud, nothing . . .

I'm telling it to you like this because it's a serious business. That's why I smile as I write. After all, a little humour never hurt nobody . . .

He took the fuses, that's why it went black, he pockets them and runs . . .

'It's alright, Steven, it's alright!'

That's my mother calling out to me, through the blackness, from way downstairs, trying to be reassuring. I have to be brave, the dark is everything . . .

19. YOU'LL NEVER KNOW IF IT'S DARK

Wednesday nights, Nana Lewis comes over on the bus and we have sausage and mash. She turns up, her hair piled up on top of her head, loads of it, brown, not a bit grey. And this soft skin, and two types of scarf, a blue net one and a coloured silky one, flowers and stuff and she holds our faces and kisses us . . .

'My angels.'

That's how she speaks. She puts her hold-all down, rummages about in it and pulls out a bag of apples. I go out to play . . . She hands me one . . . hard and shiny . . .

'Rub it on your jumper. Take it with you, you can eat it outside.'

I turn and walk out into the night.

'What if it's magotty, nan?'

'You'll never know, if it's dark.'

She shouldn't have told me that . . . I look at her and me mum through the kitchen window, the steam builds up . . . She walks over to the sink, rolls up her sleeves and starts right in mashing the spuds.

Nana Lewis: our saviour. That was true enough – an apple here, the odd half-crown there, it kept us ticking over. She could see what was going on, alright. The old scoundrel's absconded? Fine, Nana Lewis steps into the breech, and not a regular grandmother either: young, radiant, with brown hair, all her own, great piles of the stuff. Style! Something from the 1920s, a flapper, that's what she told us. She used to wear men's trousers, and that was way back in the 1930s! Then war was declared and she had to learn to drive a truck. That was her alright: wistful, exuberant. She took charge, she exercised her will. A fag, a pint of Guinness, and she was ready for anything!

'It's plain as the nose on your face what that scallywag's up to, Juny! He comes and goes just as he pleases, then clears off leaving you with the kids, the bills and I don't know what! He takes the biscuit, he really does! The boys are listless, look at the poor angels. They're sickening for something, that's for sure . . . What they need is a change of air!'

She stubs out her cigarette for emphasis, that's the way she talked. In her eyes we were always 'her angels'. As far as grandparents are concerned, grandchildren can do no wrong. The old and the young talk the same language: ga-ga!

'You need a break my girl, if not for your sake, then for the children's! You don't always have to jump to his tune you know, Juny . . . Why, you don't know where that scallywag is from one month to the next! He says he was working late and sleeping at the office! Sleeping at the office? Heavens above, he'll say he was in church next! He disappears, he reappears . . . he doesn't pay the bills! And then before you know it he's off again! Where to? Heaven only knows! And when will you see him next? Will he ever show his face again? Who can say? Take a look at yourself in the mirror sometime, love-a-duck! You're running yourself ragged, Juny – take my advice, get out and enjoy yourself whilst you still can! You're still young!'

She got through three whole packets of Guards trying to talk the old girl round. The air was blue with fag ash. The dinner would have to wait, that was for sure. Us kids couldn't get a word in edgeways. I pull at the table cloth, I nick three dog-ends out the ashtray right in front of them. I could of lit up there and then for all the notice they took of me. In the end we eat out the pans, nan still trying to talk the old girl round.

A fact is a fact, and there isn't anyone more stubborn and belligerent than my mother. If she says that there's no such thing as pure new wool, then that's that! And it doesn't matter how hard you try and cajole her, she'll have none of it. You march right up to her and plunk it down in her lap, '100 per cent pure new wool', in writing. No dice! She'll take her opinions to the grave.

'I know, I know, I know.' She nods and repeats herself. 'But the costs! the costs!'

That's another of my mother's great watch-words, 'think of the costs!' coupled with 'we'll have to economise!' I spent my whole childhood on one of her 'economy drives', limping through school in one pair of busted boots and a cheese sandwich in my brother's old blazer pocket.

'We're living beyond our means!' That was always ringing in my ears, through the power cuts and the black-outs.

The only way we got to take that holiday was through Nana Lewis digging into her nest egg. She drew the money out and didn't even consult my grandad. My mother had to be cajoled. She budgeted to the last halfpenny. I needed a fishing rod, that much was for sure. All those hard laid plans of economy and then we had to fork out another thirty quid on taxi fares. You see we didn't have a car and my mother couldn't drive. The taxi had a sun-roof, so I get to stand on the front seat with my shoes and socks off and stick my head out the roof. It helped me from getting car sick. It meant I managed not to puke.

'The air's good for him! If it cured Knut Hamsun, it won't do him any harm! If I had my time again!'

That's Nana Lewis's opinion.

I shoot my cap-gun at the passing traffic. That's what you need if you feel like you're going to chuck up, lungfuls of air! I open my trap and stare straight into the wind, both eyes streaming.

'Norm and Sue are coming as well ... You'll like the Broads, there's a lot of water there so you can go fishing.' My mother announces it to me and my brother over tea and my mouth turns to dust. 'You'll like that, won't you? And Susan's bringing Joanne with her. So you'll have a little friend to play with as well, Steven, you like Joanne, don't you?'

I swallow and manage a half-smile. 'I'm going over the back,' I tell her. I walk out, I exit, her eyes follow me, wondering ...

'I thought you'd like a holiday ...'

I keep my eyes to the ground, I give nothing away.

'We've built a camp. Can I have a tin of beans for the fire?' She looks at me, disappointed, and hands it over. I get my hat and spear, and exit.

In bed I try to imagine Joanne lying on top of me, us doing what me and Norman did, but with her, with a girl, small, my size, and no willy, just a slit ... The weight of her, the trees bowed over us, just kid's stuff, imaginings, poetry.

The taxi drops us off, chucks our suitcases on the verge and leaves us to it. My grandad holds the map upside down and scratches his head. Even after we find the right stretch of river it still takes us half the night to find the moorings. It's black on those broads, no street lights to destroy the night sky, and plenty of water. You have to watch out for that, especially the mooring ropes. We dilly-dallied about on that river bank 'til we didn't know our port from our starboard.

'Over here!'

We hear a voice off in the distance.

'That's your grandad,' says Nana Lewis.

We peer through the bulrushes, his ears and nose sticking out like a totem-pole, hawkish, blustering, snoring his big head off.

'Over here! I've found it, is this it? The right one? What do you think?'

A moor hen goes by, and a dead bream, revolving on its side, its eye missing . . . Me and Nick chuck rocks at it.

'Pack it in, you two!'

We look up and giggle . . .

'It's empty, I think it's this one . . . What's it supposed to be called again?'

The shouts and counter-shouts echo out across the still waters. The mist settling in, it starts off in the reed banks, then all of a sudden it takes over. First it's just a harmless effect, next pea-soup! The voices grow more and more muffled. You have to watch your footing, those mooring ropes, treacherous. It seems we're hopelessly lost and we'll have to re-trace our steps, it's the only chance of getting off that marsh alive. Re-find Grandad Lewis and start out all over again, but this time be methodical!

He was last seen heading towards the swamp. That doesn't bode well. We put our noses to the ground and take one step at a time, that's the only way not to come unstuck, on all fours, Red Indian-style. We zig-zag around like snakes, fog-bound, blundering through the bulrushes.

Then I run into a nest of swans – two of them, they come out honking, wings outstretched, six foot of them, going on seven. I stagger back, then I trip. They turn round and jump in the drink. I lay there 'til my heart goes normal . . . I check my sheaf-knife, a real bone handle, and dead sharp . . . I cut some bulrushes and stick them round my bush hat, for camouflage. Then I notice it, a little will-o'-the-wisp, flickering in the twilight, dancing on the opposite bank. It sits just above the water, a minute goes by and then it's joined by another. Two of the little fellows, a little ballet of the lanterns.

Then there's an almighty splash and I see him, his beak silhouetted against the setting sun: Grandad Lewis, some profile, Geronimo. I run up to him, perched on deck, sat astride his suitcases . . . I stumble up out of the mud. So, he's found it after all, it wasn't just hot air. Here he is, on the bridge, basking in the last few rays of the setting sun. He play-acts a little yawn. He double checks his time piece and shakes his head with a pretend frown.

'I thought you weren't coming . . . Did you see the rhinoceros? I winged one of them, but he got away and swam across the river. I thought maybe you'd finish him off?'

He's talking to me. I look up to my nana.

'Didn't grandad tell you he brought his elephant gun?'

They must think I'm nuts.

We climb on board, the lot of us. We go trooping up the gang-plank, I bang my feet as loud as I can, I march, I give him a sideways look but don't see any elephant guns . . .

'Which way did it go, grandad?'

'Which way did who go?'

'The rhino, the one you shot.'

'Into the swamp, to the rhinoceros graveyard.'

'Where's your elephant gun?'

'I left it at home.'

'Nana says you've got it in your suitcase.'

'No, that's my bazooka.'

'Let's see it!'

'Later . . . after tea.'

So Grandad Lewis was pulling our legs – we thought he was lost in the swamp when he's been here all along. He even had time to collect some kindling and set the stove, before dark fell. We light the lanterns and mosey around below decks. We check for rats, and I go through all the drawers and cupboards . . . All the doors are inlaid with mystic symbols, crows and dogs, Egyptian style, all one hundred per cent original. Symbols of fair sailing, that's grandad's opinion, but I've got my own suspicions, ideas not known.

*　　*　　*

Then we hear this car pull up. We see the headlights and then the doors go. I peek over the hatch, it's Norman leading the way up the gang-plank, grinning through his little specks, Himmler-ish, little, false pearls. He pats my arse and treats me like a girl, right in front of my grandad. I have to go out on deck to avoid him. Even then he follows me, he looks at me from beneath his glasses and offers me a toffee.

'Hello Fred.'

'My name's not Fred.'

'You still keeping our secret?'

I stare at the deck. He looks at me, then looks away and strokes his chin . . .

'Our little secret.'

He rummages around in his pocket and adjusts his bottle of stout. He talks in loud hot whispers. He looks over his shoulder and feels me up. I step back, then he grabs my arm and tries to pull me behind the wheel house. He snatches at my sleeve, but I shake him off and run back down below decks. I sit right up next to my grandad. I put my fingers in his beer and he tells me off.

Me and Joanne have adjoining berths right up under the bows: a little wash stand each, a triangular bunk and a crow painted on each door . . . I piss into the wash stand, I don't bother with the toilet, I do it right there, in front of her. A regular little fountain, yellowing, it goes down the plug-hole. I have to stand on my toes and fish it out, it squirts in little jets, in different directions, on account of the damaged end, where the needle went in. And a little red stain, that's blood. I don't risk walking to the bog, the gangways, ambushes in the dark. I pee in the little bedside sink instead, right in front of Joanne. I shake off the drips, dab at it, then tuck it back in my jeans. Then I walk over, lift her hair, kiss her cheek and climb in beside her. I hold her near, trembling in her nightie. Then I have to get up and take another piss.

'I got to go again . . .'

'Why?'

'I drunk two bottles of coke today.'

'Two whole bottles?'

'Yeah, and I had three on the way up here!'

I take another leak, then jump back in beside her. I try to hold her, to comfort her, but I'm nervy, too. You see, we don't know how to relax and have a good time, we're just a couple of buggered kids. All we've got to go on are rumours and hearsay, fumblings in the dark, grown ups' probings.

Then we hear someone outside – we hear the boards go, then someone taps the timber. We duck under the covers, our little hearts frozen. I take a quick peep then climb out her bunk and jump back into my own. We look to each other and try not to giggle. Then the door edges open, I put my head right under the covers. I hold my breath and listen. I hear whisperings, I make a gap and peep through.

It's Susan; she's come down here to say goodnight, and tuck Joanne in, and give her her kissing practice. 'French kissing', it's called. They hold each other, run their fingers through each other's hair and rub noses. The secret is, is to wriggle your tongue, you both do it, inside each other's mouths. You stroke them together, snake-like. Sue shows me with Joanne, then gets me to do it with her. She bites at my lips, giggles and pulls away, her hands on my shoulders. She leans in again, she sticks out her girl's tongue, I suck on it. She holds me with her eyes, dark. Thirteen years old, a real woman! I watch her tutoring Joanne, deep, long . . . They giggle and call me over, Susan pats the bed by her side.

'Come and sit with us, Steven.'

I blush and hold back.

'Come on, Joanne wants you to, don't you Joanne?'

Joanne nods and hides her face in the pillow. I grin and pad over . . . Sue holds out her hand, pulls me close and kisses me.

'Don't you think my bum's too big? Do you think it sticks out too much?'

She bends over and asks me to look at it, she twists her neck and inspects it in the mirror.

'Isn't it too muscley?'

It's true, it does stick out, and with a big split.

'Joanne's daddy makes me play with his willy when I stay round there. He sends Joanne to bed and I have to sit on his lap. He plays with my tits, then he puts his tongue in my mouth. It's horrible, like a slug! I don't like it. He sucks on my tits and makes me play with his willy, he gets it out and I have to rub it . . .'

Joanne looks down, waif-like, a pony-tail, just a kid. She looks down at my legs, my bruised shins.

'You'll get bone cancer.'

I put my hands between my thighs and hide my legs under the bunk. I cover them with my hands.

She tries a little smile, and toys with the anchor.

'When Susan isn't there I have to do it. I don't like it. He makes me feel his thing and I'm not allowed to tell my mummy.'

'I'm glad my daddy isn't like that!'

I look to Susan, I see her little woman's mouth speak, and my hand goes up to my fucked-up teeth. I feel my lips, I want to be able to speak as well, to tell the truth, to explode this world. But I can't, I just sit there dumb, staring at Joanne's bitten nails. Her fingers playing with the end of a rope, plaits, that's what they were like, lots of intricate coils, bits of cotton, frayed and dipped in tar.

'He puts it in your mouth and then it squirts, it tastes yuck!'

So Joanne's father had his monkey stick out, too? I listened with bated breath ... praying that I too could spill the beans on Norman ... that I too could speak bravely ... But the cabin turned to silence.

I keep my trap shut. I don't breathe a word, not even to Susan and Joanne. I lack all belief. We touch, we hold hands, we walk by the river bank, the occasional windmill; just kids really, kids at heart ... But somehow broken. They could share with me, but not me with them.

20. BIG BROTHER

One thing that you're never short of as a kid, is other people's big opinions: the world's full of them. The looming faces of the grown-ups – and they're all at great pains to point out the sacrifices they've made on your behalf, and all the suffering that you've caused, in particular. Parents aren't quite happy with their sprogs until they've twisted them into the same miserable, guilt-ridden victims that they are. And even then they're not quite sure that you're apologetic enough, that you quite know how to say sorry with the right amount of humility. That you understand the inherent vileness of your character and the terrible inconvenience you've caused everyone by just being born. They say it twice, they repeat themselves, pausing for maximum effect. They look away in disgust, staring out the window, fiddling with themselves and sucking their teeth.

Everyone kept telling me that I'd be alright once I'd grown out of my obnoxious adolescent ways, in ten years or so, once I'd had a few rough corners knocked off.

'He'll soon quieten down and start toeing the line, you mark my words! Or he'd better, because this world certainly isn't going to put up with him the way he is! If he thinks for one moment that it will, then he's got another think coming!'

She talks about me as if I'm not there, as if I knocked over my egg and chips on purpose.

'Shut up your whinging! Jesus Christ, that voice!' She screams and slings the saucepan at me. 'You're in for a rude awakening!

Just you wait 'til your father gets home!' She holds onto the door frame and starts to sob. 'Just bloody get out! Go on, get out!'

My brother and mother never tired of forecasting violent and merciless beatings ahead of me for the foreseeable future, and a great big one, beyond.

The old girl was more than suspicious of my involvement with the criminal element from over on the council estate. There were mysterious break-ins and disappearances. But no matter what threats were levelled at me, no matter how many times I was cross-questioned, I kept mum. I didn't breathe a word, suffering silently under a blanket of guilt. I moped about, studying the paint work.

'He'll have chronic acne when he grows up!' That's my brother's big opinion. He sidles over and stares down at me, curls his upper lip and parts his hair. 'He's just the type, and he'll scar as well, I can already see it!'

One of his many pronouncements – a blow from every direction, that was my childhood ... And always that big lug sounding off! Arrogant. Studious. And the size of the head on him, phew! It gave my mother stitches, no kidding, real ones. They had to lace her up again like an old boot! You've heard the story before? Me too, only I know it backwards, it's my history, my little thread of existence.

'He's lucky he wasn't born a thalidomide! I said you're lucky you weren't born a thalidomide, Steven! You're the exact right age!'

I looked at him. 'A what?'

'A thlid! Those kids with no arms, just little flippers – you're lucky you weren't born a flipper!'

I stared down at the deck. This was obviously some kind of a threat, something else I had to be grateful for. He saunters out the kitchen and goes for a wank. He gets one of the old man's tit books, stuffs it down his jeans and locks himself in the toilet. He's in there for two solid hours. Then he calls me over to look at it. He slaps his dick from side to side. He makes it thwack on his thighs.

He buttons up and marches into the hallway; he makes demands, swearing at the old girl. He wants to be like all the other kids at school. They have fathers who come home, who play with them and share their hobbies, fathers who don't disappear for months on end, so why can't he? He makes an extensive list of his grievances ...

He throws bigger and better tantrums: twice the beatings and twice the violence. Directed at me personally, you understand. I have to suffer by the law of succession. He instates himself as my acting father in the old man's absence. By God, he'll install some discipline into my snivelling, worthless existence! He's got all the attributes, a proper little tin Hitler. He rubs himself, he boils like a turnip . . . He shows me what for! vicious blows! twice my size! absolutely nothing I can do about it.

Plastic elephants are out for a start! No more day-dreaming about squirrels and dinosaurs, certainly not! I'm in for a rude awakening! the beating of a life-time! He draws graphic illustrations. He paints the sky, the big lug. He can't abide ignorance – a real chip off the old block.

'You can't even read or write yet? Pathetic! I could read and write when I was four, couldn't I, mother?'

He looks to her to back him up . . . She wrings the dishcloth in her hands.

'I've done all I can, I've tried teaching him . . .' She chews it over . . . 'He's not worth it! He's stubborn and argumentative! Just like his soddin' father!'

My mother stands there up to her elbows in pond water, she froths about in there fishing for potato eyes . . . She turns on the cold tap and knocks a tea cup onto the deck.

'Shit! Bugger! Christ almighty! Now look what you've made me do! Just shut up the pair of you!'

I cross my eyes and toy with my gun; I cock it . . . My brother takes a kick at me. I see it coming, I dodge, he misses. I fall to the ground and scream . . .

'For crying out loud, stop whinging!'

She comes at me, brandishing her saucepan . . . I roll in the shit of the floor; I play dead.

My brother's tempers? His kicking me? And twice my size? Not very fair . . . and I don't forget! Like my plastic elephant, that's me – memory! I pride myself on it.

Where is our saviour? The hours have ticked by and none of us have been chosen. I check my timepiece, a quarter past freckle – it is time to spit, to disentangle my damaged heart.

21. IN WHICH NANA LEWIS GETS KITTENISH

Next up, Nana Lewis pops her clogs . . . We should have seen that one coming. As far as my mother was concerned, it was nothing short of cold blooded murder: she always swore that that's exactly what it was.

'He drove her to it, as sure as I'm standing here now! And then he has the nerve to not even turn up at the funeral! Can you believe it?'

It's true that Nana Lewis took all of our tragedies on the chin – she was right in the thick of it, right in the firing line. And the old man kept heaping on new miseries; there was even rumours that he owed her money, and not two or three pounds either but substantial amounts! It seems he'd been touching her on the quiet, rifling her nest egg, and he was determined not to pay her back a single farthing, on principle!

Smoking forty Guards a day, and the old man rummaging with her heart, tugging at her purse strings like that – that's when people start dropping. A stranger feeling their wallets? – There's a snake in the grass! Money kills!

What with all the bickering and open hostilities, it was bound to affect the old bird's health, it worried away at her. Even when she was laid up, the old man was always insinuating, pouring lie on top of lie, layer upon layer; it really was worse than cement. He invented even thicker and thicker crusts. In the end she took to her bed and never got up again, only that once, to go to the loo. She lifts her head from the pillow, puts her feet over the edge of the bed and then flops back. Grandad Lewis thought she was just play-acting, getting a little kittenish.

She didn't want us kids to see her when she was laid up, she was always hoping for a recovery. 'Let my angels remember me as I was, Juny.' That's how she spoke. All her brown hair turned grey, and she flopped back on the bed, onto my grandad's lap.

'Let my angels remember me as I was.' Her last request. She'd of really liked to have seen us kids, you see, but she didn't want us to see her, to see the effect, what life had sucked out of her. The mask of life slipped – cheerio! And she flops back onto the bed, onto grandad's lap. And he thought she was only play-acting, only she wasn't, she was dead.

That morning there was a starling trapped in the chimney, just above the boiler. It was fluttering around in there, slowly dying . . . It kept it up the whole afternoon, 'til my mother took Hearboy out for walkies and when she got back it was dead. 'That was a sure sign!' according to my mother . . . An omen!

And I got out of school late because they put me in detention for crossing the school field again. Walking on the grass – you weren't allowed to walk on the grass! And I jumped the fence and that took the biscuit! First they hit me, then I had to write lines. They ask me which hand I write with, then cane the other one so's I can still write . . . And if it isn't the cane, it's the slipper. Six of the best! On your arse! We hobbled around that school blowing on our hands like a bunch of cripples.

I take my school bag off and kick it. I chuck it as high as it'll go, swing it by its strap and smack it into the wire fence. Then I see Norman revving up his old banger outside the school gate, sat there behind the hot glass. He leers at me through the windscreen, like I'm his woman or something. He opens the door and tells me to get in.

'Your mother asked me to pick you up . . . It's about your grandmother . . . Do you want to go for a little drive first?'

He pushes the bulge in his trousers down. He takes off his specs and 'hahs' on them. He looks up at me and pats the seat next to him. 'Come on Fred, we can go up the woods for a little walk.'

'I want to go home! My mum says I've got to be home for tea!'

I tell him straight, he's got to take me home right away, on my mother's orders, and no scenic routes, she's expecting me. I impress it upon him, it is as simple as that, or I won't get in his poxy car! I talk through the window, he takes his little tin out, and fiddles about with the strands . . . He rolls one, lights up and blows out the smoke. 'OK, in you get, I'll take you home, your mother's got some bad news for you.'

I climb in beside him; he looks over his shoulder and pulls away. As soon as he makes the gear change his hand goes for my dick, he spins the wheel and swerves across the road . . . He tries to get it out, there and then, the car cranking away in second . . . I get hold of the door handle and cross my legs. He slams on the anchors. He's got something jammed in his zip – he lets out a howl. I grab my bag, jump out and head straight up the road, I make a bee-line for the house. His zip goes down and I jump out the car! I don't dilly-dally: I've smelt the colour of his shit stick before and I've no wish to smell it again . . . Whoops! And I'm out the car, running into the bosom of my family, so to speak. Up the garden path, under the little arcade of trees. I go straight in without looking back.

'Nana is dead . . .' she gasps. She pulls at her face . . . 'He killed her! Sure as I'm standing here now! As sure as if he struck her down with his own hand!'

Norman comes hobbling in behind me, limping on account of his dick.

'I've already told him, Juny . . . I explained it all to him in the car, he's in shock . . . He doesn't know what he's talking about, ignore him!'

He blushes and adjusts himself. All of a sudden my little cock is the last thing on his mind. He's found a new role to play. He reads his part and steps straight in, no rehearsals. One minute he wants to suck me off, the next he's choking back a tear, dabbing at his oysters, the concerned family friend. Just like that! The truth of the matter is, he didn't dare start feeling me up, not in front of the old girl, with Nana Lewis not yet in her grave. Heavens no, there's a time and place for everything.

He puts his arm round my mother's shoulders and walks her to her seat . . . He even tries consoling me. I eye the bastard. In fact I wasn't at all surprised, the big turn-coat! He's shitting himself in case I spill the beans about the seamier side of his personality. He's hamming it up, waving his arms about, embracing and emphasising, hogging the whole fucking stage. He looks at my mother sideways, to see what kind of effect he's having – he looks away double quick and pulls a different mask. He quits undressing me and gets on with the task in hand – the family friend of the bereaved. He makes explosions with his mouth, spraying fountains of platitudes.

'I know, Juny, I know, he drove her to it . . . Such a wonderful wonderful woman . . . Yes, there's no doubt about it, death lies at his door! The martyr's death! Your sweet mother, God rest her soul!'

He bends over backwards to agree, balding, grey, the dick showing between his legs. He even invents himself a little dance, right there on the spot, a kind of jig. His cock must have gone limp. He rotates and prances, the arms go up and a little arabesque, he spins and sits down; he's fagged . . . He rolls himself another one, opens his gob, picks the tobacco from between his plate and lights up. A little lighter, embossed with a packet of Chesterfields, real charming, enamelled, intricate. He tells us the whole story about how he found it under his floorboards when he was looking for the stop cock. He tries to side-track us . . . He hands it to me to look at – OK, so it's some lighter, but that shindig? It was enough to make you puke! Really, to see that old queen play-acting like that, then fiddling with himself under the table! I look at the HP sauce bottle.

The bird died in the chimney and Nana Lewis conked out . . . and the old girl went grey . . .

'I'm going to have a nervous breakdown!' she assured me.

She held onto herself, her lungs hurt . . . The old man called up but he couldn't make the funeral. 'Business commitments', he called it. The truth is he couldn't face up to the corpse, on account that he still owed it money.

22. ANALYSIS OF A SOUL RANCID

It was at the end of the road, a barracks, low, derelict and wind-swept. You were on the scrap heap, aged eleven and a half. Dockyard-fodder, signed, stamped and sealed, and no back chat! A special mixture of emotions: Walderslade Secondary School. Northern blasts, pinning us to the hillside. Every window in that dump shook like billy-oh, rattling in their sockets. And then the rain comes in, cascading down the walls in rivulets, whole tidal waves . . . the place was awash!

You think I'm joking? It just goes to show your ignorance. You can't overstate an experience like that, it would be impossible. That special stench of doom, echoing corridors and chalk dust – this thick!

It had a reputation, alright – you couldn't just walk in there, you had to have sunk to a certain depth, to have achieved something with your life. Retards mostly, no-hopers, and even then you needed a proposer and a seconder, and not just anybody, somebody who fitted the bill. Someone with all the right attributes: vicious, villainous and petty, with just the right amount of vindictiveness. The type of character who could limbo under a dog turd without dirtying their nose.

Crowsfeet fitted the bill. One minute I'm walking up from the bus stop with the old girl, the next thing this mush runs up to us and hands me an Easter egg. I look into his dismal eyes, grey and whipped, and down at the chocolate egg, nicked more than likely. He wants to be friends . . . He wipes his gob on his sleeve.

'I got you an Easter egg.'

'Look at that, Steven,' chimes in my mother, 'isn't that lovely? Say thank-you to . . . what's your name, dear?'

'Crowsfeet.'

'Say thank-you to Crowsfeet . . . Would you like to come home with us and you can share it with Steven?'

He sucks on his snot and nods. His lips crusty round the edges, like a custard tart with hinges . . . I was planning a massive war against the ants in the front garden, and now the old girl goes and invites him back for tea!

I nod. 'Thank-you.' I go along with it: shit, I'll go along with any crappy piece of bullshit. People have a way of getting to me. My ability to say no is non-existent. Any bastard just has to walk in and rummage with my heart, turn the whole shop upside down, then wipe their stinking feet on my soul and march back out again without so much as an, 'I beg your pardon'. I've got that type of face, a jutting jawline, and a nose that's just crying out to be broken.

Crowsfeet, he called himself. We sit there chewing on it, breaking bits off, and then he takes my bit and scoffs that as well. I watch him – he does it deliberately, he picks up the chocolate and jams it in his trap along with the rest of the garbage. I watch it moving about in there, his tongue stirring through the soup. Then I have to give him my pop as well. He snatches the bottle right out my hand and swigs at it. He doesn't wipe the mouth piece either, he just lugs it back, viciously, as if it's his by birthright . . . He fucks it up with his dirty gob, bits floating, cloudy . . . contaminated . . . He burps, sits back and farts, daring me to contradict him.

I keep schtum, I pretend not to notice, so then he gets testy. He stares upwards and back, like as if he's studying the inside of his skull, a curious effect. A little scowl, the mouth twists up, the lips knot into the nostrils, then his eyes roll – presto! He pulled some pretty ugly masks, that cunt! His eyes rolling about like marbles in a yoghurt. And then the mouth, he moves it around like some kind of egg custard.

No sooner has he got one foot in the door than he makes himself right at home. He puts his feet up and lights up . . . He moves right in on the spot and starts reorganising my life: from now on all my pocket money's spent on snouts: Cadets and Park Drive mostly . . . He drags it deep then puffs it right back out in my face. Threatening. He sucks the smoke down hard and quick, then, 'Poof!' out it comes: rank, suffocating, mixed in with some old cake . . . He rolls his eyes back and then, Smack! he lets one go. I have to take it, to cry weakly, to myself . . . Bang! right in the guts.

'Stand up and take your punishment like a man!'

That was his catch phrase. 'Take your punishment like a man!' and, 'Don't whinge and don't whine.' Then – Smack! Between him and my brother, I flinched every time the door knocker went. 'Don't flinch, stand up and take it like a man!' I didn't know if it was Monday or Thursday, I was shocked, caught off my guard. He bought me an Easter egg and my mother actually asked him round to our house to eat it. As soon as I saw his weasel face coming, I should have smelled a rat.

That's all that people have got in mind when they start handing round presents: their own furtherance. The excuse to take liberties! To justify their hatred. Inflicting misery with a licence, he was just looking for an opening, for any excuse.

It was that Crowsfeet who was behind the break-ins at my parents' gaff. It all comes clear after the event, after we have the courage to admit the truth to ourselves, of our own short falls. It didn't take a genius to set it up. The old man was never home, me and my brother were at school all day, and so whenever the old girl took the mutt out for walkies it was open house. Two seconds after she went down the back alley, Crowsfeet and his mates were in through the window rifling the dump. Classes? They didn't go to no stinking classes. They were relaxing themselves at my family's expense. I saw the whole show unfolding – what I didn't know I guessed, I have a hawk on my right shoulder, no kidding, I saw the whole picture – but I keep mum. I don't breathe a word . . .

That's me, reliable and true, the eternal fall guy. Even at the last ditch, when everybody else has finally fallen, caved in and sold out. After all the love has dried up, when it's too late to say or do anything but scatter the ashes. That's when I'll be at my freshest, that's when I wake up, take a look around and announce myself: the one who remained true.

We had some pretty big bruisers in that school of ours: hefty louts, regular prize fighters. The toughest of the tough, Irish and gypsies mostly, with great shocks of red and black hair. It was sad to see our student teachers squaring up to those giants. College scarves and a few little whiffs of beard, apologetic and pock-marked. Biff! and they were down. Those third and fourth year kids could pack quite a punch. The boys with the mortar-boards measuring up to those brawny fellows? There wasn't even a contest, just threats and a yelp, a bloodied handkerchief and another kid takes a short cut to Borstal.

I was blonde and sensitive; no one looked out for me. I had to become a loudmouth pretty quick, a showman. When I saw a punch coming, I thought up a joke on the spot, I looked for the laugh, any possible means of escape ... On top of that I had to pretend to be thick.

Crowsfeet's gang mooched around the estate chucking stones at cars ... The youngest was in the same year as me, anything that wasn't nailed down twice found its way into his pockets, he had no scruples whatsoever. He really didn't give two shits! Young, old, blind, crippled, it was all grist to his mill. When it came to low-down underhandedness, he left the whole lot of us standing ... House break-ins! Petty theft! Arson! Demanding money with menaces! A.B.H.! G.B.H.! He'd have the lot, anyway. If they bent over, he nicked their piss-pots.

I get the third degree every evening, a right going over from the old girl and my brother. Cross questioning me, every word I utter was twisted and reinvented – I couldn't say meow without them drawing the wildest conclusions. They had me guilty of every crime in the book, and not even allowed the right of silence.

Apparently the house has been ransacked! Every last copper filched! They even had the cheek to check down the back of the settee! It seems that the whole of the old girl's allowance has been spirited away, and my brother's pocket money to boot!

'It's that crowd you hang about with, isn't it? That bunch of hoodlums! That boy Crowsfeet, is that what he calls himself? Well, isn't it? Steven! Answer me! He comes round here bold as brass! I caught him sitting on the gate yesterday afternoon ... He said he wanted a cigarette! What do you think of that? Asking me to finance his habits! The gall of the boy! Well, it's not the first time, far from it! It's the fifth or sixth at least ... We've lost money every month now, all last week's house-keeping gone! And where to, you might ask? Scotch mist! Your father isn't going to pay the bills ... you can be sure of that much! He's working all the hours God sends, as it is! I don't know when we'll see him next, let alone the next penny! You don't think it could be your father, could it? He wouldn't come here stealing, would he? He might, you know, as a last attempt to force us out?'

She ponders on that one. I encourage her. I put forward even more outlandish theories and accusations. I bring plots and sub-plots into play. I implicate the Prime Minister himself; I throw in the Jews and the Freemasons for good measure. Obviously, it's the old man up to his dirty tricks again! I back her up to the hilt – it's our dear father trying one last ditch effort to starve us out of house and home. Of course, the old coot's been staging the break-ins all along! I congratulate her on her shrewdness.

The old coot staging break-ins? The old girl weighs the ifs and buts, she doesn't reject the possibility out of hand, but then again, you couldn't say that she exactly swallows it whole either. In fact, she all but accuses me of lying through my front teeth. She knows the type of company I've been keeping, the exact type of acquaintances and their addresses. I was helpless, a slave to everybody's whims.

Crowsfeet and his cronies come round the house, chucking rocks at my window. They knock me out of bed, little stones, then bigger ones. In the end I have to get up, open the door and rub my eyes. They go through my pockets, nick my last few coppers and then send me packing . . . A kick and a harsh word, they send me sprawling.

I had to suffer for all the injustices that had been perpetrated against them in the name of class and discipline. Crowsfeet shows me his leg, which has been gashed open by his old man. His father beat him round the legs with a wire brush for dawdling, for punching his little brother and for asking too many stupid questions! He shows me the bruises, I see them for myself. Great welts, a million pin pricks, blue with red polka dots . . . He cowers in front of his father, then beats me in revenge. He regurgitates all the bile, he's learned it off pat. I was at the lowest end of the food chain . . . The only thing humbler was a slug.

Every game we play ends in a punch-up. We scamper about barking like geese. He chases me round the fir tree. I get half way round then change direction and double back. I run into him full tilt: smack! In the bread basket. I put my head down and charge, I'm gurgling with glee, I see nothing, then, Oof! I ground him, he's on his back, winded, clutching his guts. He goes bug-eyed and wheezes.

'Does anybody want to see a fight?'

He gets to his feet and calls all his mates together. 'Who wants to see a fight?'

He stands with his hands on his knees, he gets his wind back then moves in, he challenges me.

'Who wants to see someone get their head kicked in? Come on, put your hands up! Take your punishment like a man!'

Fight? Me fight? All I've ever done is been beaten by my friends. No, fighting's out of the question. Fisticuffs? No, it couldn't be, you see I was already a trained victim, no delusions of grandeur whatsoever. Only a bittersweet contentment in my own misery. No self-respect – content to blubber, whinge and whine myself into my own grave, if necessary ... A whipping post, with the effrontery to yelp and complain, that's me.

The punch, it whistles, it revolves, it comes out of the darkness, continuously ... I go down, but not hit, I drop to my wretched knees and beg for forgiveness, I sob. Dignity? I have none! I drop and crawl round on all fours at the feet of my bully. I implore him, worshipfully.

Forgiveness? Sorry son, in this world there is no forgiveness, only retribution for sins unknown. God looks down upon my sorry little head and doesn't even manage a half smirk. I crawl round in the dust and disgust myself.

I scrape right up next to his feet, amongst the little circle of my playmates. I sob so deep and hard that it burns. I wring my eyes out ... but no matter how long I stay down there, no matter how hard and deep I grovel, no matter to what depths I sink, one day sooner or later I will have to drag myself up onto my knees and take it on the chin.

I even offered him my bottle of pop! Everything I owned and money too ... Silver! Heavy! Round! A half crown! With Elizabeth on it ... revolving ... money, the pig! Elizabeth, the bitch! Coin of the realm? Worthless! Grief and misery is the only real currency, the only thing of any real weight in this world.

You sink and you stink? Bravo! It's your final excuse to indulge yourself, your big chance to see how utterly wretched and abominable you truly are. Drenched in shit and self-pity, and a little warm feeling ... that special tingling of self-satisfaction, that you have finally debased yourself to the limit, that you have plumbed to the very bowels of self-degradation.

Ten, eleven years old, shamelessly boo-hooing at the feet of my bully, imploring him. Too dumb and timid, too obliterated by the insidious viciousness of my family to stand up and fight like a man. That's what he said to me, my so-called friend, my very own bully. He barks it, jams open his dirty cake hole and stares upwards into the back of his skull.

'Get up and take your punishment like a man!'

He screams it at me, and I lay there at his feet, the little circle of incredulous playmates, gathered, appalled at my humility . . . sickened to the core . . .

'Get up and take your punishment like a man!'

And I groan and I gurgle in the mud, rolling in the dust at his feet.

'Get up and take your punishment like a man!'

That's the story of my life. 'Stand up and take your punishment like a man! On the chin sucker! Out your bed, you're next!' And I creep to the door bollock naked, queuing up for my personal dose of misery.

And I hold out my hands and accept it, because deep down in my inadequate little heart I believe that I deserve it, I believe in its inevitability, so that I can exist.

When all the supermarkets finally shut up shop and all the parties are over . . . When the million and one distractions of man have been used up, rinsed out and washed clean away, we will be left with nothing but Him – our dark little friend, and we'll embrace Him and take Him home with us . . . our personal little dose of poison, and we will nurture Him close to our bosoms, with some kind of half-arsed pride, yes, some kind of glowing half-arsed pride.

23. THE WLA

I starve myself so as to remember. Never to be a slug, that's my ambition. Never to be a glutton of the fat. To live with a little hunger, a feeling, always hollow in my belly. Never to become one of them, absolutely never to become a grown-up.

The woods, our woods . . . They moved in and flattened the lot! Crushed to the ground! Without so much as a 'by your leave'. Age old and noble. There's no doubt that those woods belonged to us kids, us kids, the dickie-birds and the occasional adder. One day rabbits, spiders and birds, the next: bulldozers!

People are always claiming their special prerogative to exploit and demean. They shake your hand then give you a sly one round the back, a kidney punch. People have no rights and kids have less than none. They knocked down our world with no warning, with no consultation. Their only emotion: contempt! An atrocity that should never be forgotten. I write it down, here for all to see, to be documented for future generations. The holocaust against our friends the trees, the grasses, the flowers and all their myriad of friends and relations, four-legged, six-legged, eight-legged, and wings of the sky. I swear to Christ, it makes me see red, even after all these softening years . . .

Us kids looked upon the destruction of our habitat and we saw that it was bad. We made effigies of their potato heads and dug their eyes out. The faceless men with tape-measures, they march like idiots, dealing in land, dividing it into plots and squares . . . Unasked for, and all-powerful! Unseeing of the field mice, not knowing of the jay, blind to the bluebell. They brought in their bulldozers, hideous hues of yellow, cranking their way through the trees. A man shouts, he waves his arms, they gun the motor and smash into everything, churning the forest floor into shit.

We blacken our faces with charcoal and make midnight sorties. We go on all fours. Any plot they stake out, we rip it up. We re-design their buildings for them, subtly, vandalism of the heart. We replant their stakes two or three feet out, saving the odd bush, a silver birch. Kicking over all the freshly cemented walls. Filling the mixers with concrete to set solid overnight. Sugaring the bulldozers' petrol tanks. Painting out all the windows. 'W.L.A.' we write it on all of the trucks, in olive green, in three foot high letters, dripping enamel.

The Walderslade Liberation Army. It was Goldfish's idea – he was the oldest, and he showed us how to make guns, not toys, but real guns, out of old metal pipes.

I met him in the science lab, swiping a bottle of nitric acid, right in front of Dog-Jaw's eyes. A real smooth operator, old Goldfish, on the best of terms with the lab technician. Nothing brash or showy, he didn't go seeking unasked-for attentions, he wasn't the type. Calculating, that was Goldfish; he played the swot, his fishies blinking, half under the lids, and of course, his nose dripping, the centre of activity. Then: whoops! The vanishing of the bottle. The nitric acid? It's gone walkies, my friends! One minute it's sitting on the desk in front of you, the next, presto! Abracadabra! I look again, no sign whatsoever, just thin air.

'All we need now is glycerine.' He blinks.

What's this oaf on, him with his glycerine? I nod. 'Yeah, glycerine.'

I've agreed with him, he likes that . . . He's ecstatic, over the moon! He blows bubbles, two big green ones, one out of each nostril . . . a little lava flow, they follow the line of his lip, then he sucks them back up again, a kind of see-saw effect.

That was his big problem: snot. Oozing from his neb, a regular waterfall of bogeys, truly out of control. He sucks back on it, but no matter how many snot rags his old girl stuffed in his pockets, they were always soaked through by dinner time.

'Black powder!' He explains. 'Weed-killer!'

Oh, I see, I get his drift now, now I follow him.

'Nitro!'

Everything's falling into place.

'Black powder and, of course, the weed-killer!'

That explains it. I don't let anything show on my face. He tries to read my mask, no dice, I just nod. 'Yeah ... sure ... weed-killer ...'

I'm stringing him along, playing him at his own game, I keep my hand close to my chest. 'And black powder ... hmmm ...'

He paces up and down, crashing into things. That's how he thinks. Size twelves I'd say, at least, maybe even thirteens. He flaps them around like ironing boards. The whole effect set off by his ankle stranglers, his trousers bound to his calves like bandages, cutting off the circulation. He drools at the nose and mouth, staggering around like some kind of hideous fawn.

'We need guns and we need politics! The politics of our situation!'

He certainly had some brains on him, that Goldfish. Politics? Politics? That's a pretty big word to start chucking round the classroom. I can see that he's no ordinary fish, this one, not by a long chalk. 'Politics' he said, I just heard him. 'The politics of our situation!' That was his phrase. Hey, that's not bad, that makes me look at him afresh. Prancing around in front of me, leaping from toe to toe ...

'Politics,' he says blinking through the strings of mucus. I look at him differently now. 'Politics,' he repeats it, holding a test tube up to the light, he peers into it. The way he sees it, he knows more about politics than the whole school rolled together: the head-master and old Dog-Jaw included.

'Hitler was right and Stalin was left. Conservative and Labour ... Communism's left. Socialism's left but not as left as Communism, red. Fascism is right, Liberal is in between, yellow, neither left or right. Conservatives are right but not as right as the fascists, blue. So what are you, left or right?'

Hmmm ... left or right? I try and remember which hand is which, I have to imagine I'm drawing to do that. I sort of mime it out on the desk in front of me, then look up quick to see if he's noticed anything ... I pretend to be examining the effect of the grain.

'Blue, red or yellow?'

Now that's easy, I know that one, colours, that's my department. Red, blue or yellow? hmmm? OK, hold on a minute. Red! Or blue? Or yellow? Well, give me a second to think ... Red! No! Blue! That's right, blue!

* * *

In the days before the IRA bombed Maidstone, you could walk into any chemist and buy the ingredients for black powder: sulphur, charcoal and saltpetre. We'd buy each item off a different chemist and work them in rotation, so's not to arouse their suspicions.

If they question you, you have to have the right answers right off pat. 'Saltpetre?' That was the tricky one. 'It's for dusting my mother's dahlias'. That was the answer Goldfish taught me.

'If there's any questions, tell them it's for dusting your mother's dahlias, and don't try buying all the ingredients in one shop! They'll cotton on ... And never go back to the same chemist's twice in the same month!'

I nod ... 'Yeah yeah, and the weed-killer, sure thing!'

'What do you want saltpetre for?'

'For dusting my mother's dahlias.'

'Your mother's dahlias?'

'Yeah, my mother's dahlias.'

I have to learn all the answers by heart. He sends me out on little errands with a shopping list ... He gives me half a crown and sends me across the road to Boots. He waits for me on the corner 'til I emerge clasping the sherbet.

He looks over his shoulder, opens the bag and sniffs at it.

'What did he say?'

'It was a she – she didn't say nothing.'

'Call me sergeant when we're on active service.'

'She didn't say nothing, sarge.'

He narrows his eyes at me, 'Not sarge ... sergeant!'

I have to stand back and wipe my face; I try and calm him, to stem the explosions of phlegm. The more excited he gets, the harder the taps flow. He sucks back on it, his whole mug a crusty mosaic from the nostrils out. A soldier of snot, that was Goldfish, his sleeves sodden with the stuff. He waves his arms about for extra emphasis, to get his point over, to make sure I've understood. I've got the message.

'The first thing an army needs is discipline! Discipline! Food! Guns! And Glycerine!'

HOW TO MAKE A GUN

Materials:

One length of metal tubing ¾" to 1" diameter

One nail

One length of wire
One piece of scrap timber

Tools:
Hammer, vice, drill, matches, wood for fire

To make a pistol, cut off a one foot length of metal tubing: this is your basic barrel. Heat one end of the barrel until red hot, then hammer flat for approx 3". Now hammer it back over on itself, thereby totally sealing one end of the barrel. This is now your breech. Next drill a small touch hole approx 1" in front of the folded end. It is important to make sure that the touch hole can be neatly plugged by a small nail or screw which will be your firing pin. You may find it easier to drill the touch hole after the barrel has been securely bound onto a stock with wire.

The stock may be carved from a piece of scrap timber and can be as elaborate or as simple as you wish. Once the barrel is secured and an appropriate handle has been cut, you are ready for your first firing.

Pack the barrel half full with black powder. (See earlier notes on black powder). Then plug this with a mixture of clay, shot (fishing lead) or small gravel. All that remains, is to prime the touch hole with philomites (red match heads). Insert the firing pin and find your target.

The gun is fired by striking the firing pin with a blow from a hammer. Happy shooting!

N.B. Do not lean over the gun during firing, as the firing pin has a tendency of firing upwards out of the touch hole, as happened to my brother, who narrowly escaped death. This can be remedied by securing it to the stock with a small twist of wire.

Bit by bit, we were building up our munitions, and all of them safely stowed away in an underground hide. We dug it at weekends and after school, in a small copse of saplings. It could fit two of us crouching, plus our guns and black powder. We camouflaged the entrance with a seed tray full of earth.

Goldfish shows me his patented design for exploding marbles. Rolled into the path of an oncoming vehicle, they can take out anything from a moped to a bus! It's all down to his clever little invention of a hinged pressure plate. What's more, the whole device is completely concealable in a crisp packet!

He lets go a fresh waterfall of phlegm in sheer delight. He glistens all over like a lizard. He dives in and re-shuffles his papers, blowing his nose on the blue print for his fully automatic machine pistol. He empties the contents of his schnozzle, both barrels, clang-clang! a direct hit in the waste paper bin.

'The important thing is sulphur!'

He lays his index finger alongside his snout, and winks one of his headlamps at me.

'You must learn how to acquire your chemicals! A different shop for each of your ingredients! Sulphur!'

I know, I know! For dusting your dahlias, no kidding!

'What do you want sulphur for then, sonny?'

'For dusting my dahlias!'

I've got it, that's the answer, straight back, I look him in the eye. 'I want sulphur for dusting my dahlias, Sir!'

'Dahlias? Dahlias? You wouldn't mean saltpetre, would you?'

'Yeah, saltpetre.'

There's no doubt about it, if you want to get anything in this poxy world, you've got to master the wrangles, all the little strategies of bullshit.

Goldfish takes off his peaked cap and marches over to a big demi-john full of pond water with a couple of old lilies floating about in it. He pulls the cork and sniffs at it suspiciously . . .

'Polish spirit!' he informs me. 'Distilled from dandelion roots!'

That stuff had some poke alright, it made you cough like a dog! A real hack, right at the back . . . He pours me another pint . . . Once you get over the initial vileness of it, it goes down quite smoothly. A bouquet somewhere between lavender and turpentine.

We swig at it like lemonade. I have one more hit before I have to go and take a lie down on his garden wall. I put each foot in front of me, then stand next to the rosebush, I caress it . . . I eat a mouthful of petals . . . I'm in love with the intricacy of its thorns . . . I pull two of them off, and stick them to my nose with spit. I play rhinoceroses, I go on my knees and piss myself . . . crawling on all fours . . . I go looking for pea-bugs . . . Then I remember something . . . I have to talk to the cars, to explain something . . . I climb up onto the roof and won't come down, I walk in little circles then my knees go and I hit the deck. The tarmac comes up and kicks me in the stomach! I go to puke . . . the world goes sideways, my mouth's full of dandelions . . . I eat them like grass, like a lion, mooing like a cow.

Our next jump is getting ourselves some recruits. That's a tall order for a bunch of school kids. We have to start from scratch. As Goldfish points out, 'You need some kind of discipline before you can go implementing plans for insurrection!' And raising cash for our armoury, that was another headache. That was where Crowsfeet came in. He had pinched me 'til I spilled the beans on our deal, then socked me one . . .

Naturally, Goldfish wasn't so keen on cutting Crowsfeet in. For his money, he was way too crude, piss poor and a blabber-mouth to boot! He just didn't appeal to Goldfish's finely honed scientific mind . . . But on the other hand, he did accept that we needed liberators . . . A war isn't only fought from the bunker. And as I went to great lengths to explain, you have to have foot sloggers as well as generals. You can only build so many home-made mortars.

OK, charcoal you can make, but then there's the saltpetre . . . Dusting your dahlias or not, that takes cash, big bucks. I tell you, revolution is an expensive business!

I put the case to Goldfish; I begged him shamelessly to accept Crowsfeet. I had to, you see, my life depended on it. I'd been threatened, set up yet again. I lived in a half world of fear and violence, totally under the fist of others. Opinions? I had none, my only guide was fear of the punch.

In the end Goldfish conceded the point. I was both ecstatic and crestfallen. I was on a no-win wicket: either way, I was beaten . . .

Crowsfeet chucks a rock at my window. I have to let him in and give him a cut of my pocket money. He scans the shelves and helps himself to a bottle of lemonade, he swigs half of it back and the rest he uses to clean his teeth . . . He takes a big chug, gargles on it, then spits it back in, little threads of mucus and the odd onion skin . . . He burps and wipes it with his cuff . . . He hands me the bottle, I replace it and we head out into the chill, black, night fog . . .

Crowsfeet's expertise certainly came in handy. He starts right in by breaking into the girls' school. I'm press-ganged as the look-out man, the fall guy. He nicks the rake out of my old man's shed and uses it to lean in the top window and unhook the bottom window latch. (Actually it was my idea.) We get that bastard open, look left and right, then hop in ... Goldfish nicks a set of keys from the staff room and then we have the run of the whole school ...

They've got all the gear in there, and little jam-rag bins in all the bogs ... First off, we empty the tuck shop and transport it in stages to our bunker ... Stocking up for the nuclear winter ... We ransack the whole building – what we can't flog we scoff! We go green at the gills! Our shit goes rock hard from too much chocolate.

Once we'd cleaned that dump out, we went back over to the boys' school and emptied Dog-Jaw's greenhouse of exotic plants. We wheeled the sum total of Dogs-Jaw's life's work around the Weeds Wood council estate in an old wheel-barrow. From the rarest orchids to the common aspidistra! From blooming cacti, to a slug infested geranium! We flogged the lot at sixpence a throw. We had the old biddies queuing round the block, staggering back to their cells with their arms full of lettuces. The pansies and the tomato plants were the first to go, then the rarer cacti.

That was some spring – the greening of the concrete jungle. We poured the tax payers' money back into the community and earned a bit of pocket money into the bargain. We single-handedly wrecked Dog-Jaw's life's work. The greenhouse empty, just a couple of fallen petals ...

Goldfish banks the cash at the post office and sends off thirty pounds for his special project, a pair of 303 Lee Enfields! He answers an ad in the Exchange and Mart and gets them by return post, as simple as that. He comes over my place straight after school with two parcels under his arm. We unwrap them and do a little parade round the front garden. He marches up and down yelling orders ... Then he makes me get down on my hands and knees and crawl about in the dust. I pretend to be a bush.

'The Walderslade Liberation Army incorporing The Conservative Union of Green Fascists! Attention!'

Despite the plus side of Crowsfeet's abilities, Goldfish's misgivings turned out to be well founded. It seems Crowsfeet wasn't really into revolution at all. He was more of the realist school of thinking. He wanted hard cash for snout and muff! None of your fancy ideals or politics, just fuck, fags and kip! That was Crowsfeet, alright. Gawky, hurried eyes and a mouthful of sick.

He was always shooting his stupid lip off about some junk. Mouthing off about our clandestine exploits. Playing the big 'I am'! A regular glory-hunter. Spreading his ill-gotten gains in the most obvious of places, arousing unwanted suspicions. A hideous list of righteousness, and not a bit exaggerated.

Me and Goldfish only have about fifteen minutes to empty the bunker before the whole roof caves in. If we hadn't been keeping a weather eye, we'd have lost everything, black powder, pistols, the lot!

The bulldozer trundles over and sniffs around. They get it started – it takes five or six goes. They take turns cranking it, their little puzzled faces, absolutely comical. No match for our revolutionary minds. Waving their arms about like a bunch of scarecrows.

'I bet those proles don't know the first thing about Stalin's kolkhoz!'

I nod and scratch my head . . . They start again, cranking the engine, they clean out the carbs, oily and indignant, then finally a spluttering. She coughs and hiccups, then again, teetering, precariously. W.L.A. in foot high letters, bright green, set off by the yellow of the body . . . Little puffs of blue smoke . . .

We sit parked on a felled beech, regular wise monkeys, we scratch at ourselves and eat bananas. The driver peers through his paint-splattered windscreen but we show no emotion, poker faced. Then the beast rolls. He crunches the gears, a thousand vibrations, the fear of the rabbits . . .

He lowers the mechanical crab and allows himself a half smirk. Crashing into our copse, the last remaining trees, huddled together, a few charming saplings clinging on to the past. We watch his silly little engine, so brave and full of bluster. He slews in sideways, the world turns a little circle . . . and he sees blue. He tries jamming it into reverse but it's too late, he's done for . . . the engine screaming. An unclear obstacle.

We hold our breath . . . We have to force ourselves not to get up and run. There's shouting and his mates come running, battling through the clay. They hoist him out of the cab . . .

'What the fuck's that?'

They stand around staring into the pit . . . The foreman puts his hands on hips and marches over to us.

'Alright, you kids, what does W.L.A. mean?'

We scratch ourselves and look at each other, is he talking to us?
'Dunno, mister . . .'
We pull faces, we stick our fingers in our noses and concentrate, staring into the sky.
'Na, we give up, give us a clue?'
He turns, spits and walks away. He gives us a meaningful look and strides back to the splutterings, the coughing of the yellow machine.
'You must have gone down a well, mister!' we inform him. 'There's a lot of wells over there, you has to watch out for 'em, my uncle lost his stoat down one of 'em . . . They're full of adders!'
One track spinning, through the air. A spurt of mud, the yellow underbelly exposed, helpless and ridiculous. A little crowd gathered, they come running. The men in blue, they look at each other then stare darkly at us. We jump down off our fallen trunk, we swagger, whistling a tuneless tune we carry ourselves away.

24. TB

Maybe I should've listened at school, shut my big trap, written down the lie and learned their crummy craft of omission. Then, at least, I could of transported you to someplace nice, somewhere a little more fashionable. There we go, sailing down impossible rivers! The lives of the Great Authors! Gilt edged mirrors and whores wall to wall. But no, my benefactor, you're stuck here with me, my humble observations, memories. Ten to fifteen drafts, is it? And still nothing coming through. Give up the ghost? I won't hear such talk! Onwards, ever onwards ... An all night worker. Lonely, humble and brave. That's me, ant-like, a Trojan.

I've got my own devices, to rid myself of this little burden. To drag this shit through the mire and dump it someplace deep, to let it go. To watch it sinking, settling on the river bed. It's too late to lay down the pencil now, too many years, too many sorrows and betrayals. Half a lifetime of mistakes. Irrevocable, cheeky, grinning at the wrong moments, laughing out of place, embarrassing my poor friends and acquaintances. Come my benefactor, onwards! Foot-weary; but onwards, foot soldiers, companions in a death boat!

My mother getting TB was only the beginning of our troubles. She sat with me, huffing over my little spelling book. Salt! Self! Stile! She winced at the end of every column, her throat cracking. Then a string of snot as she kissed me goodnight.

She got my brother to rub her back with warm oils, but it was plain that it wasn't muscular. She was finally buckling under the constant pressure, the old man's assaults, the break-ins. It all mounted up, it repeated on her. Then Nana Lewis dying like that, that certainly compounded everything.

After two weeks and no improvement, the quack sends her into hospital for X-rays and they keep her in indefinitely. I get home from school and the place is all boarded up ... desolate ... I have to climb up the cherry tree and break in through my own bedroom window ... No food in the house, no heating, nothing! And the mutt's crapped himself. We were left to fend for ourselves, the dog, me, and my brother as bossy boots!

With my father's miserly hand-outs we had next to nothing to live on, fresh air mostly. And after Crowsfeet's rake-off we were all but starving to death. Even he got bolshie, his life-style slumped, he had to start saving his dog ends again ... That made his face turn black, he bunched up his cake hole into a cat's arse, and Smack! Things were certainly beginning to look pretty desperate; even my brother lost some of his bollock.

Sunday afternoon, the old man drives down to pick us up and go visit the old girl. We hear his car gunning in the driveway, we get up, pull on some rags and march downstairs. We sit around, watching him ghosting round the garden, his little mush mincing away beneath his beards.

'Nichollas, the lawn! Where are the stripes?'

'Wot?'

' "Wot?" You don't mean "what" by any chance do you?'

'Where's what?'

'Aah, so you can speak correctly after all! It wasn't so difficult, was it?'

Nichollas stares forlornly out across the bombsite.

'I want clean stripes, like a football pitch!'

My father doesn't even look at me. I don't do lawns.

It's time to go. We have to go and see my mother. The old man ushers us outside.

'Come along then, chop chop! Up off the floor, Steven! And tidy yourself up, for God's sake! It looks like you haven't washed your hair in weeks! It looks like a bird's nested in it!'

That makes me smirk. A bird – is he serious? He points his eyes at me, then marches out towards the kitchen ...

'What on earth have you boys been up to? My God, you weren't born on a gypsy site, were you?!'

He throws himself onto the sideboard and pulls a great pile of dirty plates down on top of himself.

'Jesus! What have you been doing? Look at this mess! Have you been eating glue?'

He chips at a plate, congealed, enamel-like, set.

'Here! Both of you, this instant!'

We have to stand in front of him. We saunter over, me last.

'Now, take a good look around you, young gentlemen, and soak it all in. Stop fiddling with yourself, Steven and take your fingers out of your ears!' (Apparently, I've got cabbages growing in there.)

'Are you pleased with yourselves? That you can't be trusted to keep this place ship-shape? Is this what I can come to expect? Well, is it? look at it! Every single pan reeks of the stuff! It stinks like a glue factory! Everything's stuck solid!'

'It's instant mash . . . that's all there is.'

'All there is? Well, don't mope about here complaining, go out and earn a living, dear boy!' We look at him vacantly. 'If you haven't got any money, get out there and make it happen!'

He scrapes a knife through the tarmac and sniffs at it.

'So this is what you get up to whilst I'm slaving away keeping you in shoes and pocket money? Think of your poor mother! of what you're doing to her! She's ill with worry over you two! Now clear it up, the pair of you! Chop-chop! At once! You know where the sink is! Jump to it!'

We dip our hands into the water, tepid, a film of oil, not a sud in sight. We play with the dishes. That stuff certainly had a way of adhering to any surface, cement-like. The old man marches into the drinks cabinet, pours himself a treble and goes upstairs to play with his shirts.

'I'll be in the master bedroom. I'll be down in a jiffy! We don't want to be late!'

We watch him go, our skunk with the beard. Why don't we take a leaf out of his book? He only wines and dines in the finest of restaurants. Why all this damned mess eating at home?'

He checks his pornography books, then we hear him coming back downstairs.

'If you young gentlemen think that I'm going to stand any more of this slovenly, uncouth behaviour, then you're sorely mistaken!'

He grasps hold of a half-eaten pan of mash and brandishes it like a stick of celery. He wags it under Nichollas's face.

'Clean this shit up before I brain you with it!'

My brother doesn't bat an eyelid – he stares him straight back, right up his nose. The world grows hushed. The old man's hair shimmering in the lamp light. I can see all the roots, the bits where he's missed with the peroxide. His eyebrows do a little gallop, then he backs down. I can't believe it – first the old coot's bristling with it, then his cock goes soft. He replaces the saucepan. He lets it splash back into the sink and beats a retreat. One second they're eyeball to eyeball, the next he bottles out. A new and unexpected development; no blood's spilt, but something to remember, the fable of the worm. I take a swig from his whisky bottle and top it up with piss.

Once we get the kitchen halfways tidy we lock up, climb into the old man's bone-shaker, and head out towards the hospital. I stare out the window and hold my breath trying not to chuck up. The winter sun running along beside us: orange-black; orange-black; now you see it, now you don't. Some more trees and a stretch of water. I've always loathed motor cars, but hated those winter journeys in particular. The low sun glaring, always finding your eyes, and the stench of upholstery. The trees go past and you feel sad.

We pull in through the stone gates and poodle up to the visitor's entrance. The old man peers into the rear-view mirror and twists the ends of his moustache.

'Comb your hair, you boys! I want you to look like young gentlemen . . . And mind you don't traipse mud onto the ward!'

He climbs out and leads the way. He barks at us, I have to get off the grass . . . He finds the exact right corridor, and then her bed . . . He counts them off as we pass, and then there she is, laid out for all to see, ghostly.

We have to look twice to make sure it really is her. The old man beams . . . It certainly cheered the old bastard up seeing her sprawled out like that, prostrate, so to speak. He has to lean his weight on nursy . . . He goes weak at the knees . . . She brings him a cup of tea and he perks up a bit . . . even manages a few wise cracks . . . It seemed he might be rid of her at long last . . .

She tries a smile . . . We're not allowed to kiss her on account of the TB. We just sort of wave and stand back. The old man tells me to take my hands out of my pockets.

'You look splendid, Juny. The boys are doing fine at home! Don't worry yourself, you just concentrate on getting better! I've spoken to the staff nurse, I left her a little something for you . . . We'll come again when you're not tired . . . Your mother's very ill, you boys, so I don't want you worrying her! You're grown up young gentlemen now, you can look after yourselves, can't you?' My brother nods and gives me a dead leg.

As soon as we get back home, the old man starts preparations for moving in his cutie. Every evening he brings home another car-load of household gadgets. He even gives us some extra pocket money to tidy ourselves up, on condition that we try out the new Hoover.

'Steven, I don't want to see any of your council house roughs hanging about the place! We've got a special guest this weekend, so I want the place spick-and-span!'

Then, Friday night he rolls in with his Elisabuff on his arm. That makes my brother suck his teeth. Me too. To tell the truth, I eye the lot of them sideways.

The old man's eyes glint like shillings . . . He finds the sofa and sprawls out. He puts his feet up and pulls her down on top of him . . . She giggles and farts. The old man picks up the bottle and empties a pint of gin into his delicate little kisser. Damp round the edges, little pearls of moisture, his tongue lapping at the teat. He swings his head round like a cricket bat and nuzzles between her breasts, her cooing like a dove. She pushes him off and adjusts her knickers in her crack.

'Elisabeth, these are my boys! This is my eldest son Nichollas! And this is Steven, the stupidest! Boys, this is Elisabeth, your new mummy.'

'E-lis-a-buff!' She shrieks and falls back on the old man's lap . . . 'Give me a dwink, daddy!'

'Nichollas! Fix a drink for Elisabeth! A drink! Come along, chop-chop! Show her what a young gentleman you are!'

Nichollas jumps to it, he shows willing. He pours her a vodka and hands her the glass. The old man grabs it back.

'That's not a drink! That's not even an eye-wash! Fill the glass! Go on, go on!'

My brother empties the bottle, he glugs it out.

'There, that's it, that's much better, now that's what I call a measure! Pour yourself one, Nichollas, you're a young gentlemen and it's high time you learned to drink!'

He pats the cushion next to him. 'Come along, Nichollas, come and sit by your father! Father and eldest son enjoying a little aperitif together! Come and say hello to your new mummy.'

I sit and watch them from the floor. Their faces, the tongues lolling, my brother and my father, a sort of belated love affair, this new game. They clink glasses and laugh, warming to each other. The old man pulls out his onion and sticks his finger up his nose.

'Steven, it's past your bed time, it's time you were off to bed!'

I don't move, I sit tight; he looks to me, then to the others.

'I just don't know how to get along with that child!' He shakes his head. 'He smells! He's backward! And his feet are too big.' He grins, opens his trap and shows them his caps. 'Now Nichollas? – Yes! But him? – No! Not until he's twenty, not until he's twenty-one maybe, then I can see us getting along famously, but now?' He shakes his head sorrowfully . . . 'You wouldn't believe what a sickly child he was . . . Steven! I said you were such a sickly, whining child! You remember, don't you, Nichollas?'

Nichollas nods, he's in full agreement. 'He was always crying. He cried all the time . . .'

'That's right, he cried constantly! And I had to smell his nappies . . . You were both babies and I had to see your shit and piss! And you cried and you stank! When you're twenty-one maybe, but not before! My God, you used to cry so much that your mother had to kick your cot! Really, she had to! You were a thoroughly obnoxious child, Steven! And you're growing into a vulgar youth! Look at those feet! What size are they? He's out of all propor-tion!'

He slaps his thighs and puts his face right into Elisabuff's pancake. He delights himself, he re-explains, he swings his head around in ever increasing circles, spittle flying as he speaks, gesticulating, flashing sharp glances at me.

'Isn't that true, Nichollas?' Nichollas nods furiously. The show's all for him and he must show how much he appreciates it.

'Yes father, he wouldn't stop crying, and I smashed a pedal bike into his head!' He pulls me up by my jumper. 'Stand up and show her the scar, Steven!'

I pull back and sit down, a button pings off . . . I look for it . . .

'Shush, the pair of you!' The old man scans his audience. 'You're not so grown up that I can't still bang your bloody heads together!' He turns to me again. 'You were an obnoxious baby,

Steven, you wouldn't stop crying and your mother had to kick your cot to make you shut up!'

He laughs at himself, he sits back delighted. He underlines it – that's my brother's cue. He falls off his seat and rolls around on the floor. He opens his mouth so wide he almost chokes. A hard laugh, twisted, pulled from his bowels, to make believe it's the funniest thing he's ever heard in the whole history of the world. He goes pop-eyed and almost pukes with the effort, all for his daddy's benefit. The old man nods his approval, positively glowing with gin. He claps his hands and calls a halt to the proceedings.

'Come along, Steven, chop-chop! It's way past your bed time, now off to bed with you! Elisabeth will come and tuck you in, won't you, Elisabeth? Elisabeth's good at tucking in little boys!'

I get up and exit whilst they're still busy congratulating themselves. I go to my room, jam the bed up against the door, go to the mirror and stick my tongue out. I kiss it, French style, like Susan taught me. Ah Susan, unhappiness always finds us, it comes running on cold little feet, like the paws of a cat; it jumps at our throats, and then we swallow and pretend that everything's just fine.

You see, I'm writing this for you as well, Susan, for you and little Joanne, wherever you are. Because I remember everything and I promise never to forget.

25. REAL LIVE HORSES

Those journeys were bleak. All that winter, we kept driving out there, waiting for a sign, for the old girl to go one way or the other . . . And the old man swigging at his Scotch and lighting up another cigar. He twirled his whiskers and examined his onion. Sunday's the day of the dead: hell today and school tomorrow! I still can't get used to that threat, that special type of gloom that settles round the furniture, the day grows tired and any jollity seems somehow fake and hollow.

We revisited the old girl, just me and the old man – my father. He's too pissed to climb behind the wheel so he calls a cab. The sun goes down and we head out into that gloom. The taxi arrives, we open the back door, the little light goes on and that special acidic stench of new upholstery. The driver goes the long way round, the scenic route. Gradually the street lamps peter out 'til we're driving through open country . . . We pass under the trees, a tunnel through the wild wood, no other cars, no headlamps, nothing . . . Suddenly he slams on the anchors and skids into a lay-by . . .

'It's up ahead, over there . . . the back way, across the field . . . I'll wait for you. There's roadworks, I'll be alright here, don't worry about me, I've got my flask.'

The old man climbs out, me following on his shirt tails . . . He ganders about, sniffing at the sea breeze, getting his bearings . . . a clock tower and a couple of cedars . . . He heads off into the bushes following his nose. I run and catch up with him, hopping from verge to verge. A car sneaks up behind us. Hop! You have to be quick – those country lanes are narrow, footpaths unlit . . . Then we come to a stone wall, we follow it along, grey, continuous, disappearing into the distance. Then another car rushes in behind us and Hop! up onto the verge. The verge, our only hope.

'We'll be the ones who wind up in hospital at this rate,' my father jokes.

Wouldham, Burham, Eccles, Aylesford, half-way to Barming. We followed that wall for ever. The old man shakes out his handkerchief and lets off a few blasts . . . He mops his brow with it, wrinkles his nose and strides on. He decides we should take a short cut across the furrows.

'The wind's a south-westerly, so the hospital must be to the north.'

That short cut alone cost us an extra hour. We had to negotiate a couple of gravel pits in the dark, treacherous . . . still black waters . . . twenty fathoms deep, right from the bank. We swam about out there until we finally walked ourselves into a cul-de-sac, a total impasse. The only thing to do was to retrace our steps, re-find the road and stay with the stone wall. At least that way we knew where we were going. That's the only sure way of finding our Florence Nightingale. Hiking across those fields it's too easy to get yourself lost, fall down a furrow and never come up again! That was my great fear . . . And the copse, the wooded area, dying elms mostly. We didn't want to disturb the rooks' sleep.

We find the wall again, by strenuous efforts. Three barbed wire fences, and then two more. Two miles along the lane, then Hop! up onto the verge, and there it is, the hospital wall, grey stone, ominous, disappearing into the night, and beyond . . . way over there. Then something twinkling in the distance – the porch lights, they must have left them on for us. We make a bee-line in through the gate, up the driveway and there it is. Just like the cabby told us, just follow the wall and you can't miss it. Follow your noses and you're there.

Walking onto that ward made you rub your eyes: strip-lights and gleaming linen. I have to wait ten or twelve seconds before my eyes adjust. The old man's already in there getting pally with nursy, teasing her like she was a kid. He tips his hat and grimaces at her, complimenting her on her uniform, on her nails.

'There's nothing I like to see better than a set of well manicured finger nails! Take my son Steven, for instance, his nails are always deplorable!'

I have to look at the calendar on the wall 'til he quits gassing and we can walk through onto the old girl's ward. He waves to the sister and all the nurses, the old fake! I've seen the type of idiots cuties fall for and as far as I can figure it, they deserve one another! The old man's positively beaming, the lines show up round his eyes, he throws compliments around left right and centre. Then he sees her, the old girl, flitting from bed to bed, her feet in her slippers, a rosy bloom on her cheeks, and a piss-pot in both hands. She waves to us, cheerful, full of life, not in the least bit grey. She walks right up to me, gives me a peck on the cheek and calls the old man 'darling' ... That stops him dead in his tracks ... He grins all quizzical, he questions himself, like he's swallowed a fly.

'Are you sure you should be up and about, Juny? Surely you should be taking it easy? Think of your lungs, the X-rays ... Surely you should be in bed? Come, I'll help you ...'

The old girl shrugs him off, she'll have none of it, as far as she's concerned she's fit as a fiddle! The doctors showed her the X-rays; the shadow on her left lung has completely gone, vanished! They're not even sure if it was there in the first place. And the fluid around the right one is ninety per cent reduced. The old girl can't understand what all the fuss has been about ...

'I can't stand around here natting all night, there's work to be done!'

And she nips off, helping the staff hand out the evening medication, giving words of comfort and condolence. She has already cured one young Indian girl with some good, sound, old-fashioned common sense advice! A drug addict, by all accounts untreatable, a total write-off! The doctors had given up hope, but the old girl soon put her back on the straight and narrow! She won everybody over; the quacks were falling over themselves, singing her praises. She was a walking miracle. Drugs? Hospitals? Doctors? Who needs them? She cured herself!

Once the penny dropped and the old man realised that she was going to make a full recovery, the spring went right out of his step. He was crestfallen – rubbing at his eyes in sheer disbelief, he splutters and stammers, totally lost for words. He glances down at my mug, then quickly looks away. He hides his heart like a hand of cards – his mush glazes over, he stares into the distance, his little bluey's framed in between his bags, saggy, a little twitch, the dance of the blue vein. Oh, he did his best not to let his innermost feelings show, but you could read his mug like the weather. He bites his lip to hide his disgust.

Naturally, I kept schtum about the dodgy goings-on back at the gaff. There's no sense in upsetting the patient before she's even back on her feet; she might have some kind of relapse. I don't let on about the comings and goings, the clandestine meetings, the entourage of the sad and the lonely, giggling Elisabuff . . .

We leave my mother there. My father bites down and we walk out. Getting back, we didn't take any chances, we kept strictly to the wall. Re-tracing our steps, keeping a weather eye open for our cabby. We zig-zagged about in the dark for half an hour, then the old man spots him pulling away, he's given up on us. The old man leaps off the verge into the headlamps, waving his brolly in one hand and his natty little titfer in the other. His beard sparkles in the glare, and his little gold watch chain, intricate, precise, disappearing into his waistcoat pocket. I stand on the verge, almost proud of him.

'The Royal Victoria Bull Hotel, driver! I haven't eaten since luncheon! Rochester High Street!'

We take the main track out of there: Aylesford, Eccles. We circumnavigate Burham by way of the river, Wouldham, I think it's called, then up under the motorway bridge and into Borstal. That's pretty straightforward, the other lanes are dead-ends, petering out into swamps and chalk pits. Or even worse, straight into the Medway. The old man sits in the front, playing with his signet ring . . . I watch his ears in the street lamps.

We pull up outside, he extracts his wallet and tips the driver double the fare. That's his style, humbling all beneath his staggering generosity. A tinkle of silver, a superior smile, his hand goes to his wallet, buying his way with cash. The copper penny, speaking a million words! A thousand tongues! He dips in, he faffs around, keeping his man in suspense, then extracts his hand like a conjuror's glove. And brand new bank notes, mind! He pauses for full effect, then counts them out one at a time, building on the suspense. The cabby licks his lips and looks admiringly into the old man's mug, the eyes dead above the bags. I've watched this game a thousand times, a game to be played 'til the end of time: the charade of the tip!

My father has debased his man and now he must eat! We disappear in under the arch, the Royal Victoria Bull Hotel.

'The coaches used to come in under here!' my father explains to me.

I look around. 'With real live horses?'

Well, there you are, that must have been more like fun, none of your stinking cars, real live animals.

'With nose-bags? Like at the circus?'

These are questions, but there are no answers.

He sits staring into the flock wallpaper, sucking on his brandy.

'What do you think daddy should do, Steven? Do you think daddy should become a trendy?' That's the old man talking, one gargle of the grape and he's off! 'Do you think daddy should become a trendy, Steven?' He looks at me cross-eyed and lurches over the table, his bow-tie drooping in his soup. Then he sways round in a wide arc, holding onto the table in front of him, his ears burning red. 'Does Stevie-wevie think that daddy-waddy should become a twendy-wendy? Ah! Aah! Do you like your snacky-wacky? I feel kind of drunk, that's funny . . .'

He holds up his finger, white bone, knotted in the middle, perfectly scrubbed, the cuticles perfect. Unquestionably beautiful – blue under the nails, purplish at the knuckle but otherwise pure white. Virginal, long, yellowish, little scales, intricate wrinkles . . .

'I haven't had a drink! It must be the flu! Waitress! Waitress! Come here, my child! Oh, my sweet child, come and sit on Jonathan's knee . . . you see? Look, I haven't . . . have I? I haven't had one all day, haven't touched a drop! Only that much!' He revolves his finger under her nose . . . 'Not even that much! Have you got an aspro my child? It's the flu, you see . . . And my wife, that's his mother, she's got TB . . . Do you think I should become a trendy, my child?'

He paws at her apron, she unclasps his hands and breaks away.

'That's it, now run along and get uncle Jonathan an insie-winsie little glass of brandy, and an aspro . . . Will you do that for him? Because I feel kind of . . . woozy . . . I'm woozy! You're all going sideways, do you know that?'

He picks up his titfer and sends it spinning out across the tables. He hurls it double hard, with both fists. He flings it away from him with utter contempt.

'Yes, a trendy! I shall become a trendy!'

26. CHRISTIAN JUSTICE

We single file into assembly ... coughing and stamping our feet ... we won't shut up whistling ... Then Old Boyce, the head of RE, jams his gut behind the lectern and shushes us, mopping at his face ... Gradually we quit whooping and look at him, we stare at a piece of bubblegum stuck next to his thumb. He clears his throat and mutters into his collar ... He lifts his head and tries again.

'I'm afraid I have some very sad news for you this morning, boys.' He grabs hold of the lectern to steady his gut, dabbing at his damp face with his handkerchief ... The room grows hushed. 'One of the little boys ... In my school days ...' he mumbles. We listen through the gloom ... 'A brain haemorrhage, in the middle of the night! No other details! Right through the head!' My heart rises ... 'His mother, his family ... our sympathies ...' I almost laugh out loud. I'm too scared to breath. I put my fist in my mouth and gag. I have to stop myself: I look round kind of scared.

From what I can make out over the din, it seems that Crowsfeet's little lackey has copped it ... He got a headache in the night, so his mother puts him to bed, and then when she goes to wake him in the morning he's dead. That's about the sum of it. He entered our lives, ate his egg and chips, watched telly, then he made his exit.

Old Boyce announces it in assembly, and I go into a sort of glad sweat. Boyce opens his cake hole, sprays the audience, and then we have to pray, we have to pray for his stinking soul. The room grows hushed, the teacher leads us through it, and even him a non-believer . . .

We put our hands together and stare down, shamed. I bite my lips to concentrate . . . I try to imagine his dead face; I flex my retinas behind my eye lids, but nothing . . . I pretend it's Crowsfeet or my brother who's dead, or that I'm an orphan and they're all dead . . . I raise as much pity for myself as I can muster. Anything to wring out one miserly tear! I pray for the death of my brother, my father and Crowsfeet. I pray so hard my eyeballs ache . . . I peep between my fingers. Boyce stands there, head bowed, neck merging into his face, a pink mess . . . So, our little bastard's gone to meet his maker? I can scarcely believe my ears. I unplug them with my fingers; I make the sound go off and on.

'Stop fiddling with yourself, that boy!' I hear him intermittently, he glares at me. 'Take your fingers out of your ears, this instant!' I look behind me, does he mean me? 'Yes, you, boy! You can stay behind in detention . . . Four o'clock, my room! Now, if I can just have your undivided attention for five minutes, I will explain to you that when I tell you that the school field is strictly out of bounds, then that is exactly what it is! Got it?'

'Death means nothing, for ever and ever.' That's what Caroline said. Norman's face half-chewed, an eyeball missing, his belly full of slugs. I prayed regularly every night before I got into bed. I became a religious zealot.

My father kneels by a shrub in the back garden . . . he picks about at some fallen leaves . . . I stand at my bedroom window, staring into the back of his head, willing him to drop dead, for his heart to cease . . . He stands, turns and looks up at the sky . . . I move back behind the curtain and watch as he fetches his wheelbarrow.

One death had to be enough. The living just kept on living; another belch, another fart, a clip round the lug-hole and life goes on. We're left stupid and dumb – a lot more talk about nothing and a punch up the bracket, that's what we'll all get.

That fat little git preaching his way through the assembly – Mister Boyce. Holding onto his lectern, droning on about Crowsfeet's little lackey, our kid, the dead one. He mops at the moisture, a bucket of sweat; the whole thing's just a sham, a stinking act. Us kids stifling our yawns.

There's no doubt that as far as schools go, it's the religious teachers who get it in the neck. The kids just aren't interested in their useless subject. Their religion's just one mighty flop from start to finish. And no matter how hard they harp on about Christ and his idiotic cross, they can't even begin to inspire interest. They sweat and they stammer and that's when the brats take advantage: thirty-five to one, total disorder! Anarchy and chaos! Walderslade secondary school, 1972. You weren't there? You wouldn't know!

Well, that old Boyce, he kept me in detention just for the hell of it, just to make an example of me. For his money, I was an anti-Christ, a subversive and a dirty Bolshevik. He points me to my desk and then starts laying down the law, his mouth going like a sponge, like two halves of an eclair. It foams round the edges, he squirts cream, and his cheeks like luncheon meat, blending into this neck, garrotted by his tie. Some picture, a real nativity. That makes me smirk, then Biff! He punches me right on the nose for my cheek and insolence, Biff! Right up the bracket, that's the noise it makes, Doink! And there's real blood! I stand back and cup my nose in my handkerchief . . . There's Christian justice for you: 'turn the other cheek' and the 'just' war . . .

He was quite a tough boy, just that once, after school, when nobody was looking. He adjusts his dick and walks out rolling his arse. I've seen him since, I remember his face, like an eclair, and I'll confront him later, when the time is ripe.

27. GREEN JAW

I've got a face that invites wrath. I antagonise people by just being here, by having the audacity to smile and to breathe. And there's no denying that my teeth were a mess, rotted right through, gum boils, some blood and the stink! That's what got up people's noses, my refusal to care.

For my brother's money, I brought all my miseries on myself. I didn't get anything less than what I'd been asking for, he saw to that. Christ, what a stinking, bed-pissing little piece of shit I was! My mother and brother backed each other up to the hilt; they wouldn't believe that it wasn't all my own fault, that I hadn't been asking for far worse since the age dot!

It got to the point that my brother was even ashamed to bring his cuties back round the house, in case they saw what he was related to. He put on a whole show for them, curling his lip, a lovely little pout, perfected in front of the mirror, a real Brigitte Bardot with balls.

He didn't miss any opportunity to humiliate me; he made loud comments about my bed-wetting and the certainty of my impending acne attack . . .

'The thicko can't even read or write yet, can you, Steven? How old are you, eleven? And your pimples, they're coming on nicely!'

He smeared little dabs of paint onto his school trousers and always carried three or four 2B pencils in his blazer pocket . . . He ordered me to sit still – he was furious with everything, especially the pencils. I had to be drawn, regardless of my flaws . . . He draws my nose, then my eyes. He shouts at me because I'm doing it all wrong; he throws his rubber across the room and kicks at me . . .

I vowed to do everything humanly possible to be more like him. I grew my hair and walked around the house swearing at the furniture. It made me out to be more of an idiot than I already was, in fact it got me nowhere – it got me beaten up, that's where it got me . . .

My long hair antagonised Crowsfeet; he thought I was getting way too big for my boots, a little too provocative. His eyes twisted in their sockets, my golden locks drove him to new depths of spite. He punched me so hard that my jaw turned from green to purple, the teeth that didn't fall out went septic. They stuck out at odd angles; people got to notice, raised voices in public, whispered comments.

But it hasn't always been my fault, what with all those socks to the mouth. Unasked for? I should say so, an innocent abroad. What people can't seem to understand, what they refuse to get into their fat skulls, is that things can just happen to you. If somebody doesn't quite like the cut of your jib, then, Smack! And that's reason enough in this bitter world of ours. Bewildering, unfathomable, and totally unjust. Just kids, unable to grasp hold of our own sorry little existences, abused and buggered, floating in some kind of half-arsed dream world, inhabited by ghosts and half-men.

You'd think that the dentist would be a trifle more sympathetic, see that a kid's taken a beating, that he didn't bring the whole show down upon himself. But the truth of the matter is that bastard single-handedly did more damage to my mug than all the bullies put together, and that's saying something.

I walk up the stairs to the smell of disinfectant and the sound of the drill. The receptionist cracks a smile; the old girl gives her my details . . . Then we sit there raking through the heap of mouldy mags looking for a comic . . . I look up at all the posters and kick my chair. I hang around 'til doomsday, hoping the place will close down, and I can quietly slip from my chair and run.

He dives in, sticks his dirty great index in there, and gives it a tug. I smell his stink, and feel the texture, little tufts of hair on the back of his fingers.

'You need to brush properly! Once in the morning, when you get up! And once in the evening before you go to bed! Occlusal!' He tut-tuts me, he re-dives . . . 'Occlusal!' . . . that was his catch-phrase. He repeats it, mumbling through his bad breath. 'Occlusal!' He says it again, he repeats himself, then he gets his needles out.

I suck on his thumb, a really big one, it takes up nearly the whole of my gob. Then he jams his other hand back in there as well – a plug, that was the effect. All those fingers, sausagey, two or three of them, I can scarcely breathe.

'Occlusal!'

He says it again, just to remind himself. And the girl crosses her legs and writes it all down. Pink nail varnish, and she hasn't dyed her roots ... The drill screams. He slips, he brings it home, my feet twitching. I grip onto the chair ... a little blood ... some drool ... I've got a mouthful of powder. And the jolts, he leans his weight onto it ... He's drilling out the root, heading for the heart of the abscess.

'This won't take long! I've just ... got to drill down, yes ... to drain it, you see ... the pus ... on its own accord. Just don't let any food get down those holes, keep them clean, there's a good little chap. Now, just one more to go ...'

He re-seals the holes, slapping the plaster in, mercury and lead, right up to the top. He pats it down with his little trowel, one last prod, and a check with his mirror on a stick.

'That's it! All done, off home with you now!'

He grins and shows me the door. I cup my jaw, nursy helps me from the chair. I stumble out onto the stairway. I don't need telling twice, I jump up and scarper ...

'Suck,' she tells me, but I'm passing out with the pain, everything turns purple ... My whole chin starts brewing up, a moon effect, like two little beer barrels, bubbling ... and two special types of pain. It juts out in front of me like a delicate prow, I bang into things ... the world goes fizzy ... I can feel my mouth boiling over. I scream quietly, low down, between my teeth. You see, I can't get my mouth open wide enough, it's too stopped up with pus. My mother swabs away great strings of the stuff, with cotton wool soaked in whisky.

'Suck,' she tells me.

I crawl on my hands and knees, I get my head stuck under the bed, my jaw trapped in amongst the springs. My mother tries to pry me loose, but I'm hopelessly tangled. I curl up where I am ... cradling my chin ... I beat the floor with my fists.

The wind blows in the trees and the old man floats up the garden path. He rolls in drunk and stares down his nose at me. I wade around in front of him, paddling in my little pool of pus. He bristles his whiskers. I can't see him squarely because of the swelling, but I recognise the stink – brandy and Cologne. He gets down on his hands and knees and looks me over.

'There's nothing wrong with the shitty-arse, Juny! The little bastard's drunk, that's all! that's his only problem ... Why, the stinker's been at my whisky!'

He defies her, he holds out my head for inspection.

'There's nothing wrong with this child, he's drunk, that's all! I said you're drunk, Steven! You've raised a stinking wino, Juny! A juice head!' That's his diagnosis. He pushes me away from him ... 'Send him to bed, let him sleep it off! There's no use molly-coddling him. He's just taking advantage, greater and greater liberties! So, he's as drunk as a skunk as well as a thief! Bah!' He marches into the wardrobe and pisses himself.

There's no words I can say. I can't even begin to defend myself, my mouth's too stopped up. I can't really talk at all; I have to speak by semaphore. I wave my arms around, I make smoke signals. My teeth sticking out at ten different angles, like tusks, that makes me laugh. 'Tee-hee-hee! Ouch!'

Boyce! That was his name! Mister Boyce, the Religious Education teacher, Walderslade Secondary School. Boyce, the brave pugilist, the man of the cloth, who punched me square on the chin after lessons. Walderslade Secondary, 1972. Sock! Right on the button, unwinding, Christian and precise. Him and his gentle Jesus. Bam! It all comes back to me now, a flood of memories. Old Mister Boyce, head of Religious Education.

Say, he was quite a toughie, just that once, after school, with nobody watching, without witnesses. He kept me back after lessons, then set on me. He thought he could push me about, but now I pay him back, and double! The pen is mightier than the sword, Boyce! Oh ye of little faith! I remember your fat mug ... a face with a price on it, a face that will have to pay, by Christ, for no other reason than I say so! On your knees, Christian! You, who would strike one of your own flock! Yes, it's you I'm talking to, you by the surname of Boyce! Got it?

Arrr, it gladdens my heart to know you're still out there, Boyce. That at last justice will be done. That this great writer has exposed you in all your low-down glory. Well, Boyce, I might even choose to forgive you, if the mood so takes me, yes, I repeat that, if you can humble yourself. If you can still bend in the middle, you slug!

The next day I'm admitted into hospital. The old girl goes with me all the way to East Grinstead, by taxi. Of course, that sort of trip doesn't cost tuppence. The old girl has to dip into the house-keeping, something she'd put by, hidden in the lining of her coat, from the thieving hands of Crowsfeet and the old man.

The driver helps me to the car; I can just make him out through the purple fog ... I wince at every step, the jolts of my footsteps ... I roll my head on my shoulders, I gag, I hiccup. My mother strokes my brow ... I groan, I go dizzy ... I have to hold onto my guts, all the way, through Maidstone and down into the Weald ... The roads go everywhere, and my tusks, my little elephant ... I break into a cold sweat, I have to hold my vomit in my mouth, 'til we get there ... She hands me the hip flask, I take a hit, gingerly, between my lips ...

Our driver lets us know all about the blacks, and the wrongs they've done him personally. It appears that they've bankrupted his brother-in-law, and all but raped his sister ... He knows the old man intimately and has driven him on several occasions; it's his big opinion that my father is the only true gentleman left. The main problem, as he sees it, is that the streets are full of fools; no one can drive properly, and the weather's all wrong!

The old girl has to drop me at the gate ... She can't afford to hang around on account of the meter ... She can't drag her eyes away from it, every time 5p clicks up she winces ... She kisses me on the cheek and waves goodbye. She can't come in with me, she can't afford it, they have to turn round and head straight back or it'll cost an arm and a leg! She just sees me laid on the trolley, and she waves goodbye. I watch her go, she smiles and walks back to the taxi, the door opens, we turn a corner, she's gone.

'The skin won't stop growing over my eye ...'

That's my elephant talking, the guinea pig club, East Grinstead, his trunk joined onto his foot. That's what he's been trying to tell me all along, in between nodding his tusks and mouthing words. And I stare past the climbing frame, screwed into his skull. I become engrossed in the wing-nuts, one on each temple, where the metalwork disappears into his skull. I look away and try not to stare, I pretend to be reading my book. I look to his lips, to his mouth . . . He's trying to tell me something, but my eyes keep travelling back to the meccano . . . And his eye, it seems that the skin won't stop re-growing.

They cut a little pink bit out of his mouth, then fashion a tear duct out of it, just like that, intricate, crafted. A bit of glue and he's got a new corner bit. Like as if they're God, to create such a thing!

They unwind him, from the nose up, his whole trunk full of blood. Like a baa-lamb, all the wool comes out, brown and clotted, great strings of it, at least fifty foot of the stuff. And a little fresh bit, a few droplets on the bed spread, scarlet . . . He waves to us, my elephant, the scaffolding's screwed into his forehead like a block of flats. They're rebuilding his trunk, his thumb joined to his face, a few threads of skin . . . A doorway through the scaffolding – we follow the bandages, we all hold on. Nursy comes over to my bed, throws the brake and wheels me in.

They pull the little curtain round my bed, a squirt of the needle in the air. They dig it in, and we're off! Down the hallway and into the garden . . . I watch the rose bushes go past, then through the double doors, and the ceiling, six sky-lights, a hanging vase, and a face, my elephant, gentle, reassuring.

German, I think. Yes German, or possibly Austrian . . . He talks low down, monotone . . . He pries open my gob, pushes my tongue to one side, and inserts his little hand drill. He turns it between his thumb and fore-finger. I see his eye, bulging, magnified, accentuated by his eye-piece; it stares into my trap, it blinks.

Coring the root, slow turns of the drill, down the length of my tusk, taking out that other fool's fillings. Nearing the head of the abscess, like an egg yolk. I can't swallow, my head's tilted back, it trickles down the back of my throat . . . a special mixture of blood and pus. He's almost done; just a few more twists. Then he hands me over to his student – I see her standing in the wings. She glints her headlamp in my eyes and rattles her cutlass. She's champing at the bit, raring to have a go. She jumps right in and gives it a little tap with her hammer. I jolt in the chair, my hands grip the arm-rests – hey, that hurts! She messes me about, working away at the enamel, grinding, bit by bit. The Kraut straps a clamp on my forehead to hold me steady, two thumb screws and a vice.

'Ouch!' She goes into my gums, the anaesthetic's wearing off. I squirm in my seat. She holds onto my nose with her rubber glove and stares stone-like into my gob; she's all thumbs.

I wave my elephant goodbye, I slip under. He lifts his trunk in the air and trumpets. A golden sun glinting. A bird of paradise. Animal magic. I lift my hand, I want to wave too, but it's too heavy, way too heavy . . . And there's a little light in the distance and a humming noise. Someone's filled my throat with gravel.

'There, there!' I look up, her little starched hat perched on top, a charming effect, and then her nose underneath. She puts her palm to my forehead. 'There, there.' There is a real angel by my bed, hovering over me. I give her a weak smile. I'm gonna puke, I can feel it rising. I'm lost, I don't know where I am. Never fear, nursy's here, with her little bucket.

'There, there.' Here it comes. I gargle on the clots, about two pints worth. Maybe only one and a half. I have to let it go, dark brown, in hot jets. That's the stuff, I must have swallowed it during the operation. That's my blood in the bucket. I study it at close range. Yeah, that's me in there, in little clusters, coagulating, foaming round the edge. It clings to my dangly bit at the back. I let it all come out, hot and steaming, I fill the bowl.

'There's a good boy, that's it . . . there there . . .' She fondles my brow. Wow, those nurses have got some style! Warm hands, strong but soft, and not in the least bit sweaty, against my hot brow . . .

It jumps out of me, hot and sour. And in between I have to try and breathe as well. But it keeps coming, in spasms, my stomach cramping, my eyes water. It sprays out of my nose . . . It's never going to stop . . . I empty my guts . . . I sweat and suffer, pulling at the bed clothes. I fall back onto the pillow – my little rock.

I manage a weak smile, just for her, for my little nursy. She tussles my hair, her eyes travelling down over my boy's body, and she blushes. The colour rises to her cheeks, and I see it for the first time, in her eyes, and it's a warm feeling, like nothing else.

They stitch my gob back up and send me right back on the job, back to the beatings. They re-embroidered my whole mug. And a pretty mess they made of it, too. A cobweb between my teeth, holding my gums in, all hand done.

'Your teeth are a mess, Steven! My God, they're worse than your mother's! Why do you take him to the NHS, Juny? They're butchers! I, personally, see Mister Williams in his private practice. He does excellent work!'

He shows us his pearlies, every one of them a cap – a gob of gold.

My father always talked about money, but there wasn't a penny for us or my teeth.

They cut my gums away, clamp my trap open and start chopping. They peel it away from the teeth, and tuck the whole thing under my chin, then dig the poison out of my jaw-bone . . . Buff it up like new . . . and then lace the whole thing back together again. That's the way they work.

A week resting up, then off I go, a soldier, but powerless, under the rule of Crowsfeet, as if I was his girl. I wanted to have other friends, but he wouldn't let me – he guarded me jealously.

I was really very unhappy, and like I say, I have no reason to hoodwink you. You can point to my total lack of education, and my admissions of guilt, then pick up those very sticks and beat me with them all over again. I'm ready and I'm waiting; I've had every other conceivable insult levelled at me. That I smell of the shop! I'm full of humbug and know nothing! But one thing I do know all there is to know about, and that's humility. I was bullied for the best part of my childhood, and still it comes easy to me. I have to bite my lip, to quit from apologising for people walking into me, standing on my feet, and letting go of doors in my face.

28. INSPECTOR SORREL

Like any idiot can tell you, it only takes one loudmouth to start rocking the boat, and everybody winds up in the drink. He was heading for it, that Crowsfeet, but nobody dared tell him. Backchat him? It would have been more than my delicate little jaw was worth, I was still spitting out bits of cotton. I held my tongue for once, I was worried about my profile. No, when that bastard's time came, he had to 'take his punishment like a man'! By himself, standing up. Smack! Right on the chin, that rearranged his ugly mug, the cunt!

In the end he was lucky to go down for only a year. Naturally he tries to drag the rest of us down with him. We should of seen that one coming – the finger of the snitcher.

He stares into the space above my head, rolls his eyes back, open and shuts his biscuit shoot, then – Smack! I've already told you about it. Smack! A little dance of the fried eggs, then he lets one off – Pow! in my direction. To think of it, he had the nerve to treat me like that, and then to grass me up as well, if that doesn't take the biscuit! Argh, it makes me want to spit!

I just want a chance, that's all, my space to set the record straight. The use of this useless soapbox, to tell of my feelings, deep down, disenchanted and dole-ridden.

And here I am, sage-like, passing the law. No kidding, my humble remembrances. Aggressive, pissed off, but also swallowing down, studying my nails, doing my upmost, over thirteen drafts, to explain to my friends and haters alike, to a world that doesn't know and doesn't care. All the truths, half-truths, lies and despairs of my hapless childhood. I've still got a brace of home-made pistols to prove it ... Just in case I get to thinking that I made the whole thing up ... Something the law passed over, to remind myself, to prove that I wasn't day-dreaming.

Don't think that we just sat there and let events overrun us – hell no! We took precautions, me and Goldfish, doubled security! We hid up our armoury in different stashes round the countryside, Lee-Enfield 303's, 4.10 shotguns, black powder and live rounds.

We did our upmost to outmanoeuvre both policeman and peace-maker alike, but Crowsfeet's completely out of control. He's bragging and bluffing all over the estate.

He digs into his rags and pulls out something black, snub nosed, he unwraps it. A pretty little darling with a winged eagle embossed on her handle. Stolen that very morning from the old Colonel's house on King George's Road. He's looking for a buyer, a quick sale. He totes it around the council estate, and even brings it into school with him. He offers to give a display of marksmanship after dinner on the school field! He pulls it out of his duffel bag and lets us feel its weight.

'It's a Nazi revolver, a Mauser ... SS probably, or a Luger!'

He shows us the slugs, a handful, lead money, the real thing. Goldfish advises him to dump it for all our sakes, to go chuck it in the village pond.

'Wipe it and sling it in the deep end!' That's his advice. He tries to point out the whys and wherefores. But no matter how hard he explains, no matter how many bubbles he blows, Crowsfeet still knows better. The only thing he's interested in is hard currency. Why should he go ditching a meal ticket like that? A thing of beauty with a hand-carved grip.

For all the good it did him, Goldfish may as well have sung to the starlings ... He pointed out that he was Captain, the General even! But Crowsfeet just laughed in his face ... He made like a cowboy, waving it about over his head ... The whole thing gave Goldfish bad dreams; he could see all his hard laid plans being washed away. He had nightmares, in graphic detail ... all of us wiped out in a bloody siege on Week Street, Maidstone. The whole regular army versus the W.L.A. ...

We're holed up behind a barricade of bullet-ridden dustbins. I'm on the Bren gun. Goldfish's heart swells with pride. He tosses a home made nitro marble, he flings it, it bounces and it explodes! But still they pour in more and more men . . . They're massing for the big push! We're hopelessly outnumbered!

The whole place goes up in smoke, a deadly salvo. He sees me fall, I bite the tarmac. Then from out of the smoke . . . a bulldozer . . . rumbling, trumpeting like an elephant! It claims victory, it squats, crushing our barricade . . . The officer climbs down, wearing wellingtons and a donkey jacket. He forces Goldfish to his knees. Goldfish stares up into the barrel of the revolver, he hears the trigger click, then wakes himself up screaming.

He comes into school still sweating, both headlamps on full, the lashes folded back. He spills the beans, miming out the whole scenario. 'Then I look up 'n' the revolver goes off,' he stammers it out, he can't get his mouth round the words. He's trying to tell me something. 'The officer! The man with the gun, I recognised him!'

I look him straight back, I swallow down, I know what he's going to say next, I loosen my collar . . . and mouth the name as he speaks.

'Crowsfeet!'

We stare at each other. It had to be, I knew it. A premonition? Whatever, that was some dream, more like a nightmare. His mouth was the big give-away. You couldn't mistake that cake hole, egg custard – that was Crowsfeet, alright!

Then the balloon goes up. Two police cars meander into the school car park, me and Goldfish are taken from our lessons and frog-marched into Batman's office. He stands there in his mortar-board, hands on his hips, and our little cold friend sitting on the desk. We try to ignore him, to pretend not to notice. But he grins at us, he waves, he tries to attract our attention, pointing, lying on his side.

They've already taken Crowsfeet weeping to the meat wagon. His crust went completely soft, blubbering, begging me and Goldfish to take the revolver off his hands. Practically giving it away, free of charge. We bite down and ignore him, we play deaf. Slippery with sweat, his eyes like fag ash . . . We look away, the hinges of his mouth still moving, but silent, behind the rear windows, between the bars. We stand there staring at the wallpaper, repeating our yeses and nos . . . Of course, we look at the carpet as well . . . We avoid sir's eyes . . . we let him know that we're humbled . . .

It seems Crowsfeet's implicated me on several scores. Firstly, as the look-out man, secondly as a fence, and lastly as the ringleader. His accusations growing more and more outlandish, desperate to save his own skin. In fact, the more he squealed, the more guilty he became. In the end he was just firing off blanks. It came as no surprise that he fingered me and Fish. After all the big talk, he turned out to be nothing but a snitch baby.

The only thing they could hang on me, was my miserly little lady's revolver, a delicate purse pistol, bought off Colonel Snow in the Melville Court flats. The rest of the stash remained unfound. But that didn't stop them coming round my house in the middle of our tea, and start sounding off accusations in front of my mother. A real inspector too, by the name of Sorrel. I got to know his face. He bangs the table and punctuates the air with loud threats, showing off to the two rookies stood by the door, acned and feckless.

He doesn't give a damn about my hollow pleas of innocence, as far as he's concerned my goose is well and truly cooked! He pulls out his notebook and reels off places and dates, he insinuates, he paces up and down kicking at the skirting boards. I had to give it up, there was nothing else for it. If I'd have let him start rooting about there's no telling what he might unearth.

I go to my room, pull back the bed, lift the floorboards and stick my arm down by the pipes. My hand comes to it ... a leather purse with a brass clasp – my little pea-shooter ... When I get back to the kitchen, old Sorrel's wagging his arse like a dog on heat, he bounces up and down on the spot, sieving spittle through his moustache. He can scarcely believe his luck; he holds my little baby up to the light, showing it off to his two friends. He plays Cowboys and Indians, he squints at it, scrutinising the craftsmanship. He rubs his mitts together so hard that the scurf flakes off like snow, in great clouds. He scratches like a hound, pulling at his collar, choking through the dust.

It seems that there's at least two positive identifications of me as the look-out man, and still other witnesses who have yet to be interviewed. Crowsfeet painted a pretty black picture of me down at the local nick, and as Sorrel's so pleased to point out, I'm on a sticky-wicket by anyone's reckoning.

'Yes, sonny, things are looking decidedly shitty from where I'm standing!'

He takes a sip of his tea and helps himself to the plate of shortbread. He puts one in his gob and then another one, he jams them in there like he hasn't been fed for a week ... He's not bashful about it either – the rookies don't even get a look in. They watch mesmerised as each butterfinger crumbles into his salivating gob. They wag their truncheons like two doting hounds, the eyes sorrowful, waiting for the crumbs ...

Sorrel lets it be known that if it wasn't for Crowsfeet asking for the break-ins at my parent's house to be taken into consideration, he'd be more than happy to bang me up for several years, at Her Majesty's leisure!

'The Borstal is waiting! And there's plenty of beds spare for any new miscreants!'

He smiles at me without his eyes, daring me to contradict him. He sniffs as if I'm something he's picked up on the sole of his shoe, then holds out his hand, reddened, peeling, the nails eaten away, white skin hanging. And I have to hand it over, my little shooter. I drop her into his palm. Then he smiles with his teeth, yellowing, tobacco ... He shows them, gritted, the cheeks pinched.

'Thank-you!'

That's Sorrel for you, never rash. He chews everything over twenty times, pacing up and down. One minute, it looks like he's come to a decision, then he shakes his head and he's off to examine the wallpaper. He looks everywhere for the answer, chewing off great swathes of flesh from his cuticles. He winces and swears, sucks his thumb and wipes a whole new film of scum from between his ears ... He gallops around the room like a gee-gee, then pulls up short in front of me. I can hear his cogs grinding. He arrives at his decision. He weighs the pros and cons, his distinct dislike of me, against the lack of any hard evidence whatsoever.

The fact of the matter is that he can't bear the sight of me. But for now, all I have to do is sign the document authorising the destruction of my little pea-shooter. He hands me the busted stub, he takes it out from behind his ear, still wet and chewed, the leads blunt. I have to concentrate, to sign my initials, then my name. I have to sign the release sheet, to have my gun fragmented. He peers at my mark suspiciously ... He lets it be known that he's by no means convinced, but that's where he's leaving it for the moment, for the time being ... Until further evidence comes to light!

He turns to my mother, a few hushed words.

'Oh no, the case isn't closed yet, Mrs Hamperson, not by a long chalk!'

He winds her up just for the hell of it ... so she knows ...

'No one gets the better of Inspector Sorrel, madam! I have my files, my records ... the long memory of the Law! The murdering computer, Mrs Hamperson!'

He looks at her meaningfully ... puts away his notebook ... buttons his top pocket ... pats it ... smiles grimly and exits.

When the old man caught wind of this latest catastrophe, he went off like a firecracker. He interrogated the old girl all over again, via the telephone ... He got on the next train, and no messing about, he was home within the hour.

'The police! In my own house?! Didn't I say so?! Didn't I warn you?! That council estate! My own flesh and blood! A common criminal! May God be my witness! Your son, Juny, not mine! Is that conceivable?! Tell me it isn't true, I dare you!'

He leapt at the carpet and shook it between his teeth, he bit himself all over ...

'Argh! God! Thug! Thug! Hyena! Hooligan!'

He exploded like a Catherine wheel ... He chewed the end clear off his pipe and spat sawdust. He hated himself, alright. His face swelled, and he came out in bumps; he withdrew into himself, and refused to speak to any of us. He went to bed and didn't get up ever again.

29. MISS HART'S MAGNIFICENT ARSE

When people are out to save you, that's when you've got to be at your most wary, to be on your best guard! They start showing fatherly concern? That's when they're out to fix you! They're weighing you up for the chop, making little signs behind your back. They lay it on extra thick. 'We're only here to help you!' 'It's for your own good!' A smile in one hand and a knife in the other; a sweet hello and a kidney punch to boot! The 'this is going to hurt me more than it hurts you!' routine.

That's the teachers talking, the reiterators of half-truths and lies. Their masks tell one story but their actions another. They mouth off parrot-style, the same old claptrap, the soft soap of choice and freedom! They're just setting you up, a sweet goodbye and a nasty shove towards the factory gate!

Us? – Just dockyard fodder, monkeys for the treadmill. Half-arsed believers, ignorant and untutored, barely able to spell our own names.

Those smarmy cock-suckers all got together and mapped out my future for me, behind closed doors. They even went as far as to call up the old man behind my back. They made various enquiries, 'til they managed to track him down at his offices in London. Did he know that I was insolent and a back-chatter? Or could he explain why I was late for class every morning, despite only living five minutes up the road? They laid it on pretty thick; none of my positive attributes got taken into account. My individualistic spelling and sense of humour never even got an airing. Basically, those jackals cooked the whole fairy tale up between them and fed it to him like cake.

It seems that my artistic pretensions had been indulged to the hilt, and it was high time I was called to account! What I needed was a sound grounding in the '3 Rs'. Painting and drawing were definitely out! It was obvious that I'd been spoilt rotten!

That was some event, those weasels having the gumption to lay it on the line like that, to chew the old goat's ear off. And he didn't just hang up, either, he actually chewed the fat with my long suffering teachers, and even agreed to come down and pay the dump a visit.

That was a turn-up for the books. No one could believe it. The old girl unplugged her ears. For him to travel all the way down from the smoke? To hold pow-wow with those riff-raff? – Unheard of! Besides he'd always voiced his open contempt for the place. His hostilities were well known; he never failed to broadcast them, ten times a day . . . a thousand times.

He storms through the kitchen, turns on his heels and slips on a cat shit . . .

'My God, woman, the place is a pigsty!'

He throws his brolly around like a geranium.

'Who sent him there in the first place? I didn't! I always said that he should have gone to a boarding school! This kitchen stinks of cat's piss! Can he read and write yet? Well, can he? Don't tell me because I don't want to know! Jesus Christ, woman, they're ringing me in office hours, can you believe it? Telling me of his short-comings! Of his criminal comings and goings! As if I don't know already! He's ignorant? He's ignorant? They'll be telling me the world's round next! No, I won't be coming home for tea! I'll sleep on the couch in the office – don't worry yourself about me, somebody has to earn the money, it doesn't grow on trees you know! Someone has to keep that shack of yours from falling down!'

That's him barking on the telephone, explaining his point of view, his situation, voicing his doubts. That's how he communicated, via the dog, direct, every two or three weeks.

But what really knocks us sideways is that he actually does turn up to view my long-suffering tormentors. Despite my mother's doubts, he really intends to have it out with them. He comes totally togged out in his Edwardian fancy dress, right down to the side-buckle shoes and velvet collared drape.

When they clap eyes on that old cockerel, they can scarcely hide their admiration. The most immaculately dressed and mild-mannered gentleman who ever greased their doorsteps … He certainly caught them right off balance – their lists of complaints and grievances dissolved into air like milk. They'd never seen such a fancy tomato, the brims of his hat flopped right down over his ears. He peeps from beneath them, coquettish; he shimmers like a vision, his waxed whiskers blazing!

The bunch of them become self-conscious, flapping their arms about like scarecrows, and staring down at their grubby hush-puppies. They 'um' and 'arr', they fall over each other in their rush to offer him the comfy seat.

Even I have to admit that I felt proud of him, stood there like a dummy from the wax museum. The old coot certainly had bags of style. But in the end it was his dulcet tones that seduced them, the whispering voice of command. Mrs Cooper went damp at the crutch, she was literally queuing up to have a heart to heart with him, to give him the low-down on his vulgar offspring. He had them gathered at his feet, crouching on their haunches, hanging onto his every word. They wanted to know if he really did own a Rolls Royce? And how many horsepower? And the leather upholstery? A real walnut dashboard? He totally bowled them over.

And the amount of fatherly care and concern that he showered on his youngest and most beloved son! I didn't deserve him, that was plain as day!

Look at how I repaid him: a no-good, disrespectful, gun-toting truant! It was obvious that he'd been sowing his seed on arid ground. They had genuine heart-felt sympathy for him; how could a celestial vision such as his good self have had any part in the conception of such an obnoxious toe-rag?

'We're sorry to have to tell you Mister Hamperson, but Steven's progress isn't all that it could be. To say that his performance leaves a lot to be desired would be an understatement! Not that we're suggesting that you're in anyway responsible, of course … You've tried, as you know that we have tried, Mister Hamperson … but the point is, is the boy lacks discipline! He has no concept of the word respect! He refuses point-blank to co-operate! The simplest thing that's asked of him, he goes out and does the exact opposite! It's as if he takes a perverse pleasure in being different! In short he's eccentric, his behaviour's abominable and his language foul! He always has to be the clown of the class, the centre of attention! He's ruining all the other children's chances, not only his own! And I don't have to remind you, that this is exam year, Mister Hamperson! He thinks he's clever, but he isn't; he's utterly selfish and a fool to himself! He's disrupting the whole curriculum! What I'm trying to say, Mister Hamperson, is that his exam prospects look bleak, to say the least . . . I've spoken to the career office, and to be quite frank, we can't foresee any career possibilities for him whatsoever! Who'll employ such a boy, answer me that?'

The old man hums to himself, barely audible, on the edge of hearing, his fingers to his eyes, he pulls on his nose . . .

'I'm in business, in London, you understand. I have many outside responsibilities, commitments. Of course, I take full responsibility . . . If only his mother had let me know the gravity of the situation . . . No, I blame myself, I've done all I could, but it obviously hasn't been enough.'

They shout him down; they won't hear of him maligning himself in such a manner. How could he know? It's not his fault, he shouldn't kick himself . . .

The old man smiles sheepishly, nods his head and dabs his eyes with his handkerchief. He brings it forth from his drape pocket with a flourish and lets go two mighty blasts on his hooter.

'Yes, I've tried to instill good manners and truthfulness in the boy, I've tried my level best, but obviously, somewhere along the line he's gone astray. And now I just pray to God that it isn't too late to make amends, for him to pull his socks up and make a go of it . . . I'll do all that I can, I'll put him into further education if necessary – money is no object, of course . . . I feel sure that if he can only get a few decent exam results under his belt, then he can get a commission in the Royal Navy . . . Now there's discipline for you, Naval discipline! A tradition in my family, you understand. The boy's grandfather . . . I have friends at the Ministry.'

He nods and taps his nose. His audience sit there spell-bound. By the time he comes to the end of his monologue they're all hooked, lead, line and sinker! They're head over heels in love. They stand and give him an ovation, slapping each other on the back and congratulating themselves. They all agree that they've done their level best, that the only other alternative is Borstal. They wash their hands of me! If I want to go to the devil, well so be it, their consciences are clear! The more they agree with each other, the more tearful they become – a regular waterworks. Someone must have spiked their tea . . .

Just as I think that they've forgotten me, Miss Hart comes out into the corridor and takes me aside. She looks me up and down and fondles my lapels. She tells me I'm growing up to be quite a hunky fellow. She wants to know what I'm going to do with myself once I quit school? The back of her hand brushes along her thigh. She pouts and flutters her eyelashes. I wish she'd taken my head in her hands and pushed my face between those great throbbing tits.

I get literary and compose a ballad for her right there on the spot, a sonnet to her magnificent arse. She's bent over the grand piano in the main hall, she arches her back and looks over her shoulder. I stick out my tongue, the cheeks of her arse each side of my face, and Flam! She farts on my tongue!

No one was more pleased than me when they finally got round to kicking me out of that dump. The teachers and their stinking pupils? Just a lot of nodding dogs! So, they agree or they disagree? But they still keep right on destroying life.

We hung around waiting for the end of term, for our lives to just dissolve and disappear. The man from the DHSS comes into assembly and gives us a lecture on how to go about signing on at the dole office, and the rest of us are given entry papers for the dockyard. You can get so full of other people's fine ideals and crummy advice that in the end you have to walk or puke.

30. THE MURDERING COMPUTER

One thing that you can be sure of in this world, is that nobody's responsible. The starving millions? That's somebody else's fault – let them eat cake! The H-bomb? They're blown to smithereens? – God must have dropped it! The chocolate vending machine's out of order? It doesn't belong to the publican or his wife, certainly not! Nobody is who it belongs to, and nobody deals with official complaints! It restocks itself, of its own accord, totally self-perpetuating! But somebody's pocketing the non-returnable two bob bits; if you want to know their names you can go to the devil!

You won't get a straight answer – from the shop boy up, somebody else is pulling the strings. The Prime Minister? Lady luck? Don't ask too many questions, it'll get you precisely nowhere! Or at least into serious trouble. Somebody's plotting your downfall? You should of shut your mug and kept schtum! Keep your head down or you'll get it knocked off. I should know, and I should have had the sense to keep my trap shut. It always suits somebody to have you out the way. The murdering computer has his lists. It's responsible for all manner of fires and deaths. He's keeping his records, working overtime, making his plans, creating vacancies and filling them. Your national identity card's out of date? Inspector Sorrel will come to hear of it, by first class mail. By Royal protocol! By microchip!

Who's responsible for the fact that I can't read or write? OK, so I'm grouching again, we've all got our right to gripe, but who's gonna take the can for my obvious deficiencies? My mother had a go, I can verify that much. I couldn't read or write but I was as bright as a pin ... came top of the year in 1972. The teachers didn't put me up because they said that I was too eccentric and wouldn't get on with the brainy types! So, I walk home and tell the old girl, she holds onto her iron and says nothing. A big basket of washing with the cat sitting on top of it ... No one has ever stood up for me, and that's why everybody has been free to take bigger and bigger liberties!

And my father? He washed his hands and absolved himself, he went to bed and wouldn't even say goodnight. No kidding, he felt sorry for himself. But me? I only got what I deserved, and I take full responsibility ... on the chin, like a man, smack! I'll carry the show for the whole stinking lot of them! I'm young and I'm strong, a writer with a backbone, fearless and brave!

And it's no good pointing the finger at the teachers, they'll shout right back in your face, righteous to the core.

'Nothing to do with us, madam! We did all that could be expected, we wash our hands of the brat! Go fill your pipe!'

That big bitch sat right at the head of the class, skin tight slacks and cavalry boots, the piss-flaps clearly outlined like two half pound beefburgers, the nylon jammed right up the crack! And the back view – an arse like a cow! Old Ma Cooper, my form teacher, a sweet talker. You go and ask her about my so-called education.

She spent fifteen minutes every morning telling us how bright and intelligent her daughters were, how they were in private education, rode ponies and would have nothing at all to do with a prize bunch of half-wits such as our good selves! We chewed at our pencils and spat ...

Me and teachers have always hit it off badly. Teachers and Thatcherites, hate at first sight! She picked on me in particular on account that I had the nerve to answer back. From the first day of school I was singled out to be made an example of, to break my will. And they're always the big swatters as well, hysterectomy jobs. That old sow might have had her menopause but she still needs the Tampax to soak up the pus! She glowers at me, shaking her jowls with indignation, she grunts like a pig.

OK, I apologise, I've gone too far ... I take it all back and I salute you, you glorious liberals, you brave hearts and freedom-fighters, you champions of equal rights ... The anti-pornography-freedom-of-speech-lobby! Go ahead, burn all the books! Fire bomb our houses! Prove yourself heroes! No one is responsible, nobody is to blame ... Either all are guilty or none ... Nobody bore me or raised me, they just fucked and washed their hands.

31. HER MAJESTY'S DOCKYARD CHATHAM

They made no bones about it, I'd completely blown my career opportunities. I was a waster, lying around in bed 'til gone nine, playing with my dick. The only thing I learned in school was in the playground – the school yard mentality, the weight of a fist, the exact shape of a knuckle. I was late, I was on detention, I was punched.

They didn't exactly encourage creative thinking in that dump, everything they wanted to know was already sewn up and written down: dates, figures, numbers, whole lists of them. They don't ask for opinions, all they want is agreement, and they've got stacks of it, passed down from generation to generation. 'The History of the Yes-Men'. 'God, church and private ownership. Amen'. 'Utterances of the Dead'. Page after page of the stuff. I yawned and stared out the window; I was a scally-wag and a masturbator, and the teachers knew it.

Like I say, the only option open to a kid when you got out of that dump was the dockyard. Left at the town hall, tall, Portland stone, a clock tower. You'll know it when you see it, check your time piece and hurry on up Dock Road to Brompton. Now, keep a sharp look out for her on your larboard bow, arched, brick-red, authoritarian; Her Majesty's Ship Pembroke. Say, that's some gateway, a gateway to inspire fear. That's it, the only one of her kind – the main gate – I'd recognise that whore anywhere, I've passed through her enough times.

I dig for my pass, rummaging through my overalls. I walked most of it, but then I caught a taxi. I was worried about being late. My mother installed that in me, an inheritance of worry and fear. That's some word: 'fear', it has to be succumbed to, to feel its weight and obey. She painted a pretty black picture of the future in general – according to her we were going to go bust and wind up in the workhouse, as sure as shit! We lived in the honest belief of our imminent destruction.

I pull out my pass and march in, one of thousands, a whole cavalcade of bicycles and cloth caps. That certainly knocked those old lags for a six, seeing me rolling up in a limo like that, bright as nine-pence. And them peddling in on their bone-shakers, heads bowed, spitting, to see how gaily the young come to take the sucker punch.

I show my pass, I queue up at the window. Then it's my turn, we traipse through under the arch and into the sunlight, ships' figureheads beheaded, grinning ... a tit ... Old Roman Nose, gaily coloured ... Railway lines criss-crossing, a multitude skipping across the tracks ... A thousand caps, hands in pockets, dark shouldered, a countenance of gloom ... Everyone disperses to their own little corner, their own little tea hut, branching out like the finger of a hand.

We pick our way between the cranes lining the dockside, perched on stilts, beaked heads, reflected in the basins: three of them, over a thousand fathoms deep. Frigates, mine sweepers, a baby aircraft-carrier and the jellyfish. They used to hook those poor fellows out with a piece of bent wire and a string. A pile of them drying out on the quayside, kind of sad, they were alive but hard to understand.

Then the dry-docks and the nuclear sitting in the mud, right there in old Chatham, smack bang on the river, part of it. After that it's the Channel and then the German sea beyond. That's the romance of a place like that, a place of beginnings and ends.

From the dockyards of Wales and the south coast. That's where my grandfathers came from, voyaging round the shores, from port to port ... 'til finally, coming to rest here at Chatham. The dockyard's what drew them. From pub to pub, from Luton end, way up past Rochester, to the bridge ... And then some more ... Curling round the banks of the old Medway, an artery to the world.

That makes you think, a basin that deep and still. Three of them in all, one thousand fathoms deep maybe, some said more. Built by human hand, lags of another generation.

They've closed the yards down now, turned them into a museum. That's when you know a town's on the skids, when the factory gate closes and they open up for the tourists. An amusement arcade for the unemployed, that's what it will come to, along with the rest of the world. Ker-chop! Right through the head! The end of an era. The most secure jobs in the country: Ker-chop! Poof! Gone up in smoke! The dockyard? It is no more ... The little jellyfish? The homely work sheds? No more! And those dunderheads used to warn me against jacking it all in, and now it's them that's gone, and I'm still here, ticking in my corner. If only they could see me now, they'd be smirking on the other side of their faces, they'd stamp their feet most probably. The laziest of them all, nothing but a pen-pusher! With the cheek, the audacity to still be alive, to have opinions, to think, to write it down even, humph! I ask you!

Even in 1976, stonemasonry was a dying craft, a trade of yesteryear. Like most things there was only the nostalgia aspect of it left, and even that can't compete with the television. Who, nowadays, has got the wherewithal to traipse round ogling at piles of old rubble? Tombstones mostly, ruins for dreamers, monuments to a God who next to everybody's forgotten.

I mulled that one over whilst trying to fit on my father's collar. That celluloid job certainly brought the colour to your cheeks, like some kind of garrotte. I wrestled with it for half an hour, trying to jam the stud in – another anachronism fit only for the scrap heap! I busted two nails before I finally got it clipped on. My mother kisses me goodbye and wishes me luck. She's always done that, kissed me goodbye and willed me to do my best. I'm not sure it's always been for the best, but somehow I've come to rely on it.

I walked down to the old Hook and Hatchet and had a swift half before jumping on the number forty-two, and even then I was half an hour early. I sat in the waiting room staring at the paint work.

On account of stonemasonry being a craft for stiffs, it turns out I'm the only applicant, everyone else is in for bricklaying ... I checked my tie and had a catlick in the bog before going in ... The dust in that place was incredible. I had to repeat 'stonemason' four or five times before the penny dropped, then the little panel of old men quit pulling faces at each other, cleaned out their ears, re-polished their eye-pieces, nodded and looked confused. 'Stony-what?' The one at the end dropped his ear trumpet in the confusion. It must have been the dust, little particles of it, a kind of cloud, from the forms. A few moths, a mouse maybe, right at the back, under a ton of cobwebs.

'A-ha . . . here we are . . . Stonemason! Application form B1226 thereof! Yes . . . yes, this must be the fellow . . . Are you sure?'

He spoke with his eyebrows, then he blows at it, a great cloud, little flakes, mice sized bite marks . . . it rises into the air like confetti.

I'm joking now, making light of a solemn moment – the beginning of my life as a grown-up. That's why I joke and kid you about, a little tease, pulling your pigtails. Forgive me? I say this because you have to believe me, at least on this score. That's the way I am.

32. STONEMASONS OF YESTERYEAR

B ill Cubitt was the only mason left in the whole yard, and by
all accounts he was on his last legs. A snout away from death,
an old one always hanging, a wisp of smoke finding his watering
eye. A hint of blue, glittery, a little tear, he back-hands it, a
path-way through the grime. He rubs his hands together, massive
fingers, flattening out towards the ends, the nails shattered. He
picks at something, but delicately, artistically.

'We're craftsmen and don't let anybody tell you different! You
are an apprentice stonemason: be proud of that title. We are
stonemasons and we are craftsmen! Carving stones is not a trade
but a craft!'

He wheezes his words, gulping at the air. Sixty-five? Sixty-five
going on seventy, he rolls himself another snout and lights up.

'If you don't have respect for yourself, no one else is going to have
respect for you!' He stands and brushes the loose baccy from his lap.

'Between you and me, it's a dying art . . . But keep your nose
clean, and who knows?'

He lays his index up against his great hooter, blistered, a
million dots, more like holes when you stood close up. He stares
out at me through his little china blues. Yellow whites, with little
strings of red. Then he winks it, the flesh comes together, and
there you have it – a wink! That makes me flinch, I jump back
involuntarily. I stand on something and nearly slip. I nod and say
yes, and fall over it, something white, powdery and hard. He
grabs hold of my arm and steadies me.

'Mind out or you'll wind up in the oggin on your first day! That'd be some christening, wouldn't it? Mind where you're treading, this is a work area, not a playground!' He amuses himself, he looks round for confirmation. 'Now look what you tripped on, Portland Stone that is. The mason's bread and butter! Portland,' he repeats it. He taps his ash at it. 'Portland!'

I look down at it, at the 'Portland', and try saying it for myself: 'Portland.'

'That's it, now you're talking. We'll make a mason out of you yet!'

He grins at me. I can't help myself, I smile back and have to stare down at the stone.

'You see them little shells? Shale!'

I see them, little lines of them, a couple of solitary fellows, and a big one, thumb nail sized.

'A real bastard! The bane of the stonemason! You'll learn about him soon enough, he'll blunt your chisels for you, don't you worry, shale? Bah!'

I feel it with my fingertips, hard, shell-like, sitting just up out of the face. Smooth rock, then a lump, a little depression either side, and there it is, triumphant, prehistoric. The bane of the stonemason: a cute shell.

On my first day, we were working out on the Bull's Nose (September, Chatham Dockyard, 1976) where the cambers connect the inner basins to the tidal river. There's a pair of them cambers, so they have the appearance of a bull's nose, if seen by a passing crow or any other kind of sea fowl.

It was quite a hike to get out there, a couple of miles at least from our works depot. Bill puffing away on his bike, and me trotting along behind him, lugging the tool boxes. He looks back over his shoulder. 'Come on! Not much further!'

He steers with one hand and rolls up a snout with the other. He did some famous zig-zags across those tracks, a real cowboy. Cranes trundling past on rails, and then you had to keep a weather eye for the quay, on one side of the basin. On the other side, the river, broad, expanding to her estuary.

We had the whole show to ourselves – the little ships, their comings and goings, and all sorts of sea birds. A family of cormorants, sleek, oiled, a thousand commotions. And a crane lashed to a barge chained at anchor, dipping in and hauling out great jawfuls of black mud. Keeping the navigation channels open.

Apart from losing a handle off one of his suitcases, we make it without mishap. Bill drops his bike and takes a quick breather. He parks his arse on a block of granite, pulls out his handkerchief and wipes his brow, he's fagged . . .

Our job is to re-bed the granite blocks that bed the counter-weights for the cambers. That's why there was a whole army working out there, removing and re-fixing. The fizz of welding torches, power hammers . . . The big problem, it seems, is that it won't fit anymore, the camber. After a million calculations, a thousand fine adjustments, still the little baby won't sit back into her cot. The consensus of opinion is that it is all our fault. Another two sixteenths of a milli-inch needs to be sanded from the surface of the granite block. Bill lifts his left buttock and farts. It's no kind of work for a man with his artistic flair. Exacting enough to be sure, but work for a skilled labourer, not for an artisan, not for a man of Bill's calibre, a man of yesteryear educated exclusively in marble. He spits his dog-end out, goes to his baccy tin and starts rolling another. 'I need it for me concentration, to help me to think.'

He puffs out a lungful and coughs. He drags it up from deep down and spits a dockyard oyster . . . Sits for a moment contented, then pops his eyes and spouts red, a great jet of it, a beautiful plume of scarlet . . . rich, deep, liquid. It goes up, arching against the blue of the sky. A look of surprise flashes across his face, then up it goes! The sun catching it for a split second, just as it reaches its apex. For a few breathless seconds it hangs in mid-air, then the wind catches it and it spatters down in black clots in the dust . . .

'Me nose,' he explains, and puts a rag to it, 'a safety valve, de quack tells me . . . high blood pressure.' He tilts his head back . . . 'Dat's it,' he tells me, 'dat's stemmed de fucker!'

From that first day it was obvious that the yard couldn't find work for a fossil of Bill's age. I began to get the drift, to comprehend the full weight of the situation. They were basically pulling jobs out of thin air, keeping him hanging on just for the hell of it, to avoid paying him off. Skipping the golden handshake. It would be cheaper to see Bill peg out and pushing up daisies than to retire him, and the yard knew it. As far as their cheque book saw it, Bill could go stick his artistic inclinations, and learn a bit of plastering! The sooner he pegged out, the better it suited them!

I started unpacking the tool boxes, then Bill looks up. 'Don't go rushing into things, son! We'll brew up first, have a snout, 'n' ponder it over.'

He dabs at his neb, red, swollen ... He studies the cloth, a beautiful rose ... a little string of snot. He re-wipes and pockets the package.

After tea Bill sets me to carving a perfect cube out of a lump of old rock. He has to check my angles for me, biting into his snout. He brandishes his set square and steel ruler, and squints at it. The game is, that if you can pass a cigarette paper between the edge of the ruler and the face of the stone at any one point, then it's fucked! My heart wasn't really in it from the outset, the little pieces of shale didn't like me, splintery ... You catch a crab with your chisel and whoops! a dirty great hole appears. Yawning caverns, and you have to start out all over again, re-working the whole surface. Starting with the most vicious claw chisel, right down to the smoothest sand stone. That made me sigh – the cube business didn't grab me one bit.

As it was, old Bill couldn't have been more sympathetic; he takes one look at the overcast sky and decides then and there to take the rest of the day off.

'It'll be raining by three, there's no point getting our hands dirty now. You mark my words, we're in for a deluge!'

With that he adjusts his cap, puts on his bicycle clips and cycles off. We don't see hide nor hair of him for the next three days. Each morning, I come into the tea hut and there's his empty seat, and not a word of his whereabouts. He shows up on the fourth day to check my angles for me, then he's off again for another fortnight.

'It's his blood pressure ...' the supervisor explains to me. 'He might come in tomorrow.'

Then his old dear calls in to say he's had a heart attack ... He's suffering mysterious dizzy spells! And then there's the nose bleeds! I'd seen those for myself, that much was true, I can vouch for him there ... His wife phones in, 'He's sick but not so sick. He's poorly, but he could pull through, it's too early to say. We'll have to keep our fingers crossed for tomorrow'.

The yard does its best to keep me busy, they send me out labouring with the brickies. I grab my sarnies and jump on the ferry for St Mary's Island, but the crew down tools and the captain refuses to set sail. It seems that the union won't allow me to lift so much as a single brick! It would set a dangerous precedent. Why, before you know it, they'll have any old scab working for half the rate! They put their boot down ... It was fine by me, I was in full agreement, nowhere in my contract did it state that I was to lay bricks. And besides, I was apprenticed as a stonemason, and what about the insurance angle? You only have to have half a brain to see the consequences, to understand the further ramifications, the subtler nuances.

After that, the department leave me to amuse myself. I borrow a bike and go off on little excursions round the sea wall. Out on the waste ground, peaceful ... just a few seagulls and these discarded stones, regular monoliths.

I pack a flask, sandwiches and a little bag of tools, and set myself up amongst the undergrowth. I take it easy, plenty of tea-breaks, educating myself at my own leisure, no set squares, no rulers ... just a chip here and a chip there. Red Cloud, The Reclining Admiral, Van Gogh without a moustache. I stand back, I screw up my nose. I stare through half-closed eyes and jam my tongue into my cheek. I chew on it, wagging my head from side to side, making sure, checking the effect. I stand in, readjust, bring up the claw, then the mallet, and whoops, off comes his moustache! A piece of shale, I should think, more like a whole bed of it. I look at it with my fingers, little pieces. I feel him ... Hmm ... That's artistic expression, The stone speaking for itself. Who am I to argue?

I just get myself set up pretty comfy out there, becoming one of the forgotten, when the yard sends word that Bill's on the mend ...

'He'll definitely be in tomorrow, or if not tomorrow then Thursday ... If he feels up to it, that is.'

As it is, he shows up the following Monday. There's a lot of ifs and buts, then here he is! He jogs into the tea-room; we hear him coming, little wheezes, the shuffling of the pedals. He drops it, then the door opens and in comes his cap, he flings it down on the table.

'Phew, I'm shagged! Give us a mug of that brew, Charlie!'

The other grey heads come over and slap his back. They compliment him on how young he's looking, on what a fine pallor he has ... Charlie puts down Bill's char in front of him. Bill lifts it to his lips, he sticks his nose into it and breathes through the steam clouds, and sucks it down in one gulp. A purse of his lips and he drains the lot . . . sieving the leaves.

'Ah, that's it! that's better!'

He smacks his lips and sits back, a little fart of hello and he settles himself in. A sigh and a belch: Bill Cubitt.

After tea break, we cycle out round the sea wall to take a gander at my carvings. Bill points at everything, he gives me a running commentary.

'That's where the Dutch landed . . . And that, over there, was the site of the plague hospital!' He lets go with both hands . . . he almost topples . . . 'This wheel's buckled,' he tells me.

I watch him go from side to side . . . and his arse showing, both cheeks. We dump our bikes by the creek and walk over to my camp. I lead the way through the nettles, I take him the long way round just in case we're being followed. After about ten minutes we come to the clearing. Bill sits himself down, clears some space and parks his arse. He goes for the baccy, then out comes his flask. He pours me a glug and laces them both with a fist of rum. 'Here, this'll thicken your toenails!'

He opens his lunch box and offers me a biscuit, plain digestives, I think. He breaks one over the packet. A little ritual, the scattering of the crumbs, they come to rest. He shakes it . . . little taps with his forefinger and in it goes. He dips it, and then up to his open trap: the dunking of the digestive! He swallows and narrows his eyes, then picks at something right at the back of his gob. He inserts his index and fishes about in there, he extracts it and studies the end, red and slimy, a fat knuckle. He looks up.

'Na!' he says, shaking his head. 'Na, we cut in marble! Michelangelo, now that's carving! And what's it carved in? – Marble! That's right, marble . . . That's what we always carved in, forty years back, going on fifty, in fact . . . You know the Engineer's barracks? The statue of Kitchener? The frieze of the unknown warrior? Marble! That was my apprenticeship, when masonry was still a respectable craft, when you could still hold your head up in a crowd . . . You had a trade under your belt, not just some run of the mill trade, either. Artistry! We weren't treated like second rate labourers in those days, gawd no . . . certainly not! We was skilled craftsmen, artisans in fact, and paid an artisans wage, and that wasn't threepence ha'penny, I might add!' He looked at me with his eyebrows. 'Now, when I started work in the Engineers barracks, I was thirteen. We didn't piddle around breaking rocks in those days, no, we carved in marble!'

He stares into the bewhiskered mush of my reclining admiral and shakes his head. 'Fuck mine, he looks a miserable bastard!'

'He's based on my dad.'

He's at a loss for words; he goes to speak, then changes his mind, then out it comes. 'Na, na, we cut in marble!'

He's telling me about marble now, harping on about the good old days, the days of marble and Michelangelo. He repeats it, reassuring himself, to make sure he knows who he is. I nod vigorously, encouraging him. But he can tell I'm not taking a blind bit of notice. The truth of the matter is I'm arrogant, just a kid, a regular know-all. Marble? I've heard it all before, it bores me. He rolls another cigarette.

'I'm not saying anything more than that marble is the stone-mason's natural ally . . . Look, everyone makes such a hullabaloo about carving a little bit of marble, but that's because they know nothing of climatic variations. Michelangelo had it easy, what your average bricklayer and humble cement-mixer will never get into their thick skulls is that all stone reacts climatically . . . It's like a barometer . . . a simple temperature gauge, if you like . . . The watchwords are 'weather' and 'climatic variation', W.C.V! Remember those three little fellows and you won't get caught out – W.C.V! Now, in England we live in what's known as a temperate climate. In layman's terms that means it's cold and damp . . . I don't need to tell you that, do I? Good. Now OK, so occasionally we'll have a freak summer, I grant you, but on the whole it's pretty nippy, you follow my drift? Now, if there's one thing a piece of marble can't abide, that's the cold and damp. It seizes up and becomes arthritic and brittle. To all intents and purposes it's unworkable . . . But you try telling that to masons of today and they don't want to know, they're nothing but a gang of glorified bricklayers. Masons? Charlatans more like! They don't know their Jurassic from their Precambrian . . . They haven't had the training, and where are they going to get it? 'Cos I tell you, it doesn't exist these days . . . They don't know the first thing about W.C.V. Of course, the marble's unworkable, we ain't living in Pompeii, are we? A schoolboy could tell you as much! Ah, but when the marble is freshly cut from the quarries of old Carrara . . . My, my, my, it's a different fish altogether, yes, completely different . . . It's a joy, a real joy – why you can carve it with a pen knife, it's like cheese! And it doesn't flake or splinter the way it does in Chatham, my good gracious no, it cuts like a mature cheddar!'

He sits back breathless, his lids heavy and drugged. I try and picture his cheesy marble, but then he starts up again.

'Remember, the golden rules ... The stonemason's worst enemy? Weather! Frost and ice wreak untold damage on the unprotected windward face, years of work and toil gone up in smoke! The finest most intricate gingerbread work, destroyed! rubbed out for ever! in one frost! Don't even talk to me about marble, I know all there is to know about that fish, and I've had it up to here!'

He glares at me and dares me to contradict him.

'It becomes totally unworkable! Useless and double useless! Splinters flying everywhere! Slithers shooting out in all directions! And they get in your clothes, down your shirt! In your knickers! And they're sharp, too! Oh yes, they'll stick in your thumb! your arse! the back of your hand! even your eyes! That's right, your eyes! Don't talk to me about slings and arrows, you can't go pulling one of those out by brute force, oh no! Not if you value your eyesight, you don't! The trick is, you see, is to pluck a single hair from your head ... like so, make a little loop ... like that, hook it round the spear of the marble, and then ease it out ... Slowly mind! ever so, ever so slowly ... Aha! An art in itself, paid for with experience! But this stuff?'He takes a vicious kick at my Van Gogh without moustache. 'Call it stone? Stone?! Don't make me laugh, chalk more like! Only not half as useful! Give me a good bed of marble any day of the week! Oh ... oooooh! Aw, my ticker! Give us a swig of that tea!. Oooh, put a tot of rum in there for me, will you, lad ... Aaah, yes ... mmm, that's better ...'

He takes a long swig on it ... and frowns his face.

'Is it dinner time yet? Did you hear the hooter? I was lost in thought there ... I must of dozed off ... Let's get out of this swamp! You go sitting around here all day, you'll end up getting piles! Did I tell about my granny? She got hers caught in her bicycle chain and went clean over the handle bars! Har har! Aah! Na, na, don't make me laugh, ouch! Poor thing ... Na don't, aaaah, heehee! Teeheehee!'

33. THREE CORPSES IN THE SUN

O ne thing we were never short of in our situation was
something to look at, that was our advantage, overlooking
the Medway like that. The tide comes in, it goes out again. The
dredger takes a tea break. A nuclear sub surfaces and comes
alongside for a refit, engines in full reverse, between the lock
gates. A magical moment. Waves this high! Almost up to the
conning tower. The little chap with the peaked cap and spaghetti
on his shoulders, he's having a whale of a time up there, only a
speck, almost out of sight, reduced by distance, the perspective of
the quayside.

We down tools and hightail it over to the other camber.
They've caught a sub in there by all accounts, and a big one
judging by the commotion! We drop our cheese sandwiches and
make a dash. And there she blows! Bottle green, whale-like, but
no fish this one, more like a submarine. Nuclear, according to Bill.
'Winston Churchill, HMS thereof, our Prime Minister,' he explains.

I nod, I can see her with my own two eyes. She's got to slow
down, to put the brakes on, or she'll be in collision with the dock.
The commander jams her into full reverse, a million turbos, tidal
waves as high as a house. A sight to behold. Those engines kicking
up whole riverbeds of silt, acres of seaweed. Porridge, crabs and
jellyfish, bits of reef even. We stand back and savour the stink.

'Don't get too near the edge!' Bill warns me. 'We've almost lost
you twice today already!'

He smiles at me to reassure me, I take his point and take a step back. Shielding my eyes, staring up at the conning tower, two or three faces up there, silhouetted against the sun ... A flag and a loud hailer, the little men in blue and white galloping over the decks.

'Look! Can you see them?'

'No, where?'

'There behind the Big Chief ...'

'Oh ... yeah, yeah, I see 'em ...'

A murmur rises, then a hush falls over the quayside.

'There they are!'

I hear what they're saying, but I see nothing.

'Under the flags, three of 'em! Drowned on manoeuvres.'

Bill wags a truncheon in their direction, three caskets, draped with white ensigns. Bill nudges me and I doff my cap and cup my balls. The flag dips to half mast and the bugle sounds off all forlorn ...

'They rammed their own minesweeper in the night, and dragged it to the bottom of the oggin. All they found of the crew were these three poor bastards!' Bill whispers to me, almost shouting.

Three black limos show up. The relatives, white-faced, shaking hands with the top brass ... A real admiral, humbling himself ... Trying to show the sincerity of his grief ... We shuffle our feet and look away, studying old Winston. What we're standing here for really has naff all to do with showing our last respects: we're solely here for the horror show. We sit back and gawp. What we want to see is the dead, the cheerless sun bleaching out their cold faces. We want to get as close up as possible, without getting contaminated.

The corpses are trussed up on the poop, round and bloated, a whole sea of water slopping around in their guts. The wind playing tag with the flags, teasing us ... We stand there, dry-mouthed ... I have to stand on tiptoes. That's me all over, curious as a kitten. There's a sudden surge from behind when the boiler-makers show up, and we almost slip in over the edge. I cling onto Bill, short, rotund, an anchor man. He coughs and stares out past his nose. Then the wind lifts the flag clean off the fattest body, but we see no mottled corpse, he's completely swathed in polythene sheeting. A howl of discontentment goes up. The crowd doesn't get its money's worth at all, not a peek! We feel cheated, we want a refund.

Actually, we're incredulous. We stand dumbfounded as old Winnie comes in alongside, the quayside crawling with men. One minute there's not a soul in sight, the next – bedlam! The air grows dark with hemp . . .

It's time for us to get lost. Me 'n' Bill pick our way back to the quarry, we catch a last glimpse, then nothing . . . We hear the bugler playing the Last Post, there's three minutes silence, then the hooter sounds for back to work . . . The dredger starts up again; the great cycle of life, the resettlement of silt.

Did I tell you about it? A whole crane chained to a raft, a kind of floating platform, barge-like, but square. Still with the caterpillar tracks on. He sits there in his cab, a little figure at sea, working his levers . . . Mobbed by seagulls, their screams fill the air, competing with his engine. It whines in agony . . . He's caught something big, it almost pulls him in with it.

We sit ourselves down and get a brew going. A couple of card games start up. We need the rest, it's been a hard day. Bill holds out his mug and I pour the tea. One of the brickie's apprentices sounds off, 'Did you see him? The fat one? when the flag lifted . . . all green and purple, like a stilton!'

Bill doesn't even look up, he just stares into his tea. I get the message, I look down and adjust my zip.

34. SPRING-HEEL JACK

The old girl gets me up for half six. She brings me tea. I sip at it and flex my eyelids. It takes her six or seven attempts 'til I finally quit pulling my dick, get up and jump out into that iced room. No kidding, sheets of the stuff, on the inside of the windows! My damp little corner ... I grab my kacks, climb in, button up and walk downstairs. She hands me my sarnies and I head off into the fog looking for my bus ... one last cuppa and I'm off ... Thousands of us heading for that gate, into the yard, my grandfather before me, Reg, on my mother's side.

The big joke is that once we've clocked on at half seven, we go straight for our first tea break of the day. We punch in, re-find our names and head for the tea hut.

As soon as I walked in there, I felt his eyes on me like two hot stones. I tried to look away, not to notice, to laugh even, but it doesn't matter where you run to in this world, the beatings will follow you. From the schools to the workplace, from the workplace to the High Street, there's always another berk ready to stand in, punch you down and rub your nose in the dirt. Man is nothing if he's not a bully. The bully – the flunky of the ruling classes. Unavoidable! Regular as shit! Panting at the leash, ready to shut up the kid who thinks he's different. From the school yard to the grave.

'So, you think you're better than everybody else, do you? Oi, you, I'm talking to you! Are you listening to me? Answer me! Answer me boy!'

You look down and examine your feet – busted plimsolls – you kick about with your toe, chew it over, ponderings in the dust.

'Look at me when I'm talking to you!'

You check the rubber toe-cap, peeling off. You kind of think you are, but no voice rises. The truth is not required, not here, not anywhere, not now, not never, not no how.

And so I try to speak the truth, to write down the facts, but they tell me it's not true, that I'm dreaming, that I've made the whole thing up . . . And it's a tough thing to learn to shut up: tough for a kid. You can't answer back, answers aren't good enough. Answers? Just words, abstract and meaningless! You just can't nail words down, they won't do as they're told. Man: the cunt of a million colours! He'll always have another angle, a billion treacherous deceits and lies! The harbinger of grief, grief for every sorry little soul, Amen!

As soon as I walked into that dump it started up all over again, the offers of fights after work. And not skinny blokes either, big lugs, twice my size! For absolutely nothing, just for having the wrong type of hair, for wearing a hat without permission, for having the audacity to be different. That's reason enough in this world of ours, more than enough . . .

You stride out into this world full of laughter and joy, then you have to think again, to check your step and avoid the streets, the work places, the pubs, all the great festivals of the desperate and the unamused. All who demand to be entertained, row upon row of the bastards.

I saw it coming again, like a brick, in the distance, gathering speed. You make out the molecules, particles of dust, red, flaking, breaking away from the mass, heading in your direction – that's the brick. Revolving, little somersaults of doom. The brick with your name on it, cast in a kiln. Definitely a brick – awesome, regular and predictable.

You think that you left all that petty bullshit behind you in the school yard. But here it is again, alive and kicking, heading in your direction. The desperate little breaths inwards, the taste of gob, that taste of fear, and it's on you again like a hot little animal, its tongue at your neck, like a dog, tasting the salt . . . the little hairs . . . And you turn and you embrace it, because deep down in our inadequate little hearts we believe that we deserve it, like we deserve suffering, like we don't deserve love . . .

And so we encompass it, the million and one facets of the human soul, the whole stinking barrel. Opportunist, vain and antagonistic, with vague feelings of good will, but above all crawling with fear.

There were some pretty snotty fellows in that tea hut, supping from their tin mugs. One in particular, a lad of the dance-floor, little blonde highlights, a hint of moustache, two or three drawings on each arm. Red-knuckled and spitting. He eyed me and dared me to look him back, sucking the sweet stuff between his teeth. A little trickle of juice escaping, blending with his tash – cocoa. He made plenty of noise about it, a great swilling, then he stared me down. I found my seat, but no Bill. I look around, I check his locker – empty!

'Has anyone seen Bill? Is he coming in today?'

I ask about, but find only silence; I go from table to table 'til I come to my friend with the grudge. I smile and give him a good morning. I accept responsibility – it's my fault, you see, I've got this arrogance, it oozes from my pores, it comes across in conversation, in the way I part my hair. I try and humble myself before him, I mumble and apologise. But still he reads it, written right across my ugly mug: superiority! I really do try to be polite, but I'm naturally lippy. I make unfunny jokes. I go on and on, repeating myself. The truth is, I just don't know when to shut it.

'Alright mate? Have you seen Bill?'

I have to repeat it twice before he even lifts his stupid face – he shakes his head, and eyes me with his sharkies. Narrowed, pissed off . . . he swallows, sucks at his teeth and spits.

'Na, but I'll see you outside the gate at four o'clock!'

I nod and try to laugh it off. He pushes his chair back and goes to stand. It's all bravado, he's full of shit. I offer him a cigarette, I've got a fresh pack of Navy Cut. I pull off the foil and offer them around, I take one for myself, just to prove that I don't think it's below me. Charlie shouts over, one of the old lags, he steps in and comes to my rescue.

'Did you say you was looking for Bill? I thought you said Phil. Na, Bill's been taken poorly . . . he ain't coming in, it's his chest this time . . . You'd better go see the charge hand, old Spring-heel Jack . . . that ponce'll put you wise . . . His wife says he's poorly. I shouldn't be surprised if he don't come back at all this time, if you get my drift . . . Not that I'd wish him bad or nothing, not a bit of it, but . . . well, you know . . . it stands to reason, don't it?

If you weigh it all up, I mean it can't go on, can it? Your best bet is to go see old Spring-heel, that ponce'll put you straight!'

I blow out some smoke, I nod and thank him, this old dad. Bill's come over all queasy, seems like he's out for the count, hmm . . . And I should see the charge-hand, old Spring-heel Jack. That much is obvious. I disentangle myself, pluck up my flask and say my farewells . . . I pocket what's left of my ciggies and leave . . . avoiding Sharky's eyes. I make for the door, I trip and open the door in one go, casual like.

35. GOD SENDS NUTS TO PEOPLE WITHOUT TEETH

With Bill laid up for what could be the duration, they decide to send me out to Upnor, on the opposite side of the river. A six mile round trip, over Rochester bridge, Strood, then some scenery, a few hills, a little copse, down the lane, follow your nose.

'Just ask for Frank. He's making a path to the car park. He's a miserable old git. Don't cross him and you'll be alright ... You'll recognise him, a bit of a limp, but don't mention it. Tell him I sent you. What's your name?'

'Steven.'

He licks at his pencil and writes it down, he labours over it, letter by letter.

'OK, Jack, tell him that I sent you, you know who you're looking for? Up by the car park, the van will pick you up, a white van, D.O.E. ... got it?' He checks his onion. 'It's about due any minute now ... you'd best wait outside ... We'll call you once old Bill's on the mend. So don't forget, ask for Frank, he'll be wearing a cap.'

I stand around in the fog, flapping my arms about. Then I hear it, the van, it comes round the corner, D.O.E. ... This must be the fellow. It looms out of the mist, dark, menacing, I hear the engine racing, D.O.E. written on its side, a white van ...

'Jack?'

How does he know my name? I look over my shoulder, but I'm the only one standing here.

'Hop in, son!'

I climb in beside him and we drive out into the pea soup. The man thinks my name's Jack, but it isn't. There's been a mistake, it's Salvador. We head over the bridge out through Strood, and then into the open country. I take in his profile, sideways glances, trees rushing past.

He turns to me, 'You alright Jack?' I grin. 'We'll soon be there ... you'll be with Frank up in the car park, I'll drop you off. What do you do?'

'Stonemason's apprentice.' He whistles and shakes his head. 'Na, not much call for it ... not up here! not these days! You'll see.' He shakes his head, that's twice he's done that. 'Stonemason!' He makes a little explosion with his mouth and whistles. 'Well, well, well.' He re-shakes. 'Not much call for it!'

I get the message. I study my flask, red chequered, outlined in black, a criss-cross effect. We pass a sign: Upnor ... We're going pretty fast, I can't read it, I saw the first letters a 'W' or a 'Q', then nothing. I was engrossed.

'This is it, just up on your left. I'll drop you off, you just follow the track ... Stonemason!' He restates it. 'Well, if that doesn't take the biscuit!' He nods to himself in full agreement.

'Here, did you see the box last night? Swearing? I've never heard the like! And they call it music! Here it is ... Frank will be over there, on the far side.'

I walk out into the mist and the van pulls away. I see an oak tree and then a little figure whistling by the bushes, draping its hand through the nettles. He clasps hold of the stems, swathing his whole arm about in a great clump of stingers, up to his elbow. Then he pulls his hand out and looks at it, close up. He scrutinises the purple veins, old, sinuous, and the little white stings. Bumps, hundreds of them, one on top of the other, all over his mitt ...

'There you are!' He holds it out for me to take a look. 'There you are! See?'

I look at this old man's claw, he opens and shuts his fingers for me, flexing all the joints.

'Ah yes, that's the stuff ... that's better! Now I can't even feel it ... it's gone ... total control returned! Look, I can move every joint! Doctors? Doctors? Who needs 'em? I've mended it myself, perfect! And I've been to a good few in my life time, but no more, never! I'd rather die at home in bed! Oh . . . Jesus Christ, my leg, oh, oh, oh . . . bugger me!'

He hobbles off through the bushes; I have to follow after him. 'So you're the new boy are you? Bricky?'

'Stonemason.'

He looks over his shoulder. 'Oh, you don't get many of them these days. There ain't no call for 'em, there's none over here you know, not for years! It don't look like you're gonna learn much does it? Oh, bugger my leg! Pardon my French. What did you say your name was?'

'Salvador.'

'That's it, Salvador, I knew it was, I remembered . . . This is the hut.' He pulls up short in front of an old corrugated lean-to . . . 'Look out for Ivor, a bald bloke, he's the charge hand . . . He's alright, but best to introduce yourself, he likes to know who's who.'

I nod and memorise it, Ivor, the charge hand. And then we enter.

There was a lot of hot air blowing between the old lags in the tea hut that morning. We approached it. We crossed the car park, walked down the lane, in through the front gate, then over on the left, a kind of pre-fab.

'It's a pretty good set-up we've got here, son.' That's the one called Frank talking, the one with the hand in the stingers. He taps the side of his nose. 'Remote is the word for it!' He retapped his nose for emphasis. 'Out of sight, out of mind!' He winks, that makes him grin, moulded, plastic tombs. 'Keep yourself to yourself . . . just as long as you're not caught slacking, taking the piss like, you're in for life!' His whole face shines with pleasure at that sentence, at his 'in for life!' His wrinkles beam in a grin of sunny contentment. Then he turns grey again, the whiskers standing out in the furrows.

'Morning tea break,' he explains and nods over his shoulder . . . 'Morning tea break in there.' He strokes his hooter, two more hairs, right on the end. He hunches his shoulders and blows on his claw. 'Look, it's closing again!' He slaps it hard, two, three times. 'Come on!'

He pushes open the door and hobbles in, I'm left out there, standing in the blizzard. He pokes his head back round the door.

'Come on in then, if you're coming!'

I pick up my duffel and scamper in behind him. Frank first, then me in tow. We peer through the steam, there's five or six of them, talking, discussing, objecting, heads in their morning papers. Ivor seemed to be in charge of the tea urn.

'I'm Ivor,' he tells me. 'What's your name?'

'His name's Paul . . .' Frank speaks for me.

'Salvador,' I say.

'Salvador?'

'Yeah.'

'Well, I'm the charge hand, you can call me Ivor. They told me you was coming . . . Everybody, this here's Salvador!'

The herd grunt at me, mouthfuls of tea, half-eaten biscuits. They look up, and they look back, lapfuls of newsprint. Old faces, prunes mostly, the forgotten and the dying . . . Upnor, right on the other side, a marsh at the back of beyond.

The one without teeth peers at me through his specks and dunks his biscuit. He sits watching it, blinking, like a pussy cat in front of a mouse hole . . . A minute passes, he checks his wrist watch and pulls it out. He manoeuvres his gob, folds his lips back and sucks on his nose. It wobbles, swinging to and fro. First go he misses: the sodden biscuit, steaming, waving around like a banner. Then he brings up his other hand and guides it in, most of it. 'Fuck mine, that's hot!' He looks round and tells everybody, but they don't even look up.

'That's Fred,' says Frank. 'Fred, this is Salvador.'

I say hello. Fred's lips pinch together and his eyes roll round inside his specks. He pouts and rubs away the juice from his chin. He opens and shuts his biscuit shoot. No teeth, just gums, then his tongue, and then the liquid, yellowish, and the dangly bit at the back. Finally, he gets it all down and wipes his mush on his sleeve.

'Bleeding lovely!'

He adjusts his cap and puckers his lips into a great wedge under his nose.

'Lovely! Mmmm . . . nothing like a brew and a dunk! I'm Fred . . . Paul?'

'Salvador.'

'Salvador? You said his name was Paul.'

'No, I said his name was Salvador. I should know because I'm the one that went and picked him up at the car park. Wasn't I, Salvador?'

I nod quickly.

'What do you do, son?'

'He's an apprentice.'

'Apprentice what? Car-fitter?'

'Ha bloody ha! Stonemason, ain't yer Salvador . . . stonemason.'

'We don't have no stonemasons here, son!'

I kind of smile, I do my best, I've always been told to be polite.
I try it, I give him a little grimace.

'No, I told him, not for . . . what?'

'Years?'

'Yeah, must be years.'

'Decades more like!'

'That's what I said to him, I said Paul . . .'

'Salvador.'

'Alright, I know, it's you confusing me. I said, Salvador, you
ain't gonna learn much, we haven't got any, we don't need any
and we haven't had one in years!'

'Decades more like!'

'So what did they send him here for, then?'

'How do you expect him to know? They don't know their arse
from their elbow – you order spaghetti, they'll give you bandages!'

'Well, I can tell you this much, he ain't gonna learn much about
masonry here. You done any bricking son? Brickwork? He can
learn some of that.'

The one in the corner looks up, dusts his fingers, and brushes
his lap.'Why don't you let him sit down and give him a mug of
tea, it's not the bloody Spanish Inquisition! Did you bring your
mug son?'

I hold out my palms and give him a blank one.

'Never mind, we've got a spare somewhere, it's a bit chipped,
but you don't mind, do you? You can bring your own in
tomorrow.' He places it down before me . . . blue, with a floral
effect, two chips out of it, and no handle. 'There you go, beggars
can't be choosers. Oops sorry!' He spills some of it over the
Formica.

The one called Fred puts his paper down, adjusts his glasses,
and pulls his cap down hard over his dome. 'Well, I can't sit about
here all day gassing, there's work to be done . . .' He stands and
looks round. 'Well, isn't there work to be done?'

No one budges, they make a great show of poring over their
newspapers . . .

'Ivor, you're the gaffer, well, tell them there's work to be done.'

The one called Frank, he breaks the silence. 'It's twenty past Fred, twenty past. We starts at half past every day, it's twenty past now . . .'

'Well, not by my watch, it ain't!'

'The boy's got a watch, ask him.'

They all turn to me, they look me up and down, sticking their pugs right in my vision. What I'm supposed to do is look at my watch and spill my tea, that's the idea. I'm supposed to turn my wrist and pour the hot tea in my lap.

'Twenty past,' I say. I look them straight back. 'Twenty past eight.'

There's silence, the moment passes and the one called Fred sits down.

The big story is on the front cover, that's what the discussion's all about. Fred jabs at it, podgy fingers, ten of them all the same length. Brown, nicotine stained. And Frank's claw, he holds it in his lap, and massages it. It flexes and unflexes, gripping and relaxing, gripping and relaxing.

'Well, there ain't no need for any of it, is there? Who'd pay to go and see that? I ask you! Would you? Because I wouldn't, I can tell you that much!'

'Well, someone's paying for it! It says here that they got forty thousand pounds, forty thousand!'

'Yeah, and I'd like to meet the silly bugger who gave it to them. It's a bloody disgrace, in your own living room!'

'Lucky for me I ain't got kids, but still, in front of my wife, six o'clock, it's bang out of order!'

Frank lays off for a minute, looks to the one they call Fred and arches his eyebrow at him, questioningly. Fred fiddles with his gums, re-fixes his glasses and pulls his cap further down over his eyes.

'Fucking disgusting!'

'But this idiot in here, it says he kicked his TV set in, two hundred quid's worth! It says it here in black and white. Here, take a look for yourself, read it! What do you make of that? Two hundred quid's worth of television, it's a bloody joke! The man's an idiot!'

'I'd of just switched it off.'

'Exactly!'

'Two hundred quid!'

'Two hundred!'

'Fuck mine!'

'Did you see it, Ron? Ron!'

The one called Ron hadn't seen it.

'No, worst luck!'

That was a joke. That made them all cackle, brilliant! They were in stitches ... I smiled, but no one looked in my direction. I look down at my lap and sip on my brew, super-sweet, condensed milk. Gluey with leaves in it, a little pool of them at the bottom. It made you suck your teeth that stuff – liquid iron.

'You like that, don't you son!'

That's Frank speaking at me.

'That's condensed milk, that is!' I smile weakly. 'Did you see the telly?' I shake my head. 'It's in all the papers! They only do it for the publicity you know, they ain't stupid.'

'Stupid fuckers!'

'They ain't stupid!' repeats Frank. 'The stupid one is the idiot who kicked in his own TV screen, now that's what I call stupid!'

There's a general mooing of agreement, and they all lift their cups and sup as one.

'Here, you know the glass, the bit inside?'

'The tube?'

'Yeah, the tube. Well, that bit, the tube-thingy, if that gets busted, it explodes like, and sends out millions of splinters for miles around.'

Fred shows us how small between his great brown fingers.

'Minute,' he carries on ... 'tiny ...'

'Implodes,' says Ivor. 'They don't explode, they implode, it's a vacuum.'

'Do what?'

'They don't explode, they implode, there's a vacuum inside a television, and a vacuum implodes, inwards!'

'So what's the fucking difference?'

'The difference is, is that it goes inwards, like in space ... that's the difference.'

'Well, that's exactly what I said, wasn't it, Frank?'

Frank smiles at me, he shines his falsies, immaculate, gleaming in his wrecked mug. 'The boy likes his tea. Condensed milk that is, son, like we used to drink in the war.'

I take another swig, bitter-sweet, clinging. I swallow through the scum and give him a half smile, timidly, over the tea leaves.

'A lovely brew that, boy! Naffi tea, just like in the army . . .'

'Naffi tea, my arse! Naffi tea was piss!'

'Army tea!' continues the one they called Frank, the one with the deepest wrinkles.

'Naffi tea, Berlin 1945, I was there, he wasn't!'

He nods in Fred's direction and leans in confiding with me, a loud whisper. 'Still sucking on his mother's tit, he was!'

'I bloody heard that, Frank bloody Bonnington! The only reason I wasn't there was 'cos I was invalided out at Normandy, and you bloody know it!'

'I'm telling the boy my war memories, not your fairy tales!' He turns back to me . . . 'Berlin 1945, you could stand your spoon up in it! You know, after the war, they had these German women out there, rebuilding all the roads. They didn't use men, 'cos they was all dead. They used women, 'n' big old things they were too, who could piss standing up, thirty yards into a milk bottle. Without spilling a drop!'

'Bollocks!'

'Thirty yards, without squatting, standing up they was. They pulled themselves out through the front of their boiler suits and pissed straight as an arrow!'

'Bullshit!'

'Every last droplet accounted for!'

'Total bollocks!' That was Fred, no teeth just the gums, the jaw shrunken up, the lips gathered up under his nose in a wedge, a real little pug. 'Total bollocks! Don't believe a word of it, he's pulling your pisser!'

Ivor shushes him, he waves his hands about, like a pair of old gloves.

'Well, he's talking out his arse, and he knows it! Naffi tea's the same the world over, gnat's piss! I know, I did my National Service, it's the same the world over . . . Oi Ron, Ron! You did your national service, gnat's piss, wasn't it? Gnat's piss!'

Ron studies the racing form, he scratches at the end of his nose, and re-reads it with his fingers. Younger than the others, not so worn out, less dogmatic, the face less damaged. He clears his throat, folds it in his lap, rolls it thoughtfully, then places it down on the table. Removes his specks, finishes his tea, and stands.

'Come on, Salvador, it's half past, we'd best get out on site.'

I look at Ron, then to the others, the faces in the tea hut. Ivor, the charge hand, nods at me to follow.

'You go with Ron, on the walls.'

I get it, I'm working with Ron on the walls. I get up and follow him out. The others, their eyes lift from their papers and watch us go, I look back then we're off. I catch Ron at the door and follow him out. The heat is left behind, we walk into a wall of wet fog. Little shivers, crisp, damp, rising, disappearing ... We follow the gravel path up by the tower.

Ron hops onto the scaffold, follow the leader. I have to keep close or I'll lose him. Mind your head and one, two, three, four, levels. Up the little ladder, to the next scaffold, then one more and we're there, the top of the castle.

One minute we're in pea soup, the next, bright sunlight. We break through the clouds and everything goes golden. That makes me rub my peepers. We look out over the river, a great carpet of fog below us ... cottonish, spreading out, covering the Medway, the whole river ... Just odd cranes and spires jutting upwards, and us on top of everything, so to speak, sitting on our perch ...

'This is the inner wall ... You see down there? Don't look down there when the mist's gone. Are you scared of heights? Don't worry, you'll get used to it, soon enough ... just don't look down, that's the trick. If it bothers you, just keep your head up, otherwise!'

As he says 'otherwise!' he makes his eyes slant sideways and downwards, his head tilts and his mouth comes open as well. I watch him, a curious effect, out of the blue like that, animated, almost theatrical.

'You see where it's bowed? We take all those stones out of there, like this ... See, it's soft ... here she comes ... that's it! Then you carry them down there into the courtyard. But don't look down. Then you lay them out on the grass in the same order as I take them out. If any of them get busted, you knock us up a new one, OK? Out of that stone over there, the pile by the wall ... If any break up, you remake them, the same shape and everything ... And don't forget to number them ... with this ... all in a row, with this code, that's the prefix and that's the number, got it? And number the new ones as you make them, that's if we bust any. You got all that? Good! Now, don't forget, number the whole lot, and any new ones you make as well, don't forget those, it's easily done ... Say if you don't follow me, OK? Good! Right then, let's get started!' He looks at his watch. 'It'll be tea break in fifteen minutes.'

That's the way we worked, taking out the wall, the bowed bit, then laying the stones out on the little lawn. Numbering them, and if any got busted I had to make a new one. Then after we've taken the whole thing down. We put it all back up again, the whole lot stone by stone, with a plumbline, so as to take out the 'bow' that was the danger . . .

In an old building like that? It could be risky, just leaving it to chance. 'Maybe it will, maybe it won't?' – No! We took the whole thing down and started again from scratch. That's the only way to treat ancient monuments: with respect! Gently does it, bit by bit, that's how we worked. In between tea breaks, between the fog and the sky . . .

And this boy-man used to come down from the big estate, he was the gamekeeper. A man, but with the face of a kid, freakish. And his mutt, the Labrador, they walked about down there, picking between the stones at the bottom of our scaffold. That dog was pretty bright, it used to drink my tea. It had a taste for it, all that condensed milk . . . Tartar, dark brown . . . swirling in tea leaves . . . orange, heavy with a whiff of iron, the spoon stood upright! And then the mutt would bolt it down in one go! 'Good Boy!' . . . That's where Frank's army tea ended up, him and his Berlin! 'Good Boy, Good Boy!' . . . Really black, that dog was, a Labrador, I think . . . friendly, good natured, with a taste for Frank's foul brew. As soon as nobody was looking, I'd tip it in his bowl, three laps and it was gone.

We could see the whole show from up there, we had a vantage point, the comings and goings . . . The grounds, the gate house, the walls and the village beyond . . . Then the lane and the car park . . . You could even see into the squire's estate, clean over the wall into his living room . . . And the gamekeeper, way over there, checking on his pheasants, almost out of sight . . . knelt down in the bushes . . . And his dog, the black one . . . miniature, in the far distance. I watched them larking about . . . That dog, it had some fun, pouncing, prancing over the moors and through the heather. Like a little match stick dog, so far away it made your eyes ache. It was some look-out post we had up there, a crow's nest on top of the world.

'You see, over there, that's the west wing, that's where Queen Elizabeth the First took a shit . . . When she came down here to open it – the castle . . . when she visited . . .'

I give Ron a blank one . . .

'Well, she'd have to take a shit, wouldn't she?'

I nod . . . Hmmm, Queen Elizabeth, not the new one, the old one . . . over four hundred years ago, over there in the west tower.

'There's a big drop, you hang your arse over the edge, and there it goes, plop into the oggin!'

I take Ron's word for it, who am I to contradict him? But still, it sounded a bit far-fetched . . . Plausible, but Queen Elizabeth? The First, not the Second . . . Upnor Castle? Shitting over the long drop? Hmmm, there's a thought, a picture for the imagination.

'If you see Ivor coming, give us a nod and we're back to work, OK? Try and at least look like you're doing something. Now look, who's this?' He stands and peers into the courtyard . . . 'Here comes Fred, the silly berk!'

I look down through the criss-cross of scaffolding, between the planks, out through the ladder runs . . . Below us, a little to the left, I see him, hands jammed in his pockets. His lid pulled down over his ears, hobbling between one wall and the next . . . That's him alright: Fred.

'You see, he ain't got no teeth, the stupid old bugger . . . Now watch him! Look, he's taking a bite! Toffee brittle that is, he always eats that, but he ain't got no teeth. Look, he has to gum it! He can't chew it, he has to suck it . . . He can't eat the nuts . . . look . . . see?'

I look down, I can just make him out. He takes something out of his pocket and breaks a piece off.

'That's it! Look, he took it out of his pocket. That's his toffee brittle that is. He can't eat it, he has to suck on it, he can't eat the nuts, no teeth! He won't wear false ones, the silly cunt can't even chew on a sandwich! I offered him one once, ham it was, he was sucking on it for half a bloody hour, and that was only the crust! Next thing he just chucks the whole lot straight in the bin, the whole fucking sarnie, disgusting old cunt! Look, look! Can you see them, down there on the wall? You see them? Look, there they go!'

I look to the wall . . . I rub my peepers, nothing . . .

'Not there, there! Look, at least fifteen of them . . . Ha, look, look, they're following him!'

I take a second gander, double hard . . . I flex my retinas . . .

'No, over there! They've moved!'

Fred cracks off another lump and sticks it in his biscuit shoot . . . He sucks on it . . . and moves on . . . I can see him now, directly below us. He sits himself down, and takes a breather. I can just see his cap and the tops of his ears . . . his cheeks pounding on the toffee.

'There they go! They're following him! Look, look, look! Down there, on the wall!'

Now I see them, a whole flock of little brown ones ... all in a row, sitting along the wall, their little beaks going from side to side, inquisitive, expectant. A little commotion and they all ruffle their feathers and set off, two, three yards, and they perch again. Chirpy little fellows, just behind Fred, to the side and behind. Fifteen or so of them, hopping from foot to foot.

'He's going to do it any minute, watch! They know, they ain't stupid ... They're following him, they always do ... You know when Fred's coming because you see his little flock first ... Look he's chewing it over!'

I peer between the boats. You would have missed it if you'd blinked. Fred looks to his left and to his right, then checks over his shoulder, and ... Flam! a great spray of them ... brown, revolving, glistening in the sun, mixed in with bits of spittle ... He pulls his lips back over his gums, wipes his nose ... One last suck and out they come, in the wink of an eye. One minute he's still gumming, the next, a great fan of nuts ... denuded, flying through the air, in a jet of spray ... hot and wet ... little groups, single ones ... smeared with juice ...

He shakes his jowls, puts his tongue behind them and pushes. He revolves his head, eyes bulging behind his glasses, and: flam! He unplugs it and they shoot out like buck shot, scattering from the left and to the right ... They fall on the grass, in between all the green blades ... a neat little semi-circle ... Then the flock descends, they hop off the wall as one and follow their noses, pecking, scrutinising, in amongst the blades. I could see their backs, about ten or twenty of them, a mad flapping ... the eating of the nuts ... A mad flurry of the little brown ones ...

I could have been quite happy on the castle stint, sitting on the scaffolding, admiring the view. But then came news from old Spring-heel. Ivor comes out his little tea hut and gives us a wave and a shout and calls me down. It's Bill, he's resurfaced, the van's already on the way over to pick me up. I have to bid my fond farewells, pack my flask and fire my arse ... I scamper about getting my bits and pieces together, an old lump of flint I'd been carving for my father ... plus my drawings, six hundred of them in an old binder, done during the tea breaks.

36. SMASHED-UP HAND

T he weather didn't exactly get along with Bill's health, great
Northern blasts, showers of hail and sleet. He came in for a
few days and just sat there in the tea hut blowing on his mitts.

'It's the damp, that's what does it. The quack told me quit
smoking and take a holiday, Tenerife or the Riviera . . . the poxy
Riviera! Oh yeah and what on, my bike? Steer clear of the damp
he says, and what hope is there of that, we're virtually in the
bloody river!'

'Maybe you should try the Med-way, as in Mediterranean,'
jokes Charlie.

'Har-de-bloody-har!' Bill sits down, muttering to himself,
removes the lid and dips in his fat fingers, wide, yet dainty, a few
strands of tobacco. He extends his pinkie and licks: a perfect
roll-up. I watch him, studying his movements; I take notes,
learning his craft.

'There's no point you being stuck out there in Upnor, in the
back of bleeding beyond! What they want to go and send you out
there for? That's what I ask myself, as if I ain't good enough, as
if I can't teach all you need to know here.'

He wags his nose in disbelief, flicks a match and strikes it, it
flares up, a little torch. He takes a lungful and lets it out slowly,
in trickles, wisps of blue-grey, he bites at the air and makes smoke
rings. I watch, mesmerised, caught in time, my chin at an angle.

'You'd best go out on your own today. I can't go out there, not
in this weather, not with my chest! But you'll have to do it by
hand, don't use the machines! Remember all that I've taught you,

remember you're a craftsman, an artist, not a demolition mob! Keep your set-square handy ... I'd come with you, only my heart.' He bangs on his chest and coughs, to show me, to prove he's not skiving ... 'Here, pass me my tool-wrap!'

I go fetch it, and place it in front of him. He pulls on the strings and rolls it out on the bench. He smoothes out the corners with his palms, then extracts something heavy from the deepest pocket, double wrapped in chamois leather. He cradles it like a baby, removes the swaddling and passes it to me. I take the weight into my palm; burred edges, grey metal, a stick, some kind of a handle.

'My club hammer, the big boy, four pound! My master's master gave it to him, and now I'm passing it to you, a real granite smasher!' I look at it mesmerised. 'If the barometer rises, I'll be out there and help you ... But in this pea souper? in my condition? It's not on, is it? I'll give you my hammer, and you can use as many of the chisels as you like ... you with me? Use your skills, handed down from me to you. Have respect for yourself and your craft, a noble craft, no bricky, no labourer, a mason! One of the stone, a dying art, but a right royal one! From Rameses to the Acropolis, from the Coliseum to Michelangelo, from Bill Cubitt to you – the heavy weight of tradition! Shoulder your responsibilities and bear them well! Here, roll yourself one, go on, I know you've been watching me, help yourself, fill your boots ... No, like this, thumb and forefinger ... that's more like it ... but here's the tricky bit, aha, folding it back! You've got to catch the edge, and mind you don't drop none ... That's the ticket, now lick it! Ah, now that's an easy mistake to make ... look, no ... turn it round, you see the glue? It's on the other side, you've rolled it backwards, never mind, it's easily done, here take mine.'

He lights it for me, I taste it, hot and bitter.

'Go on, take it down, don't play with it, you're not a girl, are you?'

I grin through the tears, I try to hold my cough, I take little puffs. Bill encourages me with his eyes.

'That's it, that's it, take it all down! We'll make a mason of you yet! Now don't forget your tools, and give me a yell as soon as this pea souper lifts ... You know where I am if you need me, I'll be right here ... I fancy a little buttered toast and maybe some beans in tomato sauce ... Right, off you go now and don't let Spring-heel catch you! Here's some baccy for later: today this is yours, tomorrow you buy your own!'

* * *

The door goes behind me, I take a few lugs on my snout, then ditch it in the oggin . . . I grab my bike and cycle out into that fog: animal-like, trundling down in great waves, fathoms thick . . . Icy, droplets the size of stones!

Bill sending me out like that? Kicking me out into the cold so to speak? I button my collar, and shiver in that other world . . . me, the bike and just a bag of old blunt tools, next to useless. For starters, the castings are too brittle for granite . . . they just shatter under the blows . . . And that granite, a little on the robust side? Expanding, blue-grey, with a grainy finish, more like metal than rock! Two and a half foot across, exacting, precise, within thousandths of an inch, impossible!

I chew on my tongue, raise the hammer high over my head and bring it down on the chisel. There's a blinding flash – the scene's illuminated in a shower of sparks, they jump into the air and fizz to the ground. My hand is numbed by the terrible reverberations, completely peppered with shrapnel . . . I can still see lights and angels.

To get into the corners, the recesses, it's just not possible by hand; the chisels just can't cut it! The hammer slips, once, twice, real bruises! I lose my grip, numbed by the cold, I flex it, I claw my fingers . . . a dull feeling, little bits of electricity . . . I lay it on the block, lift the hammer and bring it down, three, four, five times . . . it bounces when it hits the flesh.

'Dumb hand! Stupid hand! Hand that will never hold a woman! Ugly sinful hand! Unlovable and bad!'

I grit my teeth, raise the hammer and hit it again. I increase the power. I sob and wince. I teach myself a lesson! I show my hand what for! I let it know who's boss!

I yelp and cradle it – a little tear, a tear for the self . . . One second I'm standing there, swallowing the fog, the next, everything goes in flashes. I poke my hand from my tattered sleeve, blooded and shattered. I draw it up to my breast, I whimper . . . take my scarf and wrap it, precious, a fold, delicate, I warm it . . . I leave the bike and stumble over to the medical centre on foot . . . I see snowflakes, stars, little planets . . . and something else, ghosting through the fog, over by basin number three.

Laid out flat on my back like that, I lost what little momentum for life I had. You get to sitting down for five minutes and you never want to get up again. I took to my bed and refused to budge, point blank, for several weeks . . . I wrung myself out like a rag, to the very last drop . . .

When my hand was finally fixed, and it came to getting back into my working boots, I was none too keen. I explained and re-explained. I told my mother that I just couldn't work any more. Them and their cubes of stone gave me a limp dick! A right royal pain in the arse!

It's true, I couldn't face another rock. Angles bore me; inches, centimetres, templates and set-squares! I can't even stand to look at a straight line – I go cross-eyed. The working life just isn't for me. Besides, a young writer's got things going on inside his nod, other than breaking his neck getting himself a poxy career. A young writer wants to go out onto the street, to take a gander about, to get drunk and feel sorry for himself.

37. SKIDMARK HOROSCOPES

They gave me a place but no grant cheque. My mother forked out five pounds a week pin money, but that doesn't go far, what with the cost of living. I spent mine on pointed shoes and hair dye.

I didn't get in there on maths, physics and English O Levels, hell no! I got in there on personal hard graft: one hundred per cent painter and not a qualification to my name! I learned the only way there is to learn, by myself, scribbling in the dockyard ... Six hundred drawings in the tea huts of hell! I don't mess about. Just dedication, bravery and a natural feel for portraiture. I get down the information. The look in the eyes, I capture it. The truth, the emotion, I put it down for all to see ...

The first thing that you notice when you walk into a dump like that is that everybody's flirting around the cupboard doorways, especially the tutors. Strange comings and goings, the hoarding of crayons and pencils. The world is punctuated with clandestine nods and winks, with favouritism and special favours. A young writer has no say in such an existence; the world revolves exclusively around the cunts of debutantes.

I was on my knees with unknown desires, seventeen years old. She fell for my bone structure. Love? Love? Oh sure thing, love is great when you're a kid, when you're brave and full of bluster, and Christ was I romantic ... I used to cut a graze on my wrist for every slight she did me, for every word that she spoke with another man. And those little Chinese love poems I used to send to her, laboriously copied out in long hand. I used to read those magical lines and weep with self-pity. I was in love with all those sad little Chinamen.

I'm talking about two whole glorious months of acceptance, of knowing your destiny. She was like a wolf, suckling at my dick and looking me in the eye. I tried to lick her cunt, I just got my tongue in there and she pulls me off. She was in charge, the fuck mistress, and it tasted like burnt rubber!

I embarrass myself? Too bad, it doesn't matter. She wouldn't recognise herself anyway. People's ears only prick up when you turn on the flattery. When you blab on about the subtlety of their eye colouring, the touching moments and little affections. All the things that in the end amount to pretty small beer.

When the obsession is over and the passion has passed out of us, we are left with nothing but empty love talk and lies. Later on, it's the stench that repeats on you, and you start getting to be grateful that it isn't going to be you who has to sit opposite her, and watch her slow, relentless decay. Your life twisted, out of unspoken resentments, and stomach gone sour out of denial, until one day her bowels finally drop and she keels over. Another bastard's dead and some silence comes into this world.

But I remember her eyes, her mouth, her teeth, her lips. And she said that the next time she wanted me to cum in her mouth. Only there never ever was a next time. The next time, I was sat crying on her parent's garden wall for four fucking hours, 'til her old man comes out and tells me to clear off! That I've been dreaming, that I've made the whole thing up from start to finish! That I'm just a kid, that his precious daughter doesn't love me, doesn't know me from Adam! In fact, she was a liar. From then on, I began to thinking just how utterly scummy her cunt really was.

Next to the fact that it's a knocking shop, the only other thing you need to know about art college is that everybody's a genius. Every last little tutor, every last little student, absolutely no doubts. Hanging about like pop stars, checking their profiles, waiting to be discovered. They've no time to actually do any work, shit no! It takes every spare ounce of their time and energy sounding off, being witty and polishing their name plates.

I'll tell you something else for free, all this talk about inspiration, the avant-garde and originality is all just hogwash. Rembrandt? A plagiarist! Picasso? They were doing it in the caves madam, in the dark! But that doesn't stop your aspiring famous from gassing, far from it, they become ever more bumptious.

The artists are everywhere, it's the modern plague. Standing on their heads and priming their arseholes, anticipating the big pay-off, the oiled surgical glove ... In on every sales technique, fine art razzmatazz ... Clanging awards between their legs instead of balls ... Jabbering like a thousand demented piss flaps. They don't even come up for air ... and they've no time for pleasantries. Certainly not! Accolades is what they crave, and they deserve it by holy birthright! They've seen it written in the stars, in the shit stains in their underpants: skidmark horoscopes!

Between cutting my wrists and attempting the odd doodle, I was making myself look pretty foolish; it was noticed that I was embittered, that I had green hair and an attitude problem. I back-chatted the tutors, and forgot to put my hand up when I spoke.

I hung on as long as I could in the hallowed halls of the aspiring famous, but I was thoroughly disliked. I had no talent, but worse than that, I had no money. They wanted me out.

38. EROL'S STORY

The first time I saw Erol was in the main hall, along with all the other mugs, getting the 'you don't know how privileged you are' routine from the principal, stood there, greying at the temples, stuck behind his lectern, holding us with his gentle eyes. We stifle yawns, the dust settling. He pulls out his handkerchief and dabs at his eyes, recounting yarns about the good old days. Something about David Hockney and the great fire of London, seriously.

He smiles down at us, barely containing his anger. That's some hairdo he's sporting, the old fox. A regular bouffant, blue and purple highlights ... And the sort of skin that you stare into, looking for the rouge, the blusher ... the little holes around the nose, clogged and powdery – the truth.

We file in there, me following Erol. Then the lecture and the mug shots for our passes. I was right behind him so I had a good chance to soak him in, the whole persona. Nervous round the eyes, and the flesh, a little too much of it, babyish, and his fingers in his mouth ... You go to talk to him and his hands come up and his fingers go in ... He stands there kicking at the dust, a bus ticket? a coin? No, a piece of silver paper, crunched up ... round, penny-like but false.

'Watcha!' That's me talking, and his fingers go up into his mouth, his lips, heavy and negroid ... and the teeth, white with the gap ... 'Alright mate!'

No dice, the eyes averted, the toe of his boot drawing circles. We file on in, get our mug shots. 'Fine Art', that's the sign we have to hold up, and some kind of number, a code. You see, we're artists, all us kids, we've been accepted, we are the chosen: me, Erol and all the rest. We have to have the mug shots so's we can get into the building: no kidding, security, fine art! And we're the students. Grammar school kids mostly, all except me and the kid, the one sucking his thumb.

'Alright mate?'

Nothing! We trudge in, the pep talk from the silver fox behind the podium. We swallow it hook, line and sinker, the chosen few ... allowed into the closeted, hallowed regions. Passes clasped tightly, certificates intact. We lap it all up, all the boloney, acres of bullshit. Then we go into the studios, told we're men, but in truth still sucking on our mothers' tits.

And Erol? The kid in front? Hmm, a mental age of five I should think, or maybe seven. The prodigy of the retards. Erol the orphan, short-changed ... But the drawings? Ah, they like the drawings, that's why he's here; no O Levels, just the art. That's the bit they're always making the noises about, accepting someone on their work? That's not bad for these shysters. It made you look again, that fact.

After break, I go to the office and queue up for my materials grant, sign a little slip and they hand it over, coppers mostly. I pocket them, drop the lot into my purse and head for the pub. I avoid the studios completely – I'm intimidated by the size of the canvasses and the smallness of the men. And then there's the colours, hideous hues of blue, a whole oceans worth, and the orange, sort of marigold, fifteen square foot of it, mingled in at the edges ... a brush mark, turning brownish, and twenty of those canvasses, stacked wall to wall in every studio ... all individual, none exactly the same ... Acres of abstraction, gallons of it. Witty, sophisticated, yet understated. Tactile, oblique, but still maintaining a certain lyrical quality ... A beautiful canvas, painted piss yellow from head to foot.

I stare into the paint, dumbfounded. I look to my fellows mooing in the fields, totally at home, chewing the cud, not one voice of dissent; a bunch of nodding dogs!

I have to leave, to get out of there and onto the streets, to inhale the sweetness of the exhausts. I refuse to lift my brush, to paint another single smile, another frown, to ever paint again! I won't be contaminated, I won't be tainted! It took me time to learn my craft, my friends, and plenty of mistakes, but I don't get cute, I don't wait for inspiration, I leave that to my betters. I'm not looking for immortality or one man shows at the Tate. I'm looking for that little part of me, special, laughing and proud, momentarily mislaid, but sure to be found.

We don't need interior decorators, lectures on Morse code, abstract expressionism or the tactile qualities. What we need is to be spoken to, right away, a direct line and connection, bang!

I make my little speech, I stamp my foot for emphasis. I tell them what for. I call their bluff . . . I stand back and fold my arms, they mutter under their breath and turn their backs . . . 'If you can't paint, learn to draw!' I advise them. I feel my colour rising, I blush . . . They look at me pitifully, fix their berets on straight and stare back into their canvasses.

'Can I go to the toilet?'

That's Erol talking; he walks up to Canadian Pete.

'Can I go to the toilet?'

'Sure Erol.'

Pete turns and carries on sharpening his pencils.

'Can I go to the toilet?'

'Yeah, down the corridor, straight out the door, turn left . . . and it's just across the way. Directly opposite . . .'

'Can I go to the toilet?'

We look at him again, our friend in the woolly hat. He keeps going on about something, he wants the toilet.

'Can I go to the toilet?'

'Of course you can, Erol. You want to go to the toilet, you can go.'

Erol doesn't twitch a finger, he just stands there looking at us with his big wide eyes. Canadian Pete smiles at him, encouraging him. 'It's out there, go on, Erol, you can go.'

Then he does, first the patch, then the puddle. His eyes go down and the thumb goes in . . . the knees vibrating, little tremors, coming together. Ah, now we get it, he wanted Pete to go with him to the toilet; he didn't want to go on his own, he was afraid . . . Now we get the picture.

You see, Erol was a retard, five or six years old maybe. Six foot two, but at heart still a kid. He looks down at his feet, examining his puddle, warm, increasing . . . little wisps of steam . . . trickling towards the door.

It turns out that you had to look out for him, Erol. A baby in a man's form. His big oval face, thick featured . . . He needed looking after. That's why Pete went with him after college to buy Erol's toy cars, two of them, London buses I think they were, red Dinky Toys. So Canadian Pete goes with him, to make sure he gets to the shops and see that he doesn't have any mishaps on the way.

'Buses!' He grins from beneath his skull cap. 'Buses!'

'That's right Erol, buses!'

They head off into the night, Canadian Pete walks him all the way to the toy shop and even helps him choose them, two London route masters. Erol stares through the glass, he picks them out, then they go in and pay the money. He puts them in his bag. Outside, Pete points him in the right direction, sends him on his way homeward. He waits a moment and watches him go, to be sure . . . just to be on the safe side.

Erol, wandering, meandering down the street, plastic bag in hand, a woolly hat . . . with his brand new toys, heading in the right direction, at first uncertain, but then more strident. Canadian Pete watches for a few minutes, 'til he disappears into the crowd, and then turns and heads off up the pub. And that's when they must have picked him up: The Old Bill, the squad car cruised him.

It got to be in all the papers: Erol, mental age of five, could draw a bit, otherwise a pretty simple kid. The police went through his bag and nicked him on 'suss' for the theft of the red London buses, brand new, still in their boxes.

Erol, he couldn't read or write, just an X. That's all they wanted: a confession . . . So they got him to do it, Erol, 'his mark' on the bottom of the statement. They told him they was going to hang him, that's how they got him to confess to the stealing of the buses . . . They got the confession by telling him that they were going to hang him.

The 'suss' law, the toy buses, and the threat, the 'we're gonna hang you nigger!' It all got to be in the papers, and when it came to court Canadian Pete was Erol's witness. He was there, he saw the buying of the buses. Two of them, both red, London route masters. He could swear to it on oath. And the grey-beards who ran the college got some copies of the article made up and pinned them up on the notice boards. You see, they were pretty proud of their retard, their five year old prodigy, black and arrested. They made a meal of it. Their star student – but that was before he did it . . .

But then he did. Erol, he disappears at break time with his grant cheque, cashes it and goes and buys an inflatable miss, from Soho. And he brings her into the studios with him. Pink latex, blue-eyed and a blond nylon wig. Washable, durable and double guaranteed against punctures.

Erol, just a big kid with desires, five years old, but sexist. That was the feminists' opinion. You see, harmless little Erol walked up to one of the girls and asked her for a kiss. He wanted a peck on the cheek and that was bad, because he wasn't the sweet little black boy anymore, oh no, he was a monster, a sexist, and he was out of control! That was the theory. The hero of the cells? The star of the retards? He blew it! He asked a girl for a kiss and they carpeted him, they rang up his step-parents and had him taken away.

Erol? We waved goodbye. The kid who could paint? They disappeared him. That's sad. Erol: first they liked him, then he asked for a kiss, he overstepped his mark, as long as he stuck to the crayoning, fine, but retards having sexual ideas? Copulating? Asking for a kiss? He was too husky by half, the feminists were up in arms ... What about their rights, their freedoms? Those grey-beards collapsed like wet paper bags ...

Erol, our little pissing friend, the collector of the Dinky Toys? They stabbed him in the back! And not a murmur from the liberals. Hey, that's not on! The bunch of turn-coats! So, me and Canadian Pete, we go see the principle, the silver fox of the podium. We can't stand by and see them turning our little friend over! We get pissed off! We go see the cunt and reason it out with him, to point out the fact that the prim little miss who wouldn't be kissed can piss off back to grammar school! So lay off the kid, Erol! The boy with the coloured crayons, the talent! His little hope, all gone, all washed up, on account of the asking of a kiss!

'She has to walk through bloody Soho to get here! If she can't handle being asked for a kiss, then what's she gonna do on the streets, on the tube? This is London, Soho ... There's perverts out there, killers! The pubs! The factories! What is this place meant to be, a bloody church? Erol paints, that's all he's got! No choices! She can fuck off to university or some other fucking school! She can leave! Chuck her out now, string the slut up!'

We don't get excited, we state the facts calmly and don't really swear. There's only us two, stood there, speaking up against cowardice. We let him know our objections, we paint him a picture, all the colours ... real style, but the cunt's blind ...

We traipse back down those stairs stomping all the way, we kick at thin air. The feminists won, the Erol lost . . .

That's the tight rope the liberals have to walk. They want to support the retards issue, but the feminist lobby is the loudest! They smile at everybody, they nod, they play sympathetic, but when it comes down to putting their jobs on the line, they wouldn't say boo to a goose. High principles are all very well, but they had their mortgages to consider. That's sad, our little piss-pot had to go, he outstayed his welcome. He wanted a kiss, but he scared the girls. Too threatening . . .

Five years old, maybe six, big lips and a woolly hat. He had the art but lacked the manners, the education . . . the formalities . . . The big black kid, the Erol? We didn't see him again.

39. LITTLE SHEILA

The art colleges? I don't even like to talk of them, but I do, begrudgingly, just to set the record straight. To get my views across, to set them down on paper so posterity knows that there was one, at least, a lone objector, mouse-like, squeaking in the distance.

I walk out onto Charing Cross Road, take a gulp of carbon monoxide, go down on my humble knees and beg for forgiveness. For all sins past and present. I pick up an old bus ticket and pocket it, always the artist . . . I'm joking now, I quit. I arrange to meet Canadian Pete for a coffee at the Polo cafe.

'Eleven thirty, little Sheila will be there . . . she's fourteen, still at school!' I'll tell him any old boloney, just to watch his face move, purely to string him a line. 'She finishes geography at eleven, so she'll be there by twenty past.'

He nods his head, his eyes question me but he nods anyway, the big lug. I have to look away, I can't bear anyone believing a lie.

I stand around on Cambridge Circus waiting for a car crash . . . I pace up and down with my eyes closed . . . I play blind . . . A bus just misses me, I trip off the curb and see him just in time . . . No one cares in this great city of ours. A young artist could starve, could die under the wheels of a bus, and nobody would give a tuppenny damn!

We just hold onto our own cocks and fight our corner. I spent my whole youth looking for exits, for dodges and a way out . . . anything to negate the stinking boss man and his poxy clock. And

here I am, a young writer, down on my arse ... living on a fiver
a week. Like all the greats, as brave as a Hamsun! As irrepressible
as a Fante! A lover of man and beast and good red herring! I drag
a match on the pavement between my legs and light up. I pull out
the smoke and study my fingernails; a Henry Chinaski with a
thirst for whisky and a dick like an iron poker! I puff out the
smoke and study my fingernails ... I adjust my hat, and here
comes little Sheila, plaits flailing and her school satchel slung over
her shoulder. I stand and we kiss, she takes my arm and we walk
up into Soho. We go via the back alleyways; she pulls a half bottle
out of her satchel. I take a nip of my father's poison and we go in.

'Little Sheila, Canadian Pete, Canadian Pete, little Sheila.'

I do the introductions, we sit and drink coffee ... Sheila lights
up and puffs the smoke out. Anorexic, big knees and her skin's
got a grainy feel to it. Her back's like a fish bone, every rib and
vertebrae visible. I have to feed her up, to get a square meal down
her, something to eat between the cigarettes she's always lunging
on.

'How was your geography class?'

She looks to Pete, I stir my coffee and nod.

'We finished early today, Mrs Millington was bilious.'

'This isn't hot, is yours hot? Mine's virtually cold ... here taste
that ...'

I pass my cup to Pete. I don't prejudge him, it isn't my way, at
least then it wasn't. You see, I needed a friend, but it's hard to
trust, to become intimate in a world that's been so harsh. And no
matter how obnoxious I've been, I don't believe that I deserved
every beating that came my way. I would've liked some help, a
little understanding.

Pete wants to know what subjects Sheila's taking. I divert the
conversation back to the kid Erol, the necessity of Kurt Schwit-
ters, berets and a particular brand of shoes. I tell them I've got to
go to the toilet. I've got a bit of a stiffy. I explain that I have to
leave, that I've got an appointment, that I'll see them later.

I slip out without them noticing, I offer to pay for the coffees,
but they're engrossed ... I walk out past the Gaggia machine, tip
my hat to the proprietor and exit. I take a right, then right again.
I skip onto the pavement – two taxis, in unison, that was close,
black and foreboding. The faces at the window ... Berwick St,
between the fruit and veg stalls, I walk on and on, walking funny
on account of my stiff cock.

I search out the lowest clip joints. I drag my feet through the grime, I crawl on my hands and knees. Then I see this arse up ahead, it talks to me: 'Hello', it says. I can scarcely believe my ears, and then it says it again: 'hello' . . . I put my head down and push through the crowds. Then a tit waves to me, it blows a kiss. I ignore it and scamper along after the arse. I have to outstrip the devil and his wife as well . . . to get in front, to measure up it's unholy mug, to know the truth.

I never want to be left behind in this world. I need to see everything in close-up, in the minutest detail. To shake hands with all that I most fear. Call it my artistic nature, if you like . . . I'm pushed aside, I'm slapped and trampled on . . . I want to destroy the legs, to stamp on the heels of the rich and the poor alike, to wave goodbye, to be lost in the crowds. I can never catch up, I'm done for.

'Six films, two pounds! Step right this way, sir . . . Two pounds, one fifty to our regulars! Cut price, six films!'

He winks at me with his one good eye . . . Turkish, five foot one . . . I dig into my pocket and hand him my shrapnel. I get my reduction, he can see that I'm a hard-up connoisseur of the erotic arts . . . He fingers my ticket stub, licks his lips and passes it to me, he steps aside and ushers me through the back of the shop. Up a flight of rickety stairs and I stumble into that hot pit. I trip as I enter . . . Coughing and wheezing, the smoke of a hundred cigarettes and the shining pates of twenty-two men. I stumble about in that night, the projector clattering away to itself . . . They shout at me, that mob, with no manners whatsoever.

I edge my way a bit at a time, feeling for a seat, then my head accidentally blocks the screen. I duck and weave, my companions hissing at me, I mutter my apologies, I really did do my best to explain, but my honesty fell on deaf ears. I had to find a seat all by myself, in the dark. The contrast was too much, I needed time to adjust, but that didn't get me any sympathies. And you have to watch where you put your hands in those shanties. I squint and stumble.

An almighty bang on the head, that's what my crummy childhood amounted to. That's what did it for me. Ten years in the sickest schools in Kent, in the whole country if you like. Absolutely the worst. Buggery and corruption from the Headmaster down! Education in a brothel! Not so much time for innocence or childhood games, not with my background. My childhood ended some time around my ninth birthday, shamed into sex, obedience and fear.

Us kids built this camp over the back, we take off our clothes and run around screaming, then roll down this grassy bank with our little stiff dicks. You could feel the grass on your willy as you rolled over and over, dig-a-dig-dig! dig-a-dig-dig! right the way down to the bottom of the slope. Then some big kids showed up and we had to scarper. No more fun and games. We had to leg it and cover up our dicks! 'Hide it, get it out of sight!' And my father walking round bollock naked in the bathroom, daring us to exist . . . That's some God, who makes us piss and shit in shame! Secretive, that's what we become, secretive and ashamed, ashamed of our little dicks.

The projector was clattering, in truth I was afraid. I flex my retinas, the screen in the distance . . . seen through the smoke. A movement of flesh. There's a hair in the gate.

I unbutton it, light up and swallow. I feel my brain pushing in behind my eyes. I want to disappear . . .

Hollywood can't hold a candle to those characters, cocks, cunts and agony. They've exposed the lie of the silver screen. Tinsel Town: pure hokum! Just one giant yawn from start to finish! The biggest scam of the century! The camera that lies, that duped a whole generation and three more besides!

Go ask my mother, she's still alive, she can tell you for herself, in her own words. Those flattering camera angles fooled every-body, a special effect of light and sound. And somehow, no matter what, there's always a piece of heaven, waiting for the winners, that touches you right where it shouldn't be allowed to touch you, and it chokes a man up . . . That's when every sweet little country girl got herself stitched up with a belly-ful of kids and romantic notions.

'Oh, we believed in it!' my mother tells me. 'We believed in it, alright, we fell for it hook, line and sinker!' She shakes her head in disbelief, swigging from her can of Guinness.

And now everybody's running around as if they're on TV, starring roles even! Stars? More lies, incidentally. The actors can't act so let's see what they're really made of – pot bellies and arses round their ankles! Ten cartloads of descended tits – let's see the colour of their dirty juice! Hideous grimaces, nose jobs and insertions. Let's watch them rough each other up a bit, with real blood! That would be a little bit more like entertainment, heads on sticks, a bucket full of entrails maybe? Oh yes, at the least, at the very least! Then we'd really be seeing something, we'd know that we were getting our money's worth!

I sit up the back rolling bogeys and sucking my teeth. All that vile sucking humanity, right up next to my eyes, I feel it against my face, but still I don't know if I'm alive.

I feel my dick inside my trouser leg. I flex it against the material, trying to wank it off without touching it. I sweat and I writhe. I twitch and stamp my foot. It sings through me, I grip the arm of the chair so tight that the wood cracks. My mouth goes dry. I take a swig of Scotch and the juice goes down my leg.

A half bottle of Scotch and easy love, cheaper than any whore. A little squirt onto the dust and fag ash of the floor, and it's all over, back out into the hard daylight, bang! like a dust cart! I adjust my hat, squint my eyes and take another nip.

I'm drunk, don't listen to me, turn on your tellies and forget. You see it's gone, they've closed up shop. Soho? It doesn't exist! Bistros and boutiques, new developments, the civilised face of man . . . The heart is rancid, the bowels are boiling, but the face must keep its composure . . . Everything will happen in the end, and it will happen behind locked doors . . . Now, go home and talk with your loved ones. No more fine art erotica, it's been ex-ed, not fit for human consumption! It'll turn us all wacky, we'll go blind. Heartache, cock-ache, balls-ache, cunt-ache, clap and crabs! We're all unclean, sexist and stark-raving-bonkers! The next thing you know, they'll be forcing us to talk to each other, and abuse won't be good enough, polite conversation only!

And I walk round the streets and, apparently, I require nothing. I stare in past the shop windows, my face pale and indistinct in the reflections, ghost-like, and I walk on, part of the crowd, depraved, prejudged and boycotted . . . But still the flags wave, the flags of the righteous and the good, at the head of every parade, upholding and denouncing. It's an ugly thing, trying to be a bog-man; the dignity and beauty only grow with distance. The voyeur is the only one who's got a chance, a safe seat, for the time being.

It didn't take long for my tutor to start showing his fatherly concern. He barges in and starts sounding off about my unholy absences, my lack of education, and my crummy portraits in particular! Figurative painting is one thing, but drawing pictures in front of the other students? It looked bad, my avant-garde attitudes had been noted.

He sneaks up behind me, that grey-beard, and almost makes me spill my coffee.

'Hello stranger.'

Ah, a joker, and now he's cornered me, tracked me down so to speak. I sip at my rancid brew and stare him back.

'We haven't seen your grubby little face much this term, have we? So, to what do we owe the pleasure? This is no way to go about getting a degree, you know?'

I look out the window. 'What would I want a degree for? Just so I can teach people to get a degree to teach people to get a degree, like you do?!'

'Then what the hell are you doing here?'

'Getting a fiver a week, you?'

'What I earn is neither here nor there! Do you think I enjoy coming in here and seeing empty studio spaces?'

I look to the cells of my playmates, to all those beautiful white walls – there's empty studios galore, so what's he want to go picking on me for? Just a kid, ten and a half stones. It doesn't look like he's been missing too many lunches, an arse like a cow and three chins on him. He stares up at the skylight, searching, his tongue finds one, he comes over all diplomatic.

'Look, just don't rock the boat, alright? Why give yourself a hard time? At least pretend to be working! You know your trouble? You think you're so much better than everyone else, don't you? If you're so clever, why don't you have the courage to leave? If you despise us all so much, if you're so bloody superior, have the courage of your convictions!'

'I'll tell you what, I'll leave if you resign! You're always crying about what a waste of time it is you coming in here and half the studios are empty ... Well, you resign and I'll leave!'

His little eyes dart into flame, he takes off his specks and polishes them.

'What I choose to do is not the issue!'

'Oh, so you'd teach for free, would you? It's a vocation, not fifteen quid an hour that drags your fat arse in here?'

Now I've torn it, I've forgotten the rules and gone and sworn at sir. He licks his lips and replaces his specks.

'I'll remind you that there are plenty of other students who'd give their eye teeth to have half the opportunities you're squandering! Who'd be more than pleased to take your place, put in some hard work and get a decent degree result under their belts!'

I look at him and swallow, I feel the blood in my ears . . . I go to speak, I make voice . . .

'And there's plenty who wouldn't mind your job 'n' all . . . You wander in here gassing about fuck all! You sound off, go to lunch, a few beers, and that's your day over with, isn't it? The only reason Erol got the boot is because you lot knock off early, so there's no one left here to lock up and cover your arse, because you're too tight to take a fucking pay cut! And you know it! It's all sewn up, isn't it, time to piss off back down the boozer again . . . And then you come in here whinging that there's no one in the studios. My heart bleeds, it really does! If you don't like the job, then resign!'

He puts his fingertips together and closes his eyes; he goes to speak, he coughs, and mutters in his beard.

'My mortgages . . . my work . . . my studio . . .'

'Mortgages?'

'Yes, two of them, in Clapham . . . my house and my studio . . .'

'Well, you shouldn't have been so greedy then, should you!'

He purples up, rising a little blush; he explodes in a spray of spittle . . .

'OK, I've warned you, don't rock the boat, punk, or you'll be out on your ear! Get it?'

I've ruffled his feathers, easily done mind. He puffs himself up and gobbles like a turkey.

'Portraits? Portraits? Where the hell do you think you're living, the nineteenth century? So, abstract expressionism isn't good enough for you! Well, I shit on you! If you think that I enjoy coming into this arsehole college day in, day out and playing wet nurse to a bunch of pimply-faced students, you're sorely mistaken! Give me a break . . . I've got better things to do with my time! I could have been someone, you know. My pictures sell. Sell! Sell! Sell! I sell them all! I was lionised. I am someone!'

I rinse my ears out, I stick in a finger and try to unplug the wax. I hear him on and off, intermittent.

'Obviously, I'm wasting my time pretending I can teach any of you pasty-faced pillocks the first thing about composition! You know it all already, don't you? You've seen the whole fucking world from your bedroom windows and you're sick of it, you want to pull the curtains and go back to bed!'

Now he's talking my language! This grey-beard knows his Sermon, he's got it all rehearsed.

'Fifteen pounds an hour? Can you believe it? After how many years is it? Ten, twenty? How's that going to pay the rent in central London? Don't make me laugh! Fifteen pounds? A pittance! 'But for my art and my family, I will endure 'til the end': Egon Shiele.'

He delivers his quote, he waits for the applause to subside, walking in little circles, winding himself up into new crescendos. Then he turns on me in a hot whisper.

'Did you see the colour supplement last weekend? My 'Orange on Orange' ... Did you see it? A feast for the eyes, tangerine, buttery gold, all the hues ... Mind, the colour reproduction wasn't all that it could have been, but what can you expect? They're not artists, they're printers, mere machines really. I offered to mix the inks myself, but would they let me? Would they let me, hell! I told them, 'take the slides in a natural light or you're bound to flatten out the magenta.' Argh! Such imbeciles! But did they listen? Shit, did they!'

He pulls at his whiskers and prances on one foot. 'I'll tell you what I could use right now, a drink! What this shithole really needs is a bar, bottles stacked to the ceiling, with dancing girls in all the bubbles! Move the whole fucking show two hundred yards into Soho and throw open all the doors! A tit in every cocktail! Raspberry! Mmmmm ... I need a glass of milk!'

40. TOILET WALL HUMOUR

It wasn't easy moving a dump like that; there's the plumbing and the wiring for a start. It takes the best part of the morning for the contractors to jack up the foundations. They wind her up, bit by bit, tottering on her foundations. A piece of loose masonry crashes down on Charing Cross Road and explodes like a bag of sherbet.

All nine floors staggering, she sways and shimmies like a belly dancer ... First the fire escape collapses, it becomes entangled in a passing bus and is dragged up the street clanging out like a euphonium, a whole steel band, each rail with its own special note. Our biggest single problem is the traffic, we bump an articulated lorry and all nine floors lurch like a stack of playing cards ... The doors burst open and the air rushes through her like a bellows, blowing like a concertina, a whole gale of wretched doodles from one end of the corridor to the other! She lifts her petticoats and scuttles up Wardour Street, then crouches for a piss next to the church, it's all she can manage ... She makes it inch by inch ... She dips in her toes, dainty like. It takes two hours before she finally stops shaking her tits.

We throw our bowlers up in the air and light a bonfire. We rip up all the passes and piss on them from the gantries. A gang of road workers calls in from the Blue Posts, dragging the bar fittings behind them, spittoons, foot rails and beer pumps. We scream and holler like fish wives. Everybody's welcome, beret or no beret; we crowd in, hobos and bugger queens. A visiting deputation of

Labour MPs drop in, socialists who really know what they want for lunch: 'Norfolk ham rolls garnished with Dijon mustard, and a bottle of Moet & Chandon!'

A twenty-four hour, non-stop sex show in the basement. Six films, special rate for all our regulars! The one-eyed Turk introduces us to the usherettes, two little Thai girls, cute little hats and turned up tits, their socks roll right up to here! The place is jam-packed. We literally have people queuing round the block, clogging up the corridors. Eighteen hobos fighting over two cider bottles, and a queue right the way down to Piccadilly. That's an exaggeration.

The college quack injects everybody for the clap, a giant needle right in the pecker. Elisabeth dances in slow motion, the cute little one with the gappy teeth and the sticky-out arse. She grinds it at me, both cheeks, solid muscle! It really is the morals of the gutter in here.

Apparently, a kid in the sculpture department was jogged, it was that serious! OK, I know when the game is up! I go quietly . . . there's no point in telling you that I was stitched up . . . Not one voice was raised in my defence! Even my tutor plays dumb and denies all knowledge . . . He knows that I've got no grant, and he gave his full permission for me to work from home. But when the principal questions him, he goes wet as a beer fart, can't remember a thing!

What I'm trying to tell you, in my fashion, is that they laid the whole blame at my feet. I was the one who had to carry the can for the whole rotten show. Quite frankly they were sick of my poxy attitudes, they knew all about my crummy writings and my literary pretentions. My 'toilet humour of absolutely the worst kind.'

That old silver fox, that ponce of the podium, he carpets me on the grounds that he's saving me from prosecution under the obscene publications act. That he's only got the other students' morals at heart. He comes over real polite, his little dead eyes sat in all that rouged flesh . . . In his dictionary there's absolutely no doubt of my guilt. So, if it's all the same to me, would I mind getting out of his fucking college?! His exact words, no exaggeration. He carved them into his desk with his bare teeth!

So what's new? I know their sermons back to front, before their lips even move. There's no way the righteous of Sevenoaks are going to have any sympathies for a young writer from Chatham, down on his luck. Just a kid, ten and a half stone and a fiver a week.

It's a fact, the harder you try being polite, the more unpopular you become! You try coming round to 'their way of thinking', and that's when they really stick the boot in! The lower you scrape, the harder they rub your face in it.

My mother took it the worst, she really would of liked to see me do well. She just couldn't understand.

'You're as bad as your soddin' father!'

'Your fucking husband!' I reasoned with her.

41. SANCHIA

It was winter time and they turfed me out on my ear. Snow, hail, rain and fog. Great gusts of it, whole aquariums suspended in mid-air. Only held there by the gale.

Ordnance Street, Chatham. Come out the station, cross over by the York pub, and there it is! You can't miss it, opposite the old bombsight, bombed one day in 1940 . . . And across the street the whore house . . .

You get to know what damp is all about living on a river like that. The mould takes over, waterfalls of condensation cascading out of the walls, glacial . . . We had mould growing in the bed, green fingers of rot inching their way up from under the mattress. A regular mushroom farm . . . And our breath like cigar smoke, dirty great lungfuls of it.

Sanchia stood knock-kneed in the tub. Six inches of tepid water, her teeth rattling with the cold. The water heater wheezes and dies. It just isn't up to it, it spews black smoke, the whole bathroom choking with soot. The air vent's clogged, that's my opinion. She stands back as I pour in the kettle, she goes on tippy-toes . . . The cold makes her nipples go like that! I smile at them, rub noses with them like little puppies . . . I watch her arse as she goes for the soap, but control myself. The only time she wants it is when she's bleeding, otherwise no! She doesn't like the idea of things being pushed into her. She wants me to smarten myself up, get a job and to stop picking my nose in public!

In her opinion, I'm like some kind of unruly child, the way I keep fondling myself. In fact it's true. It gets to the point that she's always making loud remarks about my behaviour and shoddy appearance in general.

I go out to the kitchen and stagger back in with another cauldron of hot water. You have to watch your step – I nearly trip on the busted tiles. Two patches of black and white and then bare concrete. Just then the flood siren goes off just outside the window . . . Sanchia clutches at her breasts.

'What's that!'

It winds up into a fearful crescendo.

'Must be the flood siren . . . They must be checking it.'

She holds onto her little teets. 'Is it the early warning siren? You don't think they're going to drop the bomb?'

'I dunno . . . I doubt it.'

She looks at me in wide-eyed panic, then bursts into tears. 'They're going to drop a bomb, aren't they? We're all going to die!'

'I don't think so . . . I doubt it . . .' I try and placate her, but she's convinced. Me? I don't know, I've got my doubts . . . I'll wait and see . . . I try and discuss the possibilities with her, but she won't have it. It's doomsday and that's that! She's written the whole planet off as dead and buried!

She falls to her knees in the bottom of the bath . . . she clings at the taps and kicks her feet in the puddle. I try and reassure her, I really do. I take a good long look at her arse, with the little bonde hairs just round the edge. I kneel and kiss it, ever so gently. I bite the cheek and rub my nose in there. That makes her jump – she nearly headbutts the sink.

'What are you doing!' She turns on me and snarls, clenches her buttocks and wipes her mouth. Her fists go into little balls. 'It's positively unnatural!' And whilst we're on the subject, she's made a few enquiries and apparently anal sex is not only perverted, it's also against the law!

So, now I know, I've been told in no uncertain terms. Nose picking isn't my only vice. I used to wait 'til she was sound asleep and then spit on it and place it between her cheeks. I used to make her blush with anger. She was irate, she made threats and ultimatums. From nose picking to masturbation! From hair cuts to pornography! It seems that I wasn't exactly to her liking.

Her mother had voiced her doubt from the outset. That bitch was out to sink me from day one! She called her daughter 'Honey' and always had a bitter smile for everyone. Fastidious and caring – a real man hater!

I tell you for free, it's the mothers who pervert their precious little darlings, not the dirty old men. It's the mothers who set the mould and administer the poison. From the nursery to the finishing school, pretending to be hurt and slighted. Handing out knowing looks left, right and centre, and sounding off guffaws of disapproval at every sentence. Hating life, hating men, but ultimately hating themselves.

It doesn't take too many wrenches of their little hearts before they become as stand-offish and ignorant as their mothers. Snorting at everything that hasn't been double sterilised and endorsed by the Reader's Digest.

It's hardly surprising that their little darlings turn to drink. Sanchia wouldn't even give you so much as a swig from her cider bottle. 'Little Miss Martini', we used to call her – it did no good, she still wouldn't part with a drop.

I only have to glance at a woman and I can guarantee she's an emotional cripple. Every girl I've ever fallen for has come from a broken home. Wrecked marriages and misery is my speciality. We stumble into each other's arms. 'Daddy left when I was nine, mummy told me over cold toast and rice crispies, snap crackle pop!' No kidding, she used to talk to her breakfast cereal. I've heard a tape her father made when she was three years old, and she sings a song … You can hear her old man muttering in the background. I've still got it somewhere. I can spot them a mile off – tragedy attracts tragedy …

How can you talk about two years of your life on a piece of fucking paper? Or even begin to discuss it? Christ we come cheap! And me? I lick the tits of a slug! It's sick, a pointless exercise, that brings me neither hope nor sustenance. Even as I offer my heart up to be absolved, I dismiss myself, for I can never be good enough, not for my father, not for my family. And so, I suffer this humiliation … daring to bare the facts … for doing my upmost … against all the odds … for daring to breathe out of turn. And so I contemplate myself in public, and hand you this stick. And love and understanding? Each must find room in their own heart.

And I used to wake up with my lap curled round the ball of her arse. And morning she'd sit between my legs, her hair gone wild, hold my balls and taste the tip of me in her mouth. Her little tits bobbing in the blue curtained light. Her hair silver blond. And it would hurt me, twisting up my legs and balls, getting in her hair and filling my belly button ... And the clothes knee-deep on the floor. And the sink blocked and the bed damp with mould and the stink of our bodies.

When Sanchia was a kid, her mother used to slice up Mars bars for Sanchia and her sister. They'd get one slice each as a treat after tea. Just one slice! It wasn't because they were poor or nothing. It was purely to control them. To make sure that they had no sense of their own worth. They got no love, and scarcely any sweets, either. Christ, it would have been better to give them nothing. Little Sanchia and her sister sat waiting for those these little bits of chocolate. Obedient, polite and frozen! Shit, it makes me want to cry.

Argh, two years of losing myself in love, goo and self-pity! And now I should talk steadily? After all this time, to come to terms? My chin trembling, no melodramatics. A fake? If anyone dares even to suggest it, I'll punch them smack on the nose! I tell you honest and true, in my fashion. I show my colours and walk on. Not for effect but out of love, without too many cheap tricks ...

Her name was Sanchia, and it meant everything to me, and her name is still Sanchia ... All the little intimacies that we held together, they belonged to nobody but us two. And now they've gone for good. If we pass on the street, we hold our heads high. We make believe and stick to pleasantries. We bat the breeze about old times, half-remembered faces, about nothing ... We steer well clear of matters of the heart; we deny ourselves.

I'm pointing no finger, I betray no confidences. We didn't have a chance ... so we wave goodbye and something dies. A little death. Numbing. A pain that kills. After two or three of those little deaths, of those encounters of the heart, there isn't so very much left to give.

We stare bankrupt and we try and lose ourselves in the streets, in the bars. But next morning we awake alone, heavy headed and thick tongued, our own personal brand of darkness. Sweet to the taste ... I hold it in my guts and bite down into my pillow, stinging tears.

It's only possible to lose yourself and your unhappiness in somebody else for so long ... basking in the first few weeks in the sun's glow of her dawn. Our souls purged, redeemed, brimming over with love, with joy for our fellow man. We allow others to hold that power over us and then we smash them, looking for any excuse to make them sorry, to make them apologise for all the past wrongs done unto us, and for having the nerve to love us when we don't even have the stomach to love ourselves. But in the end, no matter to what depths we degrade them, our unhappiness flops back into our own miserable laps. Only this time it's more stinking, foul and malignant than ever before . . . And we have to move on, to shift our gears, wounded, forever looking back over our shoulders, clutching onto those pathetic remembrances, those dreams that were never, in fact, true.

The one who plucks up the courage to leave first, the more chance they have of getting out still partially intact. Limping, a cripple, but still able to breathe. Existing through being the perpetrator.

I should've seen that kidney punch coming. Sanchia was only biding her time. The signs, the hints, building up over the months; I knew it, but I didn't want to know it. In fact to know doesn't even help in the end. I went down and I didn't come back up. That was some punch – it lasted for years, revolving, repeating on me. I can still feel it now, if I sit quietly for a moment.

I stagger, I blubber and beg . . . strings of snot . . . I crawl around in a little pool of it . . . I demean myself. I want a new role in life, the part of a dog. Only not a dog at all, more like a half-dog, too vile for the dignity of a mongrel. I howl at the moon and lick at her feet . . . I crawl in the dust and disgust myself, longing to never have been born. I swear to die, if only I can . . . of a ruptured heart . . .

The door went, her things disappeared – and my heart beat and the clock ticked. No more her hair in the plug hole, blonde and matted. I lift it out and fling it to the floor. No more the smell of her hair on the pillow. No more her drunken laughter or the white grungey stuff in the crotch of her discarded knickers. No more her eyes and lips . . . she is as dead to me as a lost hand or an eye . . .

I walk the streets like a dead man; I look for her on passing buses, in the night rain. I gripe and I complain . . . I indulge myself, boring my friends and complete strangers, licking back salt tears and staring into my whisky. The faces drift away, the place is closing up . . .

People demand success and hate a failure, but more than that they despise a whinger. So I drink and I storm, my fragile ego so ready to burst anybody else's. I live on a memory, trying to recreate those same heart-felt feelings with the next woman, and then the next. I even use the same shameful chat-up lines. The same tired conversations, until in the end I can't remember if I ever meant any of those sweet sentiments of youth.

All mine and Sanchia's young love talk was flushed down the crapper like a used Durex on the 19th December 1980.

42. LIKE CRABS

All this idiotic talk about my women, my father and my crummy beginnings, where's it all leading us? It's disjointed, I grant you, but that's the nature of dialogue. We zoom about all over the shop. Like a regular automobile. Jumpy as a field mouse. We change tack mid-stream. I overemphasise and re-emerge, crab-like, in totally unexpected places. Bear with me please, dear benefactor, my inadequacies ... my humble attempts to communicate an idea ... it has to be said, and in plain English. The unhijacked variety, yours and mine, spoken from the heart, trumpeted with zest.

I jump, I hesitate, I leap ... but I get there in the end. Bend and adapt, through a living language, incomplete, inadequate, I grant you, but it's all I've got. Crab-like, first over here then back over there. Side-walkers, they sink in, they pull themselves out again. They lift up their skirts and scuttle off. Have you ever seen them? Jolly little fellows, artists! Not straight on but sideways, like that! No noise, they're silent, walking on damp sand; tic-tic-tic-tic-tic ... The tide's coming in!

The expressions, the faces of youth and the masks of the dead. I'm a mass observer, recording all of man's low-down dealings and deceits. From the cradle to the grave. From the victims to the perpetrators, all of them lost, sad and hoping. It's my legacy, my document. Personal details of the sort that should be kept under wraps. My early beginnings, unasked for? Certainly! But I'll repeat them until I'm purged of their significance, to anybody who's got ears and time to listen.

* * *

I'm sat propped up in front of the television set. I'm one and a half years old. There's no programme playing, just the test card and this humming noise . . . I can't get up and just walk away, I'm a baby, dumb, sat there, staring into it, contemplating the snowflakes, the molecules.

Stood naked on a beach in Devon, three years old. A cheese sandwich in my little hand, and my parents are watching me, daring me to throw it away. Then a great wave comes thundering in over the rocks into the bay. It overtakes me and I drop the sandwich. I release it into the sea . . . The wave covers me . . . it foams down, and I'm left standing there. My mother runs up to me, she thought she'd seen the last of me, that I'd been washed cleaned away . . .

'I dropped my sandwich . . .'

'That's alright,' she tells me, she rubs me with a towel. 'Never mind, never mind . . .'

I'm seven years old, stood in the shallow end of the Great Danes indoor swimming pool. My mother sits on the side, and my brother and father swim up the deep end. And there's this column in the middle like an island. I want to get to it, to touch it. But I can't swim, so I make little hops, nudging closer and closer, just another couple of yards . . . Then I slide down this little shelf and out of my depth. Gurgling through the green stuff! Blowing bubbles! A terrible noise in my head! Drinking down great lungfuls of chlorine . . . I don't know that I'm drowning . . . I just watch the bubbles bursting out of me.

I'm eight years old, me 'n' me brother come out of his little tent in the back garden and watch a flying saucer come up over the trees, and disappear over the house . . . a little silver disc spinning in the clear summer blue.

'Look Nick . . . a flying saucer!'

My brother shields his eyes and squints up at the disc – slowly it revolves across the sky.

'No . . . it's only a jet.'

'But it's round . . .'

'It's a jet.'

I watch it 'til it disappears . . . a flying saucer.

* * *

I hear a great crashing of dustbins and run up the garden and out into the alleyway ... I tell the old girl I'm going over the estate to see Crowsfeet ... I hang about by the door saying my farewells and then this great noise, like dustbins. I hesitate, then run skipping into the dark, humming to myself, keeping myself company ... I just get into the alley when this little light comes rushing towards me ... It grows by the second, heading straight for me, a white light with a sort of gingery glow ... It zaps along the ground. I have to stall so as not to run into it. One moment it's trundling along towards me like a little ginger moggy, the next it towers up in front of me, the height of a man, solid and glowing ... I'm caught hopping on one foot. I skid to a halt then it just sucks itself under the fence to my left, and I start running again ... I've no time to turn for home, I want the streets, the street lamps and the people.

I tell you so that you know something of my experiences, of the faces of little men ... of dusk time and of things about which we know next to nothing ... A panther seen in broad daylight crossing my path in local woods ... Not a dog, not a rabbit, but a full grown black panther, twenty yards away ... minding his own business, stepping from one place to the next.

I'm sixteen years old living in a squat in Chalk Farm with my brother. Travelling on the tube, I pull up on the escalator behind this Indian girl. Her arse smiles at me, and slowly, not knowing myself, I push a finger into the split, I nudge it in there, my heart pounding ... We get to the top of the stairs and I watch as she walks away. I'm in love ... I look for her again but can never find her. Week after week, I scour the empty halls of the traveller, but she's gone, my angel.

Back at the squat, I lay on my camp-bed and wank to my saviour of the cold city. A real woman, to touch, to hold and to cherish ... I vowed then and there to travel to India, to leave first thing in the morning: to find my princess.

I can't bear this much longer, these remembrances, a headache, stretching back over the years, like a crusade. A crusade without money or meaning. I know, I keep mouthing off, making a laughing stock of myself, a whipping post for the liberals and extremists alike. Pissing over their freedoms and dogmas, belittling their literary traditions. I've let the mask slip once too often to pretend to hide anything from you now – it's all history. Write it down and forget, that's the rule. But it doesn't always work out that way, it isn't always that simple ... I rewrite, I rethink, and try a new perspective ... I admit to it, I try the dirtiest trick in the book: I whinge to my readers. I suppose it's too late to ask for forgiveness? 'Ah', you'll say, 'a romantic to the very end,' and you'd be right. Just one view of little Elisabeth's arse walking down Walderslade Road and I go all to pieces. I start getting all sentimental over it right away, that's my poetic nature. I crawl upon my hands and knees. I lick at the pavement. I roll over on my back and spit gravel. I beat the tarmac with my bare fists, my head bowed to God.

43. OAKWOOD MENTAL HOSPITAL

We all have our jobs of work to do. Mine was cleaning out the shit-house! Scrubbing the crappers! Sloshing round the U-bends! Ward porter. They gave me a giant passkey to all the doors in our little world. Cupboards like you've never seen. Deep, black, cobwebbed, stacked to the ceiling with every device known to fight the dripping arse of man. I've still got the key, weighty, silver, impressive.

It's just the other side of Maidstone. Five minutes from the London Road. Turn left towards Barming. You can't miss the dump. Go take a peep for yourself, borrow my passkey if you like. A big stone wall, grey, flint-like, built right round the grounds of that place, daunting . . . In Victorian times it was to keep the patients in. Now it's more out of politeness, to keep all those bits of crawling humanity out of people's faces. A junkyard for human eyesores. The busted down, the unloveable and the dead. Sapped minds, buggerists, shit-eaters and alcoholics, mostly.

Look out for the gatehouse, a hole between the stone walls. A driveway, broad, expansive, lined with great, green monsters, right the way up to the front steps. Pine trees, full of twitterings. Little brown fellows and the occasional wood pigeon, cooing their incessant little songs of freedom. The mood will hit you right away; you won't be able to mistake it. And the smell will stay with you forever . . . Lost in a labyrinth of corridors. Miles and miles of the stuff, disappearing into a point in the far distance . . . The light hits the windows, then drops off, giving up the ghost, uninterested, repetitive, never-ending. It's a place that breeds depression. And outside on the little lawn, the disused bandstand, wrought ironwork from yesteryear.

My great-gran died in this dump. The sun slanting in, yellowish, sadly . . . An acrid stench, ammonia, a trickle of piss, white ankles . . . An old guy shuffles past, he stoops and picks up a dog end. A never-ending stream of the unwanted. They stagger and drool, herded towards the canteen, towards the little grey serving hatch at the far end. Cups of dark orange tea, saccharin tasting.

You go in and sit down next to the mural the local school kids painted. The juke-box cranking out songs of young love and never-ending happiness. Blatant and unrelenting. You stare into the tea, opaque . . . And the faces tell you of failure – lined, ludicrous twitches, rockings, mutterings. And you know that the people who tell you that this world is a good place, that their days are full of hope and meaning, are just a bunch of charlatans, on the devil's pay-role, actors with cash in the bank.

Crappers! That's my department, cleaning, polishing . . . First thing, get the shit-house clean! Next, buff up the corridors! Buff up the corridors! It sounds like playing with a rag, but there's acres of those tiles: parquet. Each with its own character, wooden, stained and never wanting to gleam. And in between, I have to help serve the dinners and remove forty years worth of encrusted nicotine from the lounge ceiling. Dark brown, a billion puffs and then some more. With only a mop and a bucket. The yellow juice streaming down my arms. I wasn't laughing – that was a messy business, and as far as I could see it, a pretty pointless one.

'None of our patients are dangerous, and any that are, are kept heavily sedated.' He looks at me over his glasses, then carries on . . . 'I should also make it quite clear that we will not tolerate any kicking of the patients, swearing at the patients, or spitting at the patients.'

The wise owl holds me with his eyes, looking over his glasses. I have to say 'Yes' then he puts down his papers and smiles, dry, crumbly at the edges. He reaches over and drops my key into my hand. I take it in my palm . . . heavy, a thing of beauty . . .

'So, everything's clear then?'

I nod, 'Yes sir!'

'Now, if you'll just go along with Mrs Mop here, she'll show you to your ward, and introduce you to your supervisor.'

I re-nod, 'Yes sir!'

'And remember, no spitting at the patients!'

I salute and leave with the old bag. Once outside, I open my palm and examine my treasure: the king of keys! I pocket it and follow Mrs Mop: short, starched and threatening.

From the outset those hags in domestic ganged up on me. They took it on themselves to rubbish me at every opportunity. They were as sly as sixteen weasels and as cantankerous as a shoal of barracudas. They made faces behind my back. They insinuated. The mistresses of the pregnant pause . . . I was a boy in a woman's world, and didn't they let me know it. 'Did I think I was superior or something?' And 'why do you wear that disgusting old suit? You look like one of them, like a dinloo!'

Obviously, I was heading for a duffing, and Mrs Mop's old man would be quite happy to oblige, if I just cared to hang around outside the main gate after dark. That bitch put me on report twice on my first day for my alleged indiscretions, things that never even occurred. For getting too chummy with the patients, for back-chatting the doctors and putting them straight on a few points of patient care.

I come in Monday morning, grab my bucket and spade and there's a new face sitting on the ward . . . I see him leafing through the Reader's Digest, so I walk over and shake hands with him. Just a kid, seventeen years maybe. Gnawing at his cuticles and grinding his teeth. He wants to know if I've got any cigarettes.

I show him my palms. 'Fresh out, mate!'

'Is there anywhere I can get some?' He blinks at me and shreds his thumb. 'Ain't there a machine?'

'No, not over here . . . Have you just come in?'

'The weekend . . . Sunday night . . . Do they sell cigarettes?'

I put my mop and bucket down and park my arse. 'Shift up . . .' I sit down next to him.

'Not in this neck of the woods, you need the shop . . . over by the canteen . . . You know the canteen?'

He shakes it.

'Well, it's a quite a walk, and tricky, not at all straightforward.' I look at him and pull out my packet of Weights. 'Look, this is my last one, alright, it'll keep you going 'til nursy comes in. When she shows up, ask her to take you over to the shop, it's by the canteen, to get your snouts. She'll take you, it's up to her, I've got to go and do the bogs . . . then all the floors.'

I wave my mop in the air, I take it out the bucket, I give him an example. He smiles, me too . . . but now I have to go.

'Nursy will see you right. I've got to get going, the supervisor will be after my balls!'

I wave to my new found friend and leave him puffing on it. Just a kid, like me. Alone in the world, but not even with a cigarette to keep him company. A few sad knocks, the eyes damaged, a slight stutter. The hands fluttering, ruined. A no-hoper, with no one to care.

I give him my last snout to cheer him up, then carry on with my rounds. I get on my hands and knees and kiss the pan. I give it all I've got. I'll tell you something, half the old fools in that joint let it go before they're even on the seat, before they've even got their kacks down . . . They're not at all supervised, not in the least. They stagger about, shitting their pants to their heart's delight. They fall in it and draw pictures, finger paintings. The walls just one mass of hieroglyphs. I scrub at them, I use a paint scraper, I go to great lengths.

Then, next up, the buffing, with a machine, heavy, revolving, with a mind of its own. I have to go to the cupboard to get that. I insert my pass-key. I have to put my back into it, I lean on it, a regular Fort Knox. Finally, I get that door open and get to the machine . . . I stock up on bog paper whilst I'm at it. I fill my bags. I can't stand shelling out hard earned cash on arse-wipe! I take a dozen rolls off the top shelf, the executive variety, for doctors' use only. Soft and luxurious, not the greased sandpaper reserved for us plebs and the loonies. I bag it up for later and get on with my rounds.

That machine takes some manhandling. I sweat and I stoop, crashing from side to side, ripping great chunks out of the skirting boards. A couple of acres of parquet, shimmering into the distance. Every two miles I have to drag in the cable and plug in up ahead. I heave and pull: it spins and hums, with a mind of its own. The bastard thing nearly takes my ankles off!

It takes me 'til half eleven to even begin to get a shine on that driftwood. Then that bitch comes and tells me to go help serve up the patients' grub. Not that it's my job, mind, but I go to it. I put a final dash on, finish my buffings and lock the cupboards. I get everything done before 12 o'clock. I put on an extra spurt, unplug the machine and stow it. I chuck it into the darkest recesses of the store cupboard. I use both hands. I twist that key with viciousness, with a finality, and make for the dining area. Then I see him still sitting there, my friend of the morning. Despondent, alone, unmoved . . . staring out past the window, into the grounds, at nothing, a squirrel eating its nuts. I sit myself down, I drop everything.

'Watcha!'

He looks away and says nothing.

'Haven't you got your snouts yet?'

He shakes it.

'Didn't nursy come and take you over to the shop?'

He shrugs . . . I throw my mop down and kick at my bucket . . .

'OK, come on, grab your hat!'

I lead him, I pull him out of his chair.

'I'll just get me jacket.'

We set off, I drop everything. Stow the dinner, the boy wants his cigarettes! Been sat here waiting these past four hours, ignored and uncared for.

'Come on mate, I'll show you the way. Stuff their dinner, we'll get your snouts!'

We go out the side door and amble over, batting the breeze. Twenty Navy Cut: I have to lend him the money. His fingers tremble so much that he can't open the packet. I open it for him and we light up.

'You see, they chucked me out, I was in the hostel, but I couldn't find work. Then my girlfriend left me and I tried to top myself . . .'

I drag on it, hot and sweet, and let it out through my nose. I nod thoughtfully. Words aren't everything, for once I keep it shut and just listen. Another human being, I try and understand. His perspective, the world failing him, in his eyes.

Like I say, it's a hike over there and back, from the main hospital, but still, we didn't dilly-dally . . . We just buy the cigarettes and make tracks. We get back just as they're finishing dinner. We walk into a stack of plates, high encrusted, unwashed. And that's when they jump us. We're surrounded. They pull at my lapels. They extinguish my friend's cigarette and frog-march him back to the ward. He looks to me, desperate. They hold his arms behind him and lead him away.

It was those harpies from domestic who grassed us up – any excuse to stick their noses in! I'm dragged in front of the chief supervisor. There's already been countless reports of my attitude problem. It seems that I've been upsetting the patients, putting everybody in danger. A major catastrophe was narrowly avoided.

'You drew a picture of April, didn't you? Come along, there's no sense in denying it!'

'Yeah, so . . . it was in my dinner break.'

'And she drew a picture of you, is that right?'

I stare down.

'Is that right?'

I nod.

'Well, where is it now?'

'I don't know.'

'Look, I'm going to ask Doctor Roberts in here in a minute and you better remember pretty damn quick!' He presses his little buzzer and a black man in a white coat and glasses walks in.

'This is Doctor Roberts. Doctor Roberts, Hamperson, our new ward porter.'

Doctor Roberts shows me his teeth. 'Yes, I've seen him on his rounds. Now, Mister Hamperson, I'd like a word with you about April . . . You know April, don't you?'

I look at him, the little fellow, the little black man behind his glasses.

'It seems that maybe you know her, how should we say, too well!'

'How well is too well?'

'Look here young man, you seem to have made quite a nuisance of yourself already and this is only your first week!' He leafs through the stack of reports on his desk. 'This could look very bad for you, especially if you had to apply for a new job.' He looks at me meaningfully. 'What I'm trying to say is, if you're willing to help us, maybe we'll be willing to help you. Now this little matter of April's drawing, it need go no further. Just give us the drawing and we can pretend that this "little chat" never happened.' I stare down at my shirt front and say nothing. He clears his throat. 'We need all the information we can gather, to enable us to have a deeper understanding of April's neurosis. I'm sure you understand our situation.'

He puts all his fingers together, then takes them apart and scratches his head. 'If you know the whereabouts of this drawing, you must tell us. You can tell me in the strictest confidence and it will go no further than this office.'

'I don't know where the drawing is.'

'Ah yes . . . Well, I'm afraid that April says that you have the drawing!'

'Well, I don't.'

'I don't want to have to bring April in here. I think you will agree, that would be most unpleasant for all parties concerned.'

He blinks behind the glass, owlish, a fool in a white coat.

'I haven't got the picture . . . I don't know what happened to it. I think she threw it away.'

'I see, so you want it the hard way!'

He leans over and pushes the little buzzer. He fidgets and pulls at his nose and blinks at me again. Then they bring her in: April, the girl who eats from the bins . . . She says she loves me . . . she wants me to give her a baby . . . 'Will I marry her?' . . . She doesn't want me getting no funny ideas! She takes a handful of gunk out of the bin, scrapings, slops, she shakes it at me.

'Men are all the same!'

'Don't eat that, April.'

She holds it to her breast, she nurses it, eating from her palm, old cabbage leaves, a tea bag.

They bring her in and hold her in front of the little man's desk; it takes two of them, one on each arm. She sobs and gasps . . . I stare at my fingers, I flex them, the knuckles go white . . . The dad sits himself on the edge of his desk . . . takes off his goggles and polishes them with his tie.

'Where's the picture, April?'

She lets out a little cry, shrill, chilling.

'We only want to look at it, April, we don't want to take it away from you, we just want to see it, that's all . . . Has Mister Hamperson got it? Did you give it to him? That's all we want to know, we won't take it away from you . . . Just tell us where it is, April!'

She shakes her head from side to side, she twists it on her neck, contorting her face. She says it, she spits it out. 'No, you mustn't kill my babies!'

'Come along, April, you have to help us so that we can help you.'

She drools and splutters, sagging at the knees; she tries to droop down, but the apes hold her up.

'This young man here has told us that you still have the picture.'

He motions at me with his stupid pen, gold and glittering. He points me out, the Judas of the sketch book. I speak up, I have to, my rage. It's small but it rises. I have to say it, to spit out the lies they put in my mouth. To keep myself pure, to not be part of this world they're making.

'Leave her alone!'

I shout it between my clenched teeth, I force it through tightened jaws.

I screw up my fists, my eyes bulging 'til they ache; I can't bottle it any longer, my feelings, the disgust, the great injustice.

'You jumped-up fool, so she drew a picture? Big deal! But never again, because of you, you stupid deluded fool. It's you who's killing her, killing everybody. You're stifling all life, and you're too stupid to even fucking notice!'

I go to say it but I don't . . . I cry, I gasp, I sob. I have to leave, to be out of his dirty eyes. I need to feel the door handle, warm and friendly. To be stepping out of there, to be leaving this room, these people and their lies, behind closed doors. But I stand dumb, in turmoil, aged by guilt.

They drag her away, our girl of the bins, to be sedated. She's over-excited – they put her under the drill.

'Of course, this isn't the only matter we have to discuss with you, Mister Hamperson'

They turn on me again. I swallow down. I'm not a man, I'm not a human being, I am an insect, one of any number.

'Mrs Mop tells me that you've been upsetting not only the patients, but also the other members of her staff.' He wrinkles his forehead, the lines ask. 'She says you claim to be an ex-patient who only applied for this job so that you can 'reek your revenge on the doctors with your little hatchet!' He reads it from his notebook, the distaste showing on his lips . . . He looks up at me from under his glasses.

Like I say, toilets are my department, I'm just a shit shifter.

'Get that old, mad shit from under that rim boy! Hose it down, let's see that piss-pot shine! And don't forget the U-bend! Get your arm round there and plunge boy, plunge!'

You have to have a certain aptitude in this life, a certain belief in the superiority of your betters and a certainty in your own lack of self-worth. If they ever get even so much as an inkling that you're not content, that you're a non-believer who isn't eternally grateful for the honour of being able to serve, then boy, oh boy! You'd better watch your arse, kid! You're for the chop! Bow down on your knees, kiss the pan and don't forget to say thank-you.

44. VOICES THROUGH THE FOG

I spy suds in the bottom of my glass and hold the world in contempt. A world that doesn't measure up . . . that doesn't adore me. That doesn't get down upon its knees and kiss my loins. And I laugh and I play coy, for a young writer is used to it, to the games of this whore. And I stand worldly wise, drooped against the bar, a bitter black cigar between my lips.

'Can I get you a drink?'

I burp and look up . . . This berk wants to know if he can buy me a drink? Sure, fine! Scotch, I say . . .

'What do you fancy?'

'Scotch!'

'Great!' He hands it me. Fantastic! He lets me know I'm getting it for free, that I'm honoured and that it's him who's paying for it. 'You now who you remind me of?' I nod him to go ahead. 'John Lennon!' I look at my great patron, at his wet lips and dropping jowls. 'John Lennon, I lived with him in digs at Liverpool Art College!'

'Sure, John Lennon.' I almost spit in my beer.

'Ice?'

'No thanks . . .'

'Straight?'

'Straight!'

He hands it me, a double. I take hold of it and swill it round the glass . . . I hold it up and take a butchers through the bottom – golden poison.

'Cheers Jerry!' And suddenly it's in my mouth. I gag and swallow. I lug half of it back, that vile magical drink of my father's.

Suddenly, I have to go and take a piss. I nurse my drink close to my bosom, through the crowds. I head for the stairs. Ever apologetic, that's me ... I open doors and lower my eyes. Someone stands on my toe, pushes me aside, I apologise.

I excuse myself, holding on to my gut-rot. I make it to the stairs, go through the stable doors and head for the pan. I lay my little companion down, gently does it, with precision ... I have to concentrate, to rest one hand on the cistern, and down we go. I sit the glass by my feet ... close at hand ... within easy reach ... my little baby. Then I have to unbutton and uncurl it ... I have to coax him out, and quick ... a few droplets go down my leg. Then I stand back, and power it out through him. A little jet, then a torrent. Into the centre of the bowl, to froth up the shit, to make the loudest din, to announce myself to all the other pissers ... I drop my cigar butt into the pan and hose it down into the froth, chasing it round the pond ... It rolls over and somersaults ... I'm running out of pressure. I flex my stomach muscles and stir up that piss hole once more. It rolls over on its back, waves and surrenders ... a few more hard jets and it spills its guts, bitter leaves ... piss-laden ... mixing ... a few strands ... I shake him off, one more blast, just to let these other characters, my pissing friends, know just who's in cubicle number one: a pisser that sounds! An inspiration, with a bladder like a medicine ball!

I check his delicate little head, shake him dry and button up. Some of the droplets spraying off, caught in the strip lights ... spattering down into my Scotch. I pick it up, admire its colour and down it. Ah, fine piss this boy makes, fine piss! I knock that poison back with double vigour and head back to the bar.

Apparently, I've got to read in ten minutes. No kidding, read my verses, my little observations, humble but nevertheless relevant ... For the assembled cameras. Sure thing. Jerry calls me over, our producer, bloated, pompous, another lunch, and then it's Christmas. He sticks his nose in the trough and has a good feed, he's still feeling a little peckish so he pops another crème brûlée into his gob.

He wants to know if I need a top-up. I nod ... I prop myself at the bar, twenty years old but already a respected poet! A lover of several women! A great artist, expelled by the blinkered intellectuals of one of our finer art colleges, who wouldn't know genius if it walked up and punched them on the nose! A force to be reckoned with, King of the Pissers! Jerry refills my tumbler and leans in, conspiratorial . . . His face: jowls of desperation.

'You know who you remind me of?'

He looks over his shoulder, he has no eyes. I wait with baited breath.

'John Lennon!'

I stare through my Scotch, the light, I look it up and down . . .

'I lived with him you know, Liverpool, '61 . . . in the same digs, rough days, but colourful . . . Me and John, phew!'

I eye my assailant, put my glass down and smile into his mug. Who does he think he's trying to kid? Him with his John Lennon routine? Sure thing! Boy, you're really impressing this kid, Jerry! You knew John Lennon? Well well, you must be quite a man yourself! Yeah, John Lennon! the Cavern!

The lights go funny and I have to stop listening. I lay my heavy block in my folded arms and kiss the bar . . . And the noise goes on, the show, Jerry's mouth, the TV producer, the importance of being famous. I have to be careful not to vomit . . . In truth I'm pissed, I watch the room revolve . . .

They load their cameras. They lose their microphones. They trip over their own cables, a light explodes. A little theatre. The light meter doesn't work . . . They trip over it, acres of film, like elastic. The hicks behind the lenses.

And then I see her, three rows back, blond hair, braids of real gold and her nose at that certain angle – my Norwegian princess!

I have to turn my face in disgust and knock back another gobful of Scotch. So, she's here again, my little tormentor – Sanchia, love of my life! Well, I tell you, you will be mine tonight, my friends, that platinum princess! She will be mine again! Sanchia, the property of the Great Pisser! And she will admire me and praise me above all others! I announce it for all to hear. I stare into the bottles and tip another glass. I scowl and stare them all down: my enemies, my friends, my loved one. I give myself to you all!

Jerry takes my arm and leads me to the stage. He announces me. I turn up my collar and light another cigarette . . . I check me hair and I blow smoke like a professional. I walk up there and bark my stuff out, with venom, with zest . . . The cameras, they whirr and splutter – the tape snaps, but I carry on regardless. I kick at the chairs and piss like a fountain. A pisser that sounds!

An inspiration, with a bladder like a medicine ball! I mix my metaphors, chin jutting . . . I forget my syntax, stumbling over all of my 'f's and 'th's . . . a regular pain in the arse!

There's no sense preaching to a bunch of half-wits like that, an audience who knows nothing of poetry! Nothing of a young writer's pain and suffering! An audience that ladens its living rooms down not with real paintings but with reproductions!

I burp and bow and fall to the ground. I bounce my head on the stage and have to laugh at them all, sitting there sipping on their gins, wide-eyed and pathetic!

I walk to the bar and sulk into my beer, a pint of the dark stuff . . . I need a nurse, a cutie. I demand the attention of that woman who dared deny me! I have proven my genius, now get on your knees and admit your mistake woman! Come crawl before me and take my cock in your mouth, and maybe I will see fit to forgive you your indiscretions! I stare at the back of her golden head and will her to turn and look at me, for her throat to tighten and for her to fall to the ground, choking. And slowly, she stands and turns and actually looks at me, but her beautiful eyes don't tell me she loves me. They stare at me and scream, 'You fool! You sad stupid fool . . . How could you believe that one such as I could ever love you, for in truth you disgust me!'

She turns and walks out towards the toilets. I wait 'til the door closes behind her, then jump up and push my way across the room. I spill beer over it. I crumple toes and get to the door just as it shuts me out. I stand there, light one up and wait. I fold my arms and pace the boards.

What the fuck's she doing in there, is it fucking rag week or what? I try the door, I huff and I puff, take a deep breath and expand my chest. I practice looking nonchalant. I flick my ash and smooth my hair back, then try the door handle again. Some bloke comes up behind me and I pretend to be humming . . . staring back at his face. I dare him not to look away. I half grin and laugh to myself, just like I expected as much. To show him how lightly I take the ways of women. Then the door opens and she stands there . . . I stand back and smile.

'How did you like my reading?'

I look at her and to the ceiling, shaking my head around like a rattle.

'You're not honest with yourself!' she says, evenly.

That's the way she talks, her exact words – she doesn't beat around the bush, she comes straight out with it. She sets her jaw and defies me. I explode with laughter, loud, way too loud . . . To show I don't care, to make it obvious. What the hell do I care what a mere girl thinks about me? I examine the inside of my mouth, tonguing my cheek, I chew on something, raw, a fragment, stuck. I place my hand on hers, gently.

'OK, sweetheart, come on, you're coming home with me!'

And she laughs and pushes past me, in front of everyone. I have to step after her, to grab her arm, to force my face into hers. She gags and screams up my nose. She sets her feet and pushes me off. I claw at her wrists, dragging her towards the doorway . . . No one must see my weakness.

'You're coming home with me!'

'Let me go!'

I apologise, I plead, pulling at her arms. I follow and encircle, until the whole fucking show turns into some hideous kind of waltz . . . I grin through my mask and try some romance: I make small talk, I infiltrate . . . I light up, I offer her one, playing the big shot. I blow smoke then snatch at her bag – it somersaults and empties itself, revolving in slow motion . . . I have to make a grab, stumbling through the lipstick . . . I need air, the room is killing me! We must be outside, alone, together! I'm dying . . . I need air . . . I'm fucking dying! My legs buckle, I've no strength . . . I'm fucking dying!

The idea was for her to love me. To hold me, to kiss me – or I'll fucking kill her! And the crowd stare on in disbelief; they look from the back of my head to their drinks. Watching. The people, the audience . . . I give them a show. I panic, then grab her. I'm weak . . . weak, weak, weak . . .

The door frame saves her. She digs in her nails and grips the paintwork . . . I can't pull her through; I try, but I can't. She wedges herself in and kicks out at me. I plead with my dumb eyes then I feel it go, I'm losing my hold . . . my fingers cramped . . . I have to surrender, to help her pick up her lipsticks . . . to get on my knees and mumble, to apologise. To get out of this building, this world, this light . . . To vacate these people's faces – the eyes that accuse.

The tears sting my eyes and I exit without her. To get out of this building, to dip my body into the fog and breathe the mud cool air . . . I choke on it, burning my throat, the little iced tears. 'Good fog, you are my friend, fog, hide me, for you are my saviour!' And I sag by the doorway, wringing each of those tears from my poor burning chest. I bathe in that hot self-pity, sobbing for myself, for the terrible injustice that has been perpetrated against man. For the damning stars . . . for the rancid gift of life, the dirty trick of God!

And I long to be dead, to be truly dead, to teach that bitch some manners, to learn her some fucking pity! To show her how a real artist suffers – a young writer cut off in his prime. To sleep the eternal sleep, only to awaken to hear her apologies, her pitiful admission of guilt, crying to the world how sorry she is, and how good, brave and honest I was.

And so I walk up to God and demand an explanation, and sock him straight in his deceitful little kisser!

'You messed up when you ditched this one, Sanchia, 'cos he's a fine one, one of the best, a true one, one in a billion! Painter of poetry and a writer of vision! Artist and genius extraordinaire! But I forgive you, you poor naive child, for you are frail and mortal. And how could a mere girl realise her mistake? I shall carry this burden for you . . . Bring flowers to my grave and I shall suck milk from your unworthy bosom . . .'

I sing in ecstasy, blubbering to myself, for one so pure, yet defiled, a soul misunderstood. I suck my snot and dribble it back out through my trembling lips . . .

Dear God, that such a fine one as me could be treated so bad! My integrity questioned and tarnished by that shameless harlot! I bite down on my hanging lip and howl with the pain, crying little sobs of joy . . . I feel for the blood, looking with my fingers, but with disgust I find none.

If only you could see me now, Vincent, driven to this, to the depths of sorrow, to the edge of my own self-destruction! Ah yes, we're wed to it, boy, us artists of the heart. Our fine noble souls in abject misery! I'll give myself misery, misery for her to regret! I'll give her monumental misery, the sort to break the hearts of impossible princesses, all the princesses of the world!

I marvel at my own unabashedness. The universe could never spin above a head more sorrowful. But I accept it gratefully, for such is the weight on the shoulders of all great writers; and I wrench another great sob of pity from the heart of one so innocently true as me.

I hear voices through the fog. They're looking for me. I have to wipe my face, to smile. To light up a cigarette. They come and pull me to my knees, lift me out of my dribblings and load me in the car. They lay me out on the back seat. I want to play hide and seek, but they collar me. I let them lead me away, back through the fog, up over the escarpment.

And the one in the back, my companion, feeling the weight of the world, tries to chuck himself out onto that wet black road. He unlatches the door and pushes off. I just grab his sleeve before the fog swallows him. I drag him back in, out of the cold claws of the mist. He blubbers, he cries, he puts me to shame . . . passed out, drooling on my lap.

The bitch! And that could be me, back there, kissing the road! And her at my funeral, she would have to be there with her shining blond hair, a black veil, and a tear . . . And the knowledge in her breast of a great wrong done me . . . of her responsibility at the death of such a sensitive, snatched so young from this bitter world . . .

We zig-zag through the pea soup, my cheek on the wet window. It took us some time to find the dump. The fog lamps gave up and died, impenetrable . . . impossible meanderings in the dark. You couldn't even see to read the street signs up that mountain, treacherous! It would be easy to get yourself lost up here, to drive yourself 'til the road peters out, then nothing . . . the wolves and beyond . . . We follow the tarmac and the house numbers . . . We hang from the window with a touch 'til we find the right door number.

We lay our friend out in the corridor, adjust his collar, straighten his feet and find the Scotch bottle. I console myself. I just double check that he's OK, I look down into his kisser, such a dainty sleeper, his little tootsies crossed and two delicate mitts parked over his belly. Content in sleep, a little puckered smile on his lips. God bless you. I push a couple of coins into his pocket, light up another and give a little sigh. That's a habit I've learned: sighing . . . It comes with bitterness, I suck at my teeth and let it out . . . pour myself another drop of the poison, it's time to be off, back out into the night. It swallows us, wet tongues, hideous, all enveloping. I'm licked all over.

The driver grips the wheel and swerves through the fog; he can't see straight, a regular hovercraft. We're heading for Gillingham. Where's Gillingham? Three miles . . . through the pea soup, up under Luton Arches . . . then Chatham hill . . . From one catastrophe to the next, a big risk . . . We swerve. I check him sideways, he's pissed, bulging eyes, two closed headlamps . . .

We're cranking along in second, no breaks and he's dropping off, nodding at the wheel. I go to speak but he tells me to button it. He's not impressed with my great wit; the show's wasted on him, he curls up on the dashboard. I force a smile. I pinch the edges of my mouth together, chin up, that's it, that's the ticket! I swallow it back, staring into the passing clouds ... There must be angels out there, someone to fill my dark suit.

We're looking for luminosity ... a million lights ... hollow joys ... the gigglings of youth. The big race is to see who can destroy themselves first, our stomachs souring on cheap plonk ... To find happiness as if it were only a little mislaid trinket glittering on the street; to rid ourselves of another evening of innocent dick-pulling.

I find beer and prop myself in the doorway. So this is Gillingham, what do you know? Some place they've got here, this Gillingham of theirs. Well well ... I acquaint myself with the tin, scowling in my corner. The cuties gyrate by, all tits and arses, colliding, desperately trying to convince themselves that they're having a grand old time, that they're young and beautiful, that they shall never have to die. And I want to believe you my darlings, to become an accomplice to this lie. To drop to my knees and kiss your dimpled thighs, and implore you never to leave again, to set your feet and fly your hair like banners!

Yes, my sweethearts stay with us for always, in this house, caught for always in this very moment. Because if you ever leave, dear children, you will have to remember, and to remember – well, it's sad to remember, so sad to have been young, to have been happy, to know that everything has changed.

I bite into my cigarette and spit tobacco, flakes and paper. I flex my brain, lock my jaw and will this sick sad world to stop dead. To bring everything crashing to a halt – the talking, the bragging ... To shut up all the big shots, so that I can step in like a god and fuck their women ... But the world just carries on regardless. And the girls? Well, they pass right on by with a toss of their golden locks and a twitch of their buttocks, and they don't even bother looking back.

But one little pug, I get the notion that I know her. I recognise some of the angles. I quit picking my nose and follow her comings and goings. I've seen that delicate shape someplace before ... her arse on a spring, with a big split, grotesque! I have to sup my beer, get round in front and measure up her pug. I manoeuvre round the room, I get frantic, I can't get it down me quick enough: that's my nature.

The lights are pretty dim in this dive, and the fog doesn't help, seeping in round the window frames, coming in under the doors, mixing with all the smoke, adding to the general effect, to the haze. I push through those good timers, I forget that anyone else exists. I've no time for the dreams of others, I have to get round in front and measure up her ugly kisser.

I peer through the mist and squint; I stick my neck out, making all kinds of contortions, shameless, unabashed . . . I sniff the bottle . . . I inhale . . . I bug my eyes . . . The world goes sideways, my funny head . . . Hey, what is this shit? I make a grab, I stumble.

'My name's Dolli.'

'Hello, Rosy!'

'Dolli!'

'Hello, Rosy!' I repeat myself.

I say hello, I oggle her. I have to hold myself up, to loosen my grip and stand on my own two pins. I flex my retinas, focusing through the fog. It seems that she's not from round these parts, some kind of Turk, I should imagine. Almond eyes, black, sucking in all the light . . . and a harelip. It makes me look twice, that lip of hers. It seems to join straight onto her nostrils, that's the effect. I feel my own lip with my tongue, that's me: super-sensitive! I like to join in, to get involved, to show some sympathy. I think I recognise her, and her name, Rosy?

'I know you, I've seen you before. I asked about you. I recognised you.' I tell her, I make sure she understands my sympathies.

She looks me up and down, this little dark one, she soaks me in . . . I knew I was right, her eyes sympathise, it seems she's short-sighted.

'Are you alright?' she's asking me, she's speaking to me now. I go dizzy, I want to fall to her knees.

'Sure, I'm fine, fantastic! Never felt better!'

'Oh, you poor man, you've got a hump!'

What's that? A hump? I pull myself upright. A what? A hump? I straighten up and look over my shoulder. She's got to be kidding.

'Oh, I remember you, you're the man that does the paintings, aren't you?'

Now, she's talking to me about my paintings. I nod, light a cigarette, straighten my back and try not to breathe on her. What the hell was that stuff in the bottle, paraffin or something? It made my heart go for a gallop. I went up and I crashed down, landing on this little cutie in the process. I remember her now, I've seen her hanging around outside Chatham Station. I recognise the sea-saw between her arse and those throbbing tits. Everything teetering, balancing on that pivot . . . It all comes back to me, I've seen this one before alright, yes, my friends, Chatham station! I think.

And she likes my doodles. Say, that's not bad! That's a sign . . . I have to hold her attention, to become her centre. I do a loop . . . It's the whisky taking effect, and that potion in the magic bottle. I can't help it . . . So, I'm a pain in the arse? I've been sick and sad . . . I've been down and out, now I want to have a little fun.

I tell her of my day, this Rosy, of how it was. All the pricks and their crummy cameras! The TV men? They knew nothing, absolute jokers, didn't know their arses from their elbows! They were fools, mere groundlings, I flattened them with my superior wit! I stop in mid-sentence and check for effect; I get on my high horse and won't climb down, not for nobody . . . She supresses a yawn and excuses herself. I'm left standing at the mantlepiece and she doesn't come back.

Hey, that's twice in the same evening! I have to go in search of my cutie, through the throngs, the gyrations, the fog and the din . . . And here she is, holed up underneath the kitchen table.

'There's a man looking for me, can you hide me?'

I hear her talking to the driver. Say, I like that! I lift the chequered table cloth and play peek-a-boo . . . She's playing hard to get . . . A little flirtation, half hearted . . . I invite her out . . . I suck up . . . I can't help myself – my blood rules, my friends, not my brain.

I lead her through the throngs and out into it. Me and my little sweetheart . . . encircling . . . black . . . ice cold . . . we lose ourselves. I slip my arm round her middle, waspish . . . I lead the way, a real gent. I had the sad-sads, but now I feel a wee bit better. I choke back a tear and put a brave face on. My arm round her waist, leading the way through the fog, three or four miles . . . I find my door, the exact number.

She wants to see my masterpieces? Fine, I will lead her through the night, through this fog. We will leave these wasters and I will bask in the glory of her admirations . . . my hand on her hip. And none can say why the axe falls here or why the fearful live and the brave must die.

I bring her to my room, kneel at her feet, and in disbelief I sit staring up into her laughing gob.

'What you got in there?'

She gurgles and covers her mouth. I stare up past her tongue into the metal of her mouth . . .

'Shit, what you got in there?'

Silvery, reflecting, an armoury . . . a whole bank of the stuff! She slips her tongue in under her plate and slips it out, her front teeth sitting in the palm of her hand.

Sat crouched there on my knees I get cramps. I marvel, staring into her Turkish mug. I light up another ciggy and rest my chin on her knees, the pain shooting through my legs. But I stay there forever, my little prayer . . . martyring myself . . . because I know what's right.

'You saved my life tonight!' I tell her. 'You might not believe it, but you did, you saved my life!'

I repeat myself. I can't believe that we're alive and others aren't. The world judges and damns but here we are! I marvel at it, at cruel fortune.

'You saved my life, you really did!'

And my heart bobs to the surface like a beer bottle, and the night laughs with me, the fog, the street lights and all the angels. My face grins, I feel the skin pinching, the lines showing round my eyes.

'You see these lines? I cut them myself, with a razor, then I put fag ash in 'em, it bloody stung! the ash . . .'

And then she shows me where she got knifed. She loosens her blouse. I see her dusky belly, fuzzy, a million hairs up to her navel . . . and the scar, the raised white line, high against her ribs, so she has to lift her breast.

'A bottle,' she tells me. 'He did it with a broken bottle.'

I touch her skin. I feel it, I trace it with my knotted fingers. I weigh her heavy tits.

'You can't fuck me,' she says.

I shake my head and grin like a fool, some kind of school kid. 'I don't care. You saved my life tonight, you might not know it, but you did. The fog, it nearly got me, like a dog, crawling . . . a billion million droplets . . . You saved my life!'

I lay my head on her tit, a little bit of drool, and she strokes my hair. I think that she was a bit pissed off that I didn't make a show of wooing her . . . Just to lie there with another human being . . .

to still be alive, to wake not alone, to have a little hope ... The fog came in through the busted skirting, I could smell that stuff ... lying there, sleeping like a pup at the teat ...

The day comes thick tongued, I mumble in my sleep, somebody's shifting stuff, chucking it into a skip. I stare into the curtains. There's a rip, and a man with a beard in there, like some kind of sea god, a Neptune ... Shit, my head! It sings out, it must be gone ten. I roll over and stare into her pug, I focus on her moustache. Fine, intricate, almost invisible, and her beard, a little bit more robust. Aah, my saviour of the fog, I remember you now: Rosy of the waist of heaven ... It all comes rushing back to me; I've seen her someplace before, Chatham Station or someplace.

Christ! My head clangs and a mouthful of snot ... I go take a piss and clean my pegs. I scrape my tongue against my front teeth and spit yellow, a bit of blood ... splash my face and make tea ... a little tray, I bring the pot and wake her gently. She comes round, she smiles and she's got her teeth in, a sweet crooked smile. She sips at her tea and lights up a cigarette.

'You know, you saved my life last night. I'll tell you about it one day ... No kidding, you saved my life ... I'll write it all down.'

I say it plain, to make sure I've made myself understood.

'Really, you write as well?'

'Here, look ... I'll show you something.'

I reach for the pile of books and pull out a couple of my pamphlets.

'This is some of my stuff ...' I hand it to her. 'This is my shit!'

She beams, I've made her day. And she doesn't pretend to look out of politeness either, not like all those other charlatans. She soaks it all in, her eyes shining through the mascara.

'Oh, they're lovely! Shall I pay you for them?'

'No, no!' I hold my hand up, I shake my head.

She goes for her bag.

'No, they're yours. Here, I'll sign them for you ... No, seriously, take them, they're a gift.'

She fumbles for her purse, the stupid bitch goes for her coppers. I have to stop her, she's ruining everything!

'No, please they're yours, it's nothing!'

That's me, Mister Modest. A real big shot. She lets the coins clink back into her purse, then snaps it shut. I breathe easy again

... I shrug, I sling two of them on to the table nonchalantly. 'Yeah, this is it, my stuff, a couple of them, anyway ...' I watch her eyes, reading my lines.

'Did you do the drawings, too?'

'The sketches? Yeah.'

Oh, dear God, I've found one here, a good one, one that appreciates my art, one that understands the struggles of a young writer, not a critic, but a connoisseur! I look over her shoulder – dear Lord, let our eyes lay on that glorious page together. Ah, what poetry, what prose! Just one of my humble efforts, you understand, not my best, not my worst, but I must admit some of it I like, some of it I like very much indeed! I place my arms round her, rest my chin on her head, and I bask in it. The warmth gushes out of me ... She finishes the page, carefully closes the book and places it, as if a jewel, into her shoulder bag. She looks up and I make to kiss her ...

'Ooh,' she squeals, 'did you paint those?'

She jumps up and skips with delight in front of my canvases. I smile and wince. She enthuses, dashing back and forth, flirting between the doodles ...

'Oh, they're wonderful! You use a lot of blue, don't you? Do you like blue?'

'Sure ...' I say. 'Blue, black, red, green even, but mainly blue.'

She nods thoughtfully. I rack my brains, hungry for her attentions, trying to keep the subject on me.

'Prussian, I enjoy ... and a little cobalt. Always reminds me of Van Gogh, that cobalt.'

I bite my lips ... She giggles and her tits jump up as she goes on tip-toe, her face jammed in amongst the paint.

'I can't see ... My eyes, I'm nearly blind.'

I watch her arse, her calves flex and relax sending little shimmies right up to the divide.

'I do fashion,' she tells me. 'I make all my own clothes ... What do you think?'

She spins and twirls, still speaking, always speaking.

'What I like about your pictures are the lines, black, aren't they? Lots of black lines ... You use a lot of black, don't you?'

'Yeah, and a lot of blue, lamp for the black, Prussian for the blue, with just a hint of cobalt ... You can have one if you like, as a present, go on, take your pick ... any one you want!'

She gurgles like a child, shaking her head in disbelief.

I repeat it. 'Any one you like!'

I stick my thumbs in my lapels and swagger. The young artist, struggling, but generous. I lay it on thick.

'The green one, I want the green one!'

'Ah yes, a wise choice, a self-portrait . . . an early piece.'

I lift it from the wall and admire it at arm's length, place it at the foot of the bed and take a pace back . . . 'It's yours!' I say and let the smile come. I've been holding it off, pinching my cheeks, but it cracks, it breaks through and she smiles too and comes into my arms. I look at her little moustache, a shadow where the upper lip should be. I kiss her in the mouth, my tongue up against her plate. I push against the metal and we fall to the bed, always to bed.

45. TWO SOULS UNLOVED

It doesn't take long to learn each other, to start growing sick of all those childlike qualities which we at first found so alluring. Conquest is all to a man who doesn't know himself. To know the secrets of her unsheathed body, inch by inch, mole by mole, sag by sag. To wake to the bad breath and decay. And then you have to make the introductions, to kiss the mother and explain everything to everyone.

My little Sheila? I had to tell her of the new woman, of my twisted, self-serving manoeuvrings. And I leave her to carry my hopes, my beliefs, and my veiled betrayals. Because I'm not a man, I'm a man-boy, and to a man-boy a woman is there only to nurse his troubled brow, to understand him and to carry his vile crippling sickness.

And on the streets my head revolves on a spring, I stagger, a child lost in the realm of women. Hungry for their praise and recognition, for their bravery and forgiveness.

I've done a lot of musing over the years as to my hunger for women and hatred of self. So much so that I've grown dizzy of it. A terrible pounding fills my skull: the fear of the mother, of that power she holds over me ... And I blunder through this world, and the women walk past and the days gleam like a gun. And I go down on my knees and adore them. To destroy them, to tread them underfoot! A cunt, after all, is such a fearful thing, with its folds and counter-folds. Whereas a pretty little arsehole is a much more pleasing fellow to contemplate, so much less threatening than the slug that sets it off, so to speak.

And I was saved that night by my Rosy, my Dolli, and I kneel to it, and kiss it. Stood astride the world, to be God in her eyes, for at last the degradation to be ours.

There's nothing that bitch liked better than a thick one up her arse, looking over her shoulder, mascara like a spider. Then I'd pull it out, feeding it into her mouth, and she'd take it full in the face, laughing and coughing through the sauce ... I look round for a spunk rag, pick up my mother's kitten and wipe the gunk off her chin. Kitty springs left and right, she hops and goes meow, cute and sticky! And I fall back to the bed, and I taste myself on Dolli's lips. And we're caught here and now, trapped as two souls unloved.

46. THE FALKLANDS WAR

'You don't know how lucky you are. When we were kids we didn't have any amenities! No running water, no fridge, no bath, nothing!'

'I wish we didn't have a bath.'

She looks at me and slams down the saucepan.

'You're worse than your bloody father! You should be grateful you've got a roof over your head!'

People are always at great pains to point out what you owe them, personally. The exact date, lists of debts and accounts . . . Purely by accident of birth, you're in the red and have the honour of fulfilling their half-baked dreams. You're their property, by virtue of capitalism.

'You're using my facilities! You can mow the lawn!'

Even my mother believed in the sanctity of the lawn. Then the old man chips in. 'Straight lines, I want straight lines! And no toffee papers! Discipline! That's what you need. Discipline!'

We're caught in the gale, he's off on one of his tirades.

'Now, if you could only get a commission! You've always been interested in the sea. The Royal Navy! Now if you could just knuckle down, learn to read and write and get yourself a commission! You're interested in Nelson, aren't you, Steven? If I had my time all over again, I'd go out there, get myself a commission and go to sea! Like your grandfather! The British and the sea! Salt in our veins! You'd like that, wouldn't you, Steven? You're the expert on war! Well, aren't you?'

'I thought grandad was just an ordinary seaman.'

'Ordinary seaman! Able-bodied seaman, I'll have you know! A three striper! AB! My friend, Commander Philips, was only saying to me the other day, 'The AB's were the backbone of the British Navy!' . . . I could put in a word for you if you'd just pull your socks up! It's not too late to get a few O Levels under your belt!'

Him and his 'why don't you get a commission?' And me dyslexic, dragged through the worst schools in Kent and not a qualification to my name! It took them three years to teach me one thing, how to write 'STEPHEN'. Then on parents' day my mother comes into the school and says, 'Oh, it's not spelled S-T-E-P-H-E-N, it's spelled S-T-E-V-E-N.' Oh how interesting! 'Steven' not 'Stephen' . . . Hip-hip-hoo-fucking-ray!

'Why don't you get yourself a commission?'

I eye the cunt sideways. He's parked across the restaurant table from me, picking at his steak. 'Are you sure this is well done? What do you think? The chips?' He drops his knife and fork and swigs at the Claret. 'The Royal Navy,' he confides, 'that's the life!'

He strokes his whiskers, nods and takes another gulp . . . shakes out his napkin and dabs at his kisser.

That's rich! And me with half an O level to my name, and that's after adding all my subjects together . . . And him so interested, after what, eighteen years is it? Eighteen years going on twenty more like! Commission? Commission, humph!

He draws himself up, another flourish of his napkin, then peck-peck on each corner of his mouth.

'Now, take the Falklands War,' he announces. 'Wouldn't you like to be out there? That's where the drama is . . . it's all going on down there. Unfolding! Developing! A very good friend of mine sacrificed his life . . . an exocet right in the midships! You like guns? Well, the drama's in the South Atlantic! The Falklands! That's where the real theatre is!'

He licks his paws like a pussy-cat, pulls his tash straight, his eyes sparkling above his bags.

'I don't want you bringing your whores round Appleton Place, Steven! This is my house! Do you understand me? Get out to the Falklands! Experience some war! Get yourself a real job! Make it happen!'

47. DOLLI BAMBI

The war of more and more and sex held us, and fear too.

'If I just had a hundred pounds a week I could buy all my friends their favourite brands of cigarettes and a bottle of whisky for you.'

She dips a piece of toast into her boiled egg. 'Have you noticed that I only eat yellow food?'

I stare at her. 'What?'

'I only eat yellow food, like dippy eggs are yellow, grapefruit, banana, butter . . .'

'And?'

'Well, they're all yellow and that's my favourite colour!'

'What about toast?'

'That's not yellow!'

'Exactly! That's what I'm telling you.'

She stares into it, her little brain trying to think. She gives up and lights up another cigarette.

'If I had ten pounds a day and a hundred pounds at weekends, I could buy all my friends their favourite brands of cigarettes.'

'What?'

'I could buy two hundred Rothmans for me, and I s'pose you'd want Weights or Woodbines?'

'That doesn't make you generous, sharing what you've got when it's not enough is generous. Any rich bastard can pretend to be generous. You are generous when you give and have nothing. You can be generous with nothing!'

She wedges her lips up under her nose and turns her eyes into slits.

'But I've only got twenty cigarettes to last me! That's five for the morning, five for the afternoon and ten for tonight . . . So, I haven't really got any!'

I stare into her miserly little gob. She spoons in the last of her 'dippy egg' and, still chewing, takes a puff and blows out the smoke, still sucking her teeth.

'Jesus, you're sick! You're tight, you're stupid and you're thick!'

She scowls and sucks in another bitter lungful.

The war of more and more and sex held us, sex and fear too.

'I didn't abort that baby, I just wore my jeans tight, that's all!'

'Yeah? Well, why do I only get to hear of it second-hand? You could have asked me about it! You could of spoken to me!'

And so I confront her with it. She stands there blubbering, her mascara smeared across her face . . . All the hell and the bile of it. Righteous to the core, our Dolli never set a foot wrong in her life. I sit there mesmerised by the clicking of her plate, as she speaks, two clicks to every word. She spits it out, her dumb girlie stream of consciousness, in upper class Margate drool.

'I didn't abort that baby, I wouldn't, I just wore my belt tight, that's all! I thought you'd be angry with me and say that I'd been irresponsible, so I just wore my belt tight and drunk a bottle of Pernod! I'm not saying it's your fault, but I lost it two days after you picked me up and threw me across the room by my stomach!'

I stare at her in disbelief and her voice keeps going on and on, a mad noise like birds . . . And she repeats the whole scenario three times, four times. I'm supposed to read between the lines, to get the implications of her ongoing monologue . . . 'Til I slam my fist onto the table top. 'Be quiet!' I gasp, and drop my pen. 'Be quiet!' I stoop to pick it up. And then silence . . .

'Why do you always write those things? They're not nice! I don't understand what you're writing about or why . . .'

The war of more and more and sex held us, and fear too. And little Dolli Bambi, three years old, dressed up in white lace, ankle socks and a patent leather handbag to match.

'We were staying in this hotel in Turkey, and every morning I'd come down the stairs and the man on reception would ask, 'What's your name then?' And every day he asked me the same question 'Aren't you a pretty little girl then, and what's your name?' And I wouldn't answer him. I just put my nose in the air and walked past. We were there for a whole fortnight, and then on our final day I came downstairs at breakfast time as usual and he says, 'You're a pretty little girl, what's your name then?' and I turn to him and say, 'My name is Dolli Bambi!' then sling my handbag over my shoulder, put my nose in the air and walk out!'

The war of more and more and sex held us, and fear too. Dishing out gallons of grief, we can't quite jam enough misery into our insatiable guts ... We queue up for seconds, we dribble, aah, cute! We're helpless, whimpering like dogs in a snare ...

She held me like a vice and wouldn't let me go. That was her kind of love, alright, a self-perpetuating all-encompassing love, and damn what anybody else thinks or has got to say about it. Because it's so sensitive, so beautiful, so pure and fine. Only a limp dicked homosexual would deny her. Only a charlatan of the closet would dare renounce her sex!

She had a cunt like an octopus. The hanging gardens of Babylon! It grabbed you by the balls and sucked you in, tight as a clam.

The war of more and more and the days hold us, the weeks and the years. But they are leaving, and we too must shuffle forwards ... And I look back over my shoulder to those moments receding like a child waving. Just ten years old, stood naked in a little clearing in the woods. The cold air kissing my loins. Waiting to be adored, to be struck dead by God! And I drop to my knees and burrow a hole with my sheaf knife, tearing at the roots, then sticking my little dick into the black earth, my little arse trembling, my heart like a drum.

The war of more and more, and every time I look up that bitch is there to remind me that I am a failure in love and life ... And the day comes when I bring her gonorrhoea and herpes. And I have to quit the drink, check my sores and take my medicine. I crawl to the pisser and piss blood ... And even when I take up my pen, that bitch won't leave me be. She stalls me. She entices me.

'Why do you write those things?'

'Because they're true.'

'I'd rather you lied!'

Lying curled up on the deck in front of me, her arse dancing at the end of my nose, the cleft outlined, trembling, and, 'Why can't you just fuck me sometimes? Why can't you tie me up and beat me? Why can't you just piss on me!' 'Til I rise from my typer and unloop my belt.

'Shut up!' I scream at her . . . 'Just shut up!'

A young writer can't even breathe. I lay the strop on 'til her laughter turns to sobs, then unzip and she mumbles and moans, pushing back onto my fat dick with her bruised rump, and I finger the welts and slap her again.

The war of more and more, and no matter how much I curse, spit and hate, my heart is dragged like a stone, and we descend, broken, delirious with pain. Grateful to be half-loved . . . to be lost in this sickening mire of sodomy.

48. PAINTING THE TRUTH

And every morning she sits there munching toast, wearing your pyjamas and dressing gown. And the hairs on her chin, I count them, sixteen is it? Black and curling and the little moustache and side-burns. And all the time she's just feeding her face, totally oblivious, and I can't understand why she doesn't quit feeding, get off her arse and take a goddamn shave!

'I don't even wear those pyjamas, I only wear them when I'm ill, so what the fuck are you wearing them for?'

'I want to go to the party,' she says.

'What?'

'There's a party tonight. I want to go to it.'

She lifts her little pug and mumbles between the crusts. She dips in with the knife, takes another wedge of butter, crams it into the bread then jams the whole loaf in her face. She talks and she eats, dusting herself down. Gets to her feet, slaps her thighs, lifts the butter dish and shakes the table cloth out onto the floor. I watch her – I'm fucking speechless.

'Is it four o'clock yet?'

'It's fucking half past four! And what the fuck did you do that for?'

'What?'

'Shake the fucking table cloth out on the floor? What's the fucking point in that?'

She looks at me totally confused, like I'm talking a foreign language . . .

'You use a table cloth so you don't fuck up the table. You don't shake all the crap off onto the floor! Jesus you must be fucking stupid! I mean, I don't give a damn about the fucking table, I don't want to know about it, but I do know what a fucking table cloth is used for!'

She looks at me, folds the cloth, and lifts her little sniffer in the air. She's got this nose like a submarine, like two torpedo holes, she wrinkles it and tries to think, the poor bitch.

'I wonder what I should wear?'

She walks over to the mirror and examines herself.

Say what you like but there's something magical about the way a girl plaits her hair, snaking from hand to hand, little twists and tugs. And the neck drawn out, head cocked . . . Next, she draws the eyes in. I watch her with the pencil, black stuff, heavy, glue-like. I have to watch, to see the way they put everything on, to see their backs, the calves grow taut, she sticks out her arse, stands on one leg and the sock goes on. I sit on the side of the bed and pour three glugs of Scotch in my tea.

I'm thinking about the time she attacked me outside that house on Barnsol Road. The fat Jewish mumma and her daughter who worked in the hamburger bar. She's got this six year old kid and no husband, works the evening shifts, gets home at about three or four in the morning and brings a chocolate milkshake home for her kid. A double thick chocolate shake.

'In case he wakes up in the night and he's thirsty.'

I look at her and I almost laugh. I hook my fingers in the front of my belt and grin.

'It's no good,' I tell her, 'it won't work . . .' I say it gentle like, I don't come straight out with it, I sidle up to the point. 'Leave him a glass of water, you'll just rot his teeth with chocolate. Look, you see this mess?' I show her my fillings. I lean back and pull a face, I show her right the way up to the back, nothing but lead! 'It's no substitute for a father; my mother used to give me Crunchie bars . . .'

She looks away and guffaws. Not in the least bit impressed, as if I know nothing, as if I've spent my whole life in fairyland. I show her the evidence. I tell her about the Crunchie bars. I don't make a thing of it up, it's all perfectly true, all paid for with pain: a landslide of half-rotten pegs. I stick my fingers in, pull back my cheeks, tilt my head into the light, to get the full effect, to illustrate the point – no dice! Go fuck a porcupine kid! She turns on her stilettos and cuts me dead.

I'm left standing here sucking my thumbs. I take them out, wipe them off. I wonder if anybody saw that, a witness, people who could back me up?

I turn to Dolli. 'The stupid bitch didn't listen to a word I said, fucking chocolate milkshake!' I let her know my opinions, but she's too busy gushing, bowling everybody over. She charms and enthuses . . . The princess of tittle-tattle, she turns banality into an art form . . . But somehow cute. No kidding, even intelligent people are taken in, a girl with tits and arse and she can talk goo as well? Some kind of miracle on legs! They mistake ignorance for innocence. Me too, I don't give a shit what she says, as long as I'm putting my dick in her arse.

'If I could just have ten pounds a day and a hundred at weekends, I could buy all my friends their favourite brands of cigarettes, in big boxes!'

I wipe my thumbs on my shirt. I get the drift, we're playing that old tune again. I empty my drink, walk over and put my mouth to her ear. 'You think I don't know what you're like, but I do. You pretend that you're generous but you're a mean-spirited, spoilt little slut! All you care about is playing cute. Well, you aren't so fucking cute, your tits are round your waist and you stink! All you want is money and spunk, now shut your stupid face and get me another drink!'

She oozes and contracts, she giggles, pouts and wobbles. She's looking for a punch-up, I can tell that much. I sieve the poison, a last droplet, I lick at it, it travels round the rim, trickles down my wrist . . . I suck at it and hand her the empty.

'Go see if you can blag me a Scotch.'

I say it polite, I give her arse a slap. She juts it out against my hand and goes fetches it, a brimful. I talk to this other one with the sharky eyes, she has these pointy tits, but her eyes are too far apart. Then Dolli rolls up with my Scotch. I sniff at it, then down it in one. I leer round the room then burp.

I let them know just what sort of genius they're in the presence of. A real little Bukowski, a writer who's not to be messed with. I swig it back, oafish. I feel I have to, I'm not in control, but I desire power.

I lay my eyes on Sharky's tits; I want a bite, a little suck. I leer, and she smiles back. She jiggles them together, changing weight from foot to foot, so glad to add to the effect . . . I look around grinning, we're all hooked in some hideous game . . . I turn to Dolli, she hands me my glass, half full, I drain it.

'Give us a cigarette!'

'I haven't got one.'

'You got a whole packet, now give us one!'

'I haven't got any ... They're to last me until tomorrow. Ten for this evening and two for breakfast. So, I haven't got any!'

'You got one in your gob, give me that!'

I grab at it, I cross my eyes and make a guess – I snatch it from her lips, heavy, rouged, black blooded. I look at her and away. I puff through the bitter smoke, grinning at my new found friend. I take a deep lug. Sharky admires me, I can tell. I flick ash on the carpet and swagger. Then Dolli snatches the cigarette from my lips.

Sharky looks at her outraged. 'That isn't very nice!' she pipes up. She's got a voice, she comes to my defence, ah, touching. I give her a look, one of gratitude, weighted, of deeper meaning.

Dolli grabs my snout and crumples it, brown hands, gold rings, blood-red nails, final. Then she turns to Sharky, 'Piss off, you slut!'

One second I'm puffing on a cigarette, the next it's gone, shredded, discarded, dropped to the carpet.

Dolli jams her mug in Sharky's face. 'Go piss off, you slut! You fucking slag!'

I have to step in, to part them. I push Dolli in the chest. 'You're the slut!' I tell her. I point it out, I go to great lengths to explain, I lean my face in for emphasis. 'You're the selfish little bitch! You got a whole packet of cigarettes; I fucking paid for them and you won't give me one!'

I feel it coming, the air warms up, rushing ... I see her forearm, the hand, a shimmering of Turkish gold, then she lets it go. Doink! in my left eye. A flash of white light, something goes bang – I never saw it coming. I shake my head and let her have one straight back, dead on target. I line it up ... then she ducks. Naturally, I just missed ... I follow through, and the Jewish mumma, it was close my friends, very close! I pulled it just in time, at the last second. The old bat does her nut, she spoils the fun and almost gets a clout into the bargain. I apologise, I try to explain. I tell her to stick it! She's getting on my nerves, who's she to judge? She takes my glass in her soft fat hand.

'I think you've had enough, young man!' And she shows me the door.

I take Dolli's arm. 'We're leaving if that's her attitude, of our own accord. Bye bye, nice to meet you!' And she throws us out.

So we had a little disagreement? Big deal, it's all over now, everything's hunky-dory.

We exit, we get the hell out of there. To my mind the Scotch was watered! I let her know my opinions, from the garden gate. Then she's joined by the driver on the porch step, shouting his big mouth off.

'You touch a hair on her head and I'll fucking kill you!'

He's talking about darling Dolli; say that's nice, my own companion, my pal from old. I take a double look, I check my hearing. 'Yeah, I recognise you, you turnip!' I give as good as I get. I put him straight, my friend perched on the porch. 'Parsnip!'

I turn and pull my collar up.

It's dark out here, residential, orange street lights. A thousand hedges, green black, row upon row of them, gardens, lawns. And the noise of our revellers decreasing, grown quieter by distance. I lean against a parked car, and my sweetheart, the way her upper-lip just seems to glue straight onto her nostrils, no gap . . . a flared effect . . .

'Oi, Stingray, come here!'

'Don't call me that!'

'Stingray!' She pouts and flares them even wider. 'Stingray!'

I tell her what I think of her and her little show back there. What does she think she's playing at, slapping me in public? I've a good mind to even it out.

'Come on then, hit me if you're such a big man, come on hit me!' She turns cute on me, tilting her stupid little jaw. I put my hands in my pockets and look up and down the street. 'Come on you wanker, hit me!'

'Take your plate out your mouth and I'll bust your fucking jaw!' She's got my goat now.

'Hit me, you wanker!'

I jump and grab her arm, I lunge, but she flinches and draws back. I grab an arm and a shoulder, I tilt her, lean my weight and swing from my hips. She goes down, doubled up, a little thump. I hear the back of her head thack! against the kerbstone. 'Pardon me!'

She looks up at me, kind of surprised. I dust my hands and get the hell out of there. I straighten my collar, and run. I don't look back, just one quick glance and I'm off. Her lying on her back howling.

'Come back here, you wanker! You can't even hit me properly! You can't punch me! And you can't fuck me! Come and piss on me you bastard! Come back here and fuck me!'

I hear her loud and clear. I stop in my tracks, turn and retrace my steps.

'You wanker! You can't hit me properly and you can't fuck me properly!'

I start pacing back down the street towards her. She scrabbles to her hands and knees, she's having a change of heart, groggy, she shakes her hair, volumes of it, sticking to her face. She wants to get up, but I'm too quick, going full pace . . . I lift her with my boot, I place it under her rump. Thud-ump! That brings her to her toes, right in the arse! And another, lighter, more playful, to the guts, under her little belly. That knocks the gas out of her. She's not quite so talkative any more. She quits her monologue and rolls in the gutter, a little trail of spittle, glittery, snail-like, on her chin.

The squad car turns the corner flashing its light, real pretty, a little Christmas tree on top. And the man at the wheel, beneath his peak of gold, a familiar figure, something jogs my memory. It's the eyes, opaque blanks.

She's regretting her big stupid mouth now, only whimperings, little cooing noises, dove-like. She wants to be loved, the little darling. I drag her to her feet.

'Oooooh! Ooooh! Ooooh! I want sex, and I only want it with you.'

I pull her back by the hair. 'Quit making that racket, the fucking police are here! Shut it! Are you alright?'

The old bill rolls up, two of them in their panda car, just as I'm helping her to her feet.

'Nothing to worry about, officer, a little bit too much to drink, that's all, she tripped . . . I'm taking her home . . . We're waiting for a cab . . . Should be along any moment now . . . She slipped and banged her head . . . She's alright, she'll be OK once I get her indoors. Thanks for stopping anyways, night-night . . . Mind how you go!'

And then, magically, a taxi turns the corner. I stick my hand out and jump up and down on the spot. He sees me and I flag it down, open up the back door and lay her out on the back seat. I say my farewell to the boys in blue and leave. I convince them after many reassurances, after I show them the exact spot where she fell. Then this taxi comes along, just in the nick of time. A little face at the window, a cloth cap and blue veins on his nose. I jump in and give him the address.

That was a close call, and that police officer, I recognised his mug from someplace ... I look back at the flashing lights, receding. I wash my mind and lay back, I allow the whisky to carry me off ...

By the time we get to my mother's place, I'm spark out, dead to the world. I let Dolli drag me from the taxi, I help her carry me up the garden path. She finds my key and lets us both in. I crawl across the hall and pass out on the bathroom floor. I've gone for a loop, I sleep where I fall, I see the tiles coming up, black and white and I let myself drop. I kiss them, I embrace them ... cool ... for my battered head ...

I can't stomach climbing into bed with that hungry little bitch again, the world can stop.

Dolli goes to the kitchen to make tea. Then I hear her footsteps coming back down the hall and I feel her breath on my cheek. She's pulling at my collar. I keep my peepers tight shut. She brings water and flicks it in my face. She slaps me. I don't bat an eye-lid ... She lifts my head up by the hair and lets it drop back onto the bathroom tiles, once, twice ... This time she throws it back with force. No more experiments, with contempt. She lifts it high them smacks it back down. My jaw jars, a little bounce, the desired effect. But it gets her precisely nowhere. I'm playing possum. She begs me, she pleads with me.

'Get up! Wake up, come on! You've got to wake up!'

I just lie there, not even a smirk, not a half grin even ... Then she goes for my flies, she's turned all romantic on me ... She drags my poor little pecker out and starts nibbling at the end – hot needles ... I hold myself trance-like ... I feel her face come back over mine.

'Get up! You've got to get up! Now!'

Smack! smack! smack! My head rebounding, I keep schtum ... Then my mother's voice, I hear her coming downstairs.

'Is that you?'

'It's only us, June.'

'You haven't let my cats out, have you? Minnie, Minnie, Minnie! Nig-Nig-Nig!'

She pulls up at the bottom of the stairs and surveys the situation.

'He's as bad as his father! Worse! At least his father can still stand when he comes home!'

'Don't worry, June, I'll look after him.'

Dolli goes all lovey-dovey on me, stroking me hair.

'Take my advice and don't waste your time on him, let him rot! At least his father can still stand when he has had a skinful.'

I smile to myself, invisibly, on the inside. Oh, so she's back on that old chestnut again, the 'you're worse than your father' routine. 'At least his father can stand when he comes home!' ... All bullshit, one hundred per cent lies and deception! She doesn't mention him pissing in the wardrobe, or giving her a black eye.

'He's just like his father! Like father, like son! His father might be a drunkard, but at least he knows when to stop, at least he can still stand!' (Bollocks!)

Dolli can't wait to ingratiate herself. She bends over backwards. She embellishes. Absolutely no doubts about it, I'm a villain! A skunk! And a buggerist! An out and out queer, most likely!

'I couldn't get him to leave the party, June . . . Look, you see this? He hit me and he got us thrown out of the party! I had to call a taxi, to get him home, and I had to pay for it myself, out of my own money.' (Lies!) 'My last two pound, that's all I had! That's all I've got to last me the rest of the week, and now I've spent it on him!' (Actually, she stole the money from my pocket!) . . . 'My last two pound! And my cigarettes, I haven't got any for tomorrow! I went out with forty, but now they're all gone! I don't know how I could have smoked all of them . . . I shouldn't give so many away, I can't afford it, I'm too generous . . . I don't mind giving someone a cigarette if I've got enough for myself for later, but I've only got ten left, and I need those . . . That's fair enough, isn't it? I shouldn't have to pay for that taxi, just to get him home! I shouldn't have to pay for him!'

The old girl goes and fetches her purse. I hear her rummaging around in the drawer, then she returns and hands over the coins.

'No, I couldn't, June, I don't expect you to.'

Dolli pockets it and they chew the fat, agreeing with each other 'til they're sick. They completely sympathise with each other. I lie there motionless, memorising the bullshit, each answer. Then I feel them grab hold of my feet and try and drag me out into the hallway, they pull me by my arms . . . by my shirt sleeves. Dolli wants me upstairs but the old girl will have none of it.

'He's too heavy to shift . . . leave him here . . . he isn't bloody worth it! Let him sleep it off!'

'But I want him to go to bed with me, he's got to go to bed with me!'

'Leave him, he isn't bloody worth it!'

The old girl is convinced, besides I'm too heavy. She's all for leaving me where I am. She goes to the cupboard and throws an old duffel coat over me. 'Let him sleep it off . . . He's worse than his soddin' father!'

The light clicks off and their voices disappear upstairs. It's warm and dark on my piece of floor. I lie there, keeping dead still. I can taste the sick in the back of my throat, mixed in with the blood. Carefully, I tuck my tender little pecker away and zip up . . . Suddenly, I sense her again, a presence, a creek on the stairs, and then another . . . It's that hot little bitch on her midnight prowl. She tiptoes over, trips in the dark . . .

I feel her hot little mouth, her lips running over my face and neck, and her little worm, she tries to wriggle it into my gob. I keep my jaws clamped . . . A hot desperate whisper, low down, forced into my ear, repetitive, demanding . . .

'Come on, you wanker! Fuck me! You've got to fuck me! Get up those stairs and fuck me! Get up, you fucking wanker!'

Breathy, hissed through her falses; they click when she talks, didn't I tell you? It gives me another tune to listen to, its own little rhythm. Following behind her inanities, her demands for love and money: click-click-click! clickity-click! click-click-click! click-click-click! The dancing of her false pegs, an accompaniment, something else to concentrate on, to give a little variety.

'Fuck me! Get up those stairs and fucking fuck me!'

Click-click-clickity-click! click-click! A symphony in Morse . . . her damp little mouth against my eardrum. And then her teeth sink in. Tears well up in my eyes, but I don't let out a peep. I feel the blood, she grinds her maulers, little trickles . . .

'Get up! Fucking get it up! You've got to fuck me! Come on, piss on me! You fucking bastard!'

She bites at my neck, little explosions of pain. Then it subsides. I breathe again, I let it out slowly . . . a sigh, low down, gentle . . . not to be heard . . . Then silence, a rustle of clothing, and she slaps it in my face, holds onto my ears, squats and rubs it right round my kisser, a mouthful of hair pie! Yeasty, a special stink, smack bang in the gob! I taste her snail, riding my face . . .

'Come on, you fucking wanker, piss on me!'

She grinds her pelvis so hard you can hear the bones crack. She bounces and sighs. I'm choking on it, my mouth filling up with the glue. I can't breathe. A gallon of syrup mushed in with the thatch, a fish moustache. It tickles my throat, I can't breathe . . .

I'm suffocating ... But I daren't let on ... I gurgle through the paste ... I flap my arms ... I'm going under, one more gulp and I'm done for! She rolls off, cocks her leg and farts. She lets me out of those scissors ... Sweet air, my lungs inflate, I suppress a cough, a splutter ... She lets go my ears and my head clangs to the floor.

'You're pathetic!' she spits.

Suddenly, the lights click on, my world goes red behind my eyelids ... Then all of a sudden she's kissing me, stroking my hair, whispering sweet nothings ... making sure I'm all tucked up nice and snug. 'Am I OK? Do I need anything?' She's playing the doting lover and she's doing a grand job! What theatre, boy was I lucky! What a woman! A proper Florence Nightingale! The light goes on and in walks my mother. Dolli climbs off, she disentangles herself.

'I'm just making sure he's alright, June, that he doesn't need anything.'

'He's not soddin' well worth it!' She spits it out with venom, my sweet mother ... 'Leave him to it! You're wasting your time! Go to bed, he's worse than his bloody father! He doesn't deserve you!'

Ah, that's rich. I've heard some old truck in my crummy life, enough bullshit to fill the Atlantic, and then some more. But that little gem takes the biscuit! The 'he doesn't deserve you!' That's what these cuties will never understand. I've got names, madam, addresses, and a memory. They think I'm dozing, half-pissed, but I'm wide awake! That's right, I remember all of it, all the little indecencies, and I assure you, I'm quite willing to spill the beans, that's right, lying here, soaking in slime. I know what's been said and what's been done unto me, I've heard it all! Two earfuls! In stereo! To the very last detail!

I sit up, open my eyes and say it straight to their faces, clearly and succinctly ... I announce myself, the devil's advocate ...

'I know exactly what you've been saying and I know exactly what you've been doing, I've seen it, I've heard it and I'll remember it all in the morning, everything!'

Dolli minces up her little mush, she tucks her upper lip under her nostrils and scowls. Just then the wind changes, a perfect pug!

With that, I lie back down and continue my little nap.

You've got your face mirrors, your tweezers and your deodorants, but you'll never stop the rot! I'll strip you down and paint you as you really are, and not with gouache, madam, but with tar, this thick!

49. A SPECIAL DAY

I was half asleep, then there's this crash, like something big coming through the letter box. I go check the front door, nothing ... I go to the kitchen and put on a brew. It's freezing out here. I stand on one foot, then the other. I put one foot on top of the other, a little balancing act, then go take a piss. I take another look at the doormat, but there's definitely nothing there. I make the tea and go upstairs to Dolli.

'Did you hear anything? A noise? Like something coming through the letterbox? It sounded like something coming through the letterbox.'

I put the cups down beside the bed.

'Don't spill it, and don't get it on my books, it's not too hot, it's ready to drink ... Don't forget to drink it!'

I place it on the chair. I don't spill a drop, precise ...

'Happy birthday,' she says.

'What? Oh yeah ...'

'Twenty-two.'

'I know.'

'You're old!'

'Not so old.'

'But still old, older than eighteen.'

'I don't look it though, do I?'

I go back downstairs and check all over, even out the back, but no signs. I swore I heard something. I double check, one last look ... I make the tea and come back up. She's awake, watching me ...

'Anything in the post?'

'No, I thought I heard something. Did you hear a big bang, about fifteen minutes back?'

She shakes her head, cups it in both hands, blows and sips. 'It's your birthday today.'

'I know.'

'How old are you?' She's teasing me, playing games.

'Twenty-two!'

She whistles. I put on my shirt.

'Come back to bed.'

'I got to go.'

'What for?'

'I've got to go out.'

'Where are you going?'

'Nowhere ... Up town ... I got to meet someone.'

'Who?'

'No one ... Sheila. I said I'd meet her ... Just this afternoon ... I'll be back tonight. I won't be late.'

'But it's your birthday! A special day! You should spend it with me! Don't go!'

I slip my belt through the loops, buckle it and look down at her. Her lip, somehow it doesn't look right, something about it bothers me.

'I won't be late, I'll be back tonight, I promise. We'll go for a drink ... You can meet me at the Rose and Crown. I'll call you.'

For a man who detests a lie, I've told a few in my time, a thousand porkers ... And there's always some glee, a joy in the heart that goes with it, a little echo from my childhood.

I buckle my belt and check my teeth, scowling to the mirror ... She sniffles into the pillow. I hear it and I ignore it. I feel my bile rising.

'I'm going now ... See you later.'

I go as if to leave, look back over my shoulder. She looks up, panicked. I walk back in, lean over and kiss her. She lifts her stupid face and tries to pull me down onto the bed. I unlink her hands from round my neck, place them back on the bedspread and pat them.

'See you later.'

'I want you to fuck me! Come back to bed and fuck me!'

'I'll see you tonight.' I make my excuses and leave. 'I'll see you down the pub.'

I leave it all behind. Love lives and dies. For those first weeks we fly with our hearts, marvelling at the glorious rediscovery of ourselves, our reflection caught bright and wondrous in that gleaming new mirror. We can't believe our luck, and we thought love was lost, dead even. Oh, pity those who are not in love for we are the chosen, our bumptiousness knows no bounds!

I cross the street and buy cigarettes at the newsagent's. Eyeing the paper whores on the top shelf, then look to my fingernails and pick at the dirt. It doesn't take long to grow sick of a smile. We are filth, we demand much, and give nothing . . . Unloading our bitterness onto each other, dishing out gallons of grief. We exchange notes, we carp on about it. Never to be outdone in the realms of personal misery. But what's more, it becomes habitual – we go and queue up for seconds, for thirds and fourths even. Smack! Bang! right in the kisser! (That's where all the germs are.) We just can't quite get enough misery jammed into our insatiable guts. We're gluttons for it . . . Yet through all this, we still believe ourselves to be righteous, as if it is us who have been wronged, as if life itself had erred against us.

I get out of there and head down towards the station. I'm early and light one up whilst waiting for the train. Staring at the passing faces, shelf-stackers and till girls mostly. The old and the young, the sad and the glib. It's hard for a young writer to find himself, to find that core of love, to even believe it's there, and not just an echoing hollow. You ladies with prams, you taxi drivers, you drinkers of coke, you haters and lovers, where are the artists amongst you? Where are your gaily coloured clothes? Your smiles and your hearts? Here is a young man, doing his best, his utmost, without gods, without fear or favour. Looking for the brave.

My poor white hands, the skin peeling from my fingers. I pick at it in disbelief: Christ, I'm twenty-two years old and I'm decaying! My teeth rotting . . . headaches and herpes.

What we all need is a huge dose of luck, for it to land in our laps like a cooked ham, a tidal wave of pleasure. An impossible tit in our mouths, something to erase all our disappointments . . . But even that would never be enough, and still we'd be dissatisfied and sad, demanding yet more.

The train rolls in. Victoria? I check it, I make sure. I ask but no one seems to know, they don't make announcements; you'd think they'd do that at the least. I climb on anyway and stand by the window. Somebody sweeping under the benches, a bent back and blue overalls. A lady with a little dog, she sits and pats her lap and the dog tries to jump up, it wags its tail like a little propeller, it jumps and slips, then she helps him up, his back legs kicking . . . He licks her hand and jumps at her face . . . The carriage gives a jerk . . . I watch the platform disappearing . . . A last glimpse . . . the little dog, on her lap, and the man at work, sweeping polystyrene cups onto his spade . . .

50. THE BARRIER BLOCK

I have a photo, and photos are sad things, but still I force myself
to look, with a mixture of vanity and disbelief. And there she
stands: little Sheila, wearing her grandmother's straw bonnet, my
old donkey jacket, and a sad little posie of flowers in her whitened
hand. And that's me: skull-faced with a twisted grin. Just a kid,
twenty-two years old to the day. 1 December, a bitter cold
afternoon, bitter cold, the sun slanting in, and us stood amongst
the rubbish outside Brixton Registry Office.

When it comes down to it, maybe I should have stayed with my
wife. Maybe I'd have steered clear of some of the grief if I had.
People used to stop us on the street and ask us if we were brother
and sister. Straight up, no kidding.

'Excuse me, I hope you don't mind me asking, but are you two
brother and sister?'

At a market stall I think it was, an old man, he made the
enquiry, and we laughed and said, 'Yeah, we're brother and sister.'

And we held hands, things like that . . .

We walk into the registry office. Those places are like funeral
parlours: there's always a queue and they leave you in no doubts
that they'll be glad to see the back of you. A little man holds up
a card for us to read. We say the words and before you know it,
it's all over and they usher us out into a side room and point us
to the till. Sheila coughs up £13.50 and they hand over the
certificate, a receipt, something like that.

'Are the couple going to exchange rings?'

We shake our heads. We have to sign the register and leave; the next couple are already waiting on the conveyor belt. No time for pleasantries, just get in, fill up and get out! So we mumble the words and we're back outside, the cold afternoon light slanting in and the photographer took a photo. Us stood in front of the pillars at the entrance, a smile, crisp packets at our feet. We kissed and left.

It was a council flat – The Barrier Block – a skyscraper fallen on its side, nine stories high, curling round the back of Brixton. Sheila shows me round the gaff, built on three floors and still stinking of paint.

'Look, you see that? the little concrete forecourt? They said that was a play area in case we have children.'

I look at our children's future, six feet by twelve.

'Let's go down the pub.'

We walk out through the maze, rising columns, red brick and concrete, unlit terraces, gangways and dungeons. She knows the way, I follow.

I bring a couple of take-outs after the pub, then unpack my stuff. There's a pile of old blankets and a pillow on the floor. Sheila hangs two little plastic cherubs on the wall above our bed. I rinse my mouth with the beer and Sheila comes in from taking a piss and lays down beside me. It's half one in the morning and the dull incessant beat of reggae music is thumping out round the estate. Echoing from below, from terrace to terrace. I stare out into the night.

'Your second name's Betty, isn't it? I like that name Betty . . .'

I lift her vest and suck on her little white teat, I stare at the flesh . . . trying to find my heart, my meaning . . .

I can smell urine, the sour odour comes up from between our thighs, even the sheets take on that same sickly stench. And if I could I would pray and I would cry, but the chemicals are broken and all I know is I feel sad for something which has been inexplicably lost, a hole in my guts that can never be filled again.

I avoid her mouth and kiss her eyes. We lay back in that bed alone, the night getting blacker, the noise of the estate growing louder, the sirens sounding down on Cold Harbour Lane.

51. ELISABETH SARGENT

Before boarding the train, I walk over to the little porno shop behind the bus station, and feel the magical sing of danger in my belly. Of expectation and loss. I put my money on the counter. The character behind the till does the change, puts the magazine in a brown paper bag and hands it over. I walk out, check both ways, lift my belt and slip it down the front of my trousers.

I want to tell him that I know the mag is censored, that I'm not one of these other mugs, one of these old goats thumbing with their zippers. No, I'm not one of the duped, sir, I'm a young writer, with women queuing up to be fucked! Row upon row of them. This is purely for research purposes, you understand . . .

I pocket my change and step out onto the street. A fine rain has started to fall. I pull down my hat and wait to cross back over to the station, and then I see her: my black princess, threading her way between the commuters. She stops and speaks, she sways, and moves on. I follow her arse through the crowds. She re-emerges and starts bothering the people in the bus queue. I adjust my hat, stood in under the arcade, a light drizzle coming down. I push the brown bag down next to my throbbing groin. The streetlights flare up . . . orange . . . tail lights . . . taxis mostly.

She stops and talks with the berks in pinstripes. They wag their stupid heads and moo like cattle, adjust their brollies and look away. They make a great show of staring into the rain and checking their watches. Only when she moves on do their hungry, fearful eyes follow her. From man to man she goes, but no coins pass. Picking her way, soon she will come to me, my friends. I see the inevitability of it, position myself and step out of the shadows. I readjust my titfer, set my jaw, one leg out front, jaunty. The eyes follow her arse as she passes, but none can stomach the reality: hungry, asking, unashamed. She approaches, tottering, drugged and thick lipped.

'Buy me a jacket potato!'

I look up and stammer, caught off my guard. 'Where?'

She peers at me through dark glasses. Then she steps forward and her arm links mine; I look down at it, brown, skinny, entwining. And their eyes: the bugs of the commuters, my companions of old, are left rotting under the arcade. The rain glistening in their beards. They watch as we walk across to the station. Her brown back, then her arse, tight, muscled, a little shelf . . . resentful.

We try all the kiosks but none of them sell jacket potatoes, so we have to make do with scones instead. Dried out, yesterday's I'd say, judging by the mouldy crust. And a piece of stupid butter, hard, as if it was frozen. The scone busts under the pressure of it. I unwrap it, gold foil.

'This shit's frozen!'

I talk to myself; I press it into the scone and it crumbles in my fingers, like dust. I pass the pieces to my black princess. She wants potatoes? Well, scones will have to do, and yesterday's, judging by the texture. I put some to my mouth and swill it down with a swig of tea. Then we notice each other, under the strip lights, two ghosts, strangers who meet by night. We munch the dough, smiling. Then I light one up and offer her the packet, straights . . . She bites into it and spits tobacco, takes a lungful then lets it out slow, her nostrils flaring.

'I want to have your baby!' She says it like that, no beating round the bush. 'I want to have your baby!'

I swallow a crumb, I pick at it, right at the back, I have to jam my fingers in.

She looks at me intently. 'I'm a lesbian, you know!' There she goes again. I pull my finger out and look at it, thin, glistening, a yellow bone, five of them, a whole hand.

'A lesbian?'

'Yeah!'

I nod, put another piece of dough into my trap and chew . . . I have found another one of my friends. The mad rush to me with open arms.

'Do you smoke grass?'

I shake my head and try to swallow.

'No, drink's enough for me.'

'I bet you drink a lot, don't you?'

'Sometimes . . . now and then . . . I do and I don't.'

'Do you want to have sex with me?'

I look her straight back, I'm not afraid to do that. Then I study my cigarette. The ash, I need an ashtray . . . I blink and look away, flick it to the floor and stammer . . . There's skin coming off my fingers.

'I've got to go home. I've got to catch my train . . . tonight, to meet my girlfriend, she's expecting me . . .'

'I want to have your baby!' She places her black hand on mine and drags her cigarette down one inch in one puff, and then says it again, 'I want to have your baby.' The end of her cigarette burns red; I see it reflected in her specs. 'My dad would like you.'

'What's his name?'

'Mister Sargent.'

'Does he drink?'

'Yeah, he drinks.'

'Me and your dad having a pint together?' I smile at that.

She finishes puffing, chucks her butt into her tea, grabs my arm and pulls me to my feet. She leads me back out across the station . . . and the eyes follow us: it's the dress, her dress shows her arse, I know the score by now.

'I'm thirty-two,' she tells me. 'I'm thirty-two, and have to go up the hospital for me injections. I get them up me bum.'

She stops, twists and looks over her shoulder at it. Me too; I let my eyes rest on it.

'I dunno why, but that's where they do it. They put them in there . . . injections.'

I nod.

'Do you want to fuck me?'

My braveness drains from my limbs. What terrible disease will this girl pass on to me?

'Look, I've got to get my train, I've told you already.'

'Can I come with you?'

'I told you, I'm meeting my girlfriend.'

'Will I see you again?'

I shrug and I look away, the platform indicator clacks over. And a man in a kilt, sixty-fiveish stood to attention, every tendon in his neck showing, his tongue hanging out, with the crook of his walking stick wrapped round his neck, sticking straight out in front, horizontal, defying gravity, and his eyes staring, popped.

'Yes,' I hear myself saying.

'Buy me a snakebite?'

'If that's what you want.'

'I'm looking for a boyfriend . . .'

The man in the kilt is still stood there, his face bright red.

'I thought you were a lesbian,' I say absently.

Really, I'm trying a joke, trying to be clever. A proper smart-arse! I don't mean any harm, it's just that other people's lives amuse me, I can't help myself.

'I want to have your baby. I want you to fuck me!'

I realise I'm not helping and pull a straight face. Even I can see it's time to get serious, to make some thinking noises.

'You need someone to look after you?'

'No,' she says, 'just for sex.'

She takes off her sun-glasses and holds me with her eyes which terrify me. I dig into my pocket. I feel my way, exclude the five pound note and go for my small change.

'Look, here's a few bob for your drink, but now I've got to go, or I'll miss my last train,' I lie.

'Give us your phone number.' She holds me with her bulging, bloodshot eyes. 'You don't have to, only if you want sex.'

'I'll give you my address and you write yours here, in capitals, neatly . . . so's I can read it.'

I pass her my special writer's notebook and she scrawls it out . . . I go through my change and pass her 50p. I hand it over without a word, the coin. I drop it into her upturned palm, startlingly pink, but the lines are black. She smiles, puts on her glasses and turns to go.

'You'll be OK?' I ask her.

She nods, goes to kiss me and she tries to put her tongue in my mouth. I have to shrug her off.

'My train,' I explain. 'I'll write to you . . .'

I wait for her to leave, to walk away. I have to watch. That's my pastime, to watch her arse disappear off the station. Her back: brown, black straps, then the little shelf. First one side and then the other, beautiful, resigned. She looks back . . . We touched arms . . . she's gone.

* * *

I climb into the carriage and head straight for the shit house, pull the magazine from my trousers, rip it out of its wrapper and start wanking myself into the sink. I have to study the pictures, to find my beauty. I grit my teeth and pull. I grimace in the mirror, wishing to recognise myself, to know who I am.

I've got these two dead teeth, and this white scum, I scratch at it with my thumb nail. That makes my gums bleed. I spit pink. I look to the pictures and wring the spunk out of me. I slobber on the page ... I want this over and done with, holding my breath willing it to come. I gasp and it jumps out of me.

Dear God, I am scum, a masturbator and a whore to boot! My bloated dick, my fist gone mad, too feared to even fuck! I eye that eggwhite-like puss, lean back on my heels and spurt it into the plug hole. I smear my nob over the page. My face gone ugly. I dab at myself with a tissue. I can't breath. I am dying. I hold onto the sink and the magazine falls to the piss-spotted floor, slowly. I button up my flies and stand on the floor stud. The water comes in fits and spurts washing my children away.

I pick up the soggy magazine from the floor. I get out of there and head up the corridor, look both ways, slide open the window and chuck my ladies out onto the tracks.

'Goodbye, you tarts! You fuckers of arseholes and breast! You slags of easy virtue! Thank-you, you sluts! I loved you once, but now it's over, finito! Farewell! And I should tell you that in truth I never really loved any of you, nor you me! Our life together was nothing but a hollow sham! And to be honest, my dears, you disgust me! Your lips, your teeth, your strange bodies! Be gone with you, you harlots of the night!'

I watch the mag jerk like a white ghost, a ripped page, a sad tit, it flops and kicks on the tracks. A white torso, beheaded ... then wrapped by darkness.

'Bye bye! Farewell sweet maidens, you drinkers of spunk! I send you a kiss, for old times sake, no hard feelings ... We were once young and carefree, but now we must part! Other men shall have you, men of the tracks, tough men, wanking and hateful. You have my blessings, I wish you every happiness.'

I spit and have to duck my head, the tunnel is approaching.

52. A PIECE OF SAD CURTAIN

I shut the window, climb into a compartment and sit with my companions. The hot faces and the damp mouths. We avoid each other's eyes, staring to the ceiling, to the floor, to our papers, to our feet, but never smile or speak. Anything to avoid the eyes in case someone should read our shame.

The sweat trickles down my collarbone and licks at my ribs. I smell my own rancidness, the stench forcing its way up my nose. We're drowning in a sea of piss. It sweeps the length of the carriage, knocking seats and commuters sprawling. Everything that isn't nailed down twice comes adrift. The train crashing over bridges and down tunnels, kicking at the rails like an insane mule. Everyone's mug gets compressed into their neighbour's mug, a real chamber of horrors. Not faces at all, just monkey skulls coated in fat and fear. Their expressions melt away and drip like cooked cheese.

And it doesn't seem that the living are quite living anymore, and the dead are more than just dead. Every corpse the world's ever shunned is chattering its teeth and rattling its bones like a billion hailstones drumming on the inside of my brain box. And howling we climb out through the windows, and swarm across the tracks, storming the embankments. Chatham High Street, there's not so very much of it left, a shopping arcade, a bus stop and a blown-out pub. The town cleaved in two, whole communities erased and zeroed. Their choice of wallpaper? It's there for all to see, hanging off the wall, two storey up, cupboards, fireplaces . . .

a piece of sad curtain. Whole terraces of buildings torn down. They've been wiped out, turned into nothing, turned into car parks, mostly . . .

The whores of Padgit Street? Atomised! The Brook? Supermarketed! It's the greatest shopping expedition in the entire history of mankind! Everything must go! A last day sale at never to be repeated prices!

The air beats like a pulse, like wax in your ears. The shoppers swarm like angry flies, taking deep breaths and clasping their bargains to their chests with fear. The mayor togged out as Mister Pickwick, he inflates and turns pink as a plum. He grins, showing his teeth . . . He revolves in blue, like a television set, his head on a pole. It extends, the tongue comes out, that's for sure . . .

'Ga-ga!' he says.

He's smiling, both eyes. He blinks, he flutters, milky-white . . .

'I'm true!' he says. 'Like you said it yourself in your own head.'

53. A CIRCLE OF LUST

The first thing I do is look up Dolli. I try the pub – no dice. I walk up to her gaff and hang about her doorway, moth-like. I try the handle but the latch is down on the inside. I walk back up the entrance hall and straight into this old wheelbarrow.

'Jesus fucking Christ!'

A man could break his fucking neck on a thing like that! I kick at it, then I hear someone. I go dead quiet ... It's the old git upstairs arguing with his telly. Then I hear some footsteps. I get out of there and nip back down the boozer. A right and a left, round the side of the building, down the back alley, jump the railings and I'm on the High Street, again.

I cross to the George Vaults, take a gander in the window on tippy-toes: no one. I push the door and walk in. A regular pawn shop, busted furniture and a thousand tea cups hanging on hooks from the ceiling. I order a Guinness and a double off Old Noddy the landlord, stuffed behind the bar. He tells me all about the weather, what it's been up to all week, and what's in store for tomorrow. And all the time his head's going up and down like a dog, agreeing with himself. A thousand tremors ... I say 'yes' eight times then nurse my drink over to the corner table and hole up there 'til chucking out time. I bung a coin in the juke box to let him know I'm not for talking. I work alternate pints and doubles. I sink three of each before the bell goes and even then I have to argue the toss for a last shot, the mean-spirited old sod! Noddy takes my glass and pours it begrudgingly. One last gargle, I down it in one, say goodnight and take a stroll.

This time, I try Dolli's back door. I climb through the fire
escape and check the window. I have to flex my retinas to see past
the cobwebs. She's in there, alright, sat watching her stupid telly
without her glasses on. I've told her about that before! And it isn't
even tuned in! No picture, just this voice barking out bullshit.

Dolli pushes the cat off her lap and walks out into the hall. I
try the handle, the door opens and I let myself in. Then she comes
back in starkers, that makes my heart hurt. She does a little circuit
of the sofa, chasing pussy. I keep in the shadows, behind the
dresser. I watch her magical arse walk round the room and feel
the stout bottle in my pocket. She gives up on kitty and walks
back out to the bathroom.

The kitten runs over to me, I rough up his ears and go down on
all fours. We both go to the toilet door, listening for the little
tinkle. I wait 'til she's in full flow then stand and push open the
door. She's sitting there, brown as a berry, twiddling her toes. The
daft bint isn't in the least fazed, in fact she's pleased to see me . . .
I walk in, unbuttoning my stiffy. I wave it under her nose, her
little tongue comes out and starts to lap at it. A hard jet hits her
straight in the kisser – she screams and giggles. I squirt it over her
tits, into her lap, in golden cascades . . . Dolli shrieks and leaps
up. Still pissing, I lift her and push her down into the bath. I hose
her down from head to foot, flexing my abdomen, pumping it
over her face. She snorts it out, frothing over her lips, swilling
between her fillings. She spits it out, choking, legs akimbo, her
chin dripping. The dam has burst, I shake it, a last few droplets,
little tears of Scotch.

Dolli reaches up and gives it a pull.

'Make it thick!' she says. 'I want you to put it up my backside!'

She clambers around in the tub, banging it like a drum . . . She
climbs out and bites at it, she slaps it against her udders, bends
over the side and rubs its nose in the split. She sways it like a
Hovercraft, and the rose on her left cheek, tattooed.

'Put it in my backside.'

I kneel and kiss it, the little fan of black hair, just at the bass of
the spine, two dimples and then her arse; I put my tongue in there.
She looks over her shoulder, knees knocking. 'I want you to put
it in.'

I hop from foot to foot, I nudge it between the cheeks, but the
thing's blunt! It takes me eight goes, and then some more! She spits
on her palm and wanks it, whimpering and chewing at her lips.

'Put it in! I want you to put it all in!' She reaches round and pulls the cheeks apart. I have to ease my finger in there to release the pressure, to help tuck it in . . . And then the taps, I bang my knee. I have to climb off and try from another angle. The trouble is, is that I'm slipping in the piss, I can't get a footing . . . I have to go up on tippy toes and try lowering it in from above, straddling the universe . . . my stomach and thighs cramping . . . I breathe on the mirror. A hideous mark . . . I snort through my nose, bug-eyed and drooling . . .

'It's getting thicker!' she tells me. 'It's getting thicker and your balls are like a bag of marbles!'

I take a deep breath. I rest my hands on my hips.

'Is it all in?'

I look down at her brown arse, I slap it, it flexes . . .

'Just the head,' I tell her.

'Ooh,' she simpers.

I hold her hand. 'Feel how thick it is.'

'Jesus! Put it all in . . . please, please!'

I try, but I can't get the leverage; her arse trembling like a horse, she sways it through the steam.

'I always forget how thick it is!'

I take her hair in my fist and lift her head.

'Where do you want me to cum, in your mouth or in your arse?'

'I don't know . . . In my mouth.'

'Say "please".'

'Please.'

I ease it out of her arse, put my foot on the side of the tub and feed it to her, holding it right down at the base. I wave it under her nose, then it jumps out of me, squirting on her tongue, hot little jets and her lapping at it, slurping at the juice. It shoots across her cheek, clots of the stuff, in her eyelashes . . . I wring the life out of me . . . I twist it like a knot, my knees shaking . . . gulping for air . . . And she smiles up at me through the spunk, piss dripping from her chin. I stoop and kiss her mouth and her hand goes for my wet dong, her tongue in my ear.

'Make it thick again.' Her voice is a hot whisper. 'Put it in again, please.'

And no matter that my heart is nailed to that circle of lust, I will not, for no man can stay there. And so I stand, button my fly and turn to face the wall.

54. A TYRANNOSAURUS REX OR A SQUIRREL

Our great desire as human beings is to lose ourselves, to forget, and to rest ... To become someone or something else! We look inwards, then quickly look outwards again, double quick! We travel, we buy and sell, we indulge ourselves. You require money for that, you lose yourself a whole lot deeper and easier with money.

'What are you going to be when you grow up, Steven?'

'I dunno ...'

'Not "I dunno". I don't know ... I don't know, father ... not "I dunno" ... Juny! This child has been playing over the council estate again! And don't tell me he hasn't! I thought I'd banned you, Steven!'

'You can't watch them all the time, and he's been playing over the back. They have to have fresh air, darling.'

'Fresh air, my arse. The child's filthy! and he stinks! The boils! And look at the size of his feet, that can't be natural. Did you clean your teeth, Steven? Because they look worse than your mother's! Can he read and write yet? No, of course he can't, he's too bloody bone idle!'

My mother comes in with the clothes brush. 'I think your taxi's waiting.'

'Well, let it wait woman, I'll leave when I'm good and ready!'

... He turns on me again, 'Finish your Weetabix before you leave the table ... And for Christ's sake, don't slap your chops!'

He puts on his titfer, adjusts his Edwardian drape and consults his timepiece. My mother brushes his shoulders. He inspects himself in the mirror; he finds another speck of fluff, he points it out. 'Look, Juny, there! And another!'

He turns to glare at me, then he's off up the garden path. He boards his taxi and that's the last we see of him. His whiskers gleaming through the back windscreen. A glimpse of his umbrella, tightly furled, his great bone hand encircling it twice, three times. And he's gone.

'I'd like to be either a Tyrannosaurus Rex or a squirrel when I grow up.'

I repeat it to the door. 'A Tyrannosaurus Rex or a squirrel.'

And then the old man went into prison.

55. THE MYSTERIOUS MISTER HAMPERSON

'The mysterious Mister Hamperson', that's how he describes himself, sat opposite me. A bottle of brandy between us on the coffee table, The Bull Hotel, Rochester High Street. He offers me a peanut.

'That's what they all call me in here, you know: the mysterious Mister Hamperson!'

He looks at me and blinks. I stare him back straight in the eye. I let my mouth pinch together at the sides; I try to smile with him, but then have to look down ashamed. It's hopeless. I look up again and manage a half smirk and a nod of the head. This is his great magnanimous gesture, he has taken me into his confidences. I have to make the effort, to let him know that we're accomplices, that we share the same jokes. 'The mysterious Mister Hamperson!'

'All the staff here want to know who I am, but they just can't get it. I stay in the finest suite, I take my meals in my room . . . The best dressed gentleman in the whole damned hotel! "The mysterious Mister Hamperson", that's all they've got on me.'

He laughs fully this time. He turns to Dolli and even encourages her to join in. That was some sight, his eyes bug up and he gets his teeth out . . . terrifying!

He pours the brandies, grasps the cork, two fingers and a thumb, anti-clockwise. He seizes the bottle up in both hands, grace and finesse. Blop-blop-blop-blop! His eyebrows arching . . . blonde, golden . . . He angles the neck perfectly, wets his lips and blop-blop-blop-blop! – three goldfish bowls, perfect! The ballet of the brandy flask.

And every time he leans over to take a peanut it looks like his hat is eating it. First his eyes disappear, then his nose ... then, whoops! The nut pops into his hat. It looks as if his hat's eating the nuts, but of course it isn't, it's just an effect, a trick of the light.

'Steven, there's a good chap, run along and fetch another bottle, will you ... Mister Hamperson's bill!' He turns to Dolli and wrinkles his nose. 'The mysterious Mister Hamperson's bill!'

I leave them with the joke. I back out the room, keeping my eye on the old coot, sat there fondling his brandy bowl, his mouth going, but inaudible: the silence of words ...

I walk to the bar and buy myself a double. That's something, the old bastard being so matey, talking to Dolli, even! That's unheard of, something I'll come to dwell upon.

'That's your dad in there, isn't it?'

I look up, the barmaid's talking to me ...

'Wot?'

'Mister Hamperson, isn't it, he's your father?'

'Yes.'

She turns to her friend. 'See Joan, I told you I recognised him. He's just come out of prison, hasn't he? It was in the paper.'

I follow her now, she's talking about my old man, 'The mysterious Mister Hamperson', the fool with the nuts.

''Cos I thought I recognised him, as soon as he walked in here. Drugs, wasn't it? That's what they arrested him for. "The Downfall of Debonair Director" ... Shame isn't it? A real shame. I don't mean to be rude or nothing, but, why's he sign the register "Sir Jonathan Hamperson"? He's not a "Sir", is he?'

I drain it, I look at her face through the bottom of the glass and speak, 'The mysterious Mister Hamperson!'

56. JAILBIRDS

The old girl starts up again. She's been cranking away for ages now. For years. For decades. For whole epochs! And always the same old truck, giving me the low-down on her crummy existence and what a bum deal she's had. I sit here and nod.

Me, seven years old, looking to her tear-lined face, her nose gone all snotty. 'I'm going to have a nervous breakdown.' That's how she reassures me . . . How she lets me know that everything's going to be alright, that I'm safe and cared for.

'I'm going to have a nervous breakdown.'

And I don't know what a nervous breakdown is, all I'm sure of is that she's going to leave me, and that I'm going to die, most probably.

I duck and dive, wading through that never-ending barrage. She talks to the cat, to the teapot, anything that will sit still and listen. Humming, murmuring, twittering away to herself on the edge of hearing.

No kidding, she talks to herself in whispers, that's how nuts she is. She peters out mid-sentence, then someone sticks a starting handle in her mouth, and she's off again.

I've heard it all before, what a 'low-down crook' the old man is, and how 'I'm marching in his footsteps'. I turn off and stare into the middle distance, I suppress a yawn, I agree, I rummage under my fingernails . . . I agree! I agree! I agree! Shit, I'll agree to anything!

'Yes mum, yes mum, yes mum, I know mum. Yes mum.'

I have to check my tongue in the mirror, broad, flat, pink, very pink . . . A large tongue, a tongue screaming with blood.

'Yes mum.'

'He wanted me dead, Steven, you can vouch for that!'

'Yes mum.'

'Do you think I should divorce him?'

'Yes mum.'

I've said that a few thousand times over the years, she's not the only one content with talking to herself. 'Divorce him!' But she doesn't bat an eyelid. She's happy talking to the birds, cranking away sixteen to the dozen. But strictly in whispers mind, hushed, conspiratorial.

Didn't I tell you? Whenever his name is invoked, the holy one – 'Our Father' – only whispers, low-down, in case he's listening . . . in case he's picking us up on longwave in London. His ears are everywhere . . . She'll carry that one with her to her grave: the fear of his reprisals.

'He wanted me dead, you can vouch for that,' she whispers to me whilst polishing the saucepan, 'and now he has the nerve to want back in! After all these years! And to think, I smuggled twenty pounds of my own money into that prison, just so's his lordship could drink whisky! It makes my blood boil, twenty pounds! I could use that right now . . . A brand new note: I had to fold it up and put it under my tongue, so's the guards wouldn't find it . . . I risked my own liberty, and where does he go when he gets out? To the south of France! That's right, the south of France with her! Jailbirds, the pair of them! Well, as far as I'm concerned he can go back to her . . . for good! It would suit me down to the ground if he did . . . You know the only reason he came back, don't you? Because this is where the money is! The house, it is his collateral. It's all he's got left . . . He's squandered the rest! Well, I tell you, he isn't going to get it! She's got her eyes on the property, she's not stupid, she knows this is his only investment that hasn't turned sour . . . Well, she isn't going to get it! When I think of it, all those years, the sacrifices made! And the house wouldn't even be here if it wasn't for me! You know that's true, don't you, Steven . . . Isn't it? You know it is, don't you? Well, I can't put up with it any longer, twenty-five years is enough . . . He loses his job, his money and now he wants back in! Well, I think that's a bit rich, don't you? Do you think, I'm being too rash? Nothing would be left if it wasn't for me; I brought the pair of you up, single-handed! Up all by myself, on a pittance! On his miserly hand-outs! Whilst his lordship was out gallivanting, with his women, with his mistresses! And I was stuck down here, with you two ... Do you think I should divorce him? They'd never believe me, they'd think that I made the whole thing up from start to finish! But I haven't, have I? And my cats, they don't like him, that's a sign, they sense things ... Nigs hides under the bed whenever he's here. They can hear him coming streets away, my little early warning systems ... I stayed when he quit, and now he wants back in, that's rich! That jailbird! What type of fool does he take me for? I'll divorce him!'

I nearly choke on my beer, I spit it back into the glass. I act as if I've heard nothing. I take a sip of my tea.

'I stuck it out for twenty-seven years! And now that scoundrel thinks he can walk right back in here just as he fancies! Well, he's got another think coming! He'll sell the house and buy drugs with the proceeds, I suppose! You know he was smuggling diamonds as well, and that's on top of the pornography! He'll only fritter it all away, the same as everything else, on booze and loose women! If he'd only of listened to me, he'd be a millionaire by now, six times over! I've got money sense and he hasn't! I was on the till in Le Fevres for fourteen years you know, from age fourteen, the haberdashery department ... never a penny went astray. Only that time I lost the five pound note and I had to go and tell Mrs Wakefield. God, I almost died of fright. She was a tartar! But I'll give her that much, she was fair! And she believed me, she didn't deduct a penny from my wages, and I learned my lesson ... I've always had money sense. If only he'd listened to me ... But he didn't, he's frittered all of it all away! Thousands! Do you think I should divorce him? I couldn't, not now, could I? Not when he's down on his luck, I'd feel awful ... This is the time when he needs me the most, a time for us all to rally round and show our support ... Do you think I should divorce him? It'll all go down the drain if I don't ... everything I've worked for ... to the very last penny, you mark my words! And it's not as if he's ever cared about you or your schooling. I can forgive him hating me, but his own children! He's never looked after you, he wouldn't lift a finger, even when my mother died. He didn't even show up at the funeral. And he owed her money, three or four hundred pounds. And that was in the days when money was worth something! He didn't stand by me in my hours of need, and now he wants me to stand by him! All my work for nothing! For him to fritter away on his perversions! You may as well go and pour it down the sewer! And I've been stuck here bringing up his bloody children. I sacrificed the best years of my life! Doing his housekeeping on a pittance! And does he appreciate it? Not one bit! The place wouldn't even be here if it wasn't for me! Who paid the bills when he was off womanising? Muggins here, yours truly! Do you think it was worth it? in the long run? What would you do in my situation? No one would believe it was possible, they'd say I'd made the whole thing up from start to finish ... Fact is stranger than fiction! But who'd listen to me? He's got the gift of the gab, you can't argue with him ... You know I'm telling the truth, don't you, Steven? You know that the house wouldn't even be here if it wasn't for me, don't you. And what about my cats? What's going to become of them? I'll have to find a property with a south facing back and not too near a main road! Where are they? Have you seen the black one? You didn't let her out, did you? I don't let them out at night, they don't want to go out, there's no point, they only want to come straight back in again ... You saw what happened to Minnie's eye on fireworks night. It must have been a firework or a rose bush. And the vet's bill alone cost me a fortune! Thirty pounds! We don't want a busy road. You know we'll never get a place as good as this one, we'll never afford it ... Do you blame me? Do you? I can't afford to run this place, the rates alone ... I'm only a dish-washer you know. We need somewhere where the cats will be happy, mid-price range, I can't stretch any further, I couldn't afford the bills ... And we haven't even finished paying for this place yet ... Well, I can't be blamed for that, it wouldn't even be here if I hadn't stayed on ... He wanted it for his girlfriends and mistresses, but I stuck it out. If I hadn't slaved to keep it running on next to nothing, it would all be gone! I paid all the bills and I've got all the receipts to prove it! For the last ten years! Longer ... And his love letters. His girlfriends sent me those, a big parcel through the post. They know what he's like, they'd vouch for me, but I bet they wouldn't put up with him like I did – he'd be lucky to find anybody who would. The lies! Who would believe it? I mean the times I've taken him back, and then he's gone straight back out and done exactly the same thing again ... If it wasn't for me there'd be nothing for him to come back to, that's plain as day! All this would be long gone by now! And then there was you two, taking you to school, clothing you . . . new shoes . . . feeding you. He didn't pay a penny towards any of that, it all came out of my housekeeping, and the bills, I paid those too. We'll see how that would stand up in a court of law. If it hadn't of been for my mother we'd of all starved to death! And the way he treated her! He drove her to an early grave! And he didn't pay her back, not a bean! And now he has the cheek to say that he wants back in! I don't know why they let him out in the first place. Six months? What kind of a sentence is that? It's those friends he's got in the masons, that's what got him off, that and the Queen's Council . . . and that doesn't cost tuppence ha'penny! I could do with some of that money right now, that would suit me nicely . . . And now he has the gall to say that he wants back in! And he's been writing to her whilst they were in prison . . . Oh yes, I know! She sent me all the love letters, a great parcel of them . . . Do you think I should take him back, Steven? He might be telling the truth this time, you never know. Do you think he could turn over a new leaf? Do you think it's worth making a go of it? He wants to kick us out and move her in. She told me so herself. She rings me up in the middle of the night; she said he'd promised her the house. The diabolical liberty! If it wasn't for me, there wouldn't even be a house! What do you think of that? She's got everything going for her. For a start, she's thirty years younger than I am. And he bought her that car, do you know how much that cost? Six thousand pounds! Six thousand! Can you believe it? And now he wants to know if I still love him . . . He sent me flowers! Flowers, can you believe it? And he says he still loves me! Do you think he loves me? Do you think I'm doing the right thing? What would you do in my situation, Steven, honestly? Do you think I should divorce him? And then there's my cats to think of, they don't like him, we don't want anything near a main road . . . You didn't let Minnie out did you? Where is she? Minnie-Minnie-Minnie-Minnie-Minnie.'

I nod, I agree, I go to speak.

This is the story of my life: twenty years. Twenty years, going on twenty-two. Three hundred pages, another draft, a thousand pages more and I might be getting nearer the truth. But words are only words, they're not facts, not the real article. I've heard it all before, everything, a hundred times over, a thousand times, a million . . . I know the story backwards – talking achieves nothing, no shit!

That brought the low-down skunk running, he could sense his assets falling away ... He went all to pieces. He couldn't believe what was happening to him, his darling little Juny divorcing him? His little wifey? He blubbered, he split a gut, he gave everyone a right royal pain in the arse!

'Divorce? Divorce? You can't divorce me! Think of the house, the children!'

He looks at her sideways to see what effect he's having.

'My God, can't you see, woman? Our future, our investments! Are you thick or something? You're throwing it all away, you stupid cow! My hard work, my graft, my labour of love! Don't be rash, Juny, you're upsetting yourself. You'll make yourself ill again.'

The crown prince of treachery and deceit, stabbed in the back by his very own darling wifey. His own flesh and blood! It gave him a bad stomach, he couldn't shit straight. He rocks from side to side, holding his belly, howling ... He gnaws on the chair leg, his face like puff pastry. He's been dying his hair again, 'born blonde', a reaction to the peroxide. He pulls at a piece of loose skin, wrings his eyes out, and plucks out tufts of beard.

'Look at me, woman! Look at what you're doing to me. You're thick, do you hear me, thick!'

Sock! He lets one off ... If I'd have seen that punch ... all I was looking for was an excuse.

57. HE CAN'T FIGURE OUT WHERE MY HATRED'S SPRUNG FROM

This bozo makes me nervous, and his histrionics don't cut with me. I've been biding my time; I've walked right up behind him with an iron poker in my hand, on several occasions. Holding it up my sleeve, willing myself, but not quite able to strike. I've come that close . . . Oh no, this old cunt had better not try playing rough with me, 'cos this one's got an iron poker up his sleeve, something to rearrange your fucked up skull! I bite down, turn and walk away . . . I try to swallow but I've got no spit in my mouth.

'I can't divorce him, can I? He's up there now, in my bedroom, and he won't come down. He won't even let me sleep in my own bed . . . He's camped out under my dresser. Drunk of course, dead to the world. Do you want more tea? Some toast maybe?'

Her fingers play at her throat, she pulls at her hair, greying. That's a new development.

'Tea, toast?'

'Tea.'

'Are you sure, don't you fancy a piece of toast? Have some toast. I'll make some anyway, do you want a slice?'

I stare into my cup . . .

'And my cats, I suppose they've got to move out as well. Minnie-Minnie-Minnie-Minnie! Where's my cats? He's scared them off. Have you seen them? Nig-Nig-Nig-Nig-Nig-Nig! Come on den Minnie-Minnie, come on den, Mins!'

We look about, no signs. I go under the table, I crawl about in the gloom . . . No cats here . . .

'Maybe they've gone out.'

'You didn't let them out, did you?'

'Maybe they just went out on their own, they are cats, mum.'

'No, not my cats! Not in the dark! They don't like it, they only want to come back in again . . .'

'Yeah, they go out, then they come back again, that's what cats do . . .'

'Not my cats, not after dark. You didn't let them out, did you?'

'No, I didn't let the fucking cats out!' Her eyes flinch . . . 'I'll look upstairs, alright?' I walk out into the hall. 'Look there's the black one . . .'

'Ah, there you are, Nig-Nig . . . There you are, my girlie, yosh, yosh, yosh, come on dens . . .'

It strolls over, the Nigs, it swaggers in. Black, totally black . . . charcoal-like, a cellar . . . apart from the white under her chin, an overall effect. And two eyes and a tail like a question mark, a little black cheroot. It holds it there, erect, its trade mark.

'That's my little girlie, what's he done to you dens?'

She resumes her whisper. 'Well, he can't stay, that's for sure . . . He can go back to his girlfriend's, why should I have to put up with him? Haven't I suffered enough? He's trying to wear me down you know, the same as my mother! The house wouldn't even be here, it would have gone to the creditors years back, and now his highness wants back in! He's up there now in my bedroom! My cats won't stand for it! You can't reason with him, he's got an answer for everything, just like you! Well, he can clear off back to her! I don't want him here, I've had it up to here! Christ, I put up with it for twenty-five years, isn't that enough? Through thick and thin! And the things he's said to me, the lies . . . Haven't I fought for what I've got, tooth and nail? The truth? That soddin' bugger wouldn't know the truth if it spat at him! I know what he gets up to, he can't pull the wool over my eyes any longer. I might be blind but I'm not stupid! It's a matter of survival! What do you think I should do? His girlfriend rings me up regularly, oh yes, she gave me the low-down on that skunk. 'Tell him he's a spineless shit!' That's what she tells me, as if I don't know it already. Her with her 'tell him he's a spineless shit!' She'll be telling me how to suck eggs next! Well, I'm not moving out, no matter how many times she rings me up, let her ring away

... I know where my bread's buttered! This house is all that's left, and it wouldn't be here if it wasn't for me ... I know that goose's stinking character from tip to tail! Haven't I stuck by him? He thinks he can drive me out? Well, we'll see about that! If he thinks he's moving his floozies in here, he's got another thing coming. I haven't held on all these years just to give it all up for his little jailbird! Why doesn't he go back to her? I'll tell you why, because she's thrown him out, that's why! She's thrown him out and he's got nowhere else to go ... He thought I'd be dead and buried by now, along with my mother ... He promised her this house and he can't deliver, that's why she's thrown him out! That's why he's skulking in my bedroom ... Why doesn't he go back to her? If I hadn't stuck by him, all this would have gone yonks ago ... I'm the only reason it's still standing! And then he has the gall to lie to me again, not just the once, but a thousand times! Right to my face! As if I was born yesterday! Well, I may have put up with it in the past, but not again, not anymore! You do think I'm right, don't you? I'm not being too harsh, am I? He might be telling the truth this time ... it's never too late to change ... It is possible, there's a first time for everything ... maybe he really has left her.'

I drain my cup, and look her in the face, the black eye ...

'He hit you, didn't he?'

Her hands come up, fluttering, she fumbles with her neck scarf.

'He won't come out, he's up there now. I can't sleep up there, not with him in the room, on the floor ... I've asked him to leave nicely, but you can't reason with him ... What am I supposed to do? My own bedroom ... and my cats, they won't go in there.'

I put it down, I place it heavily, it makes a noise. I push my chair out and stand, you have to watch your head on the lamp ...

'I'll go speak to him, I'll ask him. He can sleep in Nick's room tonight, then he can leave in the morning.'

I put down my cup, stand and leave the room. I look at her and make for the stairs. I watch them as they pass under me, that's the effect, one at a time, slowly, resigned. Left at the top, across the landing. I knock, twice, three times, open the door and look in. It takes time for your eyes to adjust, to become accustomed to the gloom.

Gradually, I begin to make things out, shadowy, indistinct. Bits of old furniture, I should think, museum pieces mostly ... And that must be the marital bed, a big four-poster job. And over there, curled in a heap on the floor like a little cocoon, his head under the dresser, his golden locks gleaming, comfy looking. I walk over and tap his shoulder. He opens one eye. The bags separate, and there it is, blinking . . . blue with a little spray of red veins.

I speak to him, I summon my courage and open my trap.

'Dad, can you sleep downstairs, please. Mum wants to go to bed.'

He looks at me, a moment's recognition, then he pulls the covers back over his head.

'Look, she can't sleep up here with you in the room.'

'Go away!'

I stand there, stammering, I feel my knees going. I lean in again and re-tap his shoulder. Bang! He sits bolt upright, his dressing gown falls open, a naked chest, golden hairs, expanding, unaged.

'Go to bed, Steven, it is time all little boys were in their beds!' I feel my hackles rising. I suck my teeth, there's no spit, but I suck, that makes me curl my lip. And then I grab him. I claw at his sleeping bag.

'Listen you, you're sleeping downstairs!' I feel myself going to say it, the words jam up like a great wad of blood in my throat. I have to spit them out or I'll choke. I force myself to jump, an impossible leap, my knees knock, then I push off . . . I feel myself flying . . . a surge of beautiful hate, nursed at my bosom, matured and now full grown. It bursts out of me like a dam, rushing out through the top of my head. I spit cataracts, I snort them out through my nostrils. My ears go pop! and I pull him wriggling from his sleeping bag . . .

I feel my strength, the strength of the weakling, of the underdog. I lift him and throw him sprawling out across the landing. He scrabbles to his hands and knees, he slips in his own shit, whimpering . . .

I grab hold of his dressing gown and launch him across the floor, the blood pounding in my ears. I've got to get him up, to get him off the floor and out of this room, because I never ever want to hear my mother talk of this man, this house, this marriage, ever again!

I breathe in great gulps of cold air. He crashes down on his back and I stare at my clawed fists, his dressing gown in tatters . . . He pulls himself up and adjusts his dick . . . I don't move in, I stand off, still his son.

'Now, you sleep downstairs, alright?' I look at him in desperation . . . that this situation shouldn't turn to murder. 'Please!'

Now I think back to it, I should never of said that word: 'please'. 'Please' isn't the language of the conqueror, it's the language of the vanquished . . . Straight away he's onto me.

He re-finds his balance and comes strutting back into the room. He pulls himself up, readjusts his G-string and pats his pecker into place. He looks me up and down, finds his bluster, then starts laying down the law the way he sees it.

'You stupid little child! You think you're a man with your pathetic tattoos, don't you? But you're not a man at all, Steven, no you're just a silly little boy! I think it's past your bed time. Now, run along like a good little boy, mummy and daddy have some very important matters to discuss. Out! Do you hear me? Chop-chop! Out of my house!'

He bristles his whiskers and jams his face right into mine. I've got his gander up, that much is obvious. I let him sound off, let him have his say, but one more push, so much as one more piece of his crummy advice! I fix him with one of my stares, I hold him with it. His hands flapping at my chest. My ears go back, I can feel them burning . . . the heat rushes through to the tips . . . tingly.

'You think you're a man with your tough man tattoos, but in fact you're just a silly little boy, Steven! You think you're a man, but you're just thick! Thicko!'

He liked that word 'thick', he repeated it, 'thicko!' . . . I like it too. I lunge and groan . . . I go for his beard . . . I let him have it, twenty-two years worth in one go! He's finally got my goat.

I grab a handful of his fancy suits off the peg and ram them into his chest. I scream it out. 'It's you who's leaving, you fucking cunt!' I open my eyes so wide that they ache. His face registers panic. He can't figure out where my hatred's sprung from. He backs off, cringing.

'Steven, I wouldn't hurt mummy . . . mummy . . . I wouldn't hurt mummy!'

He's playing ga-ga now, five years old . . . And I give it to him – I put my fist in his face, five knuckles, a whole bunch . . . A perfect hatred, finely honed over years of silence and compliance. It bursts out of me like a disease, crawling and malignant.

I grab up a pile of his fancy togs and jam them into his bread basket. I shake my head and fill my veins . . . He falls back, his eyes questioning. His little world isn't functioning properly any more. He grasps at the air, he staggers, hands flapping under my nose. I cover my balls.

'Mummy, mummy . . . I wouldn't hurt mummy!'

And sock! I stick one on his bracket. I sight along my thumb and lay one on him. I coil up and spit it out. It lands, an explosion between his eyes . . . He topples, he hangs there for a moment, caught in time . . . He teeters on the brink, then his knees give way . . . I watch him go, he lifts off and flips back, bouncing down the stairwell . . . He revolves, taking three pictures with him. He cartwheels and bounces down on his bonce, one step at a time. Then crack! as he hits the bottom step. His piece of masonry, hand-built in green slate. He examines his handy-work at close range. The special type of grouting, the general effect, crack! On his final bounce.

I run down after him, leap over him, holding up my fists, bunched, ready . . . my chest tightened into a ball of fear. He's knocked for a loop, he whinnies . . . his tongue hanging out . . . his hair-do fucked, his little china blues . . . dribbling.

'If you want more, you can have it!' I'm shouting, I'm dying, I show him my stupid fists. I feel foolish, but I say it anyway. I mean it . . . He sags, propping himself on the bottom step. His left eye, it swells, a purple slug, one end of it opens and it splits its guts and starts pouring . . . He shakes his dumb stupid head and tries to pull himself to his feet.

'You can have more of it if you want it!'

The truth is, I should have killed him the instant he went down, throttled him on the spot. But the moment passed, my hatred spent, souring to my stomach.

'Blood,' he says, 'blood . . . What have you done to me, Juny, what have you done to me?'

My legs shaking, beginning to buckle . . . I drop my guard. He rolls his eyes, the blood trickling out from the crack in his skull . . . He sits back and dips his fingers into the soup . . . he studies it, he mumbles. He looks to me and the old girl, from face to face. He mouths words . . . reaches out his hand, white fingers, the blood dripping . . . He rattles those fingers, like teeth, like castanets, drumming the nails against the bone. I back off, his little death rattle . . . and he whispers something inaudible . . .

'I still love you, Steven.'

I look into this poor fool's eyes . . . It's too late, old man, too late . . . I brush my hands on my thighs to get this filth from my hands. I see my mother through the mist . . . her hands fiddling with the skin of her throat.

'He's a bully, he deserves it,' she says.

A distant voice . . . hovering . . . I leave the pair of them there and go to the front room. I'm cold, cold, my teeth clattering. I click on the TV set. I sit with my hands between my legs. I want to piss. My head's going like the clappers . . . I play with the dials.

I've been set up, a regular stool pigeon.

He's in the toilet, swathing his head in toilet paper, dabbing at the blood. I pace up and down holding myself. I can't stop rattling, I got some kind of a fever. If I lie down, I jump straight back up again. I have to sit on the side of the bed, clamp my jaws and pray.

I feel under the bed for my iron poker. I take him in my hand; I flex and I unflex. The important thing is to stay awake in case of night attacks.

The morning comes and I hear him moving around downstairs collecting his personal effects. He wanders about in the garden, his head bandaged, hiding behind his dark glasses. He dithers about, tinkering with the lawn-mower. He packs and double fiddles with everything. He tells the old girl to call him a cab and stares forlornly up the garden path. This sad old ritual, never to be played again . . .

He paces around in the driveway 'til the taxi sounds its horn out on the road. Then his face relaxes, he comes back in, sits down on his slate step, unbuckles his shoes and starts repolishing them. First the uppers, then he turns them over and concentrates on the soles. He takes his time about it, spitting and licking, as fastidious as a pussy cat. He buffs them 'til they burn like coals, then admires his whiskers in them. The meter still clicking away. That's his style, nonchalant, thirty-five minutes. He likes to keep people waiting, one of his little pleasures.

I help him carry his cases to the taxi, a suitcase in each hand. It's a tough thing to do, carrying your old man's cases, to load him up on his way to the nut house . . . He's ready to leave.

My trouble is that I'm a romantic at heart. That's what kills me. The dreams, all those little intimacies, they come flooding back to me and I'm lost. And I think of all of them, as they were. My parents, my brother, my friends and lovers, and I want to hold them in my heart forever and sob with the pain of it all . . . And I shake my fists at the moon and feel sorry for every last stinking one of us, but ultimately I feel sorry for myself.

58. IN WHICH BUDDHA AND THATCHER ARE CALLED TO WITNESS

M y brother shows up, strolling down the garden path, a face from yesteryear. I hardly recognise him. I run to the door and usher him in. I know that mug from someplace, I do a double take. It's him alright, old bro', not seen in donkeys' years. Mum joins in the party; she puts the kettle on.

'Mum, it's Nick!'

She wipes her hands.

'You answer it,' she tells me.

I fire my arse, I quit snoozing and get the door. 'Watcha Nick!'

He extends his hand, avoiding my eyes . . . 'Hello brother.' We shake.

I didn't tell you about his face, dough-like, with the two currants stuck in it. Like that! He looks out resentfully, with just a hint of desperation.

Nick sits himself down, fluffs up the pillow and parks his arse. He makes himself comfortable and squats, Buddha-like. I sit opposite, expectant. I want to know what the honour's for . . . I fish in my cup, I use the spoon, I taste it – bitter! He coughs, rubs his mitts together and half smirks.

'What's that you're writing?'

That throws me, him and his 'what's that you're writing?' I swill my tea, look down and close my notebook.

'This 'n' that, poems mostly . . . a book . . .'

'Do they sell?'

I give him a sheepish one, I hunch my shoulders and hold out my empty palms, I plead innocent.

'Have you read Burgess?'

He waves a telephone book in the air and thumps it, resounding.

'Syntax!' he says. 'Burgess,' he annunciates. And, 'What you lack is syntax.'

I nod . . . He leaves through the pages, he cascades them under his thumb, he looks up questioningly.

'Have you read him?'

'Who?' I ask.

'Burgess!' he shouts.

I shake it.

'Amis, the younger?'

'No.'

He nods his head thoughtfully . . . In truth he pities me. He stares into the print, transfixed by the effect. He comes to the end of the book and pats it like a dog. A faithful old friend. 'What you want to do is get yourself an education, boy! Get out there and read the classics: Hemingway, Amis the younger. Learn the ground rules. Syntax! Grammar! Verb agreement! Burgess writes thirty thousand words before breakfast, just to warm up!'

I ponder on that one: thirty thousand? That's a lot . . . no doubts . . . and syntax, there's a new word . . . Burgessesque, I shouldn't wonder, a puzzler. He looks at me, trying to read my mug.

'You know your trouble? You're over-competitive! You want to learn to relax a bit . . . Learn something from the Buddha . . . You're too competitive by far!' He tut-tuts me.

Obviously, I'm pushing my luck writing without his permission, lacking the correct qualifications – no wonder I get up his nose. If old bro' had his way, he wouldn't allow me to set pen to paper. He's not impressed by the writings of a dullard, no way! He's got opinions of his own, and he's read the books to prove it! Acres of them, whole bookshelves.

I put my little notebook away, shamed . . . I tell you now, the official censor is defunct. The slate's already been wiped clean, in the high chairs and the nurseries, in the schools and the playgrounds. Family and friends have been keeping each other's traps buttoned for centuries, for whole epochs! A few low-down lies, whisperings mostly, but that's about it. Mothers and sons, fathers and daughters have been tying each other up with their extravagant shows of love, loyalty and their final demands for silence and respect.

I pull faces, chewing on my pencil, I follow it around my mouth with my tongue.

I know I should quit this here and now, but in truth I've swallowed just about all the half-truths and spite that I can stomach. Just let me hear one more piece of cock-eyed bullshit from the likes of my brother, and I'll be fit to puke the whole gut load of lies back up again, half-eaten and rancid, double fermented in its own juices. One last great gob of bile to drown the universe, a mouth-wash for all the arseholes of the world!

'More tea?'

I look up, my mother's face.

'More tea?'

'No thanks, mum.'

'You said you wanted one, I've just made it. I'll pour you one, anyway, then you decide. Do you want a cup?'

My brother nods, sieves his cup and passes it for a refill.

'Have you seen the poems he writes, mother?'

My mother's eyes travel from Nick to me.

'I know, it's awful ... You shouldn't write things like that about your brother, Steven.'

She hands me the cup, a little saucer, a spoon.

'Thanks.' I sip at it – tea is life.

'The social security will be after him if he keeps writing stuff like that. They'll see it, see your name, then they'll be on to you ... They'll stop his money!'

The old girl comes back in from the kitchen, clasping her tea-pot.

'Have you seen my cats? Nig-nig, the black one?'

'It's sitting there.' I point to it, fat, licking itself.

'Oh, there you are, girlie. I've got some creams for you dens.'

'Don't give it cream, mum, Christ, look at it, it'll have a heart attack! There's a poster at the vet's, it says, "Don't kill your cat with kindness!" '

She eyes me coldly, picks it up, the Nigs, and staggers with it to the kitchen.

'Don't listen to dem dens. No, you're not fat, are you? No, you're my girlie.'

The door closes. He looks at me, the lines showing . . . He's one of these bozos who talks about Hemingway as if somebody's fondling his dick. Aggressive? Sure, he's aggressive, but what really gets his goat is the idea of me sitting here painting and writing without the correct qualifications. I'm over-competitive, I can't spell and I don't know who Burgess is. And then I have the gall to even exist. The way he sees it, I'm cheating.

He watches my pen move, I shield the page. He fiddles with himself. Something's eating away at his miserable little bean, or why's he bother showing up here, after all the fighting's over? After his great absence so to speak: old Johnny come lately.

He clears his throat and makes his forehead turn black. The big brother routine. I've heard it all before; I ignore him, I chew gum through his sermons. Apparently, I don't know what 'syntax' is. He's dead right, I shake my head . . . a lot of bollocks about adverbs and preverbs and things I've never even heard of.

Just as I'm trying to get to grips with one set of laws, he invokes another, throwing names around like they were confetti. Talking of the great and famous as if they are his personal friends.

'Anyway, I've read more books than you!' he announces.

I stare into his drinker's pimple, centre stage, smack bang on the end of his neb. I concentrate on it. He's watching to see the effect, making sure that his words of wisdom are sinking in. I don't blame him, he can't help himself. It's a habit, it dates from when we were kids.

'I'll give you a tutorial of your work.' He jumps up, claps his hands together and strides out of the room. He puts his head round the door . . .

'Come along, if you want me to take a look at your new paintings . . . I'll give you a tutorial.'

I have to rise and follow him, to comply with his enthusiasms, with his judgements.

He screws up his face and peers into the paintwork, he dissects the pictorial from the abstract, and back again.

'I mean, just look at it, that's how I sign my signature and you know it! And it isn't even composition! That river, I mean, the sail, it blends in with the bank and halts the natural rhythm. The paint's totally the wrong colour! It's OK in its own right I suppose . . . I don't mean I don't like it personally, but the way it merges with the bank . . .'

He shakes his head sorrowfully, raises his palms to the ceiling, shrugs his shoulders and droops his jowls.

'What colour is that? No, don't tell me . . . Indian red?' He nods and agrees with himself. 'Aha, hmmm . . . I thought as much, tried vermilion have you, with just a touch of burnt umber?' He turns to me and wags his finger. 'You should read the magazines, you know, wake up to what's going on out there in the big wide world! You're too . . . cynical! Don't you read the magazines? Take a look, learn something . . . You can't be the ignorant little provincial all of your life! Do yourself a favour and get out there, take a look around. Find out who's buying and who's selling, then market your goods. Hit the middle ground! You're just too reactionary . . . I used to think like you but I've learned. I've seen it, I've been there, I've done it! Don't forget, I'm four years older than you and four years wiser! You've got to learn to take advice! Don't look at me like that . . . OK, that's it! Mother, see? He isn't even prepared to listen!'

My mother's in full agreement. 'Don't tell me! you're wasting your breath, he's just like his soddin' father.'

We're onto that one again, the great list of my similarities to our dreaded father. We're both thin and I even look a bit like him.

'He's got the same hands!' My brother explodes. That's enough for them; in their eyes I'm guilty.

And my humble portraits? My attempts to communicate an emotion sincerely felt? – I'm pissing in the wind! What my talking in paint fails to do, is satisfy his hard learned intellectualism. Expression of the soul, rather than the rubbing-selling variety. My doodles of the heart leave him stony cold, the same goes for Picasso, until he reads the autograph. The connoisseurs of the blue period? Autograph-hunters more like! Naturally, I keep my opinions to myself, I button my lip and chew my tongue.

'Obviously, there is a difference between being true to your art and outright commercialism, and that's what I've been trying to tell you, if you'd only take the time to just listen! That special niche is the middle ground where all true art lies. Everybody's at it, for Christ's sake! Rembrandt, Picasso every last one of them, businessmen first, artists second!'

I can hardly believe it! At last he's got there, finally! I check my ears. For once he's playing my tune. I agree with him wholeheartedly, I fan myself, phew!

'It's pointless talking to you, you just won't listen! You're arrogant! You won't take any criticism!'

He peeps out of his skull.

Sure as shit, he's got the whole world sewn up! He's worldly wise, he exudes confidence, apart from one or two deep rooted anxieties, some of his lesser known trepidations.

'My ambition,' he states, 'is to have a one man show at the Tate Gallery.'

He's off again. I try and suppress a yawn, I pull a half smile, I nod encouragingly. He believes he's immortal, he knows he's right and he knows he'll live to be a hundred and fifty . . . a thousand maybe . . . sure as shit!

'You always have to be right, don't you? You're so bloody righteous!' He goes cross-eyed, throwing his weight about. I'm used to it, I'm the kid brother. I've told you all about it. It's his ritual, it helps him to get a stiffy. I repeat myself? Well, I'll say it again, twenty, thirty times, but it doesn't do me any good. The majority agree, and I'm in a minority of one – I eat humble pie.

He digs his fingers in, and changes tack mid-stream. He butters his words, his tongue's so thick he can hardly get his mouth round them.

'Look kid, this is our house, alright! It's as much mine as yours! Christ, you're just like the old man! I come back here, and the atmosphere's exactly the same, apart from it's you laying the law down! When are you going to grow up, get out there and see the big wide world? You can't carry on living with mummy for ever!'

He glares at me, leans in, hushed and conspiratorial . . . 'Look, one day all this is going to be ours. You understand me? You and me, fifty-fifty! Our investment for the future!' He looks over his shoulder, lifts his podgy mitt, and encompasses the whole house. 'When all this is ours,' he arches them again, 'we can sell up and get our own places . . . Think of it, something in town, London . . . the centre . . . At heart, I've always thought of myself as a Londoner, as being "of" the city.'

So that's his racket, that's what's lying at the bottom of his unexpected visit. I should have cottoned on to that one earlier. Him playing the big 'I am', with all his brotherly advice, and all the time he's been counting the family silver. So, that's what brought this hyena running. Well well, playing the doting son, whilst all the time he's fishing for sovereigns. Of course, I say nothing. I keep my trap shut. I realise that being the young brother I'm not supposed to have too many opinions of my own.

Painting pictures? Writing things down? 'You're getting a little too big for your britches, sonny Jim! You'd better save it for the birds, you low down Communist!' Oh, he's a political genius as well, didn't I tell you? He presides and lectures, he sits back. He elaborates and paints the air. His bumptiousness knows no bounds. When it comes to vanity, the bastard's insatiable. The king of the boloney! He sucks and blows, he dives in and doesn't come up for air, as gluttonous as sixteen piglets and as preening as a cage full of cockatoos. And you can't back-chat him either, no sir! Not on your life!

He expands and he encompasses. He reiterates and contradicts. He calls Buddha and Thatcher to witness. He's acquainted with the whole horror show. And all along I nod and I agree. Yes me, the one person who disagrees with everything. He's got me beat. I give him the benefit of the doubt, the big lug. So he gave me a rough time as a kid? Well, so what? He'll get his come-uppance.

He ruffles his feathers and gobbles like a turkey. He gives me his superior little smile, the one I keep going on about. It creeps in from round the edges, the fat pinches together.

'I think,' he says, 'I think that I know more than you.'

'I know you do,' I reply.

59. OUR HEARTS FROZEN

It's the memories that come for you in the night, that keep you nailed to the past. Trembling, shit-smeared and child-like. It's those dark moments of the soul that must be relived and faced like assassins. Each sickening echo grasped and denuded before it becomes yet another missed opportunity, before it's too late.

I'm six years old sat playing on the floor in the front room and my mother's lying upstairs ill in bed. My father tells me that on no account am I to disturb her. He fidgets his fingers in his eye sockets. I'm told to shush! I know that one, 'Your opinions? Stow 'em, kid!'

'Goodnight.' And I kind of blow a kiss, clumsy, in the dark. 'Goodnight, mum.' I sneak upstairs in spite of them. Who are they to tell a young kid when and where he can kiss his own mother goodnight? I sneak up there, regardless, and whisper my goodnights. I push the door to and say it to the night. I hear her stir, at the dark end, beneath the black headboard, muttering in her sleep. I guess I've woken her. I close the door and get out of there double quick. I've said what I came to say, now I exit. I skip back downstairs, with stealth, trying to whistle to myself, nonchalant.

Nichollas looks up at me with the eye of suspicion . . . I stare into the carpet looking for my soldier, the one with the bayonet . . . Then there's a thud from upstairs and the door goes. The old man stares through the ceiling, pulls at his beard and spits. We hear her on the landing, each step. And then she comes through the room like a ghost-walker and hits the bottle.

She walks into the room, grey-faced, and heads straight for the whisky cabinet. She looks neither right nor left, and my brother and father stare at me. I find my soldier, he's got a rifle and a bayonet ... She fills her glass and will talk to no one. He's got shorts on and he's charging in the carpet.

The old man tells me to clean my teeth and tidy all my rubbish away ... He marches into the toilet and flashes his dick at the pan.

'Come along, you boys, bed, bed, bed! Chop-chop!'

I cling to my covers, my little heart bruised in its chest. We can still hear her on the stairs, raised voices, the neck of the bottle hits the glass. She glugs it out, swills it back and takes a refill ...

Her comings and goings into the night. And then there's a thud and a cry ... something on the stairs ... the sound of a body falling.

Me and my brother jump up and run to our bedroom door. He shoves me, so's I can't see, an elbow in the face. He opens it slowly and we peek out ... They're both there, naked under the little red lamp shades. Him pulling at her, dragging her backwards up the stairs.

We blink through the murder, we see bodies and hell. There's his cock and his beard with teeth. He tries to shoulder her weight, he staggers ... She looks dead, our mother with her tits and arse, and him with that thing between his legs, red-faced and heaving ...

Then he turns on us and we shrivel.

'Get back to bed, the pair of you! Before I bang your bloody heads together! Now, this instant!'

We stand caught in that doorway, our hearts frozen, and we are still there. Caught in time, unable to step into our lives. Then the second clicks and we scamper to our beds and duck back under the covers.

It was my fault. I bite the sheets; I make them into fists. It was me! And the night light burns deathly red, and we hear the muffled voices, and strange thuds ... And our necks are cranked off the pillows and we don't breathe 'til the very end of night, when there's a long, drawn-out scream, wringed from my mother's throat.

60. ROSY

'You saved my life.'

And I called her Rosy. I thought she said her name was Rosy. I'd been drinking and I misheard. It was Dolli, not Rosy; now I remember, then I didn't. And then she tried to hide under the table from me, that was funny. And I sat at her knees staring up into her gob of metal and said, 'You saved my life tonight.' And it was true, I swear to God it was true. I wasn't kidding about, not trying to put one over on her . . . And the fog, like an animal at the door, right across the back of Chatham . . . rolling in off the Medway.

'What's all that metal in your mouth?'

She shows me, she flicks it out with her tongue, thumb and forefinger. It's her plate, three or four teeth attached. She pops it back in, readjusts it, pulls a face, wriggles her jaw. Me still at her knees.

For pity's sake, memories are the worst, the pits. To forget is to give it all up, to remember is to die and to suffer. I sup my beer; it's hard for a soul in this world, but for a sentimental soul it is hell. I down the dark stuff and order some poison, for my sad heart, golden, enchanting. The optic fills, and I tip it back. I like to watch the way he fills it, four little glugs, and he passes it to me and I tip it back. Hardly a measure at all.

'I'll have a double,' I tell him, and there it goes again. He catches the last drip then places it to the bar and I down it. It kicks in when it hits the bottom. That's how I know my stomach's fucked. I order the same again and smile through the tears . . .

No one's in tonight, just the fruit machine gibbering away to itself . . . and all these pretty jugs and tankards hanging from the ceiling . . . each on its own little brass hook. I lean back on my heels and hold onto the bar. I count them like gold, near on a hundred I shouldn't wonder, more like a hundred and fifty. From all round the world, the beer kellers of Munich, the watering holes of Denmark, all over . . . Intricate designs, each with their specific characters. There's fifty-two, up until the second lamp, at least fifty . . . and there's four lamps in all . . . I pull out my notebook and lick my pencil:

'The George Vaults, Rochester High Street, 2nd September 1983. Being a list and summery of all mugs, jugs and tankards held therein, for the reference and betterance of future generations to come. Item:'

I spend a lot of time staring into the mug with the four leaf clover drawn on it. That's Ireland, that is . . . and this is an Irish pub. She is number fifty-five or fifty-six, that little teacup.

I order another measure of gut rot and take a note of all the brands of whiskys held behind the bar, and how many packets of salted nuts are missing from the card. I fill in four whole pages before I down my drink and leave.

I cross by the White Heart and go up past the George Inn and that's when it hits me – you're never far from the river in this town. Like an animal it keeps itself hidden, but it's always there, with its special stink, at the end of summer.

The grey-black waters, hints of gold, the shimmerings of the night . . . The street lamps flaring up over Strood, spreading like a piss stain in the rain – the torches of man. The towns and the suburbs beyond, one giant co-operative of the disenchanted. A billion fractured, sorry souls and each locked into each other's existences, man to woman, woman to man, poor to rich and all to blind power. By hook or by crook, we've all of us been caught. Oh yes, we create our own merry little hell and everybody's implicated, the devil and his wife included.

I light up, put my hands in pockets and cross the road. I quit looking at that dirty water, the iron bridge and the ugly sky. Shit, a man could catch a chill in this drizzle, or even worse, a full blown cold!

I hunch my shoulders and stride up the hill. My way, which is a fast way, up by the castle, and under her hallway . . . Down to the end of that sorry passage, which I never ever want to remember again.

I hammer on the door 'til Dolli comes up from the basement. And she stands there, giving me that sickly 'fuck me' smile, so's I almost turn round and leave without even saying hello.

She clings to me like wet paper. I step on my cigarette, push her to the wall and kiss her roughly on the mouth. I shudder with disgust for myself. I grit my teeth and kick past her. I want to bite the hat stand. To pierce my tongue and spit blood.

I sling my coat, slump to the chair and feel my cock in my pocket. That gives me a gloomy aspect. This world is rabid enough without needs, without sex and demands, without people ordering your love and respect.

'But I only want sex, and I want it with you!' she bleats.

And I blot my mind with hate; to feel pain, after all, is better than to feel nothing. I flex my brain, and I can't even bring myself to utter it. My temples thud, and the world comes down and I sit here, silent.

She pours the tea and asks me if I want milk? As she leans forward I see her ugly tit in her open gown . . . And I taste my lips, brown. My head twitches to the left, I drop the teacup and suddenly there isn't silence anymore. There is no laughter or lightness, there is only screaming living hell. And I drag my paintings from the walls and break them apart like emptying a bottle of Scotch in one smash . . . Kicking the telephone across the room 'til it jerks like a mad head on its string. And she hovers in my face like a poisonous insect . . . And then it's her head on the end of my fist . . . I throw the punch, and at the last instant I pull it and run for the stairway, her tailing after me like smoke. Hugging her nightie to her evil body, cradling her reddened jaw . . . Out of the hallway and down the street . . . And I let her catch me, heaving and sobbing, then double back past her, out-running her again. I dive back into the hallway, down the stairs and smash my fist through the door.

She comes sobbing back into the room. I take two jumps and destroy my crummy canvases, because they're mine, because I gave them to her. Because I want to cut with a barbed knife. Because I want her to hurt like I hurt. Because she has failed me as hard as I have failed her. Because, if you can't build a true and beautiful love in this world, then maybe you can build a pure and beautiful hatred. Because after all, hatred is nearly love: it's a passion, and passion doesn't come cheap, my friends, and something has to sit in our poor trembling hearts.

There's a noise in my poor batty head, and it makes me want to punch ... And I have to go, to step out of this prison and to leave these tears, this blind confusion ... to be able to breathe.

I stagger back up the stairway into the hall ... I can't breathe, and it comes for me, that hot pain, that special pain, my little friend of hate, to kill me always ...

And the street lights rot the stars and the sky is pus. I can't breathe ... I gag, choking through the constant drizzle, 'til I go down on my knees, holding my head and nursing my shame.

I stick it out, way out over the water, and it sags and sways like a paper bridge. I shed little salt tears to that river, from salt to salt ... through the drizzle.

It's gone now, all of it ... the fields, the woods ... my butterflies, the little chalk blue, my childhood, all of it ...

I'm twenty-two years old and don't recognise a thing. Just a lapful of rancid memories, museum pieces, not even fit for the junk heap! My past has been repossessed. The woods wiped clean away, not a twig left standing; no chance for adders or little field mice, it's all gone! And I remember those fellows clear as daylight. Splat! Nothing but houses! Cardboard, twenty thousand of them staggering up the hillside! And the little chalk blue? Extinct, for all I know.

My whole childhood bulldozed into oblivion, into a shit heap ... Redeveloped ... The world carries on without us, that's what's so hard to take, that's what's so hard to get used to.

It's tough being a kid, but it's even tougher growing up. All our good intentions rubbed out, one after the other, like hillsides. Like Caroline and the little chalk blue. Only this size, no kidding! Can you imagine it? Thumb-nail size, and no bigger. And so we learn to wave goodbye.

I watch the moving blackness below, the little currents, the pieces of match wood caught down there, circling in the ink ... Whirlpools stronger than the claws of a bear, that will take a man's legs and pull him, scuffing him down to the bottom.

And my father picks me up and holds me over the river's edge ...

'Look, Steven, look at all the currents and raisins.'

And I see his bearded face ... his blue eyes and golden hair ... He holds me in his arms and his beard is prickly.

'Look at all those currents and raisins.'

And I look to the water and back to his face but I don't understand. I don't understand. And he smiles with the trickery and I don't understand ...

61. THREE PENNIES, AGAIN

People are always out to lose themselves. So much for our precious personal identities. For such vain, self-serving bastards, people are pretty sick of themselves. We set out into this world full of fine ideals and bluster, but slowly that delicate veneer is chipped away. We move on, desperate to lose ourselves, to try and forget what we've become ... And then the night, pacing the boards alone, full of remembrances.

I'm sorry, I'm drunk, crowing on about my crummy past. I repeat myself, I blow hot and cold. I laugh, I grow melancholic ... One minute I'm reeling and fighting mad, the next I come over all lovey-dovey and the world wears a smile on her lips.

The evening comes and the pubs open. A young writer has a million sites to see, but he can't face the page. I sup on the dark stuff and play with my coins. I jangle them in my pocket, I weigh them, I let them slip between my fingers. I'll write another day, on a perfect sunny day somewhere in the invisible future.

I go to the bar and I drink to it, I order Scotch, a malt. A young writer doesn't drink to his future on any old blend.

Here's to you Hamsun, you skunk! And to you Fante, brave, dumb and fearing God! I count my change, then place it on the wet bar in front of me, my three pennies.

'Warm beer and wet change', the definition of a London pub in the blitz. One of my mother's pronouncements. But this is whisky mother, and it's burning a hole right through little Johnny's heart. A little poison to warm him through this bitter night. No money, no friends, a truly melancholic time of year.

It's cold and lonely on a street like that, for a young writer who's down on his luck, to be heading home at half eleven at night without a friend in the world, not even an innocent bottle ... And only three pennies to jangle in his pocket. Such injustices shouldn't be allowed; and then to taunt someone, to make fun, a mockery.

I eye the bottles, jewel-like, row upon row of them, a million glitterings, just beyond reach. Sitting just behind the plate window ... To do such a thing to an honest fellow, a young writer. I shake my head in disbelief. When I think of myself like this, my heart fills with such pity that I want to walk straight up to myself, thrust thirty pounds into my disbelieving hand, embrace me, kiss both my cheeks and wish me all the luck in the world.

I stare down at my three pennies and back into that window. My heart thumps under my jacket and all of a sudden I know exactly what I'm going to do. I check up and down the street, pull my collar up round my ears and march straight in there.

The door clangs on me and he throws the bolt, his footsteps receding ... And another iron door ... Silence ... I stand there shivering in my cell. That unthinking bastard didn't even give me back my jacket, and it's fucking freezing in this slop hole! I walk over and take a piss in the bucket. Not so many luxuries in this department and they haven't killed the light ... No bed, not even a blanket! Just a platform, a couple of slates, stone-like ... How's a fellow meant to get his head down on that! And it's icy in this joint.

I pace the concrete floor, I prance like a flamingo, swapping feet. I have to keep moving, and not even a blanket.

OK, so I slipped up. Can't a fellow make an honest mistake? All I wanted was a drink, a harmless little nip ... And let's face it, that fat cat had plenty to spare, bottles of the stuff. Whisky galore, row upon row ... Why should he have everything in the drinks department: a cosy fire, a full brandy bowl and a cigar as well? It makes you want to kick the wall. Three worthless pennies, that's what I've got, three worthless pennies! That's if the desk sergeant hasn't already pocketed them by now.

I got to know that floor pretty well during the course of my stay; grey, concrete, with a puke trough running right down to the little drain in the middle. I counted all the ridges, different undulations. Then I have to crawl onto the bench ... I collapse.

I lay on my front and tuck my legs up under my belly. I stick my arms between my legs. A hundred contortions, anything to hold in the heat . . . to not die in this hole, to make it through the night. I shiver so hard that I almost jump off the bench.

'Oi, you, what are you up to in there!' I hear the food hatch fly back, a pair of eyes, angry and contorted . . . 'What the fuck are you doing in that shit hole, boy, playing with yourself? Oi you, you little pervert, I'm talking to you! Are you wanking in your pit? Do you want me to come in there and give you a good kicking?'

I keep schtum, I've learnt humility; he is below me, I will suffer and endure . . . A young writer . . . I see his mug at the peep hole, I will memorise it for posterity.

I mumble, I go to speak, I have to ask it, I'm delirious with the cold. 'Can I have a blanket?'

'Can you have a what?'

'A blanket, please? I need a blanket.'

'Did you hear something, Jack? I thought I heard something . . . Did you hear something squeak?'

'I need a blanket, it's cold . . .'

'Say "please"!'

'Please . . .'

' "Please, sir"!'

'Please, sir . . .'

'No!'

I hear his laughter, it cackles and recedes . . . He's delighted himself.

I count time 'til dawn by his visits, every half hour, just to make sure that I'm not getting comfortable, that I don't get my head down . . .

There's plenty of tough places to wake up in, in this world, but a police cell takes the biscuit. No bars, no such luxuries, just glass, six inches thick! Even the light can't quite make it through, thin-looking, sort of diffused, sixty watt . . . Finally, the grey dawn comes.

They re-cuff us and lead us out into the yard, the meat wagon waiting. A ten minute drive, the sounds of the world outside, over the wall, distant. Somebody else's world, but not ours. Then the court house, they drive us in there like royalty . . . round the back and into the holding cells . . . The stench of fresh paint, hushed tones, library-like . . .

It's true that you have to queue up for everything in this world, but it's a strange thing when you even have to queue up to get the chop. Funny yet grim. But that's exactly what we have to do, waiting, dry mouthed, queuing up to have our faces filled.

We sit dumb in the house of our betters. Judging by the suits of our prosecutors, we're already guilty. You won't see shoe leather like that in the dole queue. A glittering of cufflinks and signet rings, all the refinements ... Their stomachs and counter-stomachs, botty bra's and real tits ... Old guys with behinds like cows.

Tell me, which one of these gourmets is going to understand the saga of a young fellow who's down on his luck? The sort of hard-up kid who steals a bottle of sauce to keep himself company? Three measly coppers floating round in his empty pocket! I can't imagine any of these brandy swillers being stitched up for borrowing a bottle of lousy gut-rot.

They call my name and I have to stand in that little box, all alone. No one talks on my behalf. I take the oath and stammer it out, and all the time the prosecutor's willing me to make a mistake, trying to trip me up, to get me to indict myself ...

A charming little fellow, Goebbels-esque, grimacing through his specs. I can't concentrate for his cynical little eyes; they make me want to reach over and push them back into his head like currants.

I find my thread and begin. I go the long way round, to include all the facts. Then just as I'm getting to the crux he butts in and interrupts me. He draws impossible conclusions. He pulls me apart, painting a pretty black picture of a young fellow like me. He agrees with himself completely. As far as he's concerned, I should be hung, drawn and quartered!

I didn't hit anyone, I was attacked! All but mugged! All I wanted was a wee dram, a night cap, something to knock me out, to blot out my day until I had to start another.

But no one stands up for me; I have to take on the whole inquisition single-handed. Then little Goebbels gives me my chance to put my side of the case. I tilt my chin, my bottom lip quivering. I try and spit it out, to tell them of my shame, of my sincerest repentance ... of the depths of my remorse ... straight and true ... of my drunkenness and my mistake ... And please not to let my mother know, for it would surely kill her ... But my eyes tell a different story, and they can see that deep down inside I believe myself to be a man as true and noble as any of them, only finer and truer.

So, I'm down on my luck? Us young writers are used to it. I don't stand alone before you, your lordships. With me stand Hamsun, Fante, Dostoyevsky . . . and they're not owned by you or any of your so-called friends, so don't cite their dear names you humbugs! So, I hit my last threepence? Yet, still I am nobler than you assassins could ever be. You hypocrites, you citers of God who lack all compassion, all humility . . . You would crucify a young fellow who made one tiny honest-to-God mistake. Do you honestly think that I'd walk in there like I owned the place, grab a bottle of sauce and breeze back out, if I knew that the slob with his feet up and a full brandy bowl owned the dump? I apologise, humbly, deeply, sincerely. I throw myself at the mercy of this court.

Seventy-five quid they stung me for, seventy-five stinking quid! For one poxy little bottle of poison! That's four weeks dole money for the sake of a tipple, and porridge if you don't cough up, they guarantee you that much!

I can't believe my ears, seventy-five quid? If you turned that around it would mean fining a judge all of what he owns plus four years pay!

I need time for that one to sink in, they have to help me up, to lead me away . . . I stammer, I trip, I regain my footing. I see it all through a fog, but I remember their faces, I kept that little triptych photographed on my breast. Three pork heads, jowls hanging. Dead eyes that give off no light, like little piss-holes from hell: my judges! I'll remember that lot, alright, they're the types who sit around in wine bars with their feet up after hours, swilling brandies. That's the type of magistrates we've got, my friends. There you have the scales of justice: a brandy bowl in one hand and a fine Havana in the other . . . There's only two types of law in this world: rich man's law and sod's law!

They show me the door and kick me out onto the streets, blinking through the smog . . . And the sun, doing his best, a few rays . . . a dappled effect . . . The simple grace of cars, shops and people . . . The world carrying on, going about its business.

It takes a knock like that to make you see the beauty in this world, the great expanse of dull grey sky. Everything takes on a new and terrifying meaning. It fills a young writer with joy and disgust.